All she had to do ███████████████
it into the oncoming traffic. One more New Year's
Eve fatality. That's all . . . Her fingers tightened
on the steering wheel as she squinted against the
glare of headlights. It would be so easy.

Do it . . . Do it, goddamn it!

A hand quickly reached out from nowhere to
steady the wheel. *A hand! A man's hand!*

"Don't do it, Maureen," a voice beside her ordered. *"This is not what you really want."*

It was Bobby O'Connor!

She grabbed hold of the steering wheel, embedding her nails into the leather covering as she
slammed on the brakes. The car fishtailed crazily,
screeching to a halt on the side of the road.

She stared at the windshield, frozen in shock,
trying to regain her breath, her composure, her
sanity . . . and not daring to turn her head to see
if he was still there. But she felt him. As real and
alive as any living being.

Not able to stand it, she slowly looked out of
the side of her eye.

"Bobby?" her voice cracked, sounding like a
frightened child.

And then he smiled—that wonderful, brilliant
smile.

"Hiya, kid. So how's life?"

CONSTANCE O'DAY-FLANNERY

ONCE IN A LIFETIME

ZEBRA BOOKS
KENSINGTON PUBLISHING CORP.

ZEBRA BOOKS

are published by

Kensington Publishing Corp.
475 Park Avenue South
New York, NY 10016

First printing: November, 1991

Printed in the United States of America

This book is dedicated to all the women who shared their stories with me, who found the courage to lift their faces to the sun and grow. Thank you for your candor, your laughter . . . even your tears.

And also,

Robbie Kelleher, my friend.

Prologue

Florida 1970

Maureen Henessey.

God, he could still picture her when she walked into Miss Bennet's fourth grade class at Our Lady of Grace. Skinny and scared. Her blonde hair was pulled back off her forehead by a big yellow bow that was falling out of its knot. Her one knee sock had lost its elasticity and gathered at her ankle. She'd been clutching a black-marbled copybook and two sharpened pencils to her chest, as if they were a shield that might protect her from the unknown. But it was her eyes — she had the most beautiful blue eyes that flashed a mixture of defiance and fear.

Bobby O'Connor smiled as he drove up the ramp to the interstate. He loved her. Why had it taken him this long to admit it? He was twenty-one, had half a semester of college left, and here he was, driving North for spring break when all the other college kids were making their way to Florida. But he had to get home. He had to see her. He didn't care if she was engaged to someone else. He was going to tell her that he'd loved her since they were ten years old, since she had stood in front of his fourth grade class looking for a friendly face. He remembered barely listening as his teacher told them that Maureen had just moved to Makefield and they should help her feel welcome. He couldn't stop staring at her. She wasn't really all that pretty, certainly not prettier that Chrissy Wilson or Mary Anne McGee. But there was something about that face, about those eyes that stared back at the class, searching for acceptance.

And that's when they connected. Maureen had looked directly at him, and he'd smiled.

That was it. Something so simple. A smile. And he'd made a friend for life. He'd endured the teasing of the guys and became her boyfriend by the end of the school year. No big deal. They barely even talked to one another. But they *looked*. They remained a "couple" in fifth grade, broke up in sixth, danced with each other in seventh, and felt the beginnings of unfulfilled sexual longings in eighth. In high school they went their separate ways. She was a cheerleader and popular. He was a second-string basketball player, and insecure as hell. She dated his best friends and he silently endured it, too scared by that time to tell her how he felt. And yet, there was always something, something in the looks they gave each other at dances that told him she was waiting for him to make the first move.

He never did.

Well, just once, and he'd handled it so poorly that she ran away from him. It was the summer after they had graduated and everyone had gone to the Jersey shore for two weeks. You couldn't walk onto the beach at Wildwood without bumping into someone from Bishop McDevlin's Class of '66. It was a great summer, the first taste of independence. He and nine of his friends had rented the third floor of a beat-up old house on Michigan Avenue. It was a rite of passage that no respectable graduate missed—partying all night, sleeping it off on the beach the next day, only stirring long enough to set up a date for the coming night. But then he'd seen her.

Even now, almost four years later, Bobby winced as he recalled the night. Passing a station wagon, he settled back into the right-hand lane and glanced at the clock on the dashboard. One thirty-three. Not bad. He'd drive until four or five and then pull over for a couple of hours sleep. Right now he wanted to close as much distance between him and Pennsylvania as possible.

Why the hell did he ever pull her out of that party? It was raining, a warm summer rain, and Maureen had laughed, lifting her chin and letting the water run over her face. That simple carefree act had been too much for an eighteen-year-old kid with four beers in him and eight years of pent up curiosity and longing. Reacting out of need, he'd grabbed her and brought his mouth down on hers. It was a hard and possessive kiss, and it had scared the hell out of Maureen. When she had pushed him away, his pride rose quickly and he'd said, "Hey, no problem. I figured after all these years I had a right to know what it was like."

She had continued to stare at him until he felt really stupid for having put them both in that situation. Reacting out of anger, anger at himself, he muttered those fateful words, "It wasn't worth the wait."

Until the day he died, he would never forget the look of pain in those blue eyes. It could have been the rain, but he was certain that it was tears she wiped away with the back of her hand before turning and running away toward the beach. Over the next couple of years they saw each other at parties when he was home from college. They were friends. They could laugh together, tease each other, and neither of them ever brought up that night at the shore. But there was always something between them, a current of unfulfilled passion. When his mom called and told him she was engaged to Dan Malone, Bobby felt like someone had reached in and twisted his gut. Dan Malone? Who the hell was he?

That was two weeks ago.

Now when he saw her, she would see that he had changed. In a few months he would have his degree and begin looking for a job in Philadelphia. He wasn't that scared kid any longer, and now knew what he wanted. He was willing to put himself on the line, to finally find out if there really was something between them, something they could discover together.

In the warm Florida night, Bobby O'Connor never saw the truck jackknife over the median strip into the path of his Chevy Impala. He never felt pain. He never heard the crash and twisting of metal. Just as he always knew, on the day he died all he saw in the blinding white light was the haunting pain in Maureen Henessy's blue eyes.

Chapter One

Avondale, New Jersey 1989

She sat on the toilet seat, watching him shave. Her life was crumbling in front of her and she felt helpless to stop it. Fear and bile rose in her throat, yet she forced it down and pushed the words past.

"I don't understand. What are you saying, Dan?"

Her husband, this man she had loved for more than twenty years, turned away from the mirror and stared at her. Shaving cream clung to the side of his face, and she might have laughed at the thought of this conversation taking place in the bathroom if it were not for the tortured look in his eyes.

"I don't feel anything, Maureen. I want more." He looked almost desperate. "I need to feel passion. *Passion!* I want that excitement back in my life. Can't you understand that?"

She continued to stare at him, not quite believing this was happening. "And . . . and you don't think we can find that again?" The tears were brimming at her eyelids and she brushed them back with the side of her hand. Dear God, make him answer.

Finally, he picked up the towel and wiped his face. When he looked at her, she knew before he ever spoke a word. "We're not the same people anymore. Neither of us. I want to feel young and happy again. Not like this." He shook his head and threw the towel into the hamper. "God, how do I say it?"

"Just say it," she whispered, knowing she didn't really want to hear.

"Maureen, I love you." She thought he was going to cry, and a part of her wanted to reach out and comfort him, just as she had always done. Then she heard his next words. "I just don't find you desirable anymore. I want something else. I don't even know what it is. I only know it isn't this."

He walked out and left her in the bathroom, staring at the tile, at the grout that needed cleaning.

I don't find you desirable anymore.

The words became indelibly etched in her brain as memories flooded back. Memories of nineteen good years, building a life, a family, a home. They'd had their ups and their downs, just like any marriage. But the downs had been few and far between until a few months ago, when Dan became quiet and withdrawn, falling asleep at nine

14

o'clock in front of the television or staying out until three or four in the morning without bothering to call and let her know he would be late. He was drinking more than he ever did and finding fault with her and the children. He would argue at the drop of a hat to make a point, and then storm out the house in anger. She knew something was wrong, terribly wrong, but put it down to pressure. He had just received a new promotion and was afraid the job was too big. She'd walked him through this for nineteen years as he rose up the corporate ladder and he always settled in and did a great job. They were both under a great amount of pressure right now in their careers. She was in the midst of contract negotiations with her publishers for a new series of *The Cotillion Club,* her line of young adult novels. Maybe she hadn't given him enough attention . . . she believed, honestly believed, that the arc would swing up again, that everything would work itself out. Just like always.

Didn't everyone always say they had the perfect marriage? Didn't family and friends come to them for advice when their own marriages were in trouble?

This could not be happening! She wouldn't let her family be torn apart over a mid-life crisis.

Forcing herself to leave the bathroom, she entered the bedroom where Dan was dressing.

"Is there someone else?"

She said aloud the question that had been torturing her during the nights she had lain awake, wondering whether her husband was lying on a cold slab in the hospital or in another woman's arms. How many late nights at the office, retirement parties and business dinners were justified?

He buckled his pinstriped pants and shook his head. "There's no one else. This isn't about another woman. Can't you understand it's about me?" He couldn't look at her, yet she could see he was almost desperately unhappy.

She watched him dress. She had picked out the shirt, the tie, the suit. Even the Louis Vuitton briefcase that lay open on the dresser had been a birthday present from her. Suddenly it was all slipping away. This man—her husband, the father of her children—didn't want her any longer.

She felt dizzy with shock and the pain that followed the revelation. Sitting on the edge of the bed, she brought her hands up to her face and cried, letting go of the tears that were nearly choking her.

He knelt down in front of her. "Please, Maureen. Please don't cry. I didn't want to hurt you like this, but you pushed it. You wouldn't leave it alone. Just like you always do. You think you can fix everyone's problems, but you can't. Not this time." He clutched her wrist and pulled her fingers away so he could see her face. "I'm the one with the problem, not you."

Flinging his hand away, she cried, "No, you're wrong. What about Abbie and Josh? Christmas is in five days. What do you plan on telling them? That you're going to take away all their security,

16

everything they've known, because you've fallen out of love with their mother? That she isn't young enough, or pretty enough, or thin enough, to stir your *goddamn passion?*"

She sounded shrill, and she didn't care. All she could see was her life, her world, turning upside down.

He shook his head and stood up. "I knew you would make this ugly."

Her mouth dropped open in shock as she stared at him fumbling with the knot of his tie. "Ugly? It *is* ugly. It's worse than that. You're only thinking about yourself. How unhappy you are. What do you think has been happening here while you're out all night? We've put up the tree, decorated the house, wrapped all the presents and where are you? *Where are you, Dan? And what are you doing?* And who do you think has been answering your children's questions when they ask where their father is, and why they can't talk to him anymore? They're teenagers. Intelligent kids. Do you know your sixteen-year-old son asked *me* if you were seeing another woman?"

Dan turned away from the mirror, shock written on his face. "What did you tell him?" he barely whispered.

"I told him to ask you."

Dan looked away. "There isn't another woman."

She wanted to believe him. She *had* to believe him. Dan Malone was the most honorable man she had ever known. He had never lied to her. Not once, in nineteen years of marriage, had he ever

deceived her. Honesty, honor, hard work, fairness
. . . he had built his life around those principles
that had been drilled into him in the Marines.
And he had lived by them. He was a good man,
and she loved him. He was depressed. He was
forty-two years old and going through male menopause.

"I never said you weren't pretty, Maureen."

His words broke through her desperate mental
defense of him. Blinking a few times she asked,
"What is that supposed to mean?"

He smoothed down the perfectly cut jacket to
his suit. "Just that I never thought you weren't
pretty enough. You have a beautiful face."

And then it hit her. The truth. Isn't that what
they always say to fat women? She turned and
looked into the mirror and studied herself. She
wasn't fat. She wasn't thin. She looked like a
forty-two year old woman who had gone through
four pregnancies, three miscarriages, and a hysterectomy, and had come out on the other side. Her
abdomen would never again be flat and firm and
she had the scars to prove it.

"So then I'm not young enough for you, or firm
enough . . ."

"Maureen, please. Don't."

"No," she demanded. "I want to hear it. Is that
what you think?"

His expression was pained. "I want to know
what I've missed."

She felt as if he had punched her between the
ribs, taken away her breath and her self-respect

18

with one sentence. She struggled for air, for a shred of dignity, and it took her only moments to make her decision. "Get out. Pack whatever you need and leave. You can come back later and get the rest. Just leave."

"Wait, Maureen. Listen to me . . ."

She had already left the bedroom and was walking down the hallway to the kitchen. Her hands were shaking as she poured herself a second cup of coffee. You'll get through this, she told herself, grabbing the edge of the counter for support. The twins are in school. It'll be okay. It'll be okay . . .

Her coffee went untouched. She merely stood, trance-like, at the black marble counter staring into the cup. There was a sense of unreality about it. How could this be happening to them? How—

"Maureen . . . ?"

She spun around at the soft whisper, sure Dan was behind her, but the kitchen was empty. There was no one. She stared at the black and white tiles, the white cabinets . . . dear God, now she was hearing voices! Stay calm, she commanded. Keep it together. Just a little while longer. Picking up her coffee, she steadied her hand and waited.

He didn't take long. She heard him walk into the kitchen and stop. She knew he was staring at her, yet she couldn't make herself turn around and look.

"I don't want to leave," he said softly behind her.

She almost laughed with bitterness. "Oh, yes you do, Dan. You just can't admit it. It goes against your sense of honor, of right and wrong." Lifting her head, she faced him. "So I'll make it easy on you. I want you to leave. I want you to find out what it is out there that's pulling you away from us."

When she saw the suitcase at his feet, her composure crumpled and she started crying again. Dan hurried to her and held her in his arms.

"You're the only woman I've ever loved, Maureen. The only one I've ever wanted to build a life with."

Seeing him through a haze of tears, she smiled sadly, "But that isn't enough, is it? Not any more."

He didn't answer and she told herself that it was only temporary, just until he worked his way through this problem. People took separate vacations sometimes. It was supposed to be healthy for a relationship. They just needed some time apart.

Forcing a smile, she reached up and brushed a lock of sandy hair back off his forehead. Her blue eyes met his tearful gaze and held it.

"Listen," she whispered, and then sniffled. "I read somewhere that if you love someone, or something, then set it free. If it does come back, it returns because of love. You're free, Dan."

He held her, hugging her tightly to his chest, and his tears mingled with hers.

"I'm sorry, Maureen. I'm so sorry," he mumbled into her ear, before backing away and picking up his bag.

When she heard the front door close, she bent over the kitchen sink and threw up.

"I want to talk to my father."

She looked at her sixteen-year-old son and shook her head, indicating she was speaking on the phone and it was business. "Look, Taylor, you tell them I'll write the first three in the new series and edit the others. I want to finish this mainstream first and let them make an offer. I'm not signing a new contract, not for anyone, unless the mainstream is a part of it."

"They've got a good thing going, Maureen," her agent said, "and they don't want you throwing a wrench into it. For God's sake, the last *The Cotillion Club* made the damn *New York Times*. You created the monster, baby, and now everyone expects you to feed it."

"Well, I'm sick of feeding it," Maureen answered, slapping away her son's hand when he reached for more cookie dough. The buzzer went off in the oven and she shifted the pan of chocolate chip cookies to remove the chicken for that night's dinner. "I'm sick of feeding everyone," she muttered into the phone. "If I have to write another story about teenagers and the angst of first love I'll run shrieking out into the night. I want to write about big people, grown-up people. You know, Taylor—real life."

"They're offering a great deal this time. Seventy-five thousand per and ten percent royalty."

She was silent for a moment. If Challenge Publishing were offering seventy-five then she must be selling a hell of a lot of books to a hell of a lot of kids. This wasn't a gift. Everything in the business was based on numbers and hers must be pretty good. For three months they had been going back and forth with this deal and it was wearing her down, yet instinct told her to reject the offer.

"All right, Taylor, now this is what I want you to do. Thank them for their offer, but tell them no thanks. I'm going to finish my novel and if they don't want it then we can auction it. No contract without the mainstream included."

There was a loud sigh on the other end of the line. "I think you might be making a mistake."

She pushed the new pan of cookies into the oven and stifled a curse as she burnt her hand. "Well, I don't, and I'll tell you why. I own the copyright on *Cotillion* and the series. It's dead in the water without me. If they're offering seventy-five then they must be making two hundred thousand on each book. Right now they need me more than I need them, and all I want, Taylor, is to be able to write what I want to write. It's that simple."

"You're holding firm on this?"

She thought about her future, as uncertain as it was, and said what was in her heart. "Yes. Yes, I am."

"Okay, kid. Let's gamble."

She hung up the phone and turned back to the kitchen. Josh was stuffing his face with cookies and she mentally put the author on "hold" and switched back into her mother mode. Taking the cookies from her son's hand, she said, "Okay, knock it off. Dinner is almost ready. Go upstairs and ask Abbie to come down."

"Abbie! Dinner!"

Her jaw clenched as her son yelled behind her. Turning around, she took a deep breath. "I could have done that, Josh. Now *go* upstairs and get your sister for dinner."

This younger image of her husband raked his fingers through his hair with frustration. "I want to talk to Dad. There's only three days until Christmas, and he promised he'd take me to Berman's for new skis. I mean, that's all I've asked for this Christmas."

"He'll call tonight," Maureen said patiently, fighting down the feeling that this disruption of normalcy was somehow her fault. "Talk to him then. Now will you please call Abbie?"

Josh shook his head, as if to confirm her thoughts, and walked out of the kitchen. Why was it that she felt guilty, somehow responsible, for the children's pain and confusion? She didn't leave. She had stayed and tried to bring unity back into the family, and yet the looks the twins gave her spoke volumes. She must have done something to drive their father away.

She placed the platter of chicken on the table and looked at the dishes. There were only three. Fresh emotion pressed against her chest as she gazed at Dan's empty chair. He'd only been gone three days, yet everything in the house depressed her. Every room held memories. He called each night to talk to the children. When she spoke with him he sounded depressed and guilty. He said he missed them, but thought the separation was a good idea. She asked him to seek counseling. He put her off. He was staying in a hotel in Philadelphia. She was occupying their huge bed, crying herself to sleep while clutching the pillow that still held his scent.

"Mom, Abbie says she's sick. She can't eat."

Maureen looked up from the table. "Sick?"

"Yeah. She doesn't look good, even for her. She's . . . you know, crying."

"Okay. Josh, drain the broccoli and I'll go up and see about Abbie."

As she walked out of the room, she heard her son moan, "Broccoli! Dad's the only one who likes it, and now he's not even here."

"*I* like it," she yelled back, louder than she intended. Running up the stairs, she muttered, "Just do it, all right?"

She knocked softly and opened the door to her daughter's room. Posters of Madonna and David Bowie vied for room on the walls amid Mickey Mouse memorabilia and high school pictures of best friends, boyfriends and field hockey sticks. Clothes were strewn over the rug, yet Maureen had long ago given up nagging. Once every two weeks or so, Abbie tackled the job and somehow set it straight.

Stepping over the Penn State sweatshirt her

daughter had worn to school that morning, Maureen approached the bed. "Abbie? What's wrong?"

She knew Abbie was terribly upset about her father's actions and expected that whatever was bothering her daughter would be related to that. But as soon as Abbie opened her eyes and looked up at her, Maureen instinctively knew it was more serious. Immediately, she placed her hand on the child's forehead. "My God, you're burning up! Why didn't you say something earlier?"

Glazed blue eyes looked back. "I'm sick, Mom."

Gathering her child into her arms, Maureen felt the heat emanating from the young body and whispered, "I can see that. When did it start?"

Abbie's voice was hoarse, a mere whisper. "Last night. I got this terrible pain and started throwing up . . ."

Maureen was startled. "Why didn't you say something to me then?"

Her daughter started to whimper. She sounded more like a little girl than the self-confident sixteen-year-old who could argue an adult under the table over women's rights. "You know . . . because of Daddy. You have enough to worry about—"

"Shh, nothing is more important to me right now than you" Maureen interrupted, as guilt overwhelmed her. "Not even Daddy. Now why did you go to school if you were sick?"

Abbie shook her head. "I thought it would go away. Oh . . ." She curled her body up into a ball and moaned in pain.

Maureen held her until the pain subsided and then brushed the long brown hair away from her face. "Okay, I'm going to take your temperature. You'll be all right, kiddo. It's probably just the flu."

The digital thermometer read one hundred and two point seven.

"Where does it hurt, honey?"

Abbie rubbed the middle of her torso and gasped in pain. Sixteen years of motherhood, of nursing fevers and flues, chicken pox and measles, fractures and stitches, kicked into high gear. Something was really wrong here. Maureen picked up her daughter's phone and called the doctor. Within minutes, she hung up and said to Abbie, "C'mon, let's get you dressed."

On the way out the front door, she held up her daughter and called back over her shoulder. "Josh, you go ahead and eat. Get the cookies out of the oven—can't you smell them burning? And when your father calls, tell him about Abbie."

Driving to the doctor, Maureen held her child's hand when the pain returned and silently called out for her husband.

Doctor Mark Godwin had been the children's doctor since they were delivered. Abbie and Josh were his first set of twins and he always treated them more like relatives than patients. But this time he wasn't joking, or trying to make anyone laugh. After a thorough examination of Abbie, he held the results of her blood test in his hand.

"Look, it could just be a good case of the flu, but her white blood count is elevated and I don't like that tenderness in her abdomen. I don't want to alarm either one of you but we might just be looking at appendicitis, or possibly a ruptured ovarian cyst."

Abbie clutched at her hand in fear and Maureen swallowed down her own panic. "Her father had an appendectomy when he was a teenager."

Mark nodded. "Then that settles it. Let's get this checked out. I've got my nurse calling Sid Weisman. He's a good surgeon."

"Surgeon?" Maureen asked, holding back the alarm. "You're her doctor."

"I'm a pediatrician, Maureen. Abbie's dehydrated and her blood count says there's something going on in there that we have to find out about. I want you to help her get dressed and then go straight to St. Mary's emergency room. Weisman will be waiting for you."

He left them, not staying around for an argument.

She looked at her daughter. Abbie was crying, shaking with the chills that accompanied her fever. Maureen picked up the Penn State sweatshirt, and held it out. "Okay, we can do this. C'mon. Lift your arms."

The child before her stared into her eyes and mirrored the fear that was racing through her own system. "Mom, I'm scared."

"I know. Me, too," she said honestly. "But they're just going to run some tests."

27

"I'm not staying at the hospital," Abbie answered in a weak, yet determined voice. "Please . . . can we call Scott and tell him to meet us?"

Maureen pictured Abbie's boyfriend of two years. He was eighteen and after spending so much time in her house had become almost a second son to her. "If there's any reason, I promise I'll call him from the hospital. Now let's go and get it over with. I need you healthy. You were supposed to help me bake Christmas cookies, remember?" She tried smiling reassuringly.

Abbie's chin quivered. "Some Christmas," she muttered.

Maureen couldn't have said it better.

A bitter winter wind wrapped around them and she held her child closer to her body as they walked toward the emergency room entrance. Suddenly Abbie stopped and stared at the doors.

"It'll be all right. You'll see. Come on," Maureen urged.

Abbie held back. "Mom, I have to tell you something. And I didn't want to say it like this."

"What? Abbie, it's cold out here. You have a fever, and—"

"Mom, listen to me!"

She looked down at her daughter.

"They're going to ask me, so I might as well tell you. I'm on birth control pills. I have been for about six months."

Looking back, she would remember it as being the moment that changed her life. She stared at her daughter, who stood shaking with fever, fear

28

and embarrassment. An immense wave of shock and sadness rushed through her. As she stood in the cold wind, Maureen's whole life flashed before her in a matter of seconds. She saw herself as this perfect wife who rushed to the front door when Dan walked in from work, treating each night's arrival like the damned Second Coming. She kept house, built a career in between carpools, soccer and field hockey games. She'd stood in for Dan at boy scouts because he was too busy, fought book deadlines to run the fashion show for the PTA two years running and was brownie troop mother for three. She'd created this perfect little life, with a house in the suburbs, two cars, two children. Her family was supposed to be safe. She'd done everything right, everything everybody had always said was right. She had turned herself into Donna fucking Reed, for chrissake! And it was all falling apart . . .

"Mom? I'm sorry."

Blinking a few times, Maureen swallowed down the bitterness in her mouth and said, "We'll deal with it later, okay? Let's handle one thing at a time. C'mon."

When the doors closed behind her and Maureen walked up to the emergency room desk, she was certain of only one thing.

Donna Reed was dead.

Chapter Two

Enclosed in a cubicle of hospital green curtains, Maureen Malone tried to push everything out of her cluttered brain and concentrate on what the doctor was saying. It wasn't easy with a knife victim cursing out his assailant on one side of her and an old woman moaning on the other. Privacy in an emergency room was an unnecessary luxury.

"As I was saying, Mrs. Malone . . . I don't think we have to worry about appendicitis. She may have an inflamed ovarian cyst, or it just might be gastritis accompanying the flu, but I want to keep her overnight to be sure."

"Overnight?" Maureen's voice cracked. Her baby, in the hospital for the first time.

Abbie cried out, "I'm not staying. I want to go home!"

The surgeon patted Abbie's shoulder. "Just a few tests, dear."

He looked up at Maureen. "She's dehydrating

fast. I want to get her on an IV and settle her stomach. I'll check in on her again tonight." Closing the metal chart, he smiled reassuringly and walked around the curtain to the knife victim.

"I don't care what he says, I'm not staying!" Abbie moaned, "And I'm not putting on this awful nightgown either! Take me home, Mom. You said it would just be tests. You promised!"

Stay in control, she told herself. "Abbie, I never promised anything. You have to do this. You're sick—"

"Nobody is sticking a tube up my arm!" For someone so weak, her daughter's voice was surprisingly loud.

"I know you're scared, but it isn't as bad as you think. Now, let's just put the gown on and—"

"No!"

The odd mixture of anger and panic in her child's eyes was contagious, and three days of nearly constant turmoil took its toll as something fragile snapped inside of Maureen.

"Look," she yelled, "you want the truth?" Startled, Abbie shut up and stared as her mother ripped the socks off her feet and threw them on the hospital floor. "Childbirth—that's a bitch! *That* hurts like hell. This is nothing compared to that! They're going to stick a needle in your arm and that's it! Now, take those jeans off right now and put on the damn gown!"

The dead silence that followed her outburst told Maureen that everything in the emergency room had come to a halt. Slowly, she looked down to the shoes she could see on either side of the curtains. Even the guy whose friend had stuck him with a screwdriver had shut up. Her heart was hammering inside her chest. She felt dizzy and suddenly nauseated. Her head was pounding her pulse rate onto her forehead like an invisible battering ram. Gradually conversations picked up around her, as if there had never been an interruption, and Maureen wanted to tell Abbie to move over, to make room for her on the gurney because she didn't think she could remain upright. Instead, she clutched at the worn hospital sheet and swallowed back her tears.

"Please, Abbie," she whispered. "Please put the gown on. We'll get through this, honey . . . just like everything else."

Her daughter reached out to her and they held each other, crying, clinging to one another for support. Within fifteen minutes, Maureen walked out of the emergency room to find a phone. She willed her legs to move down the tiled corridor. It couldn't have been worse. The IV was in, but it had taken two attempts. She'd held Abbie, covering her child's face with her own. And never would she forget Abbie's mouth against her wet cheek, begging her to make them stop, calling her mommy . . . *Mommy.* Her sixteen year old daughter, a young woman on birth control pills, was just a terrified little girl.

"May I please speak with Dan Malone?" Maureen leaned up against the wall as she spoke into the phone. Worried families sat around the reception room talking in hushed tones, waiting for word on their loved ones.

"I'm sorry. Mr. Malone isn't here. May I take a message?"

She couldn't remember the name of his new secretary. "This is Mrs. Malone. It's an emergency. Do you know how I can reach him?"

Immediately the businesslike tone changed to one of concern. "Oh, Mrs. Malone. Gee, I'm sorry. He's—he's not here. He took a vacation day."

"Vacation day?" Maureen asked in disbelief. Dan lived and breathed for the Aviaex Corporation. He was convinced the production rate of high-tech aviation parts would take a downward plunge if he missed a single work day.

She tried to clear her brain. "Did he leave a number where he could be reached?" she asked, humiliated that this woman knew more about her husband than she did.

"Ummm . . . I know he has a new beeper number, but his secretary would have it and she's not here either."

"She's not?"

"No, Betty's out too. I'm just answering the phone."

Maureen's stomach tightened into a knot as she attempted to control her voice. "Please try and find the beeper number and let him know that his daughter is in St. Mary's Hospital."

"Oh, gosh, yes of course. Everyone's leaving for the day, but I'll do everything I can, and there's a skeleton crew on tonight, so they'll keep on trying."

She could barely talk as her throat strained against the anger and frustration. "Thank you."

"Oh, Mrs. Malone?" the woman hurried to add. "My daughter just loves your books. She'll be thrilled to know I talked to you. Wait, wait a minute—here's Hank Drayer. Maybe he can help."

Maureen heard the girl relaying the message and Hank got on the line. "Maureen. It's Hank. How's Abbie?"

"Hank," she said his name with relief. Hank Drayer was part of the new team of engineers that Dan had been working closely with over the last few months. When Dan's promotion came along, he'd taken Hank with him. "Abbie's going to spend the night. They're not sure what's wrong yet. Some tests. Some . . ." her voice trailed off as the hot taste of tears came into her mouth.

"Listen, Maureen," Hank said in a low voice. "I'll call around. I'll try and find him, okay?"

There was a moment of silence before she could answer. "Okay. Thanks."

"Hold on, Maureen. I know it's tough right now, but everything's going to work out."

She pressed her fingers to her mouth to stifle the sob, as people in the waiting room looked up at her. She had never met Hank, but she could tell by his voice that he knew about the separation. Humiliation washed over her as she realized that Dan had obviously talked about their problems with this faceless man, and she silently cursed her husband.

"I'll find him. I promise. I'm leaving now anyway. I'll check everywhere. Just take care of Abbie."

"Thank you," she muttered and quickly disconnected.

Her hands were shaking as she punched in the next set of numbers. Don't think about it now, she told herself. Don't torture yourself wondering where your husband is at this minute. Your daughter is what matters . . .

"Scott, this is Mrs. Malone. Abbie is in the emergency room at St. Mary's and she wants you here."

She hung up before the boy could ask a single question.

It wasn't until she was walking back into the emergency room that her mind screamed out the questions that were pounding inside her brain. Where the hell are you, Dan? *And who are you with?*

Over the next two hours they settled Abbie into a room. Scott arrived and Maureen gave them a few minutes of privacy before asking the boy to keep her company while she got something to eat in the cafeteria. They each filled plates and pushed around unappetizing food, and neither really ate. They talked. Somehow, she kept it together and told him exactly what was on her mind. She spoke of sex and love and commitment. Of maturity and responsibility. Part of her marveled that she could have this conversation at all when she wasn't quite sure if she believed in any of it anymore. Nothing seemed real. Her whole world was falling apart and she was fighting like hell just to keep a few rubber bands around it.

When they returned to Abbie's room, Josh was there. So was Dan. She couldn't bring herself to speak to him and the look of guilt he gave her was like a knife thrust into her chest. He sat on the edge of Abbie's bed and made small talk while Maureen stood up against the wall and looked at her family. How was this happening to them? What had she done wrong? Unable to watch any longer, she walked up to her daughter and kissed her forehead.

"I'm going to go home now and pack some things to bring back. Can you think of anything else you'll need?" She had to get out of this room before she unraveled completely.

Abbie shook her head, and Maureen was pulling away when her daughter reached out and grabbed her hand. "Thanks, Mom," she whispered. "Thanks for everything."

Maureen nodded and tried to smile as a knowing look passed between them. There was a difference now. It was more than mother and daughter. It was woman to woman. She knew what Abbie was saying, what she didn't want her to forget to bring back. Ignoring her husband, she kissed Josh, patted Scott's arm and walked out of the room.

Now she had to go home and pack a robe, slippers and underwear. She would bring everything back and spend the night with Abbie, like a good mother. And inside the box of tissues on her daughter's night table would be a white plastic case of birth control pills.

What a perfect little family, she thought bitterly. What a perfect little lie.

She awoke with a sense of unreality. It was New Year's Eve and the sun was shining as if it were the middle of July. Nothing about this holiday seemed real. There was no snow, not even cold weather. No children had come running in on Christmas morning, shaking her awake in eager anticipation of gifts. Josh and Abbie had slept until ten o'clock. There had been no frenzied ripping of paper and squeals of delight over presents. It had been very civilized, very quiet. And very strange.

Turning her head, Maureen looked at the man sleeping next to her. Dan had come home the night she stayed with Abbie in the hospital. He had quietly moved back in, without fuss or much of an explanation—other than to say he wanted to come home. He was sorry. He would try and work out his problems. He needed his family.

Studying his face in repose, she saw a stranger and once more felt the now-familiar tightening of her stomach. The man she knew, the one she loved, was disappearing before her eyes each day. In his place was a desperately unhappy man. Oh, he tried to participate in the holiday, but more often than not she would find him sitting in the study staring into space. When she realized he was suffering from depression, she had taken charge and found a counselor for him. Dan actually kept his appointment, but he didn't seem any less discouraged when he returned. If she tried to discuss their problems, he would immediately become defensive and tell her it wasn't working, and maybe he should leave. In the last week, she had heard those words no less than ten times. He went through all the motions like a stoic soldier, as if he were making a sacrifice for her and the children. Yet his strong sense of honor refused to allow him to go.

In all honesty, she hadn't been the picture of serenity herself. On Christmas morning when she had opened his present, she'd been unable to hide her feelings. He'd bought her a wildly extravagant emerald and diamond ring. At the time she didn't see it as anything more than a guilt ring, the typical type of jewelry a wandering husband would present his wife. She had nothing to prove otherwise, yet some inner voice told her she would never see the ring as anything else. It would sit in a drawer, a reminder of this pain and suspicion. When she returned the ring for a simple heavy bangle of gold, some crazy surge of hope rose up inside of her, inspiring her to spend the difference on a plain gold wedding band for him. Of course, the ring was too small and needed to be sized.

That's what she was going to do today. She

would return the ring, get the right size, keep her hairdresser appointment and tonight, at the stroke of midnight, when the new decade approached, she would present it to him and tell him it was a new beginning for them both. She would make the effort, extend herself, because this was a good man that shared her bed. For nineteen years he had been a good husband and father. He had stood by her through all the miscarriages and the hysterectomy and now it was his turn. He was depressed and deserved her support and understanding. Now she had to be the stronger one. Isn't that what a partnership was all about? Somehow, she would heal this marriage and keep the family together.

A wave of sympathy and love overwhelmed her as she looked into his face and she reached out to lightly trace the lines at the corner of his eye. At her touch, he immediately awoke and flinched away from her fingers. Refusing to take offense, she merely smiled.

"Good morning," she whispered.

He moaned sleepily and muttered the same. "What time is it?"

Maureen glanced at the clock by her bed. "It's early. Eight forty-five." She forced herself to snuggle next to him. Wrapping her arms around his chest, she said, "It's New Year's Eve. Can you believe it? Any hints where we're going?" She had left the plans up to him. She didn't care if it was only dinner at a restaurant. She just wanted to be alone with him.

He quickly expelled his breath and shook his head. "No. Not yet."

She was about to remind him that he might have a problem at this late date without reservations, but kept it to herself. She was not going to nag. Instead, she ran her fingers over the small patch of hair on his chest and kissed his shoulder. "The kids both have parties tonight, so we could have a quiet dinner here, if you want."

She touched him, ever so lightly, allowing her fingernails to graze over his chest. Quickly his hand reached up and closed over hers, stopping her, as if the action were more annoying than tender. "Look, I said I'll take care of tonight, and I will." He squeezed her hand and added, "I feel like I haven't slept, that's all. I just want to go back to sleep."

She lay behind him, staring at his back, frozen with rejection. Once more she had to talk to herself, tell herself that she had to go slowly, that she couldn't expect to fix everything in a week. All they needed was time—and understanding.

Pushing the comforter away, she sat up. "I'm going to go to the jeweler's this morning, and then keep my hair appointment. I'll be back this afternoon."

He made a noise to let her know that he'd heard.

She stood up and stared down at him. "You do want me to get the larger size, don't you? I mean if you don't like the style or—"

He spun around so quickly that he startled her.

His face showed anger and annoyance. "I haven't worn a wedding ring in ten years, Maureen. What the hell makes you think I'd start wearing one now?"

She stared at him for a good twenty seconds, numb with shock, until the pain crept in and took hold. Without saying a word she turned and walked toward the bathroom.

From behind her she heard him curse and mutter, "Christ! Everything's a confrontation. This isn't working. This is not working . . ."

It took every ounce of will power to quietly close the bathroom door and shut out his words. Leaning up against it, she felt a wave of pain and sorrow so strong, so nauseatingly real, that she slowly slid down the wall and huddled on the floor like an abandoned child.

"God, I can't take this." The fist against her mouth started to bleed. The despair was so overwhelming that she thought she was about to pass out. And she might have, if it were not for the tiny enameled nightlight flickering on the wall. Maureen stared at it in disbelief. The nightlight hadn't worked in months. She'd been meaning to replace it. Oddly, there was something comforting about the light. Yet, even as she stared at it, the iridescence began to die out. *It's only your imagination, Maureen. Don't get crazy. You have two children. You must hold it together.* Wrapping a towel around her hand, she pulled herself up from the floor.

41

* * *

Within the hour, she walked into Bailey, Banks and Biddle and placed the velvet boxes on the glass counter.

A beautifully dressed woman in her fifties smiled and asked in a perfectly cultured voice, "May I help you?"

Maureen tried to return the greeting. "Yes, I hope so," she managed to get out. She would not cry again. Not now. Not yet. "I would like to return these, please." Her hands were shaking as she pushed the boxes forward, and she quickly withdrew her fingers and clenched her fists to steady them.

The saleswoman opened one case and then the other, examining the contents. "Is there something wrong with them?"

Maureen shook her head. "No," she whispered. "I just don't want them."

"It's a beautiful bracelet," the woman admired, holding it up to catch the store's light. "So simple and elegant . . ."

"I don't want it," Maureen insisted, fighting the damn tears that were quickly forming at her lids. "Nor—nor the ring." She hated the fact that her voice cracked with emotion. Fumbling in her purse, she took out the piece of paper. "Here's the receipt."

The woman looked at her for a moment longer than necessary and as the understanding passed between them, it was another humiliation to add to the others. "Can I show you anything else?"

Maureen shook her head. She wanted to get out, to run away from the memory of this latest revelation about her husband. "I would just like the money."

"I'm sorry, but we don't keep this amount in the store safe right now. If it were the holidays . . ." The saleswoman shrugged her shoulders. "I can give you a credit, or they can send up a check from the main store in Philadelphia."

She looked directly at the woman and said, "Send the check." In a stronger voice, she added, "And I would like it made out to Maureen Malone."

The woman nodded and picked up the boxes. As she watched the ring disappear, Maureen silently cursed her husband. *Damn you. It was the sentiment that went behind the ring. You could've worn it. You bastard—you could have worn it.*

She glanced down to her own wedding ring and slipped it off her finger. There was an indentation on her skin from almost twenty years of wear. Twenty years . . .

Without another thought she tossed the ring into her purse and waited for the saleswoman to return.

"God, Maureen. I can't believe it. What are you going to do?"

She finished her tea and stood up. "Well, I'm going to get my hair done in twenty minutes and after that . . ." Her voice trailed off and she shrugged her shoulders. "I don't know, Lisa. I honest to God don't know."

She had come to her friend's house for tea and sympathy and direction. Lisa Costello was the most sensible, grounded, person that she knew. She was also divorced, making a better living than most men and had turned her own life around in less than three years, Maureen had tried to be there for her when Lisa's marriage fell apart, and it had seemed the most natural place to go after leaving the jewelers.

She didn't want to leave Lisa's cozy new kitchen and go back home. She wanted to run away. "I don't know," she said in a tired voice. "Maybe I just let myself go. I wasn't exciting enough. I was preoccupied with the new contract, and writing—"

"Will you stop?" Lisa interrupted, standing up and picking up the empty cups. Lisa was short, voluptuous as Italian women tended to be, with long curly black hair. She also had a quick temper and was known to be brutally frank. "Will you stop blaming yourself for your husband's problems? Christ! He's going through male menopause, treating you and the kids like strangers, and *you're* standing there making excuses for him."

"Do you think there's another woman?" Maureen finally said aloud the words that had brought her here.

Lisa shook her head. "I don't know. Maybe I'm not the one you should be asking."

Nodding, Maureen picked up her purse. "All

those late nights. Retirement parties. Playing cards. Out drinking with the guys from work. He came home two weeks ago at six o'clock in the morning. Six o'clock! I was frantic. I thought he was dead. And he says he was playing cards and fell asleep."

"Did you believe him?"

She answered honestly. "I needed to believe him. Then, I needed it."

"And now?" Lisa asked gently.

"Now I want the truth."

Lisa wrapped her arms around her and Maureen felt her eyes once more fill with tears.

"Listen," Lisa said softly. "Maybe this is premature, but I want you to know you're not the only one going through this. Remember that support group I told you about? The one that helped me?"

Maureen nodded.

"I'm going to write down the phone number. I'm not telling you what to do, but you'll know when the time is right. You'll feel it yourself."

"God, I hate this crying! That's all I seem to be doing lately." Maureen sniffled, wiped at her eyes and stood back. Smiling, she added, "Hey, I never even asked you what you're doing tonight."

Pouting, Lisa made a face as she wrote down the number and handed it to her friend. "Brenda from accounting is having a party. It isn't bad enough I have to spend five days a week with those people from the office, now I'm so desperate I'll be ringing in the new year with them."

"It's better than being alone," Maureen offered,

though she knew Lisa would argue the point. "Who knows, maybe there might be someone interesting there."

"Maureen, it's been over two years since I've been laid. Do you really think Prince Charming is going to magically show up at this New Year's party and sweep me off my feet? This isn't one of those books you write. This is real life. And real life, when it comes to dating after thirty, sucks."

Laughing, Maureen hugged her friend. "Thanks. I needed that. I knew if I came here you would somehow make me laugh." She looked into Lisa's eyes and said quietly, "Happy New Year, Lisa Costello. Thanks for listening, and for being my best friend. My wish for you is that in the coming year you find someone to share your life. You, above all people, deserve it."

Walking her to the door, Lisa answered, "Hey, I'll settle for achieving occasional multiple orgasms. I'm not greedy."

Maureen was still laughing when she started the car.

"Your hair looks nice."

He was watching television when she came home. "Thanks. Where're the kids?"

"Josh is finalizing his plans for tonight and I think Abbie's still drying her hair. Do you think it's a good idea to let her go out so soon after the hospital?"

She barely looked at him as she dropped her packages onto the couch. "Abbie's fine. It was only the flu and it's almost ten days since she left the hospital. I can't keep her in on New Years."

"I just asked, Maureen. You didn't have to snap at me."

She looked at him then, really looked. They could have been related by blood. They both had the same brown hair, highlighted with blond. Blue eyes. And he was only about five inches taller than she was. He had aged gracefully in the last twenty years, his added weight only making him appear more manly and sturdy, while hers . . .

"I didn't think I snapped at you," she snapped at him, angry that she was comparing herself to him.

"Well, you're obviously angry about something."

"Have you made plans for tonight?" she asked, ignoring his words.

He shook his head. "Everywhere I called was filled up. I guess I should have made reservations earlier."

"You're right. You should have." She was too annoyed to hide her anger.

"Look, we can't even talk without arguing," he pointed out. "It isn't going to work like this. Maybe I should—"

"You should what?" she interrupted. "Leave? Again?"

He stared at her, not saying anything, and she walked over to the study door and slammed it shut.

"You want to talk, Dan? You finally want to talk? Fine! Let's do it. Let's find out just what the hell is going on here, all right?" Her hands were starting to shake, but she willed them to stop as she sat opposite him in a chair. "And why don't we start with the truth, for a change? Instead of sweeping everything under the rug. Like where were you the day Abbie went into the hospital? I called work and was told you took a vacation day. Where were you, Dan?"

He continued to stare at her as if seeing a stranger, and Maureen was glad. The understanding wife and partner seemed alien at the moment. Now she wanted answers.

"I was Christmas shopping. That's when I bought the ring."

"Really? Did you pick it out alone?"

"What's that supposed to mean?" She could hear the anger in his voice, but it was no match for what she was feeling inside.

"It means exactly what I said. Did you pick it out alone? Or did you have help? Did your new secretary, who was also conveniently on vacation, help her boss pick out his wife's Christmas present?"

"What were you doing, checking up on me?" he demanded bitterly.

"Your daughter was just admitted to the hospital. I called you because I thought you should know. But you weren't there. Neither was she. And no one knew where to find either of you."

"You'll believe what you want to believe, Maureen. You're too upset right now to logically discuss this."

"That's an evasive answer, and you know it."

"Look, what do you want from me?" he challenged.

"I want the truth. I want my husband back."

"You're asking me to make a commitment to something I don't know if I want anymore."

Her heart beat furiously in her chest, yet she had come this far and couldn't back down. "Let me get this straight. You don't know if you want to be committed to your wife and your family? Is that it? Is that what you're saying?"

"I don't know, Maureen."

She came as near to hatred as she was capable of feeling. "And exactly what am I expected to do until you find out? Am I expected to continue to hold this family together, to make your meals and clean your dirty laundry, while I wait to find out if you still *want* me? If I'm *good* enough for you?" My God, the humiliation was complete!

"We can't even talk!" he countered. "This isn't working and you know it. I—"

"Don't!", she shouted, jumping up and holding out her hand like a traffic cop. "Don't you dare say it again. You want to leave?" she demanded in a voice that was becoming a shriek. "I'll pack your goddamned bags for you! Because this time you're not coming back to pick up anything. This time you're out of here for good!"

She ran out of the room. Like a woman possessed, she raced into the kitchen, threw open a cabinet, and grabbed a box of Hefty garbage bags. She raced upstairs, taking the stairs two at a time, and once in the bedroom, she flung open the armoire and started emptying a drawer into a bag.

It became a fast routine. Flip open a bag. Dump in a drawer. Pull the yellow plastic string. Begin again. Three drawers were lying empty on the rug when he caught up to her.

"Maureen. It's New Year's Eve. This can wait! I'll do it!"

"Get the hell out of here," she snarled at him. "Go say goodbye to your children. See if you can explain to them what you're doing to us!" She felt wonderful. As crazy as it seemed, she felt like a million bucks taking some action by standing up for herself and her family.

"Lord! It's almost laughable," she breathed, riding high on the adrenaline as she attacked his closet. "A forty-two year old man who can't accept the fact that he's getting old. You're so typical, it's pathetic!" She threw the suits, the crisply laundered shirts, the designer ties, into the huge plastic bag.

"Mom! What're you doing?" Josh stood next to his father and stared at her as if she'd lost her mind.

Even though she was sobbing, Maureen felt terrific. She didn't stop tearing apart the closet as she ordered, "Josh, take these bags out to your father's car. He's leaving. And he's not coming back in a few days. This time he's leaving us so *he can find himself.*" Throwing another bag at her husband's feet, Maureen didn't bother to keep the sarcasm or ridicule out of her voice.

Within twenty-five minutes, everything that was Dan Malone's had been removed from the bedroom. She hauled down the heavy bags herself when Josh and Dan didn't do it quick enough, and she wasn't satisfied until every Hefty was out of her house.

As she stood heaving from the emotion and exertion, Maureen tearfully watched as Dan said goodbye to the children on the porch. She refused to allow her children's feelings to sway her. She knew it was right. It felt right. Hell, it felt wonderful to physically exorcise the demons that had been living inside of her for weeks.

When the kids went back inside, Dan turned to her. He was about to speak when she held up her hand to stop him. "There's nothing you can say that I want to hear. And there's only one way for you to ever return—you have to choose *us,* want *us,* over whatever it is out there that's pulling you away."

She shut the door and turned to the remainder of her family. Her entire body was shaking, as if from a chill, yet she willed the tremors to cease.

"I want you two to help me with something."

"Mom, this is only temporary, right?" Josh asked, wiping at his eyes. "I mean Dad just needs help and—"

"Shut up, Josh," Abbie snapped and reached for her mother. "You don't know what he's been doing. None of us do! All we know is that he argues with everyone—"

"You shut up. You've been a whining witch since you've come home from the hospital!"

"All right! That's enough!" Maureen interceded. "We're all upset. Let's not attack each other." *Keep it together,* she told herself. *Only a little while longer. You can do it . . .*

She wiped the tears away from her cheeks and looked at the twins. "I want to get that armoire out of the bedroom. We can put it in the hall and use it for linens."

"Mom, have you gone nuts?" Josh demanded. "That thing must weigh five hundred pounds."

She spoke in a determined voice. "We can do it. I want it removed before the two of you go out tonight. Do you understand?"

Abbie threw her hands up in defeat. "We'll help you, but we can't go out now."

"Why not?"

Her daughter gave her the same look of disbelief as her son. She glanced at her brother for confirmation. "We can't leave you like this. Not tonight. God, Mom . . ."

Abbie started crying again and Josh shifted his weight as he swallowed down his own tears. Coming back to them, Maureen wrapped the children in her arms.

"Listen to me, you two," she whispered, sniffling away the emotion that threatened to overwhelm her. "It's New Years Eve. A new beginning. Right now, there's just the three of us. But I don't want either one of you to think you have to baby-sit me through this. I appreciate your concern, but I won't have it. You both have plans, and you're going. I would feel worse if you stayed home." She kissed them in turn. "Now, c'mon. Let's get that sucker out of my bedroom."

She walked through the living room, then stopped and touched the flowered chintz loveseat that Dan had always thought was too feminine. "You know, I always wanted a place to have morning coffee while I was getting dressed. Do you think we could get it upstairs?"

Josh and Abbie looked at each other. It was her son who said it aloud. "I think you're losin' it, Mom."

She didn't drink. She never liked the taste of it. Standing at the kitchen counter, Maureen filled half the tumbler with Irish whiskey, dropped in a few ice cubes and a splash of diet 7Up. She stirred it with a spoon and brought the glass to her mouth. Taking a healthy gulp, she realized it wasn't that bad. Certainly not as bad as the first batch.

She was getting drunk.

She couldn't remember the last time. Was it before she was married? It was certainly a long time ago. The house was quiet, unbearably so, yet she was glad the kids went out. She needed this time alone. Taking the glass with her, she wandered into the living room and flipped on the stereo. Classical music flowed out of the speakers. It was sad and beautiful, and she didn't want any part of it. She punched another station and listened to a split second of rap music before switching.

"Not tonight," she said aloud, searching for an oldies program. "Tonight is for me." She didn't care that she was talking to herself. It felt good. It also felt a little silly, but good. When "Shake a Tail Feather" blared out of the speakers, she smiled. "All right. This is more like it."

She took a large swig of her drink and set it down on the highly polished antique end table. She didn't care if it left a ring. Hell, she didn't care if it ate right through the two hundred year old wood. Might add character. Turning to the stereo, Maureen started singing with the music. She couldn't remember all the words, but instantly recalled the carefree feeling of her youth. Within seconds, her body started moving with the beat and, suddenly, she wasn't Maureen Malone any more. She wasn't the good wife and mother. Not the author, or the PTA volunteer. She was Maureen Henessey, boppin' and shakin' her tail feather at Hugh Carcella's dance Hall in Fallsington, Pennsylvania. She must have danced for fifteen minutes straight, moving to the empty place on the rug where the loveseat had been. It was only when the music slowed to a Righteous Brothers ballad, that she fell onto the sofa, dizzy and breathing heavily.

It was a live broadcast from a Philly nightclub and she could hear the crowd of people in the background as the DJ asked if everyone was having a good time.

"Hell, yes!" Maureen shouted drunkenly to the stereo. "I'm havin' a bloody party here!" She giggled. Dan and the twins would be shocked by her actions and her language, but she honestly didn't care any more. She was always so good. So proper. Always doing what everyone thought was right. She had followed the unwritten rules and it still fell apart . . .

"Hey, everybody," the DJ called out to her. "It's New Year's Eve. In forty minutes, we'll be ringing in the new year. We're down here at the Grapevine Cafe, and there's still time to come out and join us."

Voices in the background cheered and it sounded like the best-invitation Maureen had ever heard. She listened to the tinkling of glass and the laughter. The buzz of excitement. New Years Eve. She was all alone, but what was Dan doing? *And who was he doing it with?*

She cursed him again with language that would have made a sailor proud and stood up. What was she doing getting drunk all alone? Hell, there were people out there waiting for her. The Grapevine Cafe. She knew where it was. She could do it. Throw some water on her face. A little makeup. Her hair was already done. She wouldn't even have to change. Let the rest of them wear their silks and gold lamé. She'd wear her jeans and sweat shirt and to hell with tradition.

Making her decision, Maureen shut off the stereo and raced upstairs.

* * *

Fifteen minutes later, she was on Route 130 heading toward the Betsy Ross Bridge. She opened all the windows and turned the car radio back to the oldies station. The music of her youth was blaring in her ears, reminding her of happy times, of innocence, when her feeling of euphoria suddenly vanished. What in the world was she doing? She was as bad as Dan, trying to recapture something that was forever lost. She wasn't an eighteen-year-old kid looking for a party. It was her children's time, Abbie's and Josh's, not hers. Hers was long gone. Just like her marriage. Everything familiar and secure was gone, wiped away because she wasn't young enough or pretty enough any more. She had lost more than her husband. She had lost her closest friend. She had trusted him, and he betrayed her. The immense weight of sadness returned and Maureen started sobbing while searching for a place to turn around.

And then it hit her.

The thought.

As the pain and betrayal became unbearable, crushing against her until she thought she would surely die, Maureen realized there was a way to end the sorrow, to stop the excruciating grief.

All she had to do was turn the wheel, just turn it into the oncoming traffic. One more New Year's Eve fatality. That's all . . .

Her fingers tightened on the steering wheel as she squinted against the glare of headlights. It would be so easy. Just turn it, she told herself, and

56

it's over. You don't have to think about any of it anymore. Do it. Do it, goddamn it! Her heart pounded in her ears as the temptation became so strong that even mental pictures of her children weren't enough to stop the thought. Staring at the white lights in front of her, she became mesmerized by the idea of darkness and freedom. No more pain. No betrayal. No anger. Just peace. Serenity . . .

The concept held such appeal that she almost didn't notice when a hand quickly reached out from nowhere to steady the wheel. *A hand! A man's hand!*

"Don't do it, Maureen," a voice beside her ordered. *"This is not what you really want."*

Staring at the hand for only a second, her mouth opened in disbelief and shock, and she jerked her head toward the body in the passenger seat.

It was Bobby O'Connor!

"Holy shit, Maureen, will you stop screaming and take the wheel? I don't know how much longer I can control this thing! I already went once this way; I'd rather not repeat the experience."

She grabbed hold of the steering wheel, embedding her nails into the leather covering as she slammed on the brakes. The car fishtailed crazily, screeching to a halt on the side of the road.

She stared at the windshield, frozen in shock, trying to regain her breath, her composure, her sanity . . . and not daring to turn her head to see if he was still there. But she felt him. As real and alive as any living being.

Not able to stand it, she slowly looked out of the side of her eye.

"Bobby?" her voice cracked, sounding like a frightened child.

And then he smiled—that wonderful, brilliant smile.

"Hiya, kid. So how's life?"

Chapter Three

She couldn't move. She could barely breathe. He was sitting next to her in the car, as if it were twenty years ago . . . Maureen stared at the apparition. Dear God, he didn't look much older than Josh. A lock of thick black hair fell over onto his forehead. His blue eyes sparkled with mischief and those damn dimples that had driven her crazy so many years ago now appeared on either side of his mouth as he continued to smile at her. This was madness! Insanity! She was losing her mind.

"Bobby?" Her voice was a mere whisper of disbelief.

He chuckled. "One and the same. God, it's good to see you, Maureen."

"You — you're supposed to be dead," she cried. "I went to your . . . your funeral."

His smile disappeared. "Yeah, I know."

She said aloud the question that was uppermost in her mind. "Did I die? Is that why I can see you? How else can this be happening to me?"

His smile returned and nearly lit up his face. "I'm dead, Maureen. Not you. Though, you scared the hell out of me for a second there." He shook his head. "Nah . . . I don't think you would have done it. Your kids mean too much to you."

"My kids?"

"Yeah. Josh and Abbie. Good kids. Josh reminds me of myself. I couldn't get along with my sister either."

She started crying then. It began slowly, yet quickly built into full-blown sobs. Her children . . . what would become of her children? Surely, they would be taken away from her.

"Hey, don't cry. I didn't mean to scare you. I just didn't know any other way to stop you. You were pretty close to blowing it there, you know?"

Leaning up against the steering wheel, she buried her face in her arms. "I've lost my mind," she sobbed. "They're going to take my children away from me . . ."

"Aw, geez."

Suddenly, as if it came from somewhere outside herself, Maureen felt a warm peacefulness invade her body, wiping away the fear and panic. It was so tender and gentle, wrapping around her like the arms of a lover, that she slowly lifted her head to see if Bobby had touched her.

He was still seated in the passenger seat, but the look on his face made her softly ask, "Was that you? Did you do that?"

Shrugging, he nodded as if embarrassed. "Feel better?"

Maureen sniffled and wiped at her nose with the back of her hand. Sitting in the dark with him she could almost believe that he was real, that he existed, that this young man of her youth, the one she had loved for so many years, was alive.

No longer afraid, she tried to smile as her throat nearly closed with fresh emotion. "Oh Bobby, I've missed you." She reached out to touch him and was amazed as her hand passed right through his shoulder. Her jaw dropped open in shock as a warm tingling spread up her arm and settled in her stomach. Snatching back her hand, she stared at him.

"What did you expect?" he answered her look of astonishment. "I haven't come back to life. I wish I could, but—"

"Then what are you doing here? In my car? Why are you here, Bobby? Why am I seeing you, talking to you . . ." Her words trailed off as she silently begged him to answer, to let her know that she wasn't losing her mind.

His gaze was filled with tenderness and compassion. "I came back to help you." Smiling sympathetically, he continued, "You've had a pretty rough time of it lately. We thought you could use some assistance, though I didn't plan on being this direct. I'm telling you, Maureen, you really scared me. For a second there I thought you might turn the wheel into—"

"We?" she interrupted.

He appeared uncomfortable. "You know," he answered evasively and nodded out to the sky.

"The higher-ups. The ones with all the power."

"Like God?" she whispered, staring beyond him out of the car window. Was the Supreme Being about to materialize on Route 130?

Bobby nodded. "God . . . that's a pretty good name. But my direction comes from a little lower than that."

"Lower?" she insisted. "An . . . an archangel, or something?"

He laughed. He threw back his head and chuckled, and the action brought a smile to her lips.

"You sounded like Sister Carmela in religion class." He took a deep breath, as if to stop the laughter. "Okay, if that's the way you want to think, then yes. And I've been sent here to watch out for you."

She stared at him for a few more seconds. "Then you're my . . . my Guardian Angel?"

He returned her look with one of affection. "Yes, Maureen, I'm your Guardian Angel. I like that—Guardian Angel. I hope they're paying attention up there."

Turning her head, she stared out of the windshield and into the night. When she spoke, her voice was a whisper of awe. "What's it like, Bobby? Heaven? Is it real? Does any of that stuff they taught us really exist?"

"I can't tell you, because . . . because I don't know."

She looked back at him. "You don't know? But you're—you know—dead." It sounded so impolite to use that word.

He didn't seem to take offense. Instead, he shrugged his shoulders. "It seems that I have a selective memory. I can remember the past. I can remember everything about the past, even the color of the ribbon you wore in your hair the first time I saw you." He raked his fingers through his own hair, as if in frustration. "But I can't remember anything since the night of the accident, although I know it's in my mind. It's like I can't retrieve it, or something." He looked out to the night. "Maybe it's one of the conditions of me being here with you. Hey! Listen . . ."

When Bobby looked at the radio, its volume suddenly increased. She hadn't even noticed that it had been silent.

The DJ she had been listening to earlier yelled out in a ridiculously joyful voice, "Happy New Year!" The crowd around him broke out into cheers. Noisemakers and laughter rang out along with the traditional playing of "Auld Lang Syne."

She felt the tears well up at her eyes as she stared at the radio. What was happening to her? Nothing was right anymore. Where was order and normalcy? She had just thrown her husband out and was sitting on the side of the road talking to a ghost!

"Be happy, Maureen. You just made it through one of the toughest nights of your life." His voice was low and rough with emotion, and when she looked up from the radio, he was no longer there.

She sat in the car for more than five minutes,

trying to reason out what had happened. Staring at the empty seat, she willed him to materialize, to show himself again, just so she could know she wasn't crazy. Bobby O'Connor was her Guardian Angel? He had come down from heaven, or wherever, to watch out for her. But it was impossible. Angel or ghost, it didn't matter. This sort of thing just doesn't happen. Her life was orderly, structured. There was always an explanation for everything. She was drunk! That was it! There. That was an explanation.

It had been fifteen or twenty years since she'd had that much to drink. She'd never had a vision before, even a drunken vision, but she was older. That's right. Older. Her body chemistry had changed.

Maureen giggled to herself. She really was losing it if she believed any of it actually happened. Taking a deep steadying breath, she turned the key and jumped as the ignition screeched. The car was already on; she'd never shut it off.

"Okay, calm down," she said aloud. "You can do this. You're not crazy. Slightly drunk — that's all." She took another deep breath and turned on the left hand signal as she slowly pulled out onto the road.

Clutching the wheel in a death grip, she didn't relax until the car was safely in her driveway. When she leaned back against the headrest, Maureen shut her eyes and allowed the tension to drain out of her body. This time she didn't even bother to stop the tears.

Bobby O'Connor. Dear God, how she had once loved him . . .

As the middle child she had always been the practical one, the quiet one, the child who didn't want to cause trouble or gain attention. Life was easier that way, especially since her mother had died. Her brothers were a handful and their dad figured the best way to get through the coming years was to run the family like a military camp. His position as commander-in-chief was never challenged and he bellowed out orders with every confidence that they would be carried out. Everyone had their assignments, both in and out of the house, and the slightest infraction was always met with the dreaded grounding. It seemed like she could never work off her punishment before the next was attached. God, it had been over two months since she was allowed out — legally that is.

Standing at the dining room window, Maureen watched the street outside her house for Bobby's car. A knot of fear formed in her stomach as she silently prayed that Bobby would come before her father returned from the store. It was almost a year now since she had invented the Andersons. John and Ann and their two children Bill and Tracey. The fictional family was her excuse to get out of the house on Friday nights, whether she was grounded or not. At sixteen, when all her friends were dating and going to dances, Maureen had been on perpetual grounding. She would finally work off two weeks when she'd forget to peel the potatoes for dinner, or something equally stupid, and two more weeks would be tacked on. Her entire existence involved school or the running of her home. Seventeen years old and she had the same social life as a cloister. Her father was trying to keep her away from the world, to protect her from the unknown, when all she wanted to do was run straight into it. Thank God for cheerleading, an extracurricular activity that her father endorsed since it provided the way his only daughter could participate in the male sport of football. She missed her mom. She missed freedom.

One day she sat in her room and tried to figure a way to have a normal life. Babysitting, a job, the chance to earn money and instill responsibility — now that was something that would gain her father's approval and freedom for one night during the weekend. So every Friday night for almost a year, Maureen babysat for the non-existent Andersons. She'd even had her father drop her off the first time at an old grade school friend's house. Waving to her dad as he drove away, she'd had a moment of guilt but told herself that the deception was necessary if she were to grow up normally, to have any teenage experiences that involved a male outside of her family. For ten months she kept the same two dollars inside the zipper of her purse. She didn't care how many lunches she had to skip, her babysitting money was safe and secure.

Seeing a car drive up the street, Maureen was

sure Father Fidelias would tell her she was committing a grievous sin. It was for that reason that she never mentioned it in confession.

When she heard the horn beep, Maureen jumped into action. She grabbed her coat and called out, "I'm leaving."

Joey looked up from the TV. "Babysitting?"

Maureen opened the front door. "Tell dad I should be back around midnight," she instructed her younger brother. Again, the guilt. No matter how many times she told herself that she was seventeen and had no other way of getting out of the house, she was always hit with shame when she left.

Running to the car, she opened the passenger side and slid in. When she saw Bobby wearing his father's hat, she burst into laughter. "Mr. Anderson, I presume?"

He glared at her with impatience as he backed out of the driveway. "Look, your dad knows my parents. I'm not taking any chances." He made a disgusted noise with his mouth before adding, "Why can't you just get out like normal people?"

"Because I don't live in a normal house, with normal people. You know my dad. He makes General Patton look like a sissy."

"And he'd beat the crap out of me if he knew I was doing this."

Seeing the old-fashioned hat atop Bobby's head, Maureen again laughed, but the amusement was short lived as two headlights quickly came up behind them.

"Holy shit! Is it your father?" Bobby demanded, jamming the car into first gear.

Maureen looked back and all the fear she had stored up for a year slammed into her chest. "Get out of here," she ordered in a strangled voice.

Bobby's foot smashed into the gas pedal and they left rubber burning on the road as they lost Maureen's father three streets later. Out on Route 1, Maureen finally found her voice. "Oh my God, what should I do?"

Bobby's breathing slowed close to normal. "What do you want to do? Do you want to go back?"

"Go back?" To Maureen, it was the equivalent of facing a firing squad.

"Maybe you could explain—"

"To *my* dad?" she interrupted, fighting back tears. He was going to kill her. There was no doubt about it.

Bobby threw his father's hat onto the back seat. "I'm picking up Muzzy and Ted and Colleen. If you want my advice, I say if this is your last night of freedom, then you'd better have fun."

She stared out the window and nodded, that nauseating feeling of dread settling in her stomach and taking hold.

"Hey," Bobby added in a falsely cheerful voice. "At least we're going to Philly. I mean, you could've been caught over some stupid movie. We're going to the Boulevard, girl."

She tried smiling.

It didn't work.

To kids from the northern suburbs, the Boulevard Ballroom was a teenagers' Valhalla. Music blared so loud you had to shout to be heard. Wall to wall young people filled the immense room, stomping so hard on the wooden floors that the intense beat was felt in one's solar plexus. It was where dances that would spread across the country were originated. Styles of clothing were conceived in a single night. It was time of conservatives and jives, when what you wore also stated what you stood for. Motown reigned supreme and the Beatles still looked like preppy bad boys. It was the last breath of innocence, a time when grass was still something you had to mow for your father on Saturday afternoons. No one had ever seen a joint of marijuana, and half of the kids in the place probably couldn't even find Viet Nam on a map.

1966 . . . the last trace of naivete.

Maureen should have been happy. Everyone around her was having a great time laughing and dancing, yet she stood in the middle of the floor with her arms crossed over her chest. From time to time she was jostled by the dancers but she ignored them. Her last night of freedom. She should be enjoying it, yet everytime she thought about going home her stomach knotted with fear. It didn't help that the air was heavy with the cloying scents of *Ambush* and *Canöe* emanating from the bodies of three hundred kids tightly packed into one room.

"Hey, how come you're not dancing?"

She turned, looked across the dancing bodies that separated them, and saw Bobby staring back at her. He had laughing eyes, wonderful blue eyes that lit up when he smiled. A lock of black hair fell over onto his forehead and he was sweating, just like everyone else. But his mouth . . . how she loved his mouth. He could have done a Colgate commercial. And those dimples. You just couldn't help grinning back at him when he smiled. How many years had she fantasized about those lips touching hers in a real kiss? It seemed she had wanted him forever. She counted off the years in her mind. Eight. For eight years now they'd had this weird relationship. Boyfriend. Girlfriend. Going steady. Dancing. Then, just friends. She was never sure of him, never certain just what those looks they shared really meant.

Like now. What was he thinking? If he wanted to talk, why didn't he stand next to her, instead of shouting? As if from far away she heard the music change and people paired off into a slow dance. She held her breath as she waited for him to make a move. *Just once, Bobby,* she silently pleaded as she continued to hold his gaze. *Just once make the first move . . .*

As if reading her mind, he slowly made his way through the dancers. Standing in front of her, he stared into her eyes and said, "I thought you were going to have a good time."

She shrugged her shoulders. "I can't," she said over the music. "Everytime I think about going home . . ." Her words trailed off helplessly.

He smiled, shook his head, and pulled her into his arms. "C'mon," he muttered into her ear. "Let's dance."

He held her softly, almost reverently, and Maureen slipped her arm over his shoulder, pulling him into her. She felt the length of him against her body and held her breath as a rush of excitement raced through her. Tears formed at the corners of her eyes as she sensed his hand tighten at her waist. The language that could be transmitted during a dance was amazing. Two young bodies moving together, slowly, sensuously, could speak to each other in a way that defied explanation.

He took her hand and brought it to his chest, leaving it there to wrap his other arm around her back. Beneath her palm, she felt the beat of his heart and the heat of his body. It aroused her more than she thought possible. His breath was above her ear, sending shivers down her spine, when he whispered her name. "Maureen?"

She pulled back and looked into his face. They stared at each other for timeless seconds, unaware of anyone else in the room, until Bobby lowered his head and kissed her.

It was everything she had imagined, and more. His lips were soft and tender, yet soon became demanding. She parted her lips, allowing him entrance to her mouth. God, he tasted wonderful, and she was hot and hungry for him. With a shocking boldness, she wound her fingers through his hair, pulling him tighter against her as she devoured him in a hot, wet—

"Mom? Mom, wake up!"

She moaned, angry to be jerked away from the best kiss she had ever experienced. Blinking a few times in confusion, she stared at the young boy in front of her. It wasn't Bobby O'Connor. It was her son, dressed in sweats and carrying something orange under his arm.

"Are you going to take me to basketball practice, or should I wait for dad?"

"Dad?" she repeated, thoroughly dazed.

"He is coming, isn't he? It's Saturday. He said he'd be here this morning."

Maureen nodded and turned over, snuggling into her pillow. "Ahhuh. Give me ten minutes more, okay? I'll get up," she mumbled. "I promise."

She dismissed her son and tried to get back to the dream. She was filled with happiness. Her whole body seemed content and a smile appeared at her lips. She wanted to get back; she needed to find out what happened after the kiss.

But Bobby never kissed her that night. She opened her eyes and stared at the watercolor on the wall across from the bed. They had danced and then he took her home. Her father was waiting for her in the dark, sitting in a chair with his belt in one hand. He demanded to know who was driving the car, but she had never told him. It was a matter of honor. She wouldn't rat on Bobby, no matter how hard her father beat her.

Maureen sighed and turned over as she remembered the beating and the three months of punishment that followed. Her feeling of euphoria vanished as reality set in. *It was just a dream, Maureen,* she told herself. Bobby never kissed you that night and you never saw him three days ago on New Year's Eve. All of it is your imagination. That's why you're a writer; you invent this stuff. Now get a grip on yourself. Get up and get ready. Your *husband* is coming to see his children.

Throwing back the covers, she raced for the shower.

Chapter Four

There was no one left. He'd have to deal with her. Josh was playing basketball, and Abbie talked to her father for less than five minutes before announcing that she forgot her promise to Scott that she'd go to the mall with him. Now there was just Maureen and Dan, alone for the first time in over a week.

When he sat at the kitchen table, she asked, "Would you like some coffee?"

Glancing at his watch, he nodded. "Sure. Thanks."

She hated it when he looked at his watch. It always made her feel that he was meeting someone, or at least had somewhere more important to go. She was also aware that Dan felt like a stranger in his home and as she brought the mug to the table, she forced herself to smile before sitting opposite him. Once seated, she finally stopped sucking in her stomach, but she was careful to hold her chin up, to straighten her shoulders, to present herself in the best possible light. She hated the fact that she couldn't relax in front of him. He had once been her friend, her best friend, but now she made sure that her makeup was perfect and her hair in place. She'd dressed in black jeans because they were slimming and a red silk blouse because someone had once told her that red was her color. A part of her knew she was trying to win him back, and it seemed so shallow and pathetic that she quickly dismissed the thought.

"Abbie's angry with me," Dan said, picking up his mug.

Maureen didn't reply. She noticed that he was drinking his coffee black, something new, and that his hand was shaking, as if tremors were passing up his arm.

"What's wrong with your hand?" she asked out of concern.

He quickly put the mug back on the table and shook his head. "Nothing. There's nothing wrong. I'm just tired."

She nodded. Why was it so hard to hold a conversation with him? Why was her brain searching for a neutral topic . . .

"How have you been?" he interrupted her thoughts.

She shrugged. "All right, I suppose." She wanted to get up and ask him to hold her, to reassure her that everything would work out, that she wasn't losing her mind. But she couldn't. Not now. Now they were like two strangers that were forced to endure each other's company.

"How about you?" she asked. "How are you doing?" God, even this conversation was strained.

"Okay," he answered quietly. "The kids look good. So do you."

She was right about the red blouse. "Thanks."

"Listen, Maureen, I have to talk to you about something."

Her heart tightened with hope and she smiled. "All right." Even though she was the one that had told him to leave, she didn't want to let him go. She didn't know how. Twenty years of her life were wrapped up in this man.

He didn't look up from his coffee. "We need to talk about finances."

"Finances?" she asked stupidly. What about starting over? Seeing a marriage counselor?

He finally raised his head and looked directly at her. "I've found an apartment."

Her stomach recoiled and she felt as if he had punched her. It took several attempts to swallow before she could mutter, "Where?"

"In Philadelphia, a few blocks from work." He sipped his coffee and then added, "It's really a dump, the third floor of an old brownstone. Eddie Munster could have lived there."

She failed to see the humor in his statement and her jaw tightened with anger. He was really going to do this . . .

"What about us?" she demanded. "What does this mean?"

He sat back in his chair and looked around the

kitchen. "It means I need a place to live. I can't keep staying in a hotel."

"You didn't answer me," she insisted. "What about us?"

He shrugged his shoulders. "I don't know. I need some time."

"To do what?" Maureen asked quickly. "To get some help? Or to play with the secretary?"

She immediately knew it was the wrong thing to say, yet she didn't care. What was he doing to them? If he got an apartment, they might never get back together.

"I told you before," he answered in a tightly controlled voice, "this isn't about another woman. I wouldn't do that to you."

She couldn't keep the sarcasm out of her tone. "You wouldn't?"

He pushed the mug away from him. "If that's what this was about, do you honestly think I haven't had the chance before? There's been plenty of women that have been attracted to me, but I never did anything about it."

"You haven't been with any other woman?" she asked directly.

"No."

She wanted desperately to believe him. "Then what is it about?"

"I don't know." His face was red and his hands were starting to shake again.

"Well, try to find out, goddammit! You're destroying this family." She fought back the tears and the burning in her throat. "Dan, go back to the counselor. Get some help. Don't let this just happen . . ."

"You can't make me feel any more guilty than I do already." He looked at his watch again and stood up. "I've got to leave," he said in a strangled voice. "I just wanted you to know that I'll continue to pay all the bills. Money will be deposited every month into the checking account—just like always."

"I don't care about money," she said through clenched teeth. "I care about my family, about us. Please, Dan, think about—"

"Just leave me alone!" he shouted. "God Almighty, Maureen, what more do I have to do to you?"

She stared at him, feeling battered and alone, as a numbing chill spread through her body. "Nothing," she said distantly, nearly choking on unshed tears. "I—I believe you've just done it."

He threw a piece of paper on the table and said in a shaky voice, "My new number. For the kids. I—I have to leave."

Staring at the paper, Maureen blinked away the film of tears covering her eyes as she heard the front door slam. It was only then she leaned onto the table and buried her face in her arms, sobbing and crying out her anguish. The hoarse moans that came out of her mouth sounded like a wounded animal. Her heart was breaking. She could feel it tighten painfully with the same kind of grief as when her mother died.

It was a death.

The death of her marriage.

She wanted to yell with anger and denial, to rage at her helplessness, to scream at the unfairness. Why was this happening to her? What had she done wrong? Why—

Music invaded her ears, making her sniffle and raise her head to listen. She hiccupped and wiped at her eyes as confusion replaced outrage. From a distance she heard music, soft familiar music. Did Dan turn on the radio in the living room before leaving? Getting up, Maureen walked out of the kitchen knowing full well he didn't have time. Then how . . . ?

As she neared the living room she recognized the song. It was a Temptations ballad, "My Girl." She hadn't played that oldies station for a week, since New Year's Eve. Wiping the tears from her cheeks, Maureen felt the muscles in her chest contract with fear. She was afraid to turn the corner and look in the room. But she did.

He was there! Sitting in the wing chair, Bobby grinned and indicated the stereo with his head. "Now *that's* music, right?"

She held onto the wall for support. Oh, God . . . please, make him go away! Please let him be gone when I open my eyes! Maureen clamped her lids shut for a few seconds then popped them open.

"Aw, c'mon and sit down," Bobby said gently and held his hand out to the opposite chair. "I'm telling you, Maureen, I don't know what you ever saw in the guy. He's a real jerk."

Holding her waist to stop the sudden cramping that comes with fear, she fell into the chair, staring at him, willing him to fade away. She had nearly convinced herself that Bobby was merely a figment of her fertile imagination. Ghosts didn't exist. They didn't! But then what's he doing sitting in her living room chair?

"What are you doing here?" she cried, staring at his jeans and Madras shirt, his leather bomber jacket, the way his black hair fell onto his forehead before he raked his fingers through it to push it back.

"I told you. I'm here to help you. Hey, listen to those lyrics . . . *I guess you'd say*—

"If you want to help me," she halted his singing, "then leave me alone! This is insane!" She covered her face with her hands and chanted, "He's not here! He's not really here. This is stress. That's all. You are not crazy—"

"I'll tell you what's crazy," Bobby interrupted. "You getting yourself all worked up over this guy. Maureen. Give me a break. I told you. He's a jerk."

Spreading her fingers, she peeked at him.

He waved, to let her know he was still there.

"He's my husband," she mumbled behind her hands. "He's not a jerk." She brought her hands to her lap and nervously wrapped them around her waist. "Well, he is a jerk now," she amended, sniffling and wiping her cheek on the shoulder of her silk blouse. "But he wasn't always—why am I talking to you?" she demanded. She brought her hand up, as if to ward off an evil specter. "You don't even exist."

"I exist for you, Maureen. You can see me and hear me, can't you?"

She stared at him, at his disarming smile. "That's because I'm going crazy."

"You're not crazy."

"I have to be," she cried out, feeling the tears return. "Why else would I be sitting in my living room talking to a dead man?"

He winced, as if she'd hurt his feelings. "That's the second time you've said that. We don't like to use the word dead," he stated in a gentle voice. "It sounds really flat and forgotten. We prefer something a bit more upbeat."

"Upbeat?" she asked stupidly, wiping at her nose and trying to control the hiccups that always followed a crying jag.

Smiling, he nodded. "Sure. Something like departed, resting, or spirit-filled."

She couldn't help it; her nerves were shot. She giggled. "Spirit-filled? You sound like a television evangelist."

His eyes lost their friendliness and turned angry. "Don't get me started. Thank God, everybody comes full circle and has their day." He shook his head, as if to clear away the disturbing thoughts. "Anyway, that's not why I'm here."

"Why *are* you here, Bobby?" she whispered, feeling the lump come back into her throat. "Why am I talking to someone that's . . . that's *resting?*"

He grinned. "See? You're getting into this now."

"Bobby, why are you here?" she demanded. Her panic returned and she started crying again. Just as she was about to run from the room, from the incredible sight of her old, "rested" boyfriend sitting in her home, a warm, steady feeling started in her legs and slowly crept up her body. When it reached her head, she felt bathed in a secure and peaceful glow. She looked over to him and murmured, "You did that again, didn't you?"

"We have to talk, Maureen."

"What else can you do?" she asked, fascinated now that she wasn't frightened anymore.

He looked puzzled. "What do you mean? I came here to talk to you."

She shook her head. "You turned on the stereo—"

"That was to get your attention."

"You got my attention. Then you do this . . ." she looked down to her body as she searched for the words. "This relaxing thing. What else can you do?"

He stared at her. "Are you asking for proof? You want me to perform for you?"

She felt childish, yet fascinated, as she stared back.

"I'm not Mary Poppins, Maureen. We don't come equipped with a bag of magic tricks to entertain."

"I didn't mean it like that," she said, and it suddenly occurred to her that she was calmly conversing with him as if he were real. "I'm sorry."

He continued to stare at her for a few moments

and then shrugged. Looking about the room, he muttered, "I can't believe I'm resorting to this."

Suddenly the lamps on the end tables flickered on and off several times and Maureen's mouth opened in surprise. "It was you!" she declared in an excited voice. "In the bathroom that time. *You* made the night light work. I was sitting on the floor thinking my life was over and then that old night light started flickering and I felt better just by staring into the glow of it. That was you, wasn't it? And—and when Dan was leaving the first time. You called out my name in the kitchen. It was you, wasn't it?"

"It was me, Maureen."

He said it simply, honestly, as if that sort of thing took place every day. She wanted to hug him, to thank him for looking out for her. She remembered their conversation in the car. "You really are my Guardian Angel, aren't you?"

He almost laughed. "If that's how you want to think of me." He seemed to collect himself. "Now, Maureen, we have to talk—"

"Mom?" The front door was flung open. *"Mom?* Where are you?"

Panic returned three-fold as she stared at Bobby. "Oh my God," she muttered, as if her son had caught her with another man. "It's my son!"

Bobby nodded, frustrated that his important talk was being delayed. "Terrific. It's Josh."

She frantically waved her hand at him. "Go away! Vanish! Do whatever you—"

"Who're you talking to, Mom?"

She stared at her son in his dirty sweats, bouncing his basketball on the hardwood floor. She glanced at the chair by the stereo and her eyes widened at Bobby's wave of familiarity. Looking back at her son, she asked in a frightened voice, "Do you see anything — anything strange in this room?"

Josh captured his ball and held it against his hip as he surveyed the living room. Finally he shook his head. "The only thing weird is that music. You're not going to start listening to *oldies,* are you?" The way he said oldies made it sound worse than opera.

"He can't see me, Maureen," Bobby said. "Though we're going to have to teach this kid how to appreciate fine music."

She stared at the young man in her chair, then at her son. Josh didn't see him!

"Dad leave?"

Maureen blinked a few times, trying to get it straight in her mind, and nodded. "He . . . he has an apartment. In the city. He left his . . ." she waved toward the kitchen, ". . . his new phone number on the table."

Josh looked at her and shook his head in disgust. "Shit! What is wrong with him?" He threw the ball toward the kitchen and walked after it, leaving her alone with Bobby.

Turning to look back at him, she whispered, "Why didn't he see you? Aren't you real?" Her earlier feeling of panic was fast returning.

"I'm real for you. That's all that matters."

"But —"

He shook his head and pointed to the stereo. "You wanted tricks, Maureen? Here's one. Listen . . ."

She looked at the radio and heard a vaguely familiar song. It was slow and sensual.

"Till Then" by the Duprees. That's the song we danced to at Boulevard Ballroom. That was some kiss this morning." He sighed loudly. "I only wish it were real."

When she looked back to the chair he was gone.

She sat for endless moments, listening to the song, to the drumming of her heartbeat in her ears. He knew! Somehow, he knew her dream! Her hands were shaking as she covered the scream that was threatening to explode. It couldn't be! It couldn't! Maybe it wasn't too late, her mind reasoned as she pushed herself out of the chair and raced to the foyer closet.

Maybe there was still time to save her sanity, she prayed as she searched the pockets of her coat. She saw herself dressed in a dingy white hospital gown, haggard and lifeless, staring at the bars on a window and talking to a ghost when her children came to visit. The graphic vision filled her brain and she actually sobbed with relief when her exploration proved successful. Clutching the paper in her hand, she ran into the kitchen and picked up the phone. It took her two tries before she correctly dialed the number for Lisa's old therapy group.

If any sanity remained, she was going to fight like hell to keep it.

She fell asleep thinking about the insanity of attending a therapy group in the morning. How could her ordered and structured life have fallen apart so miserably? As sleep softly wrapped its blanket around her, Maureen realized her dreams were as crazy as reality, for there was Lisa standing before her with an ecstatic look on her face as she gazed up at a fairy tale prince, complete with ermine robe and crown.

Lisa turned to Maureen, smiled sweetly, and said, "I'm so excited! I finally got laid by Prince Charming, and I'm going to have a baby." A beautiful infant magically appeared in her best friend's arms.

Maureen stared at the child in amazement as Lisa added, "Don't worry. I haven't completely turned into Donna Reed. Look." Lisa parted her gown and stuck out her ankle. "I'm never shaving my legs again."

Thoroughly confused, Maureen looked down and stared with wonder at Lisa's short limb, covered in hair that would have made Joe Namath jealous. What the hell was she dreaming? It was ridiculous, crazy and made no sense. Lisa with hairy legs? Maureen turned to run away while hearing her friend shout after her, "Doesn't that prove it? I'm still a feminist!"

It was insanity.

Her heart was slamming against her rib cage as she ran into a dense fog, anywhere to escape the lunatic that had once been her best friend. Her breath came in short, ragged gasps and Maureen slowly came to a halt while struggling to expand her lungs. She stood still as the thick fog swirled around her. Just as she was feeling lost, with no way back to reality, she spied lights in the distance and began walking toward them. Surely here was the way out of the nightmare.

It was as if an unknown force had blown away the fog for she was suddenly standing in the parking lot of a shopping center. Maureen's jaw dropped in amazement as she read the neon sign over the last store.

Joe's Pizza.

It couldn't be! She looked around the parking lot and saw old cars, cars that had been manufactured before head rests or seat belts were mandatory. Kids were standing beside them, kids the same age as Abbie and Josh. They were talking and laughing as she walked up to the front door of the restaurant.

"Hi, Maureen," a girl called out. The girl looked vaguely familiar as she stood next to a boy whose arm was casually draped over her shoulders.

The boy winked at her. "How's it going, Irish?"

And then Maureen recognized them. Mary Lou Stewart and Jimmy Scanlon. Jimmy had always called her Irish.

Maureen tried smiling, but her expression was

frozen stiff as she mumbled "Hi" and hurried past. What the hell was going on now? She stared through the glass window to the inside of the pizza parlor and saw all her old friends from high school. They were jammed into booths, laughing and eating and calling out to one another. She saw someone waving to her and a feeling of awe swept through her as she recognized Margie McKee, her closest friend since freshman year.

Touching the cool glass pane, Maureen smiled and found herself waving back. Margie pointed to the empty place next to her in the booth, indicating she was holding the space for Maureen and gestured for her to come inside. Without reasoning it out, Maureen nodded back and opened the door.

Her senses were immediately assaulted by the aroma of Italian food and the level of noise, a mixture of youthful voices and Motown coming from the jukebox in the back of the room.

Had she somehow slipped into another nightmare? As she walked down the center aisle, Maureen crossed her arms over her chest for protection. No one seemed to notice that she was old enough to be their parent, or that she was wearing a thin cotton nightgown that clearly outlined a body well past its youth.

"Where have you *been?*" Margie demanded, moving over and patting the place next to her.

Dumbfounded, Maureen slipped into the booth as she stared at her friends. Margie, the prettiest of them all with her long, straight blond hair, flawless complexion and dazzling smile; Colleen, the smart one, who hated her red hair and freckles, but never lacked a date. And Robin, earthy with dark brown hair and eyes, the most adventurous and experienced of all of them, the one who had taught them how to smoke and who stole her father's liquor supply to give them their first taste of alcohol. They were all together again, as if the last twenty years had never happened . . .

"Okay, so she's here now," Robin said impatiently. "Let's get back to business. Do I, or do I not, go all the way with Mike?"

"God, I wouldn't," Margie whispered. "What if he tells everyone? You know how guys talk."

Colleen shook her head. "It's supposed to be the most wonderful experience of your life. Why waste it on Mike Higgins?"

Robin leaned closer to the table. "Wonderful experience! Oh, yeah. Right. Rita Carmeletti says she bled like a stuck pig, and that it hurt like hell."

"Then why are you even considering doing it?" Margie asked.

"Because Mike's pressuring me," Robin answered. "And I like everything we've done so far. I also don't intend to be the last virgin in Levittown, Pennsylvania."

No one said anything until Robin looked at Maureen. "What do you think, Henessey? Do I cave in and do the dirty deed?"

Maureen looked at the wall mirror on the sides of the booths. She saw her own image, a woman in her early forties. Tired. In her nightgown. With

89

her hair all messed up. Why couldn't anyone else see she didn't belong here? That this was all a dream?

"Maureen?" Margie nudged her for an answer.

Blinking a few times, Maureen tried to focus on Robin. "Why are you letting a guy pressure you? If you're not ready, tell him no." She thought of her own daughter on birth control pills and added, "What if you got pregnant? Do you want to be married to Mike Higgins for the rest of your life?"

All of them slowly glanced to the back of the restaurant where Mike was sitting with three of his friends. The girls looked at each other with an expression of horror on their faces.

"Hell, no," Robin nearly hissed across the table and everyone broke up into nervous giggles.

"And what will your husband say when he finds out your not a virgin?" Margie added, trying to be serious. "I mean, what will he think on your wedding night?"

Colleen stared across the table at Margie. "I can't believe you said that. Why is it okay for Mike to have all the experience and his wife is supposed to accept that, but Robin's husband can't accept that she isn't a virgin! This world's screwed up if a guy's experienced, but a girl's a slut."

"Hey," Robin interrupted. "I am not a slut! I haven't even done anything yet. I'm still ninetynine per cent Ivory pure. I'm just saying the one percent so far has been pretty nice."

"You girls ordering something, or what?"

They all looked up at Bella, Joe's wife, as she stood at the front of their booth.

"Yeah," Robin answered. "I'll have a cheese steak and fries. Vanilla Coke."

"Same," agreed Colleen.

"Meatball sandwich and a Vanilla Coke," Margie said.

Everyone looked to Maureen. "Ahh . . . I'll just have a Diet Coke."

"What?" Bella stood with her hand on her ample hip. "What are you talking about, huh? I got Coke. Pepsi. 7UP. No diet anything. Now, what is it? I don't have time for you kids and your games. You don't wanna eat," and she indicated the door with her thumb, "then you can go out with the rest of them."

"C'mon, Maureen," Colleen urged. "Don't make trouble."

Looking around the table, Maureen said, "I—I guess I'll just have a Coke."

"Oh, I know what it is," Robin told the group. "She doesn't want to touch her babysitting money. Gotta show up at the old homestead with some bucks tonight, huh?" She reached into her purse and took out a five-dollar bill. Pushing it across the table, she said, "Now order what you want. You can pay me back later."

Robin was an only child and never without funds.

They all looked at her and Maureen stammered, "I—I'll have . . . a . . ."

"She'll have a cheese steak and a Vanilla Coke,"

Margie answered for her and smiled at Bella as the woman walked away. "What are you trying to do? Get us thrown out? You know how impatient Bella gets."

And then Maureen remembered trying to stay on the good side of the owner's wife so they could sit and talk and not give up their booth to the crowd waiting outside. It was all coming back to her.

As Bella placed their Cokes in front of them, Robin held out a pack of Winstons. "Who wants a cig?"

The sweetness of Vanilla Coke awakened her taste buds and Maureen felt a wonderful sense of nostalgia as she sipped through the straw.

Colleen and Margie were already lighting up. "How about you, Henessey?" Robin offered the pack to her.

Maureen shook her head. "No. I quit years ago."

Everyone stared at her as Margie whispered, "But we only just started smoking two months ago."

She saw the confused expressions of her friends and nearly giggled. Instead, she shrugged her shoulders. What the heck? It was only a dream, right? Pulling out a cigarette, Maureen smiled. "Just kidding, guys. Can't you take a joke?"

They looked suspiciously at her until she lit up. Deeply inhaling, Maureen closed her eyes as she blew out the smoke. It sent a rush traveling through her blood stream and she felt as if she'd just had a drink. God, it tasted good! Bringing the cigarette back to her lips, she didn't know until this moment how much she had missed it.

"Okay," Robin pronounced. "Now back to my problem. The consensus is that I shouldn't do it. Right?"

"Right," Margie said.

Colleen put her cigarette down in the ashtray. "I wouldn't. Not with Mike Higgins."

"Maureen?"

She wasn't sure what to say. Should she talk to her as a friend, or like she had talked to Abbie? "Look, Robin, I don't think you're old enough to handle the emotional responsibility of making love to someone. What's the hurry? So what if you're a virgin? Don't do something you're not really ready to do. Wait until you don't have to ask anyone else's opinion. When it's right, you'll know it."

Robin looked disappointed. "You know, you sound like my mother!" She took a drag off her cigarette and glared at Maureen. "And why do you know so much? Have you been keeping something back from us, Henessey?"

They all stared at her, examining her face as if it would tell them something until Maureen actually felt herself blushing under their scrutiny.

"Oh, my God!" Margie blurted out in a hoarse whisper. "She's *done it!*"

Colleen picked up her cigarette and puffed crazily. "I can't believe it! How could you do this and not tell us? Who was it? I bet it was Joey Harrington, wasn't it?"

Maureen wanted to laugh out loud as Robin sat back in the booth and smiled across the table to her. "Well, well, Henessey. Still waters do run deep. You've just gone up a notch in my book."

"You're all making a big deal out of this and it's—"

"It is a big deal," Colleen interrupted. "This is supposed to be the most important moment in a woman's life and you've kept it all to yourself."

This time Maureen did laugh. "I'll let you in on a secret," she said, crushing out her cigarette. "It is *not* the most important moment in a woman's life. I don't know what is—maybe the birth of her children, or finding out what she's really meant to do with her life. Maybe it's even her marriage. But I do know it isn't losing her virginity. In fact, in most cases, the first time is awkward, uncomfortable and leaves you feeling distinctly dissatisfied."

Margie was looking at her as if seeing a stranger. "How do you know all this?"

"I've read a lot."

"Yeah? Like what?" Robin demanded.

Maureen looked at each one of them with fondness. They were so young, so innocent, so full of dreams. "Like Masters and Johnson. The Hite Report."

"Never heard of them," Robin announced as their food was placed on the table. Everyone ignored their plates. The discussion was far more interesting than french fries.

"I know you haven't. But you will someday. Pay attention," Maureen advised. "You'll learn a lot about yourself."

Colleen leaned closer to the table, so not to be overheard. "I don't want to read about it. Not when I have someone sitting here who can tell me first hand. How *was* it? Did it hurt?"

"Did you bleed like a stuck pig?" Margie asked anxiously.

Maureen smiled at their innocence. "No, I hardly bled at all, and yes, it did hurt. The first time."

"The *first* time?" All three girls asked the question in unison.

"Jesus, mercy," Margie looked to the others. "She's done it more than once."

"Oh, who cares, Margie," Robin said, her eyes lighting with excitement. "Tell me, what's it like? After the first time? Is it like all the books? Fireworks going off and all that?"

Maureen chuckled. "It can be if you're with the right man, a man who understands a woman and how her body works."

"What do you mean?" Colleen asked. "How her body works?"

Nodding, Maureen figured she might as well tell them. "Everything you've been taught? By your mothers and the priests and nuns?"

"Yes?" they answered, waiting for her revelation.

"Well, it's all bull."

"What do you mean?" Colleen demanded.

"I mean Father Fedalias standing in front of a classroom, telling us that the momentary pleasure a man feels when he's having intercourse is God's way of paying the man back because he'll have to raise children for eighteen years is bullshit. That's what I mean." Without asking, Maureen reached over and took another cigarette. Robin pushed the pack at her, eager for more information.

"How can a man that's never had a lasting relationship with a woman possibly teach sex and marriage to girls? No wonder we're all warped." Maureen held the match to her cigarette and took a deep drag, without the slightest feeling of guilt. "Listen to me. A woman probably enjoys sex even more than a man because she's capable of multiple orgasms and a man needs time between his."

"Multiple . . . what?" Robin looked to the others to see if they understood. No one did.

Okay, this could prove delicate, Maureen thought. But what did it matter, if it was only a dream? "According to the experts, there are two kinds of orgasms. Clitoral and vaginal, though vaginal seems to be rare—"

"Oh, my God," Margie moaned, clearly embarrassed and looking around to see if anyone overheard.

"Shut up, Margie," Robin snarled, suddenly hungry and picking up her cheese steak. "You'll never learn this from your mother or religion class. Go ahead, Maureen. Two kinds. What's that clitor stuff?" She took a huge bite from her sandwich.

Maureen laughed. "Clitoral. And this is going to be tough to explain." But she did, and Margie, Colleen and Robin listened with rapt attention for the next fifteen minutes as she revealed the biological differences between the sexuality of a male and a female.

"So we're supposed to *tell* them?" Colleen asked in a shocked voice. "I couldn't. I'd die of embarrassment."

"Most of them will never know how to please you unless you speak up." Maureen toyed with her food, but didn't eat it.

"And you've done this?" Margie continued to stare at her. "You've actually talked about this with a guy?"

Maureen nodded.

"Who?" Robin wanted to know. "Was it Joey Harrington?"

Remembering the tall handsome football player she had dated in her senior year, Maureen smiled but shook her head.

"I know," Colleen said. "It was Bobby O'Connor, wasn't it? There was always something going on with you two."

"No it wasn't Bobby," Maureen answered. She wished it had been, though. "It was someone none of you know."

"We might as well eat," Robin pronounced. "She's not going to tell us."

In the silence that followed, everyone picked up their sandwiches. Maureen could tell that they were thinking about what she had told them. They were so innocent, holding the same misconceptions that had been passed down through the ages. It would take ten or fifteen more years before women were honest enough to talk like this, to admit to each other and to men that they were highly sexual creatures with unique wants and desires. Maybe it was only a dream, but she felt better for the conversation.

"Why aren't you eating?" Margie whispered. "You're not . . . pregnant . . . or anything, are you?"

Maureen smiled as she held the greasy cheese steak before her. "No. I'm not pregnant. I was thinking about cholesterol and fat and calories. And about how much I want this sandwich."

Sliding the bottle of catsup down the table, Robin shook her head. "What are you talking about? If you want it, just eat it."

Maureen looked at them as they devoured their food while talking about the guys in their crowd—who was dreamy looking, who was a good dancer, who was a good make-out artist—and wondered how it was possible that she was once this young. Was there ever a time when her only concern was boys, when she never worried about her children, her husband, or her figure? It seemed so long ago . . .

Opening the bottle of catsup, she poured it over the cheese steak and took a bite. It tasted scandalously sinful and wonderful.

"Hey, Henessey," Robin pointed out with a grin, "You've dropped catsup down your front."

Maureen looked down and saw the thick, red spot on her nightgown. Grabbing a handful of napkins she blotted the dark stain while a distant ringing started in her ears. As it became louder she looked up, only to see Colleen disappear before her eyes. She started to say something, but the words caught in her throat as Margie and Robin also quickly vanished.

The sound became piercing and more insistent, annoying her to the point of anger. Suddenly she sat up straight and opened her eyes.

Daylight surrounded her bed and she blinked several times with confusion.

"Hey, Mom," Josh yelled from his bedroom across the hall. "You gonna turn that alarm off, or what? I've got fifteen more minutes to sleep."

She automatically reached over to her night table and slammed the clock into silence. What a weird dream! She collapsed back onto her pillow and tried to recapture the closeness she had felt with the friends of her youth. A smile appeared at her lips. But it was only a dream, probably brought on by falling asleep while thinking about meeting with the therapy group this morning.

Her eye lids immediately snapped open and she groaned out loud just thinking about it. Maybe she could cancel? Say she was sick? Knowing how childish it would sound, Maureen threw back the cover and decided to be an adult for the day. Her life was a mess and she had sought them out. The least she could do was show up. But that didn't mean she had to like it. In fact, as she made her way into the bathroom, she realized the notion of spilling her guts to strangers filled her with absolute dread.

She stood in front of the mirror, feeling more tired than when she had fallen asleep the night before, and slowly turned on the cold water. She squeezed out a small amount of Crest onto her toothbrush and was about to bring it to her mouth when her hand froze in midair as she stared at her reflection.

There was a deep orange stain on the front of her nightgown. She dropped her toothbrush into the sink and grabbed the material at her chest. Bringing it up to her nose, she inhaled the spicy scent of catsup!

"No," she whispered in a terrified voice. "This is not happening to me." She dropped the front of her gown and it fell back into place. Standing closer to the mirror, she tried to read some sign of insanity in her eyes. Maybe she had been sleepwalking during the night. Maybe she'd gone into the kitchen and ate catsup because she was dreaming about her old girl friends. There had to be an explanation . . . somewhere. Why the hell couldn't she find it? Terrified, she covered her mouth with her hands to stop the scream that was threatening to explode from her throat.

And that's when she smelled it. The distinct aroma of cigarettes clung to the fingers of her right hand.

"Oh, my God," she moaned and collapsed onto the toilet seat. Staring at the rug beneath her feet, she took it as a sign from above that she desperately needed the help of a trained professional — someone who dealt with delusions and ghosts and maybe split personalities. Well, the same personality, but split ages. God Almighty, they really were going to lock her up!

Bolting upright, she picked up her toothbrush. She would not lose it. Not yet. First she'd get the kids off for school and then she would get ready for the crazy ladies of the therapy group. Crazy ladies? Hah! Maureen could guarantee nobody crazier than she would show up.

What was *really* nuts was that she had the sudden, overwhelming urge for a cigarette!

Chapter Five

"I don't know how to trust a man again."

"Trust? You can't."

"Well, I don't know why they risk everything for a piece of ass. It makes no sense."

"Because a man's brain is centered between his legs. It rules him. They're all bastards."

Good God! Maureen looked at the woman seated next to her and cringed as the rest of the group laughed. Never in her life had she heard women talk about men like this. It was certainly open and honest. But it was also intimidating. There were five of them: Etta, a displaced homemaker in her fifties, whose husband had left her six months ago; Janet, an attractive, friendly-looking woman in her late twenties, whose husband had taken to beating her before bedding her; Casey, an attorney, had just left her live-in lover of six years because they'd grown apart; and Melanie, in her mid twenties, had walked in on her husband in bed with her neighbor. It was Melanie who had made the last remark.

"Maybe men aren't meant to be monogamous," Joanna threw out. Joanna Dunne was the psychologist who headed up the support group. She was the one Maureen had talked to on the phone, the one who had urged her to join the others for a frank discussion. It was certainly frank, and as of yet Maureen hadn't joined in. She couldn't understand how these woman could talk so openly about such personal things. She felt like an outsider, maybe even an innocent.

Her attention turned to Casey as the woman leaned forward. "Maybe no one is meant to be monogamous, women included. Maybe it's just an unnatural state. We're the only creatures that demand faithfulness. Is it possible we've become too damned civilized?" Casey looked about the circle of woman for an answer and grinned. "You know in ancient Celtic times, women were only monogamous until a son had been delivered, an heir. After that, a woman was free to take as many lovers as she wished."

"I think that's disgusting," Etta remarked, crossing her arms over her ample chest. "And the only reason you brought that up is because you're trying to justify breaking up with Jack."

"What do you think, Maureen?" Joanna asked softly in an attempt to draw her into the conversation.

She felt everyone's eyes on her; she sensed their

expectation, and said the first thing that came into her head.

"The trumpeter swan."

Everyone continued to stare at her as if she'd wandered into the wrong conversation. Blushing, Maureen tried again. "The trumpeter swan is monogamous," she said shyly.

Etta's grin was triumphant. "There. See? That shoots holes all over your theory, Casey."

Casey glanced at Maureen before turning her attention to Etta. "Why? Because some bird mates for life? Give me a break, Etta. You were married for over thirty years and you thought it would last forever, but it didn't."

"Casey, don't be cruel," Janet interjected, then smiled at Maureen. "How long were you married?"

"Almost twenty years," Maureen answered easily. She smiled back at Janet, glad she was seated next to her. She liked the woman, at least she felt more comfortable with her than the others. "We had a good marriage until a month ago. Then everything started to fall apart." *I've also started to lose my mind,* Maureen thought, but kept the knowledge to herself. How could she explain to these women about ghosts and weird time travel dreams where she visited her high school friends? A strait jacket would be slapped on her before she could finish a sentence.

"What happened?" Melanie asked. "Did he cheat on you?"

"No." Maureen's answer was quick. "He started

staying out late, arguing with everyone, drinking . . ." She shrugged her shoulders and glanced about the room. All the women were looking at her with pity, as if they knew something she didn't. The small room was filled with silence, and even Joanna didn't try to fill in the void. Finally, Maureen realized why. "Really," she said defensively. "I asked him directly and he said it had nothing to do with another woman."

"And you believed him?" Melanie asked in a skeptical voice.

Maureen swallowed. "Yes, I do."

They all broke eye contact with her, everyone but Casey. The lawyer smiled in sympathy. "It's not you, Maureen," she said, as if explaining to the others. "You see, they all have similar stories. It seems to follow a pattern—working overtime, staying out late with the boys, arguing, disinterest in sex or anything that has to do with the family and home. They're really very unoriginal."

"Martin used to come home and within a half hour he would start an argument." Etta shook her head at the memory. "It took me over a month to realize he had planned it that way. Before he pulled up in the driveway, he knew what he was going to do. Pick a fight, storm out of the house in anger, and then he was free to meet his secretary at the Sheraton."

"They're all selfish bastards," Janet spat. "Every single one of them."

"I don't think you can condemn all men," Joanna advised.

"Well, I do!" Janet countered. "I can't find one man that I can respect. Not my father, my uncles or my husband. Priests are molesting young boys. Evangelists are caught in motel rooms or cars with whores. Politicians don't even try to hide their mistresses. Everywhere I turn marriages are falling apart." Janet looked like she was about to cry. "It's hopeless."

Melanie sighed deeply. "I think we should be looking for trumpeter swans."

"Maybe men are just different than women," Etta offered. "With women everything is wrapped up together — work, family, love. It's all intertwined. I think men are more compartmental. Their job comes first. They leave that and come home to their families —"

"I think they define themselves by their possessions," Casey interrupted. "If someone asks a man to define himself, he doesn't say I'm a husband, a father and a CPA. He says I'm a CPA. He thinks what he does for a living tells the world who he is. Not whether he is a decent human being, a great husband or partner, or a good parent. His job is a possession. Just like the car he drives. How many men drive the Mercedes to work while the wife is stuck with the Escort, lugging the groceries and his kids all over town? Even his wife is a possession and a reflection on how successful he is. If she's gorgeous, he'll show her off. If she's a dog, he hides her at home."

There was a moment of silence as everyone digested Casey's words until Etta almost whispered,

"I don't know why you're so bitter, Casey. You left Jack. It wasn't the other way around."

Casey shook her head. "You don't get it. You aren't out there, Etta. You don't hear them, or see the way they behave with each other."

Casey leaned back in her chair and reached into her pocket for a cigarette. She lit it almost in defiance and blew the smoke toward the ceiling. "You remember me telling you about Steve in the office?" She turned to Maureen and explained, "This guy's married and has been hitting on me for months."

She looked back to the rest of the group. "The senior partner in the law firm is retiring and there was a party for him last Friday. Everybody was drinking and Steve comes up to me and starts. I told him again that I wasn't interested and why didn't he just go home to his wife instead of trying to cheat on her." Casey deeply inhaled the smoke and held it in her lungs before exhaling in disgust. "Do you want to know what he said? He leered at me and said oral intercourse couldn't be counted as cheating."

The room seemed to explode in anger and disbelief until Joanna held up her hands for silence. "What did you do, Casey?"

The tall attractive woman crushed out her cigarette. "I got my coat, wished Sam Briskin a happy life in retirement and went home and took a bath." She looked across the small circle to Etta. "You're not out there, Etta. You still believe in men with honor and respect. Try walking into a

107

singles bar where over a third of the men are married and don't even bother to remove their wedding rings. There's almost an arrogance about it."

"She's right," Melanie broke in. "God, I hate it! It's as if a parade passes in front of them and they have the right to look you up and down and then dismiss you if you don't make the grade. Who gave them that right to judge us so openly, so quickly?"

"Maybe we did," Joanna said. "Do you think we fought so hard for equality that somewhere along the way, in gaining equality, we might have lost their respect?"

"Why can't we have both?" Melanie asked.

"Because now we're competition," Casey answered. "Now they don't only have to compete with each other for jobs or placement in the pecking order. Two days after I bought my BMW, Joe Gardner pulls into the office parking lot with the same car, same color, only a larger engine. Why? What did he feel he had to prove?"

No one offered an explanation. The women sat in silence for a few moments until Melanie said in a quiet voice, "Maybe Janet's right. Maybe it is hopeless."

"Or could it be," Joanna asked, "that they're really just as insecure as we are?"

Janet shifted in her chair and smiled at Maureen. Totally confused by the conversation, Maureen could only smile back. These women were so angry. She couldn't help remembering her dream of the night before, how different these women were from Robin and Colleen and Margie. Her friends were so filled with hopes and dreams about their future. Guys were dreamy, and the perfect one would be the answer to their prayers for a life of happily ever after. But now, looking about the group of older women; she could see how dreams had gone awry and expectations were never met. The result was disappointment, bitterness and anger. Feeling more than ever like an outsider, she realized that she wasn't angry with all men—just one in particular.

"Well, I'm not insecure any longer," Janet pronounced. "I'm very happy now that I know who I am."

Etta shook her head and Melanie groaned before saying, "Oh God, Janet. Not again! You think you're the first abused woman to feel that way?"

It was Casey who again explained it to Maureen. "Janet thinks she's a lesbian."

A lesbian? Maureen's eyes widened with astonishment and she couldn't help straightening her body, an unconscious effort to slowly move away from the woman who was sitting next to her. It also didn't help that Maureen had felt more comfortable with Janet than the others. It was Janet who had smiled and seemed most friendly. It was as if there had been an unspoken affinity between them. *A lesbian!* She had never even seen a lesbian before today. Too afraid to sneak another look at the woman, Maureen stared down at her own tightly clasped hands. What was happening to her? She'd come here for some help and now she was more frightened than before. If she felt such empathy with Janet, then what did that say about her? Were there secret, latent desires lurking within her own heart? Did she—

"Okay, that's enough."

Maureen stiffened as she heard the familiar voice behind her. Her eyes again widened with shock as she saw Bobby walk around the women's chairs.

"You are not a lesbian! But what I want to know is how long do you intend staying at this male-bashing party?" He glanced at the circle of women and shook his head.

Casey was trying to explain to Janet that the only reason she felt more attracted to women was because she had been so abused by her husband and her father before that. Maureen didn't even try to listen any longer. She felt dizzy and frightened. Her brain was spinning and she could only stare at Bobby as he stood behind each woman and made his own explanations.

"This one," he said above Etta, "lived her life through her husband. His walking out is probably the best thing that could have happened to her, only she doesn't know it yet. She loves the theater and good old Martin refused to go. She was an art major in college thirty years ago and has done nothing with her talent. Tell her to go back to school and rediscover what made her happy.

Grasping the arms of the chair, Maureen was riveted to its seat. She couldn't escape Bobby, even here in a therapy group. What other proof did she need? She was truly and verifiably insane.

He moved on to Casey. "Look at her. She's pretty, intelligent and successful and can't make a commitment because she's looking for her father in every man she meets. And she's always going to be disappointed unless she deals with—"

"Stop it!" Maureen jumped up and glared at him while the others gaped at her in astonishment. She looked at Etta and the rest of the group and saw their surprise at her outburst. Unable to take any more, Maureen pressed her fingers against her temple and muttered, "I'm sorry," before running from the room.

She raced down the stairs of the building, pushed open the huge glass doors and gulped in fresh air, as if the action might wipe out the craziness taking place around her. She fumbled with her car keys and wasn't satisfied until she was clutching the steering wheel in her hands while resting her head against it.

"Please God, help me," she cried. "How much more do I have to take?"

"Just start the car, Maureen. Let's go to the lake."

Her head snapped up. He was there, back in the passenger seat! "Leave me alone," she pleaded, her chin trembling with the effort to control her tears. "You can't be real, because I'm certifiable if you are!"

Bobby sighed and closed his eyes for a moment, as if gathering his thoughts. "I am real," he said slowly. He opened his eyes, looked at her, and smiled. "Why are you putting yourself through this? Just accept that I'm here for you and then we can get on to my real purpose for coming back."

"And what's that?" she asked sarcastically. "To drive me insane? Because you're doing it. Look at me," she exclaimed, waving her hand toward the window. "People are staring. They don't see you. They only see me talking to thin air! They lock up crazy people, and I don't want to be locked up."

"Go to the lake."

"Go to hell."

He laughed. "That's good, Maureen. And I'm not even offended, 'cause I've got that one safely behind me." He straightened and said in a more serious voice. "Now, c'mon. Just drive to Strawbridge Lake and we can discuss all this."

"How do you know about Strawbridge Lake? You never lived here." Instead of an answer, the engine turned over and Maureen jumped in fright. "Damn it! Will you stop doing stuff like that?"

"I thought you liked tricks. I bet your favorite show growing up was Bewitched." He was teasing her, trying to make her laugh.

"Yeah? Well, she was a witch."

"And I'm not."

Maureen tried to make her voice as scornful as possible. "Oh *right*—you're my guardian angel."

"Look, I thought you'd enjoy seeing an old friend when you're going through a tough time. And the only reason I brought up the television show is because you've got this thing about Donna Reed."

"How do you know about that?" she demanded.

"I told you I know your past, but not your future. I know that you grew up without a mother so you modeled yourself after a dumb television show, instead of following your instincts. I'm just here to help you." He jerked his thumb toward the office building. "And I also thought you wouldn't mind being rescued from that hen party. Man, those women are bitter."

"Those women have each been hurt by men and are trying to recover."

"Look, I don't want to argue with you. If you'll just do as I ask then I can get on with my job and leave you alone."

She glanced at him with suspicion. "If I go to the lake, you'll disappear?"

"Hey, I'm just trying to do my job, Maureen. Now can we go?"

It took only a moment to decide. Pulling out into traffic, she vowed that she would go to Siberia if it would make him disappear.

She was on Route 38, a mile from the lake, when the radio came on. Smokey Robinson's smooth, sensual voice filled the car.

"What is it with you and oldies?" she mumbled, no longer shocked by his ability to turn things on without touching them. Pulling into the right hand lane, she sniffled and glared at him from the corner of her eye.

"I like Motown. So did you."

"That was twenty years ago. A lot's happened in twenty years. Most of us grew up."

He didn't say anything and, as she turned into the entrance to the lake, Maureen shook her head. "I shouldn't have said that."

"Pull in here," he said, pointing to an old oak tree.

It was early in the day and Strawbridge Lake was deserted, except for the large gathering of ducks that made their home there.

Turning off the engine, Maureen stared out at the water, dark and murky in the cold winter afternoon. It seemed to match the depression that was settling over her. "I'm sorry for that remark about not growing up," she apologized. "No matter who I'm with, I can't seem to say or do the right thing."

He turned to her. "Look, Maureen, I didn't come here to make your life miserable. I came to help."

"How can you help me?" she cried. "Every time I see you I think I'm slipping further over the brink of sanity! Do you know what I did last night?" Not waiting for an answer, she told him. "I—I dreamed I was with the old crowd again. Margie, Colleen and Robin. I was there, Bobby! I had a—a cheese steak and spilled catsup over me and when I woke up this morning my nightgown was stained. Can't you see? I'm losing my mind! How can you help me?" she asked miserably. Looking out to the water's edge, Maureen thought

114

of all the happy times when she and Dan had brought the children here. "Can you blink your eyes and make everything right again? Can you wipe out the last few weeks? Can you make my husband want me again? Or can you erase the fact that he's destroyed my self-confidence as a woman? Do you possess some magic, Bobby, that will give my children back a stable home?"

He smiled at her. "Only you can do that, Maureen."

"But how?" she demanded, as the tears slipped down her cheeks. "Do I become someone I'm not? Change my body and my mind, so I can compete with a twenty-five year old? What happens when I slip? When I look my age? Do I spend the rest of my life in fear that Dan's going to turn to someone else? That isn't a life. It's a prison sentence." She stared at him, fighting back the choking sobs. "And what did I do, Bobby? What did I do, except grow old?"

He reached out and touched her cheek, wiping away a tear, and Maureen felt a warm tingling sensation pass through her body. She wasn't surprised any more, or even afraid.

"You're not old," he whispered. "I think you're beautiful."

She felt an odd sexual drawing at his touch and, confused, she pulled away. Issuing a nervous laugh, Maureen countered, "Oh, right. What are you—twenty-one, twenty-two years old? I must look ancient to you." She pushed the hair back off her face and shrugged. "You don't know what it's like."

"You're right. I don't. But I'd give anything to know what it feels like to have someone love you for twenty years, to give you children and watch them grow, to build a life . . ." He shook his head at her foolish thoughts. "Damn, think about what you've had, Maureen. You've been given more than most."

"And it's all been taken away," she said in anger.

"No it hasn't. You just haven't stopped feeling sorry for yourself long enough to realize it."

"*Sorry for myself?*" The anger in her built. "You don't think I've had reason to feel sorry for myself? My entire world has been turned upside down and I'm fighting to hang on."

"Then it's up to you to turn it around again."

"Hah!" She couldn't keep the sarcasm out of her laugh. "You're my guardian angel. Why don't you tell me how."

He smiled again, and it was brilliant, holding the same boyish sensuality that had driven her nuts twenty years ago. "That's what I've been trying to do for the past two weeks. You have to start rebuilding your life, Maureen. You can't put everything on hold while you wait to see what your husband's going to do. Get back to work."

"Work?" The very last thing she wanted to do was write about young love.

He nodded. "You have a deadline coming up. Are you going to jeopardize everything you've done, the career you've built? Think of yourself for a change, or if that isn't enough, think of your kids. They're going to depend on you now. What are you going to do to support yourself if you don't write?"

Deep in thought, she could only stare at him. There wasn't anything else she wanted to do. The idea of working for someone else, of punching a time clock or leaving her children made her break out in a cold sweat. He was right. She was in danger of ruining everything she had worked so hard to achieve.

"Okay. I'll go back to work."

His smile turned into a grin of pleasure. "Good. But first I want you to do something."

"What do you mean?"

"I want you to start doing things for yourself, things that will make you feel good."

"Feel good?"

He nodded. "You know—pamper yourself. Go get your hair fixed, or go to a movie. Buy something special that will make you happy. Don't depend on anyone else for it. Replace the attention that you lost by getting it back yourself."

Thinking, she looked out to the lake and twisted a strand of hair around her finger. "I could get my hair done, I suppose."

"That's a beginning. And then go out and meet people. Get back into life, Maureen. You have the time and the opportunity to find out who you really are, what you really want. You've got *life*. And it's too precious to waste on self-pity."

How could someone so young be so wise? She turned her head and looked at him. There were tears in his eyes. Without thought, she reached across the seat and fell into his arms. "Oh Bobby, I'm sorry—I never think about how you must feel, to have had everything taken away from you when you're so young." Holding him tighter, she murmured, "When you died I thought a part of me went with you. I missed you so much, Bobby." She felt as if she was melting into a soft, warm cocoon, where nothing could ever hurt her.

"Don't think about me," he whispered above her head. "Think about you. It's got to be your time now, Maureen. Now . . . or never."

"Hey—I can touch you," she marveled, lifting her head to see his face. Yet when she did, he faded from her arms and she fell over against the passenger door. With her cheek pressed to the window, she blinked a few times in disbelief, until she caught her reflection in the side mirror. She stared at herself for a few moments, trying to see the insanity in her eyes.

"162-80-0056," she muttered. There! She had read somewhere that if you could remember your social security number without hesitation, then you weren't crazy.

Maureen pushed herself upright and looked back to the dark water as it moved down the lake toward the waterfall. After a few moments she realized that she wasn't afraid any more, at least, not of Bobby. It went against everything she was raised to believe, everything she held true. But he *was* real—he simply had to be! He'd been her first love and he had returned to her life when it was falling apart. He'd come to help her, to guide her. For whatever reason, he had been sent to her. Instead of fear, she was filled with wonder and a smile slowly crossed her face. He was a miracle, and maybe so were the dreams, or at least a phenomenon that defied explanations. And she didn't care any more. She'd be crazy to reject this gift.

"I'm going to do it, Bobby," she whispered out to the lake. "You just watch." Throwing the car into reverse, Maureen headed for Main Street.

Toppers at Main Street was a replica of the well-known Philadelphia spa where the rich and famous submitted their bodies for head-to-toe pampering. As soon as you walked into the place it spoke of wealth and the quality of indulgence that kind of money could buy.

Maureen walked up to the reception area made up of deep green marble and glass. There were three women working behind the huge circular desk—a blonde, a brunette, and a redhead, each of them intimidating. Their makeup was applied with professional skill. Not a strand of hair was out of place, unless it was intentional. Even their fingernails were uniformly long and manicured to perfection. They were sophisticated women, beautiful, poised and polished.

The redhead looked up and smiled. "Yes? May I help you?"

Maureen smiled back, wishing she had taken more care with her own makeup this morning. "I don't have an appointment. I—I guess you could say this is a spur of the moment thing, but would it be possible for me to see someone about my hair?"

"Your hair? Do you want it cut?"

The woman's smile was friendly and Maureen couldn't help admiring her shining red hair. She took a deep breath and said it before she thought any more. "Maybe shaped. But what'd really like is something different. A little color, some high-lights . . ." Embarrassed, Maureen shrugged. "I need help."

The receptionist checked the huge book in front of her and asked Maureen's name.

"Well, Maureen," she said in a warm voice, "I think Mario can see you in an hour. Can you come back, or would you like to wait?"

She looked about the spa, seeing woman milling about in thick white terrycloth robes. They appeared happy and rested. She recalled Bobby's voice, telling her to do something special for herself and, without further thought, she heard her voice asking for a massage.

"Perfect," the redhead announced as she stood up and came around the desk. She signaled to someone behind Maureen and hands suddenly appeared at Maureen's shoulders.

Startled, Maureen turned and saw a young, very handsome man smiling at her. "It's okay. Relax," he said in a low, calming voice. "I just want to hang up your coat. You're here now. We'll take care of you."

The coat slipped from her arms and the man smiled again before walking away with it. *We'll take care of you*. That's what she wanted. Would it be so wrong? For just a few hours?

"If you'll follow me, Maureen, I'll show you your locker."

She turned back to the receptionist as the woman added, "Would you like herbal tea, or juice? Perhaps a glass of white wine?"

Maureen shook her head as she walked through the spa. "Nothing, thank you." She was nervous, and it obviously showed. "I've . . . ah . . . never had a massage before."

The woman stopped and turned to her. Suddenly, she held out her hand. "My name's Kathie. Goodness, your hand is freezing!" she exclaimed, while rubbing it as if to get the circulation back into it. It was a warm and friendly act, meant to put Maureen at ease. "Everyone's a little nervous the first time. You don't know what to expect. But, believe me, you're going to love it."

She opened the door to the locker room and Maureen saw several women in various states of undress. She tried to concentrate on Kathie's words and not look at the others.

"Here's your locker and your key. You'll find a robe and slippers inside. Get completely undressed, remove everything, even your jewelry. When you finish your massage, there are showers right beyond this wall. Did you notice the small area outside the door when you came in?"

Maureen nodded, even though she hadn't.

"When you're in your robe, come back out there and someone will get you for your massage. Do you have any questions?"

"No, none."

Maureen smiled back at Kathie as the woman said, "Enjoy yourself. That's what you're here for." She left her in front of the locker.

Opening the door, Maureen looked at the thick robe and took a deep breath. What had she gotten herself into? The last female she had undressed in front of was her daughter, someone who looked at her with loving and noncritical eyes. Now she was required to do so with strangers. And a massage? Good grief, was she paying someone to touch her body when her own husband didn't want to any longer? What had sounded like a great idea only minutes ago now seemed like a form of self-torture for someone who had no confidence in herself as a woman. She could always go back out and tell them she'd changed her mind. But she knew she'd be even more embarrassed to admit her inhibitions.

Unbuttoning her blouse, she shyly glanced at the other women. They looked rich and pampered and confident, as if this were a weekly ritual. Leaving her blouse open, she sat down on the leather bench in front of the locker and removed her shoes. If she couldn't strip nude in front of strangers, then she'd simply take her time and wait them out. As if fate were suddenly on her side, one of the women finished dressing and left. The other went into the bathroom and the third abandoned the locker area to apply her make up in front of a huge mirror, flanked by exquisite floral arrangements. It was just the chance she was waiting for. Someone whose clothes were on fire couldn't have ripped them more quickly from their body. She threw them to the bottom of the locker and whipped the robe around her, tying the belt tightly around her waist. Straightening, she casually picked up her blouse and hung it up, along with her slacks. She removed her earrings and gold necklace and placed them in her purse. After slipping her feet into the thongs, she closed the locker and pocketed the key. Her heart was pounding; she was breathing heavily, but she had done it. Her moment of triumph was short-lived, for a knot of apprehension was tightening in her stomach.

She still had to get through the massage.

Maureen sat in front of the three doors, waiting to be called. She learned from one of the other women that there were two men and a woman who performed this particular service. Please God, she prayed while staring at the doors, please let me get the woman. She simply couldn't bear the embarrassment of a strange man's hands on her. Concentrating on the doors, she felt trapped. Was it to be the lady or the tiger . . . ?

The door on the far right opened and a small, fragile looking woman came out.

"Maureen?" she asked with a smile.

Grateful, so very grateful, Maureen jumped up from the chair. "That's me," she answered quickly, as if one of the other women might try to take her place.

"Hi, my name is Lynn. Why don't you come in?"

She followed the younger woman into a small, dimly lit room. There was soft, relaxing music playing and a scented candle burned beside a table that was draped in sheets.

"You can hang your robe on the back of the door and lay down. I'll be back in a moment, all right?"

Staring at the table, Maureen swallowed. "Okay," she muttered.

"Kathie told me it's your first time. Don't be nervous. It's really quite nice."

She exuded friendliness and Maureen nodded as the masseuse left her alone and closed the door.

Removing her robe, she slipped between the sheets. They were warm and soft, like fine, old cotton. The music was soothing, a New Age composition that seemed to tranquilize. Taking a deep breath, she tried to relax. There was no way out now. She had to go through with it. But why did it feel like the feminine equivalent of losing your virginity at a house of ill repute? Because it was the first time, she thought and she was nervous about handing over her body to a stranger's ministrations.

There was no time for answers as the door opened and Lynn walked in.

"Comfortable?"

Maureen tried to smile. "Yes. The music is very

nice."

Lynn walked over to a table and picked up a bottle of oil. She poured a small amount into her hand and worked it between her palms. "I try to put my clients at ease. The music helps. I want them to enjoy the hour to the fullest." She came over to Maureen. "Now close your eyes. Take a deep breath, and relax."

She did as she was told and soon felt small fingers massaging the oil onto her forehead, gliding to her temples and ears and back again to the spot between her eyebrows. It was as if the woman possessed some magic, for Maureen could feel her facial muscles relax and she had to stop herself from moaning at the pleasurable experience.

"I use a combination of Shiatsu and Swedish massage," Lynn said matter-of-factly. She went on to explain both types and the philosophy behind them.

Maureen barely listened. She was too absorbed in the wonderfully relaxing sensations as Lynn worked over her face, her neck, her shoulders. It was sheer heaven. There was something faintly sexual about it, and the image of Janet flashed before her closed lids. No. Maureen dismissed it. This wasn't anything like that. It was more nurturing than sexual, more soothing . . . almost like a mother.

Suddenly, Maureen's throat tightened with the realization. She had skin hunger. She missed her mother's touch, her husband's touch. How long had it been since someone had given her this attention?

She remembered Bobby's words about doing it for herself, and right then and there, Maureen decided to stop thinking and just enjoy. Her whole life she had given this to others, trying to take the place of her mother with her younger brother. Then it was Dan that she soothed and caressed, followed by the children. But who did this for her?

It took the full hour to work all the stress and tension from her body and when Lynn left her alone on the table Maureen felt totally drained, as if she'd just had the best sex of her life, but somehow missed the sex part. Alone in that room, with the scent of jasmine in the air and the soft sounds of nature filling her ears, Maureen closed her eyes and sobbed for everything she had lost and for the terrifying journey she had just begun.

Chapter Six

"Hello, Maureen? This is Casey. From Joanna Dunne's group?"

She pictured in her mind the attractive attorney who had been so outspoken. Cradling the phone on her shoulder, Maureen pushed the save button on her computer and sat back in the leather chair. "Of course. Hi, how are you?"

"I'm fine. I'm calling to see how you are. I got your number from Joanna. We were all a little worried."

Maureen closed her eyes as the memory of her bizarre exit flashed before her. "God, I'm sorry I ran out like that. It isn't like me."

"Don't be sorry. That's the whole purpose of the group. You can say and do anything you want, and no one holds it against you. I guess we came on a little strong."

"No, not really," she lied. "All of this is just so new to me. I suppose I've lived a pretty sheltered life. Everything you discussed seemed so foreign

. . . singles bars, dating. I can't even imagine it."

There was a pause and then Casey said, "Listen, would you like to meet for a drink? See it for yourself?"

Maureen thought about it. She couldn't picture herself in a bar without her husband. But she didn't have a husband now. What was holding her back? And in truth, she had to admit a certain curiosity. Maybe it was the writer in her that wanted to see what Casey was talking about. Or, perhaps it was just the lonely woman she'd become that made her answer, "Okay. Sure, why not?"

"Great. How about tomorrow night? The Woodcrest Inn? Do you know it?"

She'd driven by it a hundred times on the way to Philadelphia. "What time?"

"How about nine o'clock? I'll probably have to finish some work here at the office. But I could be there by nine."

Nine o'clock. Dinner would be over. The children would be settled for the night. "That sounds fine."

"Terrific," Casey said. "I'll see you then."

Maureen hung up the phone and stared at it. Now that was surprising. Out of all the women in the group, Casey was the last one she thought would want to start a friendship. Smiling, Maureen turned back to her computer. How nice. She had plans for tomorrow night. She suddenly felt happy, almost young again. It was time she took control, instead of letting things control her.

* * *

Maureen pulled the blanket over her shoulder and cuddled the pillow under her head. Even as she drifted off to sleep she was aware of a knot of apprehension in her stomach. Tomorrow she was going out. For the first time. And as a separated woman. Images swirled before her closed lids, of herself as a young mother carting the children in twin strollers through the zoo, of her wedding day, trying to get in step with her father as he led her down the aisle. And even further back, back before Dan, when she was young, and pretty, and secure in her attractiveness . . .

It was the summer after her graduation from high school. She knew she was dreaming and went along with it happily, eagerly, knowing she would see her old friends once more. Fireworks sprinkled the night sky with diamond sprays of colored lights, and the aroma of cotton candy and hot dogs filled the air. It was the Fourth of July and she was standing in front of a booth with Robin at St. Michael's Fair.

"Do you think he'll come?" Robin asked, an expression of excitement reflecting on her face.

Maureen had only a moment of surprise as she gazed down at her silky pink nightgown. At least this time she knew she was dreaming. "I don't know," she answered evasively, since she couldn't remember who Robin's boyfriend had been at the time. "Who are we waiting for again?"

Robin cast her an incredulous look, before turning her attention back to the swelling crowd.

"What's wrong with you, Henessey? Timmy Fennerty."

It all came back to her. "Oh, that's right," Maureen murmured. "Timmy . . ." Didn't Robin wind up married to him?

"There he is," Robin announced and nearly punched Maureen in the ribs. "Oh, he's so cute!"

Maureen searched the crowd until she saw Timmy Fennerty with a group of boys making their way through the heavy throng of people. They were taking their time, messing around with the younger kids they passed — pulling down the visors of baseball caps, delivering fake jabs to the shoulders of underclassmen . . . This was their summer. They had made it out of high school and were entitled to their fair share of respect. There was Timmy and Jake and Mike. Muzzy, Ted and . . . and Bobby.

Bobby!

He was laughing with the rest of them, carrying a small yellow teddy bear under his arm. They walked up to the two girls, and formed a circle around them. Timmy gave Robin a kiss, while Maureen stared at Bobby.

He looked away, as if embarrassed. Needing to know if he was participating in this dream, Maureen walked over to him.

"Bobby?"

"Hi, Maureen."

She stared at him. "Bobby, are you real? Or — or you just part of this crazy dream?"

He stared back at her, a confused expression on

his face. "What are you talking about — am I real? You been drinking?"

He didn't know . . .

She shook her head, more to clear it than to answer his question. He seemed uncomfortable around her, looking over her head to the gambling wheel behind her. Finally, he shoved the teddy bear at her stomach. "Here. I'm sorry, okay? I'm sorry about everything. Now let's forget it ever happened."

Her hands automatically grasped the furry stuffed animal. "Forget what?" she whispered, completely bewildered.

Bobby took it as an acceptance and nodded. "Look, I've got to go. I'm meeting someone over at the dancing. I'll see you later," he said to the others. He never even glanced at her before turning and disappearing into the crowd.

What was that? Maureen stood, confused, hugging the bear to her chest, and shaking her head.

Robin leaned close to her ear and said in an undertone, "I think he's sorry about the shore."

The shore? What was Robin talking about? And then she remembered. Bobby had kissed her. He'd been drunk and she had pushed him away and run to the beach. It was silly — kid's stuff. But that's what they were then. Young kids with their first taste of freedom at the shore. He had said something to her, something that had hurt her feelings, but she couldn't remember what it had been.

Going along with the crowd, Maureen looked

for Bobby as they passed booths where pennies were pitched into tiny bowls of goldfish, rings were tossed onto green glass Coke bottles, baseballs were thrown at burlap cats that never seemed to fall over. It wasn't until they reached the area where the dancing was taking place that Maureen saw him.

He was dancing with Sherry Margolis. A crazy, totally irrational, surge of jealousy swept through her as she watched the two of them together. She was an adult. She had the mentality of a grown woman, a woman who knew that Sherry's loose reputation was probably false and spread by immature boys who liked to brag, yet she could barely stifle the desire to pull Bobby away from the girl. It was stupid and she forced herself to look away.

The Supremes sang of young love and the youth of the time seemed at their prime. Everyone was in Madras shorts, pastel oxford shirts and penny loafers without socks. Future Yuppies, who would find themselves in their thirties and forties dressing exactly the same way. Observing them gave her a weird sensation.

"Hey, look at Dominick Wallinski!"

Along with the others in the group, she turned to the right and tried to pick him out of the three-deep line of kids that circled the dance floor.

"He is sooo jive," Robin pronounced with disdain. "God, even after he's graduated, he still dresses like he's in eighth grade."

He was quite easy to spot. Poor Dominick was

cursed with a terrible case of acne, black horn-rimmed glasses, tight curly hair and absolutely no taste in clothes. She remembered hearing in school that his mother bought them for him because she worked at F.W. Woolworth and could get a discount.

As the others ripped the poor kid apart, laughing at his clothes, his hair, the dripping chocolate ice cream cone that he held with a napkin wrapped around it, Maureen suddenly realized that twenty-five years ago she probably would have seen the humor in their remarks. But not now.

Now she knew the pain of rejection, the anguish of insecurity. She felt closer to Dominick Wallinski than Robin, or any of her friends. And as a loud voice announced a ladies' choice, she knew exactly what she was going to do.

"Where are you going?" Robin demanded, as she started to walk away.

Maureen turned around and said, "I'm asking Dominick to dance."

The hoots and howls of laughter that followed her announcement didn't faze her in the least as she walked across the dance floor.

He saw her coming and she watched as he looked away, as if he were very interested in the dancers.

"Hi, Dominick." She stopped in front of him and smiled.

Startled, he dropped his ice cream cone and held onto the napkin, staring first at his cone lying in the dirt, and then back up at her.

"Would you like to dance?"

He looked behind him to see if she was talking to someone else. Spinning back around, he mumbled, "Me?"

She nodded. "You. C'mon. Let's dance."

His eyes narrowed suspiciously. "Why? So you and your friends can make fun of me? School's over, okay? I don't have to put up with that anymore."

Maureen felt her throat tighten with emotion. By her superiority, her attitude and her ignorance, she had contributed to his suffering. Smiling sadly, her heart filled with remorse. "I'd like to dance with you because I want to, because I'm sorry I never got to know you in high school."

He stared into her eyes. "You're serious?"

Nodding, she held out her hand. "C'mon. The song will be over before we get out there."

She took the napkin out of his fist and blotted a smudge of chocolate that clung to his cheek. He blinked rapidly, and then wiped his hands down the front of his shirt.

"Okay," he said in a nervous voice. "If you really want to."

Grinning, she said, "I do. Let's go." Still holding his hand, she led him to the middle of the dance floor and turned to him, clutching the teddy bear in her fist. She put her left hand on his shoulder and felt a small tremor in his arm as his right hand touched the small of her back.

She wanted to tell him to relax, but knew he'd

be embarrassed. Instead, she asked, "What are you going to do, now that you've graduated? Have you made plans yet?"

He was still looking at her as if he couldn't believe she was in his arms. "I . . . ah . . . I'm going to Community College in the fall."

"No kidding?" Maureen asked, her expression brightening with friendliness. "What courses are you taking?"

Dominick shrugged. "I don't know yet. I want to be a lawyer, specializing in criminal law."

She smiled. "I think you'll make a great lawyer," she said truthfully.

"You do?" He was searching her face, trying to see if there was a hint of ridicule behind her words.

She nodded, and without further thought, brought him closer, so that they were dancing cheek to cheek. He wasn't a bad dancer, but who would have known that? She had never seen him dance with anyone in four years of high school.

Maureen danced with him, filled with remorse, listening to the sexy voice of Smokey Robinson. She wished somehow that this dance had really taken place, that she could wipe out the wrong she had done to this boy in her youth. As she heard his heavy, nervous breathing in her ear, she bit her lip to stop the tears from coming. Poor Dominick wouldn't feel so fortunate if he knew he was actually dancing with a middle-aged woman in a thin silk nightgown, a woman whose body was no longer firm and young. But what did

135

it matter? It was only a dream, wasn't it?

From across the dance floor, her gaze connected with Bobby's. He was dancing with Sherry, but looking straight at her. And he was smiling, as if he understood it all, everything she was feeling. She started crying, for herself, for Dominick, for Bobby. In a few years Bobby would be dead and she had never told him that she loved him . . .

What if she told him? Would it change anything? Suddenly it was very important that she warn him. Maybe if he never went to college in Florida? Maybe he would live. Wiping her eyes on the teddy bear, she called out his name.

"Bobby?

"Bobby?"

She bolted upright in bed. Her heart was pounding; she was gasping for breath, and tears were streaming down her cheeks. Dawn invaded her room, casting a gray shadow across the bed, and Maureen stared in disbelief at the yellow teddy bear laying in her lap.

"Oh, my God!"

She flung it across the room to get it away from her, and grabbed a pillow. Hugging it to her chest for protection, she stared at the stuffed animal that lay upside down on the loveseat.

Bobby gave it to her, *but in a dream!* This couldn't be happening. Reality seemed beyond her grasp as she continued to stare at the teddy bear. Okay, remember the dream, Maureen, she mentally instructed. It was a gift. He wasn't mad at you. Remember that look, that smile, at the end?

He gave it to you with love. Realizing that, she wasn't quite as afraid.

Still, it took every ounce of courage she possessed to throw back the covers and get up. Very slowly, she walked toward the loveseat and reached for the small toy. As she picked it up, she felt the plush fur, the stuffing inside of it, and knew somehow it was real. She hurried to her closet, put it on the top shelf and quickly shut the door.

Racing back to bed, Maureen pulled the covers up to her chin and stared at the closet. She would simply ask Bobby about it the next time he appeared. That's all.

Don't think about it now, she told herself, for there was no logical explanation, not for the stuffed animal nor the fact that she was actually waiting for a ghost to reappear.

Pull yourself together, Maureen Malone. Yes, you've seen a ghost. Yes, you're having crazy dreams. But outside of that, you've always led a sane life. Just get through the day like any other and tonight you won't dream—even if you have to stay awake all night.

Tonight.

Oh God. She was supposed to meet Casey at the Woodcrest Inn tonight. Had there ever been a time when her life was simple? When she thought it might be boring?

Going to a nightclub. Alone. At her age. She stood in front of the mirror and stared at herself.

All her earlier feelings of excitement died as she saw her reflection. What was she doing? She was a middle-aged woman with children and responsibilities, not a young girl. Last night had been a dream. This, unfortunately, was reality. She didn't even know what to wear. Maybe the dark green dress was too much. Maybe she should be more casual. She ripped the dress off and threw it onto the loveseat that had taken the place of Dan's armoire, then searched through her closet and pulled out black silk pants. She tossed them over the dress and continued her quest for the right top without daring to look at the teddy bear that she knew rested on the highest shelf.

White blouse? No. Red? No, she'd never wear the red again, not after that fiasco with Dan in the kitchen. Black, then? With her good black paisley jacket? So what if she looked like Johnny Cash? Didn't she once read that dressing monochromatic made you look taller and thinner?

"Why do you care?" she muttered, pulling the slip up over her head and grabbing the slacks. She was meeting a woman for a drink, not looking to pick up a man.

"Mom?" Abbie burst into her room. "Josh still hasn't done the dishes. I'm not doing them. It's his turn and—hey! You look great."

Slipping her feet into her heels, Maureen glanced up to her daughter and smiled. "Thanks," she said, though she didn't believe her child. Love really was blind.

Abbie stood behind her and looked into the

mirror as Maureen checked her makeup. "The best thing you ever did was go to Toppers."

Her hair was highlighted in auburn, making a nice contrast with her fair complexion. After the massage and hair style, Maureen had treated herself to a makeup session and watched carefully so she could duplicate the transformation. She learned that she had used all the wrong colors. That brown eyeshadow was perfect for her blue eyes. That she could wear bright lipsticks. She did look different. She looked . . . together, confident, attractive. Too bad she felt silly, insecure and pretentious. And, maybe, just a little crazy.

"Before you leave will you do something about Josh? Or we'll fight all night about it."

Maureen nodded as she picked up her purse and checked her watch. She'd wasted too much time on clothes and now she was late. "Abbie, will you turn off the light?" she asked, leaving the bedroom. "Josh? Where are you?"

Walking into the family room she found him sprawled over the sofa, reading the latest issue of *Sports Illustrated*. "Will you please do the dishes? It's your turn."

"I will," he muttered from behind the magazine.

"When?" she asked impatiently. "Dinner's been over for two hours."

He threw the magazine onto the sofa and sat up. "Why are you going out?" he asked in a resentful voice.

She took a deep breath and held her purse

tighter to her side. "I told you. I'm meeting a friend."

"How come we don't know this friend?"

"Because I just met her last week. What does this have to do with the dishes?"

Her son stood up and faced her. "Where are you meeting her?"

She stared back at him, wondering why he was drilling her. "I told you. I'm meeting her at the Woodcrest Inn for a drink. That's all."

"The Woodcrest is a pick-up joint, and you don't drink."

She continued to stare at him, seeing the hostility and indignation in his face and his body language. She instinctively wanted to lash out at him, to tell him that what she did, or did not do, was none of his business. That he was her son, not her husband, and he had no right to speak to her like this. Instead, she took another deep breath and said, "Listen, Josh. I'm going to meet a friend for a drink. That's all. And I have every right to go. I know all this must seem strange to you and I can't tell you how sorry I am that your life and Abbie's has changed because of the problems of your parents. But I can't sit home and feel sorry for myself any longer. I need to be with friends, people my own age." *And I'm going crazy in this house,* she mentally added.

"Why can't you invite her here?"

She smiled at him. "You want to know something? I'm forcing myself to go. It would be too easy to stay home and pull the covers up over my head and pretend that all this is going to magically work itself out. But I've got to grow up, too, Josh." She kissed his cheek and walked to the foyer. Pulling out her black raincoat, she turned back to her kids who stood watching her.

She smiled at her son and said, "Do the dishes, okay? I'll be home early."

As she buttoned her coat, Abbie called out, "Have a good time, Mom."

"Thanks," she muttered quickly, and opened the front door.

In the car, Maureen swallowed down the taste of tears. They were a mixture of sadness for the confusion her children were suffering, and anger toward her husband. He had wanted this separation, and he enjoyed total freedom. He could go anywhere, do anything, and never have to answer to his family. His children didn't grill him before he left his apartment to meet with—no, don't even think about it, she scolded herself. Don't start fantasizing about Dan with other women and everything he had put the family through so he could regain *passion!* If she continued to dwell on it she would drive right past the Woodcrest Inn and go straight over the bridge to Philadelphia to beat the hell out of him.

No. This was her night, she thought, as she resisted the urge and turned into the massive parking lot of the Woodcrest. Tonight she would have a drink with a new friend, listen to music and maybe laugh a little. It had been too long since she'd laughed. And wasn't this exactly what Bobby had been talking about at the lake? Pushing herself back into life? Good God, she was actually believing in ghosts! Even the dreams didn't seem so frightening now. What the hell, the rest of her life was screwed up, why not a ghost popping in and out, day *and* night?

She told herself that she didn't check her coat because it was a six-hundred-dollar gift to herself when she'd signed her last contract. Some women had furs. She loved the simple, elegant lines of the Japanese designer. In truth, Maureen knew she didn't plan on staying that long. One drink, and if she didn't like it, she was out of here. She could hear the music from the lobby, and it took an extraordinary amount of courage to walk toward it.

The room was large enough to hold six bars, all in a row, and there was a mass of people crowded around each. The music was loud, lights were strobing and the heat of so many bodies pressing together nearly unstrung her. It would be impossible to find anyone in here, she thought in a panic. She should just turn around and leave. Go back home where it was safe and familiar.

A swarthy Mediterranean-looking man glanced at her, sized her up from her knees to her head, and just as quickly dismissed her to see who was behind her. She felt insulted by his pointed inspection and lifted her chin in anger. Taking a deep breath, Maureen pushed herself forward. If a man could go out for a drink and listen to music, why couldn't a woman? Without every male thinking she was only there to find a man? As more and more men did the same thing, she began to feel she was part of a parade that passed before them, waiting for that look, that smile, that nod of approval. It was humiliating, and thoroughly degrading. Realizing that she would never find Casey in this madhouse, she turned around to leave, but passage back was nearly impossible. She felt like a salmon trying to swim upstream.

"Excuse me."

"Pardon me."

"I'm sorry . . . excuse me."

She was bumped from behind, turned completely around twice and was fighting down real panic when a hand reached out and pulled her away from the flow and toward one of the bars.

"Maureen! Are you okay?"

Breathing heavily, Maureen managed to smile at Casey. She felt as if the woman had just saved her life. "My God, what would happen if there were a fire in here?"

Casey threw back her head and laughed. "You take a chance on getting bruised just going to the ladies room, but don't worry—there's plenty of exits, they're just not opened right now. Seriously, are you okay? This can be an eye-opener for the novice."

"I'm all right," Maureen said, holding her coat closer to her stomach. "I didn't think I'd ever be able to find you."

"I saw you when you walked in, but I couldn't get to you until now. What would you like to drink?"

Maureen looked at the three bartenders working furiously to fill orders. She remembered her son's words, telling her she didn't drink. He was right. She didn't like the taste of alcohol and usually settled for a fruity drink to disguise it. But these young men working behind the bar didn't seem to have the time for anything so exotic, and she found herself saying, "I'll have a rum and Coke." It was what she drank twenty years ago . . . twenty years ago when she was young and confident, and places like this would have seemed exciting.

But she was no longer young or confident and the past minutes had been painful proof that she was out of her element. Suddenly she knew how Dominick Wallinski felt at those dances in the high school gym.

"Here you are," Casey said while handing her the drink. She held her own up in a toast. "Here's to discoveries."

Maureen thought it was an odd thing to say, but she raised her glass and smiled. Just as she brought the glass to her lips, someone bumped her arm and she spilled a mouthful down the front of her blouse. She stared at her chest as the dark stain grew larger.

"Damn, people are so ignorant," Casey muttered as she handed Maureen several napkins.

A voice at Maureen's shoulder said, "Maybe you'd like some help cleaning that up, honey."

She and Casey looked over at a middle-aged man who practically leered back at them. He was

144

dressed in a three-piece suit, but had removed his tie and opened his shirt so that his graying chest hairs mingled with the multiple gold chains that hung from his neck. On top of his head was a toupee that closely resembled a burnt pancake. Maureen found herself staring at it with a sort of horrified fascination.

"I think we can handle this, thank you," Casey pointed out.

The man wasn't about to give up. "Ahh," he said, holding up his large hand. "But I'd like to handle you. Either one of you would do."

"Beat it," Casey said, matter-of-factly and turned her attention to Maureen's blouse. When the man walked away, Casey asked, "Was that not the worst toupee you've ever seen?"

Maureen couldn't help it. She laughed, giggling in a nervous release of tension. "It was pretty bad."

"When I first saw it I thought it was a beret. I mean, the guy's hair was obviously gray and he's wearing a dark brown toupee." Laughing, Casey shook her head. "I'm telling you, Maureen, the male ego is staggering."

Touching the shoulder of a woman on her other side, she added, "Listen, I want you to meet some people from my office." She drew the attention of a young blond woman and the two men who stood beside her. "Maureen Malone, I'd like to introduce Carrie McBain, Tom Davis and Tony Polletti. They're all lawyers, so only believe half of what they say, especially if it's about me."

145

They shook hands as Casey remarked, "Maureen's a writer."

The lawyers appeared impressed. "No kidding?" Tom asked. "What do you write? Novels? Articles?"

"Novels," Maureen answered, raising her voice to be heard over the music. "Children's books." This wasn't the place to try and explain the young adult romance market.

"I can't even write a letter to my mother," Carrie moaned. "It really must take discipline."

Maureen smiled at the pretty woman. They were all at least eight to ten years younger than her.

"Who are you kidding, Carrie?" Tony teased. "You can't even write a decent memo. What was that thing you put on my desk this afternoon?"

Carrie playfully slapped his arm. "It was a note reminding you that we were meeting tonight for drinks. Oh listen—I love this song. C'mon, dance with me."

The two of them pushed their way through the crowd to the dance floor and Tom pulled Casey's arm in that direction.

"Let's dance."

Casey shook her head. "Not now." She glanced at Maureen, as if to say they shouldn't leave her alone.

Feeling like the fifth wheel, Maureen insisted, "Go ahead. Enjoy yourself. I'm fine."

"You're sure?" Casey asked, concern in her voice. "I don't feel right about leaving you. I mean, you just got here."

Maureen smiled. "Look, I wasn't going to stay that long anyway. One drink. That's it. If I'm not here when you come back, call me."

"Maybe we can meet somewhere a little more quiet for dinner?"

"I'd like that," Maureen said and looked at Tom. "It was nice to have met you."

Tom smiled as he drew Casey into the crowd. "You, too," he called back.

When she was alone, Maureen felt a wave of depression fall over her as she glanced down the bar and saw Mr. Bad Toupee smirking back. Hanging on his arm was a woman in her early thirties. His look clearly said, "Hah, I found someone younger and prettier. Your loss."

Casey was right, she thought—the male ego was staggering. She ignored the man and turned her attention back to the crowd.

She was completely out of her place and time. She felt more comfortable in her dreams than here. Having spent the last two decades pretending she was Donna Reed, she'd had her head buried in the sand, believing that places like this only existed for the young, that middle-aged men didn't go around trying to pick up woman half their age. But she couldn't deny it. The proof was before her eyes. It was like the cantina scene in *Star Wars,* and she felt transplanted to another world, sent to observe the alien life forms.

There were the Spandex Queens with their *Fatal Attraction* hairdos. The young women in bustiers parading before older men in three-piece suits or tee shirts that said *Plumbers do it deeper. They clean out your pipes.*

It was impossible not to overhear the conversation of others and she found her back teeth grinding together as she listened to one man say to another, "She may have a good ass, but you haven't even seen her face yet."

His companion, a man whose jacket couldn't close over his beer belly, retorted, "Look, I don't want to marry the broad. I just want to get to know her for fifteen minutes in the parking lot."

And that was it. That was the look they gave you as they passed. It was an appraisal, as if to say, "I don't want a relationship, just a quickie in the parking lot."

Two women in their mid-twenties, both of them beautiful, took the place of Casey and her friends at the bar. After they ordered drinks, one said to the other, "But he's so old. Are you sure?"

The brunette glanced at her friend and shrugged. "Listen, he's a ticket. I'm with him *because* he's not young. He won't be screwing everything that can walk. Plus, he's settled in his job. He's got the money to take me to nice restaurants, maybe even an occasional weekend in the Caribbean. I'm telling you Denise, older men are the way to go. They're so damn grateful, they treat you like a queen."

"How do you know he's not married?" the woman named Denise asked, lighting a cigarette.

The brunette shrugged again. "Hell, I hope he is. Married men are even better. They don't take up too much of your time. Look . . . here he comes."

Maureen watched as a man in his late forties joined the women. The brunette gave him a brilliant smile and the man practically beamed as she wound her arm through his and rubbed her breasts against him.

Maureen placed her drink on the bar and stared into it. Was that what Dan was? A ticket? The thought brought tears to her eyes. She glanced up again at the brunette and watched her artful flirtation. The brunette could have any man her own age. Why was she wasting herself on someone old enough to be her father? What had happened to society in the last twenty years? The writer in her wanted to figure it out. The woman in her was desperate to know. When she saw the way the man held onto the young woman, almost like a trophy, Maureen had her answer.

It was ego. In spite of the Woman's Movement, things really hadn't changed. This woman had to have a man, anyone's man, someone to take care of her. And the male, going through a mid-life crisis and terrified by his lack of appeal, manages to get his manhood back. With a young woman on his arm, what better proof could he send to his peers that he is still vital? Still virile?

Looking around the huge room, Maureen felt the burning in her throat from unshed tears. No matter how hard women worked for equality, it was still a man's world. All you had to do was walk into a singles bar to see it. The options were all in a man's favor. He could be old, out of shape, wearing a disgusting tee shirt or a pathetic toupee, but he still thought he had the right to approach a young woman. But what do middle-aged women do? Do they walk up to twenty-five year old men? Maureen looked up and down the length of the bar and smiled sadly. Women who could no longer compete with the Spandex Queens were standing alone as men their own age passed them over.

It was sad, depressing, and demoralizing.

Angry, and making up her mind that she'd had just about enough of feeling like the wallflower at an eighth-grade dance, Maureen took the coat off her arm and swung it over her shoulders.

"Hey, are you all right?"

Realizing she had hit someone with her raincoat, she quickly turned and apologized.

"I'm sorry," she muttered, pulling the edges together. And then she looked up . . . and up.

He had to be over six foot five. And huge. He had dark blond hair, ruddy cheeks, hazel eyes and was built like a professional football player.

He grinned. He wasn't exactly handsome until he smiled. Great smile, she thought, taking in the Colgate-perfect teeth. He looked as out of place as she did. Amid a sea of chest hair and gold chains, he stood out like an Ivy Leaguer in a dark green sweater and Ralph Lauren shirt.

He leaned down to her so he could be heard. "That's okay. Listen, can I ask you a question?"

She could only nod.

"Do you have a strange mistrust of coat-check girls, or were you using your raincoat for protection so no one would ask you to dance?"

He had a brain, too!

"A . . . a little of both," she managed to say. Why did he look vaguely familiar? "I'm not staying."

"You don't like it?" he asked, nodding out to the crowd.

"This place . . ." she said. "It's every woman's worst nightmare. I was just leaving."

He smiled again. "Then I guess you wouldn't be interested in dancing?"

She considered it for a mere second then glanced out at the floor where Casey and her friends were still enjoying themselves. Each song led into another, and she didn't want to make a fool out of herself. Shaking her head, she said, "No, I don't think so, but thanks."

"Can I buy you a drink then?"

Again she shook her head. "I was just leaving." Didn't she already say that? At least three times?

"That's right. You were."

Was that actually regret she was seeing in his eyes? She mentally sighed. Don't flatter yourself. Just find the door.

"Then the least I can do is run interference for you to get you out of here. It's pretty crowded."

She knew that was a football term and smiled back at him. "I'd appreciate that. I was wondering how I was going to manage my escape." There. That sounded fairly intelligent.

151

Grinning, he took her hand as casually as if they had known each other for years and held it behind him as he opened a path for them. She noticed several people, both male and female, staring at him with recognition as he pulled her through the crowd. A few even seemed to know him and patted him on the back as they passed. In a surprisingly short time they reached the lobby and he released her hand as he turned to her.

"There. Mission accomplished."

Even in heels, she only came up to his chest. Tilting her head up, she smiled. "Thank you."

"You're welcome." He held out his hand, a little embarrassed. "By the way, I'm Matt Shannon."

She took his hand. "Maureen Malone."

"It's been very nice meeting you, Maureen. Drive carefully."

He held her hand a few seconds longer than necessary and then quickly released it.

She nodded. "I will." Suddenly she didn't want to leave. She didn't want to turn around and go home to her house and all the memories. She didn't want to fall asleep and have another crazy dream. But she had said she was leaving, and would look stupid if she did anything else. "Well, goodbye," she muttered and turned toward the door.

She had only walked four feet when she heard him call out, "Maureen?"

She spun around.

"You can't stay for one drink? Right here in the lobby?"

Her mind raced. What should she do? What was the proper etiquette? Should she ask if he was married first? Should she tell him she was married, but separated? How old was he? He was younger then she was, she was sure of it.

"Would you like to have coffee?" she heard herself asking, and was horrified that the invitation came out of her mouth.

"Coffee?" he asked, closing the distance between them. He was so *big!* All the men in her family, including her husband, were under six feet, and none of them were built like this.

"Ahh, there's a diner right down the road," she mumbled, hating the fact that she could feel a blush creeping up from her throat. What the hell was she doing, inviting a total stranger to meet her at a diner? He could be a serial killer, a mad rapist, a—

"I know the one. Sounds great," he quickly agreed. "Just let me get my coat."

"I'll—I'll meet you there," she nearly yelled and ran for the door.

Once in her car she grabbed the steering wheel, while waiting for the heat to begin thawing out her numb fingers.

She was definitely losing it. Did she need further proof? She had just invited a man, a big man, for coffee! Lord . . . what had she just done?

Chapter Seven

"Would you like something to eat?"

She shook her head. "Just coffee. Thanks." God Almighty, why did she do this? She had no idea what to say to him. What must he be thinking of her? Going around picking up men—

"If you don't mind, I'm going to order a hamburger. I didn't have dinner."

"You didn't eat?" Terrific. She sounded just like a mother!

He smiled. "Didn't have time. I didn't feel like going straight home from work, and once I was in the Woodcrest, I guess I really didn't feel like staying."

He had a great voice, kind of low and intriguing. She thought he would probably make a good public speaker. The waitress came and took their order. When the woman left there were a few seconds of strained silence and Maureen struggled to fill it. "What do you do?" Geez, she might as well have asked his astrological sign. There was no doubt about it. She was definitely on foreign ground here.

"I'm in communications."

"Communications?"

He nodded. "Television."

"Television?" She sounded like a myna bird repeating every statement. And then it hit her. Her mouth opened in surprise as she stared at the man sitting in the booth across from her. She pointed her finger at him. "You're—you're Matt Shannon," she said in astonishment.

He grinned, showing those perfect teeth. "And you're Maureen Malone. I think we've already established our identities."

"No, but you're *Matt Shannon!* Wait until I tell my son. He'll never believe it!"

The waitress delivered their coffee and Maureen watched as the older woman smiled shyly at Matt. No wonder everyone recognized him—he was the sports announcer for a Philadelphia television station.

"How old is your son?"

Maureen still couldn't believe she had practically picked up this local celebrity . . . and he was here with her. She felt like a fool. She had probably startled him with her bold invitation, and he was too nice to refuse. She could sense a warm blush spread over her face and she looked into her coffee cup while trying to settle down and collect her thoughts.

"Maureen?"

She glanced up at him. He was smiling.

"Your son? You were going to tell me how old he was?"

She swallowed down the tightness in her throat. "Josh is sixteen."

"Sixteen?" He looked surprised.

She nodded. Now it would come. He'd ask her age. He'd—

"Does he like sports?"

Grateful that he didn't bring up the age issue, she returned his smile. "Loves sports. All sports. But baseball is his favorite."

"Do you have other children?"

"A daughter. Abbie. She and Josh are twins."

"No kidding? Twins?"

She grinned back at him. "No kidding. They're good kids. I'm lucky."

He nodded. "They must be a handful."

"They were when they were young. You know, there were times I used to think I'd give anything for some peace and quiet, to get away from it all, and now I realize they'll be going off to college in another year. And it doesn't seem like I've had enough time with them." Knowing she was rambling, Maureen murmured, "It sounds silly."

"It sounds normal . . . like a mother." He studied her. "What else do you do, besides raising twins?"

Staring right back at him, she smiled. "Are you interviewing me?"

Now he looked embarrassed. "I'm sorry. I guess it sounded like that, didn't it?"

Suddenly relaxed, Maureen laughed. "Don't be

156

sorry." At least she didn't have to worry anymore. He wasn't a serial killer or a rapist. Heck, he'd already been in her home by way of the television. "Besides raising children, I write young adult novels."

It was his turn to appear astonished. "You're a writer?"

Nodding, she said, "I have a series of books for young girls called *The Cotillion Club.*"

"Well . . ." He seemed surprised. Sitting back, he stared across the table at her. "I'm impressed. I spend hours writing my own copy each night and once a week I do a sports column for the newspaper. I'm telling you, I spend more time trying to get what's in my head onto the computer screen than I do going out and getting the story. And you write books? A series of them?" He shook his head, as if amazed. "That's why I didn't eat dinner."

"Why?"

"I was writing, or I should say trying to write, an article for Sunday's paper on the continuing debate concerning academics and college basketball."

"And you ran into a problem?" she asked, interested.

He nodded and thanked the waitress as she put his platter before him. Picking up the bottle of ketchup, he said, "I couldn't find the right angle for the story. I tried three different approaches and none of them worked. I intended to see the problem through the eyes of the administration and coaches. I interviewed a few but all I heard was rhetoric. I got sick of the topic even before I started writing it. So, I finally just gave up and left."

She smiled. "I know what you mean. When I'm blocked I'll do just about anything to avoid writing." Maureen watched him fix his hamburger and pick it up. He had the most amazing hands. The palms were large, yet the fingers were long and finely shaped. She imagined her own hand being lost inside of one that looked so strong, yet suggested tenderness. Damn, it was the curse of being a writer, fantasizing all the time. *Get a grip on yourself, Maureen,* she mentally scolded. Desperate to get back to a sane discussion, she blurted out, "Have you thought about doing it from the kids' point of view?"

He swallowed and wiped his mouth. "What do you mean?"

She shrugged. "I don't know. Maybe it comes more naturally for me because that's the way I write, but what is it really like for them—you know, kids who've worked for years building their skills and their reputations. I don't know that much about sports, but doesn't it all come down to scholarships? A college team either wants them or they're done. Where do they go from there? What kind of pressure or stress are they under with SAT scores and waiting for strangers to decide their lives?"

He put his hamburger down and just stared at her. Finally he muttered, "Where were you three hours ago when I needed you?"

She grinned. "I was making dinner."

He smiled back and held her gaze. Something passed between them. They connected on some level. Maybe it was friendship, or their ability to communicate so easily . . . whatever it was, it was scary. He seemed to sense that in her and picked up his hamburger again. "You know, I think you've got something there. And it won't be that hard to write. All I have to do is recall how I felt."

"You played basketball?"

He laughed. "You really *don't* know that much about sports, do you? Look at my size. I'd be winded before the first period. Football was my game. And, no—I didn't play pro ball. I wasn't good enough. But still, I remember what it was like during the drafts. Thank God I made friends with some sports writers and changed my major in college to communications."

"But you're still involved with sports. You're one of the lucky ones, doing something you love."

He nodded. "You're right. What about you? Do you love writing?"

Placing her coffee cup back on its saucer, she admitted, "I love it and I hate it. But mostly, I love it. I'm fighting right now to change genres. To only edit the children's line and write mainstream fiction. It's something I've wanted to do for a long time."

"Then you should do it."

She grinned. "That's easier said than done. As my agent puts it, I've created the monster and now

I have to feed it. I should be flattered instead of frustrated."

"You're books are that successful?"

"They've done well," she conceded shyly. "My last made the *New York Times* list for six weeks."

His mouth hung open. "I'm sitting here with a genuine celebrity! Do you realize how many people I know that would kill for that kind of recognition?"

She was embarrassed for wanting to impress him. She rarely told strangers about making the *Times.* "Hardly a celebrity, Matt Shannon. I would think a celebrity is someone who's seen every night in hundreds of thousands of living rooms."

He leaned his elbows on the table and looked at her with intense interest. "Would you like to go to the movies sometime? Or dinner?"

He left the invitation hanging, waiting for her response.

Holy shit! Was he asking her for a date? A date? *Her?* Just like that, from out of nowhere, he just blurts it out? Speechless, Maureen could only stare back at him. Finally, she stammered, "Excuse me, I—ahh, I have to use the ladies room," before quickly sliding out of the booth.

Her brain refused to work logically. Her heart was pounding furiously against her rib cage as she escaped through the diner to the restrooms. Once inside, she ran up to the sink and turned on the cold water. Staring up at her reflection in the mirror, she murmured, "What are you doing here, Maureen? What the hell are you doing?"

"That's what I'd like to know."

She spun around to face him. *"Bobby!* Have you lost your mind? Get out of here!"

He looked over his shoulder to the empty stalls. "Big deal. Nobody's in here."

"What are *you* doing here?" she demanded, anger creeping into her voice. "I don't need this right now. Just leave. Disappear!" She waved her hand, as if the act would make him vanish.

"Oh, yes, you do need this. And right now," he countered. "The singles bar was one thing. But this . . ." He shook his head. "What do you know about this guy?"

"What do you mean, what do I know? I know he's an intelligent sensitive person who's safe. He's on television."

Bobby looked over her shoulder and fixed his hair in the mirror, running his fingers through it to push it back off his forehead. "Oh, and that makes him safe? Because his face is on the tube? Get with it, Maureen."

She glanced at the door, terrified someone would come in and see her talking to thin air. "Look, if you want to discuss this we can do it later. Just not now. Okay? I can't handle him *and* you at the same time. Go away. *Go* away!"

"I repeat, what do you know about him?"

"That's none of your business. I'm having coffee with him, not an affair."

"Did he tell you he's married?"

She stared at Bobby, her mouth opened in denial. "He's married?" she whispered and wondered why she should feel such sharp disappointment. "Is he really?"

Bobby shrugged. "Ask him."

"No, I'm asking you. You seem to know so much. Tell me."

"I've already told you more than I should. Just don't be stupid this time, okay?"

The hairs at the back of her neck rose in anger and resentment. "What is that supposed to mean—*this time?*"

Bobby didn't answer her.

"You think my marriage was a mistake? Is that it?" Indignation surged through her body. "Well it wasn't! Do you hear me? I was married for almost twenty years, and most of them were wonderful. I have two great kids who I wouldn't have had with anyone else. How can you possibly understand? Look at you. You're still a kid. You have no idea what it's like, what I'm feeling or thinking. I'm an adult, a—a mature woman, and you're still stuck in the sixties!"

She was fighting back tears and she pressed hard on her cheekbones to stop them. "Leave me alone, Bobby," she pleaded. "Let me live my own life." Wiping her nose on the back of her hand, she added, "And stay out of my dreams. Take your teddy bear and go away. I'm tired of being scared. I just want to be happy."

Turning away from him she walked out of the bathroom.

He looked in the mirror and saw his reflection.

What are you doing here, he asked himself. You should back off now. Maureen's on the road to recovery. Why can't you just leave her alone like she demanded? Isn't that what you wanted? If you wanted her back on her feet, taking control of her life, then why are you arguing with her?

Because you love her. The answer was strong and swift.

He had no right to love her. Not anymore. His chance was twenty years ago. *But it was torn away from me,* he thought in anger. *I never had the opportunity to tell her anything, and now she doesn't want to listen because in her eyes, I'm just a kid.*

A kid . . .

He continued to stare at his reflection, concentrating, visualizing fine lines around his eyes and mouth, a lack of firmness in his skin, graying hair around his temples. His eyes opened in amazement as he saw the change actually taking place. *Hey, I can do this!* Leaning closer to the mirror, he smiled at the accomplishment. Who knew what other powers he possessed? He ran his fingers through his hair, noting that his hairline was back about a quarter of an inch. But this gray . . . too much gray he thought, and was satisfied with only a few distinguishing strands. He was fascinated by the transformation. He didn't look like a kid any more. He looked like—*my God, is this how I would look if I were alive?* He tried to close the front of his bomber jacket but found it was too tight. Put on a few pounds too . . . but not bad for a forty-two year old man.

Looking back into the mirror, his grin widened. How could anyone not want to grow older, he thought in amusement. Only someone who never had the chance could appreciate each line, each extra pound or gray hair.

Now Maureen would have to pay attention to him. She'd be more comfortable. She'd listen. He only wanted her to be happy. Isn't that why he was sent back? He just couldn't show her that he loved her, and he'd have to control his jealousy every time she showed interest in another man. But he could do it. He had no other choice.

He'd have to do it, if he wanted to stay with her.

She slid into the booth and stared down at her empty coffee cup. What could she say to him?

"Hey, are you all right?" Matt asked. "Look, I didn't mean to frighten you. If you'd rather not go out, just tell me."

She looked up. "Are you married?" Those were the words. That was the question. Now, what was his answer?

He held up his left hand. There was no ring. "I'm separated. Three months now. What about you?"

"I . . . I'm separated. Since New Year's Eve." It was the first time she had said those words to a man, and a wave of sorrow for her marriage washed over her. Would she never get over it?

"New Year's Eve? That's a hell of a time to end a marriage. I'm sorry."

She smiled. "I used to believe in marriage. Now I don't know what to believe in anymore. It's as if someone changed all the rules and forgot to tell me."

Nodding, he agreed, "I know what you mean."

"Do you have children?" she asked, wanting to know him better, to prove Bobby wrong.

"I have a daughter, Kelly. She's five years old."

"Really?" Maureen grinned. She couldn't help it; she loved children. Especially since she couldn't have any more. "Do you have a picture?"

He took out his wallet and flipped it open to a small photo of a little girl. She had blond hair and big blue eyes and a wonderful smile. "She looks like you," Maureen murmured, studying the child's face. "You must miss her."

An expression of regret passed over Matt. "I do," he answered honestly. "She's everything to me. I hate it that I only get to see her on Saturdays. And I hate not being with her at breakfast, not seeing her going off to kindergarten . . ." He left his words trailing as Maureen handed him back his wallet.

"Isn't there a chance you and her mother could work things out?" She could actually feel his sorrow, and it was for that reason that she asked such a personal question.

He shook his head. "I wish we could, for Kelly's sake, but I don't think a reconciliation is possible. At least not at this point. It's a long story . . ."

"Aren't they all?" she asked with a smile.

"So what's yours?"

"My story?"

He nodded.

"I'm afraid it's not very original." She toyed with the handle of her cup, deciding what to tell him. Finally, she looked up and knew, even though they had just met, that she could trust him. "My husband is going through a mid-life crisis and has decided I'm not attractive enough any longer. He wants . . . I don't know . . . I guess he wants anyone but me." She was embarrassed, nervous, and tapped her fingernail on the cup. "I'm sorry. I don't know why I'm telling you this."

He reached across the table and stilled her hand. "Don't be sorry. And, Maureen?"

"Hmm?" He really did have a great voice and great eyes . . .

"You're husband's a blind fool."

She stared at him then, fighting the sudden taste of tears at the back of her throat. Dear God, he would never know how much she needed to hear that. Maybe that's why she had told this stranger such a personal thing. Maybe she was looking for a denial, to prove Dan wrong. In that moment, she realized how her husband had robbed her of self-esteem, how her confidence in herself as a woman had been shattered.

"This is embarrassing," she muttered, pushing the hair back off her face. "I never should have said that to you. And I don't know why I did."

"I'm glad you did," he answered. "If nothing else, it shows you're not scared of me anymore."

She looked surprised. "I was never scared of

you."

"When I asked if you wanted to go to the movies, you ran out of here pretty fast."

Grinning, she said, "Look, Matt, you're very nice, but I don't go around picking up men in singles bars and inviting them for coffee in hopes that they would ask me out."

"I don't think that."

"Thank you. Since I'm being so painfully honest here, I might as well tell you that tonight is the first time in twenty years that I've been out as a single woman . . . well, separated woman." Her expression was self-deprecating. "I guess it showed."

He didn't say anything for a few seconds, just continued to hold her gaze. It was exciting, yet frightening, and Maureen felt her muscles tighten while she waited for him to answer.

When he did, what came out of his mouth was unexpected.

"Maureen, I'm here because I want to be. Now, I'll ask you again. Would you like to go out sometime?"

She blushed, and was humiliated by the visible evidence of a forty-two year old woman that simply couldn't handle the situation. "I haven't dated in twenty years. I wouldn't know how to do it again."

He laughed. "I think it's still the same. Two people meet and have dinner, maybe go to a movie and get to know each other. It's not really that hard."

"Maybe not for you. Look, I don't understand. You were very nice to come here with me tonight, but don't feel obligated or anything. You're well known. You could go out with anyone—"

"I don't believe this," he interrupted. "I'm asking you because you're a beautiful, intelligent woman. You're easy to talk to and you made me laugh. Do I have to go on? I want to see you again. It's that simple."

He was doing it again. She could feel the tears of gratitude welling up in her eyes. "That's one of the nicest things anyone has said to me in a very long time."

He smiled back at her. "Is that a yes?"

She shook her head. "It's more of an I-don't-know."

Matt let out his breath, showing his frustration. "Okay, let's leave it like this. If you want to see me again, even if you just want to talk, I'll be at the Woodcrest on Sunday night. Unless, of course, you want to give me your phone number?"

She liked him. A lot. But she just wasn't ready for this. Not yet. "Maybe I'll come on Sunday." Picking up her purse, she slid out of the booth.

When he made a move to follow her, she put her hand on his shoulder to stop him.

"I'll walk you to your car," he offered.

She shook her head. "That's okay," she said quietly. "Thanks for the coffee. I'm really glad I asked you."

When she walked out of the diner, she could feel his gaze following her, and yet she wasn't nervous. She felt warm and almost happy. In fact, she was so pleased with the evening that she found herself giggling like a teenaged girl as she drove home.

Well, well, well . . . Matt Shannon.

Who would've thought he'd be such a nice man? He may have only been trying to be kind to her, but sitting in that diner tonight was a hell of a lot better than staying home and feeling sorry for herself.

And to heck with Bobby, too. He'd messed up her head with those dumb dreams and showing up when he wasn't needed. She refused to let him rain on her parade. Not tonight. Her entire life she had listened to men telling her what to do. First her father and then her brothers. Dan was more subtle in his manipulation of her, but he usually got his way too. And now Bobby was telling her how to lead her life. Who to see. What to think. *And he wasn't even real!*

She shook her head as she turned onto her street. Not this time. Tonight she had laughed and felt pretty, and connected with someone.

Even if she never saw Matt again, this happy feeling was a welcome change.

Chapter Eight

When Dan called and told her that the windshield of his car had been shattered and his good
leather jacket stolen, she'd sympathized and even
lent him her car until his was fixed. Two days
later the phone rang again. The water heater in
his apartment burst and half his clothes were ru-
ined, or in the cleaners. The next day he lost over
two hundred dollars to a pickpocket on the street
outside his apartment. Then his tires were slashed
in the parking lot of work. All of this in less
than a week.

Each time she hung up the phone, Maureen's
belief in a God of justice was a little more firm.
She even wondered if Bobby was somehow causing all this to happen to Dan. And when her husband called her on Friday, she had to bite the
inside of her cheek not to laugh out loud.

"You're not going to believe this, Maureen."

"What happened?" Maybe it was cruel, but she
couldn't wait to hear the latest disaster.

"I left the apartment to go to work and the car wasn't there. Somebody stole my car!"

She could sense the near hysteria in his voice and she had to hold the phone to her chest so he wouldn't hear her laughter. Taking a deep breath she managed to say in a shocked voice, "No! I can't believe it," and quickly covered the mouthpiece so he couldn't detect the laughter that was threatening to overwhelm her.

Yes, yes, there is a God, she thought, collapsing onto the kitchen chair as she listened to him rave.

"First they break the window and steal my coat. I get that fixed and they slash my tires. I only just got the car back yesterday and this morning they steal it."

"Gee, Dan, who do you think *they* are?" she asked, trying to sound sympathetic. "Whoever they are, they certainly have it in for you."

"What do you mean?" She could hear the anger in his voice.

"I don't know—it could just be a run of bad luck, but it sounds to me as if you've made someone very angry. I don't know what you've been doing. Only you can answer that."

He paused, as if considering her words, or maybe he was merely trying to control his anger. "Look, Maureen, I didn't call to argue with you so that I can feel more guilty."

"Then why did you call, Dan? You already have the number for the insurance agent."

"I called to see if I can come over for the weekend."

Her brows knitted together with confusion. "The weekend? Here?"

"I — I thought maybe we could go out to look for a new car tomorrow. And then have dinner at Chez Robèrt?"

She didn't answer immediately. She knew why he wanted her to help him look for a car. It was familiar, something they had always done together. But why did he want to take her to her favorite French restaurant? Was he reaching out? Or was he so overwhelmed by his misfortunes that he just wanted to come back home where it was safe?

"Maureen? Did you hear me? Can I come over this weekend?"

She took a deep breath. "The children would like that," she answered.

"Would it be all right with you, though? I've missed everyone."

As she felt her throat tighten with emotion she silently cursed. Damn, she'd thought tears were behind her. "Sure, Dan," she whispered. "You can spend the weekend."

"Great. I'll be over tomorrow afternoon then."

"Okay, I'll tell Abbie and Josh."

She stared at the phone after she hung it up. At the end there it had sounded like the old Dan, the husband who had called her every day from work. Maybe he really was thinking about coming back . . .

Trying to reason out Dan's motivations, Maureen started dinner. Josh would be happy for his father's company, but Abbie? Abbie deeply resented Dan's abandonment and let him know it at every opportunity. Maybe it was because her daughter was almost a woman and felt Maureen's pain and anger. Even though she had never put Dan down in front of the children, she could still see the resentment in their eyes. Because of their parents' inability to work out their problems, the children's lives were painfully disrupted. But that was just it. They weren't really children any longer. They were on the brink of adulthood and intelligent enough to figure things out on their own. One couldn't hide and make excuses and say Daddy was on a business trip. The truth was their father left because he wasn't happy any longer. And they knew it.

Through the jumbled thoughts racing around her brain, a sound registered, familiar music announcing the five-thirty news. Dropping the potato peeler onto the counter, Maureen raced into the family room. It was silly, even immature, but she sat glued to the television set. Dan was forgotten as she waited for Matt Shannon's face to appear. She had done this every night since Sunday. Like a star-struck teen, she admired his confidence in front of the camera, his friendly way of speaking, his eyes, his hair, his mouth . . . and she remembered the gentle touch of his hand upon hers. She found herself almost giggling, keeping this secret all to herself. Josh wouldn't believe her even if she had told him that she'd met Matt Shannon and the man had asked her for a date. But she knew, and she kept the knowledge close to her heart. When she felt insecure and lonely, she brought out the memory of the diner and found herself smiling. If she never saw him again she would always be grateful for that one night, when a stranger, an intelligent handsome man, had told her she was pretty.

She sat, mesmerized by his voice, as he spoke of the upcoming Spring training in Florida. She wondered if he ever thought of her. He'd probably forgotten—

"I'm not even going to watch the Phillies this year if they trade Ricky Jordan. Everybody talks like Dykstra's the whole team."

She turned at the sound of her son's voice. Josh collapsed onto the sofa and scowled at the television set. "How come you're listening to the sports?"

It would be the perfect opportunity to tell him, but she didn't. "I'm waiting for the weather. Your dad called," she added.

"Yeah? What happened to him now? A building collapse around him?"

"His car was stolen this morning."

Josh sat up straight. "No kidding?"

"No kidding."

"Boy, talk about being snakebit." Her son shook his head, as if pondering the mysteries of the world. "Why do you think all this is happening to him?"

She pictured Bobby in her mind but merely shrugged her shoulders. "Who knows. Anyway, he's coming over this weekend to look for a new car. Maybe you'd like to go with him."

Josh shook his head. "I can't. Me and Mike talked to Coach Kowlecki about using the gym tomorrow after the wrestling meet. We're going to play some kids from Moorestown."

Maureen stood up, ready to go back into the kitchen. "Basketball?"

He nodded. "Hey, Mom, what did you mean dad's coming over for the weekend? He's staying here?"

"That's right."

"Why? Is he coming back?"

She wanted to take him in her arms and hug him to her chest. She wanted to feel his skin against hers, to comfort him and wipe away all his confusion, just like she had done when he was little. But he was nearly grown now and would die of embarrassment at such a display. Instead, she could only smile sympathetically. "I don't know, Josh. I guess it's just easier to sleep here this weekend while he looks for a new car."

"Who's sleeping here?"

They both turned at the sound of Abbie's voice.

"Dad's car was stolen this morning," Josh said, wanting to be the first to tell his sister this important news.

Abbie merely stared at her brother. Very slowly she looked from Josh to Maureen.

"And he thinks he's staying here?"

Maureen took a deep breath. "I told him he could. He said he misses everyone."

"Hah!" Abbie gave her mother a sarcastic look. "Yeah, right. He misses us. That must be why he's living in Philadelphia."

"Hey, give him a break, will you?" Josh demanded. "His car was just stolen."

Abbie glared at her brother. "Good," she muttered through tightly clenched teeth. "He deserves it." She held her school books close to her chest and scowled at Maureen. "And you're crazy if you allow him to stay here." Walking out of the room, she didn't wait for a response.

"Why is she so mad?" Josh muttered. "He didn't do anything to her."

Maureen glanced at her son. "Be patient with her, Josh. She's hurt."

"*She's* hurt?" Josh demanded. "Everybody's so worried about Abbie. Well, what about me, huh? When dad left I didn't lose just a father. I lost a friend. How easy do you think it is to be here without him, living with two women? We always talked. About sports and . . . and everything . . ." His voice broke and tears welled up in his eyes.

Maureen rushed back and gathered him in her arms. She didn't care that he initially stiffened, for she refused to let him shut her out. "It's okay, Josh," she murmured against his hair. It's okay to let go. Say whatever you want. Just don't keep it in."

Her son sniffled, fighting the tears. "How long is this going to go on? Can't you two work it out? *Please . . .*"

Her heart broke listening to him. It was so damn unfair that children suffered like this. "I don't know if we can, honey," she answered honestly, swallowing down the tightness in her own throat. "But we'll try. I promise you that. We'll try."

"Look at it, Maureen. Isn't it beautiful? Let's take it for a test drive."

It had called to her from across the car lot. While Dan was wandering through rows of corporate-looking sedans, she had turned her head and caught sight of it. Tiny. Red. And shining in the winter sun. Ever since her twenties, she had harbored a desire for an MG sports car. It was silly to be forty-two years old and to be gazing so lovingly at a car. All her life she had settled for what was serviceable; for the last ten years she had driven around in a station wagon. First a small one for all the groceries, the car seats and playpens. Then a larger one for the football equipment, the baseball bats, the hockey sticks and all the car pools she had become a part of. Her present car was a small wagon, one that she intended to pass on to the twins when they got their licenses in six months. And in all those years, every time she had seen an MG on the road, a part of her had yearned to be behind the wheel of such a classic automobile. She had thought it was forever beyond her reach, and now she was too old.

"Did you hear me, Maureen? Let's take it out."

She blinked away her daydream and stared at her husband. He'd changed in the time he was away from her. He'd lost weight. His hair was shorter and styled like Josh's. Even his clothes were different. His conservative clothing was replaced by more young, today, with-it apparel, from the leather bomber jacket right down to the Air Jordan sneakers. But what irritated her the most was the gold chain around his neck that glared at her in the sunlight. It was almost laughable. He looked like a typical male in a mid-life crisis, a strutting peacock trying desperately to attract the younger hens.

She realized again with great sadness that Dan Malone was, in the words of the young women at the Woodcrest Inn, "a ticket."

"Are you all right? Didn't you hear me?"

Smiling, Maureen nodded. "Sure. We can go for a test drive if you want."

Ten minutes later, Dan was speeding down a back road with a look of excitement on his face. "God, this is great. You always liked an MG, didn't you?"

There was a tight band of pain around her chest and Maureen glanced at the car's interior, the leather steering wheel, the wooden dash and gear shift. This was not a car for groceries or children. This was a car for fun. "Yes, I did," she answered in a subdued voice.

"Is something wrong?" Dan asked slowing down for a red light.

She noticed the way he looked at the cars that turned onto the road, seeing the way he tried to catch the eyes of women drivers. It made her sick. This was not the man she had married. He was a stranger. "You're not seriously thinking of buying this, are you?"

The light changed and Dan peeled out. "I don't know. It is a great car."

"Dan, if your old car was stolen, how long do you think this one would last in the city?"

"I'd garage it."

Well, there it was. He had no intention of coming back home. "Then do what you want," she said. "But I wouldn't rush into anything."

He turned around and headed back to the dealership. "Yeah, you're probably right. This is the first day I've looked at cars. It'll be here next week. But it sure is a lot of fun, isn't it?"

She gazed out the window to the barren, winter trees, so undressed and vulnerable. That was exactly how she felt inside. Empty and cold. "You're right. It sure is a lot of fun, Dan."

Dinners at Chez Robèrt were reserved for special occasions—birthdays, anniversaries, the signing of a new contract or wining and dining the boss. The restaurant was renowned for its French food and people came from as far away as New York City to enjoy its cuisine. As soon as you walked into the place it spoke of wealth and luxury, from the two-inch thick carpets to the exquisite floral arrangements that graced each table. Waiters in impeccable tuxedos hovered over you, making sure every detail of your meal was perfect while a pianist rendered Baroque pieces that quietly enhanced the romantic mood.

It was a place that Maureen associated with good memories and she smiled brightly at the man across from her. "It's nice to be here again."

Dan smiled back. "It's nice to be here with you."

The admission was so unexpected that Maureen looked startled.

"I mean it," Dan said. "I've missed everyone . . . missed you."

"You have?" Dear God, why did hope spring eternal? Why did she feel like she was on an emotional roller coaster, plunging into depression and quickly rising again with expectation?

He nodded. "It isn't as great as you might think out there, Maureen."

"You've had a pretty rough week." She wanted him to come home because he loved her, because he wanted her, only her—not because he felt beaten up by a run of bad luck.

He picked up his glass of scotch and drank deeply. "I want . . ." He looked at her, then down to his plate. Lifting his head he held her gaze. "I want to sleep in my own bed. I want Abbie to talk to me again. I want Josh to look at me like his father, not an outsider. I want my family back, Maureen."

Not once did he say anything about her. Inside of her there was a nagging doubt that something wasn't right, but she instantly pictured Abbie's anger and Josh's frustration, and pushed her doubts aside. If Dan was reaching out, trying to undo the damage, then how could she slap his hand away?

"You want your bed and you want your children. But do you want me?" Her heart slammed against her rib cage as she waited for his answer.

He looked like he was going to cry. "I love you, Maureen," he whispered. "I never stopped loving you."

Loving and wanting were two different things. His answer didn't tell her what she needed to hear, yet he was trying. His face looked like it had aged five years since he had left. His hand shook as he held onto his glass. Knowing at this moment she was the more stable, Maureen smiled shyly.

"Then why don't we skip dessert and go home."

He was visibly relieved and smiled broadly while signaling to the waiter for their check.

They would heal their marriage and put their family back together. They would all be happy again, just like before. She would push the nagging doubts out of her mind and just go for it. This time she would make it happen. She could do this. She had to—for herself, for her husband, and especially for her children.

It was as if fate were suddenly on her side. Abbie, not wanting to be around her father, was spending the night with her best friend. And Josh, seeing how friendly his parents had suddenly become, abruptly announced that he and Mike were going to Mike's house to watch *The Godfather,* parts 1 and 2. Everyone agreed that he might as well just sleep over. She and Dan were to be alone for the entire night.

She suggested that they get comfortable. Dan changed from his suit to a pair of jeans while Maureen made tea and set a tray in the family room. Still not exactly at ease with him, she gave Dan his privacy in the bedroom.

When he joined her, she felt nervous and mumbled something about having only Pepperidge Farm cookies in the house for dessert. She noticed that he ignored the tea and walked over to the liquor cabinet and poured himself another drink. As she left the room she told herself that he was probably as apprehensive about the evening as she, and it was silly for two people who had shared twenty years to feel so anxious. Yet when she was in the bedroom and opened her lingerie drawer, she stopped and stared at the fragile, ivory silk nightgown.

She loved him, didn't she? She wanted her family back, didn't she? Then why was she hesitating? Picking up the gown, she slipped it over her body and looked in the mirror. She ran a brush through her hair and applied blush to her cheeks. Did she look young enough, pretty enough?

God Almighty, don't think about it, she mentally scolded and grabbed the matching kimono robe. *Just do it. Get your husband and your family back. It's worth it.*

She started yawning during the last half hour of *Saturday Night Live* and looked across the sofa to her husband. He seemed mesmerized by the show. This wasn't working out like she had planned. Instead of watching television and drinking scotch, why didn't he sit closer to her, put his arm around her and talk to her, or at least touch her hand? Something was very wrong. Had she read the wrong signals? Did he really just want to spend the night . . . alone?

No longer able to handle the suspense, Maureen rose and picked up the tea tray. "I'm really tired, Dan. I think I'll go to bed."

He glanced at her, as if he had simply forgotten that she was in the room. "Oh, okay. I'll be in a minute. Just want to finish this drink."

She nodded and walked out.

She would not cry. Snuggling deep into the feather pillow, Maureen vowed she would not unravel. He didn't want her, and it was painfully obvious. She didn't know how she was going to get through the night and prayed that he would fall asleep in the family room, for she didn't think she could stand to be in the same bed with him.

The hall light turned on and she could hear him climbing the stairs. *Oh God, he's coming in here,* she thought in a panic. What was she supposed to do? Pretend she was asleep, confront him?

He moved in the moonlight like a weary apparition, dropping his clothes onto the loveseat and feeling his way to the bed. When he laid down, she held her breath, waiting.

"You asleep?" he whispered and she could smell the scotch on his lips.

She turned to him. "No. Not yet."

Sighing deeply, he put his arm around her waist and pulled her close to him. He didn't say anything, not about love or wanting, or how sorry he was, or how glad he was to be back. Nothing. He kissed her, gently at first, and then with an urgency that surprised her.

In that moment, she surrendered her anger, her confusion, and told herself that in his own way he was talking to her, letting her know how he felt. She kissed him back, trying to put twenty years of love into it. She wanted him to want her, to think she was a desirable woman, and Maureen left his mouth and trailed kisses over his cheeks, his eyes, his ears. Very slowly, she moved down his throat to his chest, teasing his nipples, feeling them harden with her tongue. She smiled. It was going to work. Starting to become more confident, she moved lower and made love to him in as intimate a way as she knew possible.

He never made a sound. He didn't whisper to her of his passion, nor touch her hair, her skin, anything to make her feel he was responding. It seemed to her that ten minutes must have passed and she was beginning to sweat with the exertion of trying to make him acknowledge the passion she knew he was feeling. Exasperated, Maureen straddled his hips and he entered her.

She watched his face in the moonlight, willing him to open his eyes, to look at her, to communicate something. All he did was fold his hands behind his head and let her work.

The tears welled up her eyes, bitter and painful. She felt, watching him ignoring her, like she was all alone. For the first time she knew what a prostitute must experience. Sobbing, she pulled off him and collapsed onto the bed.

"I can't," she cried, curling up into a protective ball. "I just can't do it anymore."

Chapter Nine

Dan leaned over her. "What? What's wrong?"

She clutched the pillow tighter to her chest, trying to muffle the sounds of her grief. Shaking her head, she couldn't answer him.

"Maureen, talk to me. Tell me what's wrong."

She spun around and faced him. *"Now* you want to talk? You want me to tell you what's wrong?" she cried. Gulping down tears, she whispered, "You're what's wrong, Dan. Who were you making love to? It wasn't me. You didn't even know I was there."

He slumped back against his pillow. "What are you talking about?" His voice was defensive. "I thought it was terrific."

"Of course you thought it was terrific. Do you know what you were doing?" Silence. "I'll tell you. You did absolutely nothing. You isolated yourself from me. You put your hands behind your head, as if you were taking a nap on a Sunday afternoon."

She wiped the tears off her cheeks and looked at him. "That wasn't making love. That was little more than masturbation on your part."

"Jesus Christ, Maureen!"

"Do you know how you made me feel?" she demanded, anger creeping into her voice. "Like you should leave money on the dresser when you leave. I can't do it all alone, Dan. I can't try and hold this family together by myself. I can't keep reaching out to you when there's no hand to grab hold of." Her throat nearly closed with emotion. "And I refuse to make love alone. I—I respect myself too much for that."

Silence filled the bedroom. The absence of sound was so large and threatening that it seemed to envelop her and press down on her chest.

Finally, he whispered, "I'm sorry. I thought we could make a new beginning. I don't know . . ."

"How?" she whispered back. "All day long we act like brother and sister. You never touch me. You ignore me. And you expect me to turn into a siren because you come to bed and finally kiss me? My God, why can't men realize that if they want to make love to a woman then they should begin when they walk in the front door, not when they walk into the bedroom? You want to make love to a woman, Dan, then make love to her mind first, before you ever touch her body."

"Is this the writer talking? Is this the result of all your research for some novel?"

"This is a woman talking. Honestly. It used to be good between us, wasn't it? We made love together. What happened? What's wrong?"

"I don't know."

"I think you do. I just don't think you want to tell me."

"Look, Maureen, I came over here this weekend because I wanted to be with you. I wanted to see if we could begin again. Maybe we can't . . ."

His words trailed off, leaving a void that needed to be filled.

"We can't begin on quicksand, on lies, or try to put a Band-Aid on a gaping wound. We can only begin on truth. And that's what you're keeping from me."

"I don't know what you mean."

"I think you do. I think you're consumed with guilt, and it's changed you, made you defensive and angry, and it's pushing me away."

"I don't want to push you away. Not any more."

That one phrase *not any more* spoke volumes, and a tight knot of fear formed in her belly, yet she couldn't stop now. "Then let's begin with the truth. I'm not stupid, Dan, but I've tried to ignore my instincts where you're concerned. I know there's a woman behind all this. There has to be. I can feel it. Now, I'm asking again for the truth." She paused for a moment, trying to still her heart. "Because I deserve it."

He didn't say anything. She wanted to hear a denial. She wanted him to tell her that she was crazy, that he hadn't broken his marriage vows, that—

"I . . . I've been with three women."

She felt the weight of it again, that heavy, crushing weight of pain pressing her into the mattress. "With? Like in the biblical *with?*" she muttered stupidly.

"Yes."

She didn't move. She could barely breathe. It felt so unreal. None of this was happening.

"Maureen?"

It rushed at her then. The pain. The deception. Sweeping over her like a tidal wave of betrayal. Bolting out of bed, she rushed into the bathroom and knelt in front of the toilet as her body revolted against the shock. She clutched the smooth porcelain, as if it might ground her to this world, while her stomach muscles contracted and heaved. From very far away, she heard Dan telling her that he was sorry. He sounded like he was crying. She didn't care. She thought she was dying.

Minutes later, she pulled herself up and washed her face. Her legs were shaking, her entire body was trembling, yet she forced herself to go back into the bedroom.

He was sitting on the loveseat, dressed in his jeans. She could only stare at him, this stranger who had betrayed her.

"God, Maureen, I'm so sorry. You'll never forgive me, will you?"

Who was he? Where did her husband go? How could this stranger have taken over?

"That's why I couldn't tell you. You've always been so good, so perfect . . ."

When her voice came, it was hoarse and raspy,

and not all of it was from being ill. "When did it start?"

"October."

It was just one word, yet the power of it almost brought her to her knees. Holding onto the wall for support, she forced her lips to move. "How could you have lied to me like that? All those nights I laid awake thinking you were hurt or dead, and you were in bed with another woman. How could you do it? How could you come home and tell me lies about playing cards or retirement parties, and then come into our bed?"

He didn't answer her.

"When I asked you about another woman you denied it. You looked right at me, Dan, and said you would never do that to me while you were living here. But you were fucking around for months before I asked you to leave!" Her last words became a scream of outrage.

"Who are they?" she demanded.

"Maureen, that won't serve any purpose—"

"I said, who are they? I have a right to know!" The words were torn from her throat.

Even in the moonlight she could see him squirm and a blind fury built inside of her that he would protect those women.

"They didn't mean anything," he began.

"They must have meant something to you. You threw away your family for them. Don't try and be honorable now, Dan. It's insulting that you want to protect them when it's okay to shit all over me."

His voice was so low she had to strain to hear it.

"One was Kathy. I used to work with her before the promotion. The other's name was Ellen. She's with an outside firm that's doing business with us." He took several deep breaths. "The last was Betty."

"Your new secretary," she whispered, her statement filled with bitterness. "Christ! It's so typical, it's pathetic."

"Maureen, please . . . I'll do anything to make it up to you. Just tell me what I have to do."

She could hear the desperation in his voice, yet she felt nothing for him. In that moment, something fragile died inside of her. She wrapped her arms around her waist and rocked back and forth with sorrow and anguish as a deep sobbing began.

"I'll—I'll tell you what to do, Dan," she managed to say. "You get the hell out of my house and stay away from me. I can't handle any more. I can't . . ."

She looked at the bed, wanting to collapse and die, to wipe out the memory of his betrayal. But she couldn't go back there. Not now. Not tonight. Instead, she slowly walked into Abbie's room and pulled down her comforter.

Sliding under the cover, she smelled her child's scent on the pillow and broke into uncontrollable sobs. God, even Abbie knew. How could she have been so stupid? So trusting?

"I'm sorry, Maureen. I don't know what else to say."

He stood in the doorway for a moment, but she couldn't answer him. She didn't want to talk, or think, or feel. She wanted to die from the betrayal and humiliation that sliced right through her heart.

She didn't even care when he walked down the hallway and out the front door.

In her heart, she knew it was over. Forever.

She was dreaming. She had to be dreaming, otherwise why was Bobby standing beside her bed, looking years older?

"You're okay, kid," he whispered, sitting on the edge of the mattress and gently pushing her hair back from her face. "You'll make it through this."

"Bobby?" Her voice sounded strained to her ears.

He smiled. "Right here."

"You . . . you look different. Older." Or was it just the moonlight casting shadows onto his face?

"You're the one who said I looked like a kid. Now maybe you'll listen to me."

She remembered their argument in the ladies room of the diner. "I'm sorry I yelled at you," she murmured, and felt the tightness return in her throat. "I'm sorry for a lot of things. Dan—" She couldn't finish her thought. It was too painful.

"Shh . . ." He soothed her by running his fingers through her hair. "I know about Dan. Don't think about it now."

She started crying again, deep, sorrowful moans of anguish. Instinctively Maureen reached out and pulled him closer, needing to feel him against her.

He cradled her in his arms, consoling her, soothing her with soft sounds of comfort. "It's okay. It's all right now."

"It—it'll never be all right," she cried, burrowing her face against his chest. She tried to stop crying, but found she had to push the words out. "I feel like such a fool. I trusted him, and he betrayed me. I believed him. How could I have been so stupid?"

"Because you loved him. Because we never want to believe that someone we love can betray our trust. But you'll get through this because you're strong."

"I'm not!" she moaned, shaking her head in denial. "Everyone thinks that, expects that. But I just want to crawl up and die. I can't survive this, Bobby. Not this kind of pain. I can't!"

"Yes, you can," he countered, holding her closer. "And I'm going to tell you why. Because you have two kids who need you. They need stability in their lives right now and you're the only parent they've got that can provide it."

Maureen groaned. "Stability! I'm seeing a ghost in the daytime and dreaming about him at night. Half the time I'm scared to fall asleep because I wind up wandering around in my nightgown with my old high school friends. My husband just admitted he's been cheating on me for months. I feel like my life is over and you think I can provide stability?" She closed her eyes to block out the mental image of Dan with another woman. "I want to die . . ." She shuddered, and curled up in his arms like a grieving child.

"Listen to me, Maureen, I think human beings are just like anything else in nature. We're resilient. What's you favorite flower?"

"What?" the question was so unexpected, she lifted her head to look at him.

"Just tell me. What's your favorite flower?"

Sniffling, she wiped her nose with the back of her hand. "I love zinnias and poppies. I have them planted all around the house."

"And what do they look like now."

"Now?" She couldn't figure out where this conversation was leading. "Now they're all, you know, withered."

"But they're not dead, are they?"

She shook her head and placed it back against his chest. "No. They look like it, but they aren't. They'll come back in the spring."

"That's you, Maureen," he said slowly, gently, while running his fingers through her hair. "You're a beautiful flower and you're going through a tough winter. But you've got to push away all the dirt and crap around you. You've got to fight like hell against it, clawing for your own survival, until you break through. Even then your head's going to be bent; you'll still be fragile. But then someone's going to rain love on you, and you'll find yourself lifting your face to the sun and growing again, taller and stronger than before. And pretty soon you'll open up, and you'll be a beautiful flower, ready to accept love or whatever life hands you."

She was sniffling, listening to his soft voice. Finally, she said, "They teach you how to do that? Talk in parables, like in the Bible?"

She felt the laughter start deep in his chest. "Boy, I hope they hear this. Maybe it comes with age. You think? I probably wouldn't have thought of it at twenty."

In spite of everything she found herself smiling. "What would I have done without you?" she whispered, wishing she could see his dimples in the moonlight. "I don't care if you are only a figment of my imagination, Bobby O'Connor. Now this is twice I've felt like you've saved my life."

"You still don't get it, do you kid? You're doing all the hard work. I'm only here for guidance. Now go back to sleep. You're going to need all the strength you can get."

He lifted her shoulders and placed her head back against the pillow.

"Am I going to dream I'm back in high school again?"

He smiled. "No."

She gazed at him and said what was in her heart. "I've always loved you. Did you know that? Ever since I walked into Miss Bennet's class at Our Lady of Grace and you smiled at me."

"I've loved you, too, Maureen."

Her throat constricted, but this time it was with a bittersweet pain. "All those years. Why didn't you ever say something? I waited for you, for some sign. I wonder how different my life would have been if only—"

He put his finger to her lips. "Don't. You can't change the past, only the future. But maybe you're lucky. Maybe you can look back on the past and learn from it." A warm feeling of peace passed from his finger to her lips. It entered her brain and swept down her arms and legs, relaxing the muscles and making her sleepy.

They stared at each other in the moonlight, until Maureen reached for his hand. "Will you stay with me until I fall asleep? I want to feel loved again, even if it's just for tonight." Her voice was low, a mere whisper, yet she knew he heard her.

She could tell he was thinking about her request, but it didn't take long for him to say, "Sure. Move over."

He laid down behind her, pulling her back against his chest. Wrapping his arms around her, he thought of all the years he had fantasized about doing just that. It was better than he had imagined. She was warm and soft and her hair held the faint scent of flowers.

Picking his hand up from her waist, she brought it to her lips and kissed his fingers. "Am I dreaming, Bobby?" she asked sleepily.

"What do you think?" he answered in a rough voice, more moved by her simple act of tenderness than he thought possible.

She sighed deeply and snuggled against him. "I must be dreaming," she murmured. "And if I am, I never want it to end."

Moisture filled his eyes and his mind whispered

back to her, *But it can't even begin, Maureen . . . it's too late for us.* He was surprised that he was still capable of feeling such deep emotions — love, anger, regret. But just for tonight . . . for tonight maybe he could hold her and pretend. He looked up to the ceiling of the bedroom and beyond. Was it so much to ask? Didn't he deserve one night with the woman he loved?

She awoke with a sense of peace and a smile on her lips. Stretching, Maureen felt a deep contentment inside her and grinned as she opened her eyes.

Abbie's room? Why was she in here?

Immediately the memory of last night rose up and seized her brain, filling it with images . . . the fiasco in bed with Dan, his betrayal of her with other women. Three other women. Crawling into her daughter's bed. And Bobby. She had dreamed of Bobby. It was just another dream, wasn't it? It was becoming more and more difficult to tell her fantasies from reality.

Looking at the huge posters of Madonna and David Bowie, Maureen shook her head. Of course it was a dream. Bobby had looked older, had told her a pretty story about flowers, or something, and she had asked him to hold her until she fell asleep. But in her dream he had seemed so real. She had felt wrapped in a warm cocoon of serenity. She remembered the muscles in his arms, the beating of his heart as he held her tightly to his chest. He had given her comfort, told her he had loved her. Why was it that her dreams were better than reality?

She covered her face with her hands and slowly ran her fingers through her hair. Digging her nails into her scalp, she tried to blot out the memory of Dan's betrayal with the pain she was inflicting on herself. But nothing could banish from her mind the images of him with younger, prettier, thinner, women. The heaviness in her heart returned and settled like a weight upon her chest.

"*This* is reality, Maureen," she muttered to herself, as the tears returned. The silence of her house was almost oppressive as it closed in around her. "You're alone," she admitted. "The hope that your husband will come home is gone, because he's not the man that you once loved. And the one you do love, the one you dream about, is a ghost. You can't have either of them; they're both lost to you. It would be easy to stay in bed and cry, to curl back into the warmth of the covers and lick your wounds. But it wouldn't change anything. You'd still be alone."

Throwing back the comforter, Maureen rose. With a deliberate slowness, she carefully remade Abbie's bed and then left the room. She still couldn't look in her own bedroom. Not yet. The nightmare of last night was too vivid. Instead, she walked downstairs. She would make coffee, read the Sunday paper, and maybe call Lisa before the children came home.

She felt like a robot, going through all the motions, acting as if it were a normal Sunday morning. She made coffee, brought in the paper, but found her hand reaching for the phone instead.

"Lisa? Did I wake you?"

"Maureen? What time is it?"

"Eight-fifteen. I did wake you. I'm sorry."

"What's wrong?"

Maureen paused. "It's Dan. He . . . he finally admitted that he's been cheating on me since October." There. She had said it aloud. "I feel like a fool. I believed him when he said all this had nothing to do with another woman."

"Oh God . . . I'm sorry, Maureen. Do you want me to come over?"

Tears welled in her eyes but she shook her head. "No. I think I just needed to tell someone. I'm sorry it had to be you. It's a hell of a thing to wake up to."

"Are you all right? What can I do?"

"Hell, Lisa, I don't know what I can do. I feel so helpless. I have this rage building up inside of me and I don't know how to release it."

"Listen, I know this isn't going to help, but I remember a friend of mine in college who believed his mother was a witch."

"A witch?"

"Yeah. It seems his mother had a running feud with their neighbors. One day she cut up a lemon and carved this neighbor's name on it and sat it on the windowsill to dry out. Every day, as the lemon dried up, the man got more sick. Until he died."

Staring at her coffee cup, Maureen laughed.

"So I should start carving women's names into lemons?"

Lisa chuckled. "It might make you feel less helpless. You can't walk up to them and punch 'em out, but who knows—maybe they'll just dry up. It would sure make sex unpleasant."

Shaking her head, Maureen giggled. "I knew you'd make me laugh. That's why I woke you up."

"Seriously, let's go to lunch. How about Tuesday? Leave the kids, the house. Just get the hell out. The two of us. Okay?"

"Okay," Maureen answered. "I'd like that."

"Do you want to talk about it now? About Dan? Or anything?"

"We'll wait until lunch. The kids are going to be home soon. I can't stop crying and I don't want them to see me like that anymore. God, Lisa, I'm so tired of being unhappy."

"It won't last. I promise you that. This is the worst part. I know it sounds like a cliché, but you'll get through it."

"See you Tuesday then, all right?"

"One-thirty at Cafe Gallery?"

Maureen smiled. It was their favorite restaurant for lunch, a lovely place on the Delaware River. "One-thirty. I'll be there. Thanks."

She hung up the phone and poured herself a second cup of coffee. Her heart wasn't in the newspaper or its blaring headline. Feeling sorrier for herself than anyone else, she dismissed a major fire in Philadelphia and idly flipped over the different parts of the paper.

200

His face looked up at her from the front page of the sports sections. Matt Shannon. And there was his story on academics and college basketball. She sat down at the table and started to read. When she saw that he had taken her idea and wrote the story from the kids' point of view, her smile became a wide grin.

Matt Shannon.

It was Sunday and he would be at the Woodcrest Inn.

He said he would be there, waiting for her answer . . .

She thought of Dan. His lies and betrayal. She thought of Matt. His concern and his kindness. She had two choices. She could stay home and feel sorry for herself, or she could go to the Woodcrest and see if Matt Shannon really meant what he said.

Chapter Ten

She had enough concealer under her eyes to spackle a wall. Unfortunately, she was one of those women whose face mirrored her state of mind. The lack of sleep brought dark circles and her eyes were puffy from crying. Why, in the name of God, was she back at the Woodcrest Inn looking for a sportscaster, when she could have been home where it was safe and warm? *And lonely and filled with memories,* her mind quickly responded.

That was true, Maureen admitted while walking through the front door. She could not sit in that house tonight. It felt like a prison, every room holding painful memories.

"Check your coat?"

Maureen turned at the masculine voice by her ear.

He towered over her, looking handsome and happy to see her. Dressed in tan pants and a brown sweater, Matt Shannon held his jacket over his shoulder and smiled down at her.

"Hi." Her stomach seemed to flip over, and she told herself it was nerves and not that she was actually flattered to see him waiting for her.

"Hi. I'm glad you finally showed up. Every woman that passed through that door tonight must have thought I was giving them the once-over. I was beginning to think you weren't coming."

"I—ahh, I had some things to do at home. The kids, and everything." God, she was flustered just by being around him.

"Well, look, you're here. Now, are you going to trust them with that coat?" When he smiled he completely disarmed her. It was the kind of smile that made her feel like she was important.

Handing her raincoat over to him, she said, "I believe they look trustworthy."

"Good. That means you're staying," he answered, folding her coat over his brown tweed jacket and motioning toward the coat-check room. "Let's get rid of these. You look really pretty, by the way. Green is a great color for you."

She unconsciously touched the silk lapel of her deep green jacket. Now she had two closets. One for everyday clothes and the other, which used to be Dan's, was now used for her expensive author's clothes. "Thank you," she muttered, trying to remember the last time her husband had given her a compliment. How sad that she couldn't.

Matt gave the girl money and was about to pocket the tickets, when Maureen held out her hand. "That's okay. I'll hold mine. Here's the dollar."

He placed the ticket in her hand. "Put your money away."

"No. I insist. I don't want you paying for me."

He stood, staring down at her. "You're not going to be militant about it, are you?"

"Please understand. All of this is new to me. I'd just feel better if I paid for myself."

He grinned. "You mean you'd feel safer."

"Okay. I'd feel safer."

He took her money and put it in his pocket. "I can see this is going to be a cheap date."

Walking toward the music, Maureen corrected him. "This isn't a date."

"Oh? What is it?"

"It's two people meeting, talking, getting to know each other."

"Sounds like a date to me," Matt said, taking her arm and leading her through the crowd.

"It's not a date," she insisted. But she didn't think he heard her.

When he found a place at the bar, he made room for her next to him. "Am I allowed to buy you a drink?"

Still smiling, she shook her head. "No, but thank you for asking."

He gave her a confused look. "Okay. Can I at least order a drink for you?"

"That you can do," she said with a laugh. "I could stand here for ten minutes trying to get the bartender's attention. You won't have that problem." In fact, as she looked around, she could see people staring at them. At him, to be more exact.

"What do you want?"

She turned her attention back to him. "Rum and Coke," she said easily. "Diet Coke, if they have it."

He handed her the drink and she put a ten-dollar bill on the bar.

"This is going to confuse the hell out of the bartender," Matt remarked while waiting for his beer.

She leaned closer to him to be heard above the music. "I'll tell you what we can do," Maureen offered. "I'll pay for this round and you can pay for the next."

He shrugged his shoulders, as if giving up. "Whatever you say, *Ms*. Malone."

She left the change on the bar and sipped her drink. He was smiling, but she hoped he really understood her intentions. She just couldn't think of herself as being someone's date, of feeling obligated at the end of the evening. He was right. She felt safer.

"I read your story this morning in the paper. It was great."

Holding the mug of beer to his chest, he leaned down so she would hear him. "I have you to thank for it. As soon as I thought of the story from the kids' point of view it just started coming."

She nodded. "You did a good job." She could detect the faint, spicy scent of his cologne. It was very appealing and very masculine.

"I bought one of your books."

She straightened. "You did? Why?"

Shrugging, he said, "I wanted to see what you did, so I went into a book store and there you were. It's really impressive seeing your name like that. How many have you written?"

"There's twelve in the series, so far. But I'm working on a mainstream now."

"What's that?"

She smiled. "That's an adult book that has a broader audience. At least, I hope it will." He had to be interested in her. He must have thought about her during the week. Why else would he go into a book store and check her out? She was flattered and nervous. What if he thought her books were silly, or—

"Do you like to dance?"

She stared at him. "I haven't danced in years. Unless it was at a wedding, or something. I think I'm out of practice."

He put his mug on the bar and took her hand. "It's like riding a bicycle. Comes right back," he said, while pulling her toward the dance floor.

She pulled back, not wanting to humiliate herself, but it was as if she were trying to resist steel. He was stronger than she thought, leading her through the dancers to the middle of the floor.

He leaned down and nearly shouted, "No one will notice us here. C'mon. They're playing oldies tonight. You should remember this."

Maureen looked around her to the other dancers. "This isn't an oldie," she shouted back.

Those in their twenties were dancing like Abbie and Josh, moving their heads and shoulders like Paula Abdul worshippers. Yet those in their thirties and forties were doing something a little more familiar.

Matt grabbed her shoulders so she would look at him. "If we just stand here shouting at each other, then everyone's really going to notice us. They'll start pointing and whispering. *Look at the sports guy and the famous writer. They're making a spectacle of themselves.* C'mon, Maureen, our reputations are at stake here."

Laughing, she gently pushed him away and started to move. He joined her and she was surprised that he was such a good dancer. For some reason, she thought someone so tall and muscular would look awkward. But he didn't. He looked comfortable, and at ease with himself and his frame. And when he smiled at her, she felt something weird taking place inside—something that started way below her belly and spread like delicious ribbons of excitement through her body.

"See," he shouted, half laughing as he tried to be heard. "It all comes back. And you're good, really good."

Embarrassed, Maureen could only smile her thanks and look away She used to be good. She had even won dance contests in high school. She'd loved to dance, relishing the freedom of movement, the joy of expression. But Dan didn't dance, unless he'd had too much to drink. So for twenty years she'd sat on the sidelines and tapped

207

her toes, watching others enjoy themselves. Now she was dancing again. With a man other than her husband. And she liked it.

Just as before, one song led into another, and Maureen looked around her as everyone started to form some sort of line dance. Gazing up at Matt, she shrugged her shoulders and turned to walk off the dance floor.

He took her arm and said, "C'mon. Let's try it."

She looked at him as if he'd lost his mind. "I can't," she protested.

"Yes, you can," he insisted and pulled her toward the back of the line. "We'll learn together. I think it's called The Electric Slide . . . or something." When the woman to his left danced right into him, he looked at Maureen and laughed. "If we don't join this thing, they're going to dance all over us."

"I feel stupid," she muttered, sure everyone in the place was watching as she tried to follow the woman in front of her. Within minutes, she thought she had figured out the steps and was feeling pretty good about herself, only to suddenly lose it and bump into Matt. He was having more trouble than she and, when he caught her attention, they both burst into laughter. Yet they kept at it until they had mastered the dance. Three steps to the right. Three to the left. Up. Back. Slight dip forward and then turn and start again. It wasn't really hard. Just confusing when a mass of people are trying to do the same thing in unison. Every once in a while Matt would mess up and he looked so flustered that Maureen would erupt into giggles, laughing so hard that she had to press on her diaphragm to stop.

It seemed incredible to her that last night she had thought her life was over. She had cried so long and hard that she had wanted to die. And tonight, she was dancing next to a slightly clumsy, though funny, man, and laughing so much that her sides ached. How could that be, she wondered, moving smoothly with the rest of the crowd.

Don't question it, a small voice inside of her commanded. *Just enjoy it. Laughter's better than tears.* And it sounded like good advice to her.

When the music suddenly became faster, half the crowd quit the competition and Maureen pulled on Matt's arm. "That's it," she announced in a breathless voice. "I surrender to youth."

He was breathing hard from the exertion. "I agree. I was hoping you would have given up sooner."

She was sweating as though she'd just run a mile. It wasn't very feminine and she grabbed a couple of napkins from the bar and patted her forehead. When she looked at the rivulets of sweat running down Matt's face, she laughed and handed a few to him.

"Thanks." He wiped his face and picked up his beer. "Well, I thought we were pretty damned good."

Grinning, she nodded. "So did I. Thanks for

forcing me into it."

Several men surrounded him, patting him on the back. "Hey, Matt, how do you think the Sixers will do? Think Barkley's the best forward in the league?"

"What about the Phillies? Goin' to spring training?"

Picking up her drink, Maureen watched as he tried to answer their questions. He was very polite, even a little shy, as if he didn't want their attention. He glanced at her several times and she smiled back at him, letting him know it was okay. When the DJ played a slow song, he excused himself and grabbed her wrist. She followed him, knowing he was making an escape.

He put his arm around her back and held her hand. "Sorry about that. Thanks for saving me."

"That's all right," she answered, immediately nervous at his close proximity. Slow dancing was so damned intimate. Could he feel the sweat running down the center of her back? The bulge at her waist because her pantyhose suddenly felt too tight? God Almighty, he probably dated sleek, beautiful women, and she felt fat and lumpy and sweaty. She wanted to run off the dance floor and out into the winter night where it was cold and—

"Are you okay?"

She glanced up at him. "Yes. Why?"

"You're so tense. Your muscles are—I don't know—rigid." He smiled down to her. "Relax, Maureen. I'm not going to attack you."

She felt like crying. All her self-confidence vanished. "You don't understand," she muttered. "I haven't done this in a very long time."

"Danced?" He was trying to make a joke, but she didn't laugh.

"No. This—this ritual. Meeting. Getting to know each other. Dancing. Slow dancing. It makes me nervous. I don't know what to do."

"You move your feet the same time I do. In fact," and he looked down to the floor with an astonished expression, "I believe we're doing it already."

She slapped his arm, but couldn't help smiling. "Will you stop it? I'm serious."

"That's your trouble. You're too serious. What do you want me to tell you? I respect you? I won't put any moves on you? You've got it. Now, just relax and enjoy yourself. We're dancing, Maureen. It's as simple as that." He pulled her into his arms, before she could protest.

She found herself enveloped by him. It was the strangest sensation. The side of his chin rested against her temple and she stared at his shoulder and up to his neck. Even though he was obviously strong, he held her lightly, almost protectively, and when he whispered in her ear, "We'll just take it slow, that's all," she had to gulp down her tears as she placed her hand on his back and felt the texture of his sweater.

He was a nice man.

They shouldn't have moved this well together. He was so tall. She was so short. It shouldn't have felt this good . . . this right.

But it did. Good God, it did. Because of his size, she felt small and feminine . . . almost fragile. Relaxing, she closed her eyes and moved with him, thinking how wonderful it felt to be held with such tenderness. He didn't talk to her. He just held her, leading her in small circles around the dance floor. It was slow and sensual. The scents of their bodies. The texture of their clothes. All of it mingled with the heat they created between them. It was exciting and scary, and she felt a longing deep within her as they continued the ritual. If she moved her hand closer to his neck, his tightened at her back, running his fingers over her silk jacket as if he liked the feel of it. Her breasts were pressed against his chest. His belt buckle dug into her stomach. They were so close, yet careful to keep more intimate parts of their bodies apart. She never expected this instant turn-on, this immediate arousal of all her senses. She had thought herself immune to another man. But it had been so long . . .

When the dance was over, he took her back to the bar and picked up their drinks. "C'mon, let's find some place a little more quiet where we can talk."

She followed him to an area in the back of the room where there were comfortable chairs and small sofas. They found one in a deserted corner and sat down. They both sat facing each other with their arms on the back of the sofa.

"Tell me about yourself, Maureen. Tell me why you came here tonight."

He wasn't trying to be funny anymore. Now he was serious. The expression on his face was of intense interest.

"I came here tonight . . ." her words trailed off and she shook her head. "I guess I just needed to get out of the house. I don't know. Maybe I wanted to find out if you were going to be here."

He picked up his beer and took a sip. "Why did you want to get out? Was it the kids?"

Again she shook her head.

"Your husband?"

She stared at him and blurted out what was on her mind. "I found out last night that he's been cheating on me for months." As soon as she said it, she wanted to take back the words.

"Oh, Christ . . . I'm sorry."

Shit! Why did she tell him? Now she felt stupid—the poor little wife is always the last to know. "Don't be sorry. I guess I knew it. I felt it instinctively. I just put my head in the sand and made excuses for him."

"Are you all right?"

She smiled sadly. "I don't know what I am. I just feel so betrayed, and humiliated. And I shouldn't have told you."

He touched her, running his hand up and down her arm in comfort. "I guess you can't help feeling betrayed, but don't feel humiliated. I told you before. Your husband's a fool."

She continued to stare at his hand. It was impossible. Matt Shannon had her touch. As crazy as it seemed, his touch, the way he softly ran his fingers over her arm, was the exact way she touched others.

"What kind of music do you like?" she asked crazily, anything to change the subject.

His eyebrows lifted in surprise. "I like Motown, 'cause it reminds me of when I was young and happy. I like Elton John and some of Tom Petty. Sometimes I like reggae, and sometimes classical. Depends on my mood."

"Me, too." Okay, let's probe further. "Who are your favorite writers?"

"Writers? Mostly I like newspaper columnists. If I were to read a book? A book that had nothing to do with sports? I'd have to say Dick Francis, although strictly speaking horse racing is a sport." He thought for a moment. "Straight fiction? Herman Wouk, Andrew Greeley, or Maeve Binchey. I like books with Irish characters. But I guess my favorite author is Michener. He writes a great story, but I think he gets bogged down with all his research."

It was spooky and a shiver ran up her back. He had named all of her favorite writers. "I've read *The Source* twice," she whispered.

He looked impressed. "No kidding? It's over a thousand pages: For a good read, though, I'd take Greeley. He really has that Irish Catholic thing down pat."

"Are you Irish Catholic?"

He grinned. "Twelve years with the Dominican nuns."

She stared at him. "Twelve with the Sisters of

Mercy." It was uncanny. "What about movies?" If he said Woody Allen, she was running out, because this guy was too good to be true.

"Now who's interviewing whom?" He was smiling that drop-dead, Colgate-perfect, smile.

"I'm sorry," she said, a little embarrassed because that was exactly what she'd been doing.

"Don't be sorry. I thought it was funny, because everyone always accuses me of it. Movies, huh?" He looked out to the main room and thought for a moment. "I like comedies. I hate horror. I see enough of that in the news room. Any movie about sports. *Bull Durham* and *The Natural* are my favorites. Oh, yeah, and Woody Allen, especially his early ones. What about you?"

Her jaw dropped as she continued to stare at him. This could not be happening. But she wasn't getting up and running away. If anything, she wanted to know him better and that frightened her far more.

"Maureen?"

"Huh?" It was too weird. It was like he was the male version of herself!

"We were talking about movies."

"We were?" She blinked several times. "We were," she corrected. "Right. Let me see . . . anything with a good story. I have a terrible habit of trying to figure out the next scene. Second-guessing the plot. It must be the writer in me."

"Or if something's out of line? Like if the guy's carrying a seven iron in one scene and then in the next he's pointing out something with an eight

215

iron. Or if he's wearing a handkerchief in his pocket and in the next scene it's gone." He shook his head and laughed. "It drives me crazy."

"I know," she agreed. "Details. It's a curse. Everyone else seems to sit there and enjoy the movie and my brain is working overtime trying to figure out the plot, or picking up flaws. Like when I first saw *Three Men and a Baby,* I saw a child standing by the window, but I thought someone's kid wandered onto the set and the editor didn't pick it up. Then it comes out on video and there's a national story about ghosts."

"I saw it, too," he said in an excited voice. "I kept my mouth shut because Claire, my wife, says I ruin every movie by nit-picking."

His wife. There it was. He said her name so easily, without bitterness. Did he miss being a daily part of his family? Maureen couldn't imagine not being able to see her children every day, to walk into an empty house or apartment. It must be terrible.

He grinned at her with affection. "Is it just me, or has it occurred to you how alike we are?"

She smiled back. "It's occurred to me."

"So then why don't we go out to dinner and then take in a movie and drive ourselves crazy?" He waited for her answer, looking at her with expectation.

"Why are you separated, Matt?" She knew it was personal, damn personal, yet she needed to know.

He took a deep breath and closed his eyes for a

moment, and his whole expression changed. He looked pained. "Claire and I are entirely different," he began slowly. "I guess we don't have much in common anymore, except Kelly."

"Every marriage goes through rough times—"

He shook his head and interrupted her. "No, it's not just that. I think we expected something different from each other, and both of us are disappointed. She thought marrying someone in television was going to be more glamorous than it actually is. And I thought . . . hell, I don't know what I thought." He ran his hand over his eyes, as if he were tired.

When he again spoke, his voice was rough with emotion. "She uses people. It took me a long time to admit it, but she does. She has a catering business. I was really proud of her when she started it after Kelly was born. I put up the money for it, supported her every way I could. But she expects me to introduce her to the right people or, as she puts it, 'those dumb jocks with more money than they know what to do with.' I did it a couple of times, but she wasn't satisfied."

He looked at her, wanting her to understand. "I can't use my contacts like that. If I did, I'd lose all credibility with them. Claire doesn't recognize the distinct line between my professional life and my social life. Unless I'm on the road with them, I don't hang around with the players. They don't come to my house for dinner and I don't go to theirs."

"You don't break up a marriage over something

like this," Maureen said quietly. "Maybe you two should go to a counselor."

He shook his head. "It's not just that. I don't think we like each other any more. We've grown so far apart, I can't even remember what we ever had in common. I don't have a nine to five job and she says I was never there when she needed me. We couldn't connect with each other, so we immersed ourselves in our careers, and it got worse over the last year. The arguments. The accusations. Neither of us could take the sniping anymore, so we agreed I should move out."

"I'm sorry," she said in a sympathetic voice.

"Yeah, so am I. I miss my daughter."

"But you do see her."

He nodded. "But not enough. Kelly . . ." He said his daughter's name with sorrow and regret. "How the hell do you explain it to kids?"

Looking out to the crowd, she said, "I don't know. I guess we just do the best we can. My daughter resents her father and barely speaks to him, and my son can't understand why his life has been disrupted because his parents can't get along. Even though I wasn't the one that broke the marriage vows, I still feel so damned guilty."

He shook his head. "God, we're a pair, aren't we? How did we slide into this depressing topic? Do you want another drink?" He signaled the waitress.

Maureen looked to her drink sitting on the table. "To tell you the truth, Matt, I really don't like the taste of alcohol. I'd prefer just a straight Diet Coke."

He threw back his head and laughed. Confused, she looked at him until he stopped when the waitress came.

"Two Cokes," he said to the scantily dressed young woman. "One diet." As the waitress walked away he turned to Maureen and added, "I rarely drink. Maybe a beer every once in a while. Now, c'mon, Maureen . . . neither one of us drink. We don't smoke. We both think Michener's great. We've each survived twelve years of Catholic school. You're separated. I'm separated. We both work in a form of communication. We pick apart movies. My ancestors were Irish. So were yours. We like the same kinds of music. And we dance well together. Now why the hell are you fighting me so hard?"

She held his gaze, not sure how to answer.

"A dinner and a movie, Maureen. I'm tired of being alone and unhappy. Aren't you?"

She nodded. "Yes." *God, yes!*

"Is that a yes to a date, or yes to tired of being unhappy?" He was still smiling.

"I know I'm making this difficult for you. You probably could go out there to any of the bars and find someone who would say yes without a second thought." She wanted to say it right. It was important to her. "But I'm not like them. At least I don't think I am. I'm so damned scared. I haven't dated in twenty years. Which brings me to another point. Exactly how old are you?"

219

He gave her an exasperated look, as if he couldn't believe she was putting him through all this. "I'm thirty-seven."

She knew it. He was younger than her. "I'm forty-two," she said. "I'm five years older than you."

"So?"

"So you could find someone closer to your own age. Someone younger and prettier. I've got two teenaged children. I wouldn't know what to do on a date. I—"

He grabbed her forearm to stop her words. "Why are you doing this? Do you want to know what I thought when I saw you last week?" He didn't wait for her answer. "I saw a very beautiful woman who looked frightened and yet angry, who looked so out of place in here that she wanted to run. I was attracted to you *because* you were different. You didn't act or look like you wanted to pick up a man."

"I didn't," she cut in. He said she was beautiful! Her?

"I don't give a damn if you're five years older than I am. I don't care how old your children are, or if you wear false teeth. I can talk to you. You make me laugh. And it's almost uncanny how much we have in common. What I can't believe is how hard you're making me work at getting a date."

The waitress delivered their Cokes and after Matt paid her, Maureen took a deep breath and whispered, "You do realize we'll have to split the dinner check and I'll pay for my own movie."

Bringing his glass up to his lips, he stopped and glanced down at her. A slow grin spread over his face. "Is that a yes?"

She started to smile. "That's a yes. Now when are we going to do this?" Good God, what is she doing? Making a date, *a date,* with someone who's practically a stranger? But he didn't seem like a stranger. He seemed like an old friend.

"What about tomorrow night? I have to do the five-thirty and six o'clock programs, and then I'm free."

"Tomorrow?" That soon? He wasn't giving her much time to get used to the idea.

"Tuesday, Wednesday and Thursday I also do the eleven o'clock sports. So it's Monday or Friday, and I don't want to wait until Friday. There. I ought to get some points for honesty."

She laughed. "Okay. Tomorrow then. What time?"

"Is seven too late for dinner? Where do you live?"

"Avondale. Why don't I just meet you at the restaurant? It'll save time and—"

"And it's safer," he finished her sentence. "And you'll have your own car. I understand."

"As long as we're being truthful, I might as well admit that I'd rather you didn't come to the house. I don't know how my children will react to their mother dating." She knew, she just didn't want to tell him he would be considered a threat.

"That's fair. Now where shall we go?"

Maureen thought for a moment. Matt Shannon attracted too much attention and she didn't want to go anywhere close to her home. Very few people knew she was separated, and she didn't intend to deal with strange looks if she were recognized by a neighbor. "How about Gina Rosa?"

It was a new restaurant in Voorhees, right next to Toppers and close to the movies.

"On Main Street? Good, that's close to the Marlton Eight Theater. What about the movie? Is there anything you want to see?"

She shook her head. "I thought of the restaurant. You pick the movie."

He laughed. "Okay. It'll be a surprise."

A slow song came on and Matt looked into her eyes. "Would you like to dance, Maureen?"

She held his gaze for just a moment, a thrilling moment, and admitted, "Yes. Yes, I would."

He nodded and stood up. Holding out his hand to her, he said, "Now this one is definitely an oldie."

Walking with him to the dance floor, she listened to the song, an old favorite called "Try the Impossible." Sounded sort of prophetic to her. As he gathered her into his arms, she again felt surrounded by him. They moved easily together, falling into a slow, sensuous rhythm, and Maureen immediately relaxed.

"Who sings this?" he whispered into her ear and delicious threads of pleasure raced down her body.

"I think it's Lee Andrews and the Hearts," she whispered back. *What are you doing, Maureen?*

her brain lectured. This is too unexpected, too good. Why was it that Lisa hadn't been with a man in over a year, the women at the therapy group had all reported horror stories of meeting the wrong men, and here she was dancing with Mr. Perfect? It was too good to be real. Something would happen. She'd discover he was on drugs, Charles Manson crazy or bisexual. The ridiculous image of Matt Shannon, sports jock, in the arms of another man made her giggle.

He pulled back from her. "What? Did I step on your toes?"

She smiled and shook her head. "No. You're doing everything right. And that's what scares me."

He gave her a look that could only be taken as extremely flirtatious and pulled her back into his arms. This time their bodies brushed intimately, only for a second, but a rush of sexual heat flashed through her like a bolt of lightning, making her fight the urge to lift her face to his. She knew, instinctively, that if she did he would kiss her. It wasn't vanity. It was hunger. She felt it, and a woman knows when a man experiences the same. It's in the friction of skin against skin. Heartbeat against heartbeat. The overwhelming desire to become more close, more physical . . .

She was in trouble.

Monday morning she awoke with a sense of urgency. She packed the kids off for school and raced into the shower. By nine o'clock she was walking into First National Bank. She opened a savings and checking account in her name and deposited a check for forty thousand dollars drawn on their old account at another bank. Since most of the money was hers, she felt absolutely no guilt. Besides, she had left Dan ten thousand. Considering everything, she thought it was generous. It was time she started thinking with her mind, instead of her heart. She had a life to rebuild, a life without a husband. The thought scared the hell out of her, but she had to force herself to go on. She couldn't wallow in self-pity any longer.

She might have forgiven him for having affairs. Mistakes happen. What she could not forgive were the months of lies and the betrayal of her trust. Whatever drove him away from her was still there. He wanted to be young again. And she wasn't. He was tired of responsibilities. She had the children, her home, her career. If he intended to play around, she couldn't stop him. But she wasn't about to help him become some young woman's *ticket*. And if he wanted to take his secretary to the Caribbean for a weekend of passion, he'd have to do it with his own money. She was going to protect herself and her children.

An hour later she drove up to the car dealership and took the little red MG to her mechanic. Thirty minutes later she bought it.

MORE PASSION AND ADVENTURE AWAIT... YOUR TRIP TO A BIG ADVENTUROUS WORLD BEGINS WHEN YOU ACCEPT YOUR FIRST 4 NOVELS ABSOLUTELY *FREE* (AN $18.00 VALUE)

Accept your Free gift and start to experience more of the passion and adventure you like in a historical romance novel. Each Zebra novel is filled with proud men, spirited women and tempestuous love that you'll remember long after you turn the last page.

Zebra Historical Romances are the finest novels of their kind. They are written by authors who really know how to weave tales of romance and adventure in the historical settings you love. You'll feel like you've actually gone back in time with the thrilling stories that each Zebra novel offers.

GET YOUR FREE GIFT WITH THE START OF YOUR HOME SUBSCRIPTION

Our readers tell us that these books sell out very fast in book stores and often they miss the newest titles. So Zebra has made arrangements for you to receive the four newest novels published each month.

You'll be guaranteed that you'll never miss a title, and home delivery is so convenient. And to show you just how easy it is to get Zebra Historical Romances, we'll send you your first 4 books absolutely FREE! Our gift to you just for trying our home subscription service.

BIG SAVINGS AND FREE HOME DELIVERY

Each month, you'll receive the four newest titles as soon as they are published. You'll probably receive them even before the bookstores do. What's more, you may preview these exciting novels free for 10 days. If you like them as much as we think you will, just pay the low preferred subscriber's price of just $3.75 each. *You'll save $3.00 each month off the publisher's price.* AND, your savings are even greater because there are never any shipping, handling or other hidden charges—FREE Home Delivery. Of course you can return any shipment within 10 days for full credit, no questions asked. There is no minimum number of books you must buy.

4 FREE BOOKS

TO GET YOUR 4 FREE BOOKS WORTH $18.00 — MAIL IN THE FREE BOOK CERTIFICATE TODAY

Fill in the Free Book Certificate below, and we'll send your FREE BOOKS to you as soon as we receive it.

If the certificate is missing below, write to: Zebra Home Subscription Service, Inc., P.O. Box 5214, 120 Brighton Road, Clifton, New Jersey 07015-5214.

FREE BOOK CERTIFICATE

4 FREE BOOKS

ZEBRA HOME SUBSCRIPTION SERVICE, INC.

YES! Please start my subscription to Zebra Historical Romances and send me my first 4 books absolutely FREE. I understand that each month I may preview four new Zebra Historical Romances free for 10 days. If I'm not satisfied with them, I may return the four books within 10 days and owe nothing. Otherwise, I will pay the low preferred subscriber's price of just $3.75 each; a total of $15.00, *a savings off the publisher's price of $3.00.* I may return any shipment and I may cancel this subscription at any time. There is no obligation to buy any shipment and there are no shipping, handling or other hidden charges. Regardless of what I decide, the four free books are mine to keep.

NAME

ADDRESS _____ APT _____

CITY _____ STATE _____ ZIP _____

TELEPHONE (   )

SIGNATURE _____ (if under 18, parent or guardian must sign)

Terms, offer and prices subject to change without notice. Subscription subject to acceptance by Zebra Books. Zebra Books reserves the right to reject any order or cancel any subscription.

GET
FOUR
FREE
BOOKS

(AN $18.00 VALUE)

ZEBRA HOME SUBSCRIPTION
SERVICE, INC.
P.O. Box 5214
120 BRIGHTON ROAD
CLIFTON, NEW JERSEY 07015-5214

Chapter Eleven

She was stopped at the light right before the bridge when she heard him.

"You're riding the clutch. You'll burn it out if you keep it up."

Startled, she nearly jumped out of her skin as she stared at him. "Damn it, Bobby! One of these days you're going to get me into an accident . . ." Her words stopped as she continued to stare at him. "What have you done to yourself?" He looked older, just like in her dream.

He smiled, causing dimples to appear at the corners of his mouth. "What do you think, huh? Not too bad for an old man." He raked his fingers through his black hair.

"But you're not an old man," she insisted, rattled by his appearance. He looked good, like a man in his early forties who had aged extremely well. Too good, she told herself. She preferred to be haunted by a young ghost, a safe ghost, one who stirred nothing but memories. "You . . .

you're supposed to be in your twenties."

"Yeah, well, you seemed to have had a problem listening to me then. Now we're the same age. I did it for you, Maureen. The light," he said, nodding toward the windshield as a horn blared in back of them.

Easing her foot off the clutch, she muttered, "Well, turn yourself back."

"I can't."

She glanced at him as she pulled a dollar out of her coat pocket. "You can't?"

He shook his head. "Nope. Tried it, just for the heck of it, and nothing happened. Guess I'm stuck with being forty-two. Great car," he added, running his hand over the dash. "You always wanted an MG, didn't you?"

"Yup. And now I've got one." She paid the toll and drove over the bridge into Pennsylvania.

"Geez, it costs a dollar now? I remember when it was a nickel to get into Jersey."

She smiled, recalling all the trips she and her friends had made over this bridge. "That was twenty years ago," she said, "when all of us came over to Jersey because the legal age was eighteen and we could get into clubs." Looking out to the Delaware River she murmured, "I wonder what ever happened to everyone? Muzzy, Ted, Colleen, Margie . . ." Once, so very long ago, they had been the best of friends, and her recent dreams had made her curious.

"Why don't you know? Why didn't you ever

keep in touch with any of them? You don't live that far away."

She stared at the car in front of her. "I don't know. I guess we just lost interest in each other." Not more than fifty yards past when she shook her head. "That's not true. It was my fault," she admitted. "Dan was from Philadelphia. When I started to date him, he just seemed more comfortable with his own crowd."

"You mean you never even introduced him to Margie? Wasn't she your best friend?"

Guilt set in and she tried to explain. "I did introduce them. Once. And Margie came to our wedding, but it was different then." She pictured dating her husband twenty years ago, and suddenly she straightened in the car seat. "You know what? I just remembered something. Dan lived in Philadelphia and every time we went out, sometimes three and four nights a week, he would drive all that way from Philly to my father's house. It had to be over twenty-five miles. He would pick me up and drive all the way back to northeast Philly. That's . . . why that's over a hundred miles a night so we could be with *his* friends."

She glanced at Bobby. "Why did I let him do that? We never double dated with any of my friends. He never wanted to go to a club in my neighborhood, where I might know people. Why didn't I stop that? I gave up my friends for him. I gave up everybody I knew."

"Did he ask you to do that?"

She shook her head. "No. I just did it. I accommodated him, but I lost Margie and Colleen and Robin. What ever happened to them? To Ted and Muzzy? I'll never know . . ."

"Everybody turned out okay." Bobby took a deep breath. "Except Muzzy."

She downshifted as they came off the bridge. "What happened to Muzzy?"

"He committed suicide after he came back from Viet Nam. Drugs." Bobby's voice was low, almost bitter.

Shaken, Maureen pictured Kevin Reed, star baseball player in high school with a shock of wiry red hair that had earned him his nickname. "My God, Muzzy . . ."

"Why did you get the car, Maureen?" Bobby asked, and she knew it was an intentional change of subject.

"I wanted it."

"Yeah, I know, but that too was twenty years ago. It couldn't be because Dan wanted it?"

She glared at him as she turned onto Route 13. "No, it was because I wanted it. Because for my entire life I've always put everyone else first. Now it's my turn."

She expected some comment, but when it was obvious none was forthcoming, she glanced at him and said, "You think it's selfish, don't you? How can you, when you were the one that said be good to yourself?"

"Did you buy it in anger, or with happiness?"

She passed a huge truck and settled back into the right-hand lane. "Maybe I was a little angry, but it's going to bring me happiness. In fact, I was pretty happy until you showed up and started questioning my motives."

"Would you like me to leave?"

She shrugged. "I guess not. Just tell me something. Are you doing all this stuff to Dan? Are you the one making his life miserable?"

"Dan's making his own life miserable. I have nothing to do with it."

"Okay." They rode in silence for a few minutes, enjoying the peace and quiet. Finally, Maureen decided not to let anything spoil the day. Smiling, she turned to him and asked, "Want to go to Washington's Crossing? I was going to go to my father's house and tell him about my separation, but I have time for visiting old haunts. How about you?"

"Strange choice of words, Maureen, but yeah, sure, I guess it's time I went home again."

They were two old friends, pointing out familiar landmarks—like their high school, where he and Ted and Muzzy had spray-painted "Class of '66", got caught, and spent the first month of summer vacation under Father Wilfred's eagle eye while they scrubbed the parking lot clean. They lamented the fact that the woods were being taken over by shopping malls, that their favorite movie house no longer existed.

"It's sad, isn't it?" Maureen asked as they turned up River Road. "They say you can never go home again, and I guess they're right."

"Maybe if you're lucky enough to hold good memories of your past, you should never try." Bobby looked out to the Delaware River and sighed. "It's like when we went back as seniors to Our Lady of Grace to talk to the kids in eighth grade. Do you remember when they made us do that?"

She nodded. "They made us feel it was our obligation to convince those kids to go to Catholic high school. We were marched in there like the ROTC of Catholic education."

"The point I'm trying to make is that we all couldn't believe how much smaller the room had become, how tiny the desks seemed. But it had never changed. We did. You can go home again, Maureen. You just can't look at it with the eyes of a child."

She thought about it for a moment and said, "Speaking of going home, I'm not looking forward to facing my father."

"You're a grown woman now."

She laughed. "Sure. You know that. Even I believe it most of the time. But my dad?" She shook her head. "He is the quintessential patriarch. He'll never understand."

"Then why are you doing it?"

"Because I have to," she said, turning into the entrance of Washington's Crossing. "Josh has a regional championship game next week and my father will be there. He never misses a chance to cheer on the male members of his family. I don't want a scene in front of the children, so I've decided to confront the lion in his den, so to speak."

"Maybe you've misjudged him. He might understand."

She shot him a disbelieving look before pulling the car off to the side of the road and parking under a huge maple tree. "Let's get out and walk around."

Bobby glanced out the window to the winter scene. "It's cold."

She almost giggled. "I didn't think cold weather would bother someone like, you know, . . . like you."

"It doesn't," he answered. "I was thinking of you."

She opened the door and pulled on her gloves. "Then come with me. I want to climb Bowman's Hill."

"You're kidding?" he asked as he left the sports car. "It was tough going when we were teenagers."

Walking up to him, she reached out and took his hand. What did it matter? The park was deserted and no one would see them. "I want to do it again, Bobby. I want to stand at the top of the tower and look down on the world, feel the wind in my hair and know I'm okay, that I'm going to make it through this bad time in my life. Please?"

Shaking his head, he held her hand in his and led her to the hill. "This is crazy, Maureen," he mumbled. "The tower's probably closed for the winter."

She smiled, liking the feeling of friendship that they shared as they walked up to the old tower. "I know it's crazy, but I don't care. I'm through doing what everyone else expects. I've tried that for forty years and it doesn't work. Not any more. Today I took some important steps. I opened my own bank account. I bought a car. And now I'm going to climb Bowman's Hill in the winter. And you know why?" She didn't wait for him to answer. "Because I want to, that's why."

"That can be a dangerous philosophy," Bobby advised. "You can't just do whatever you want and disregard rules. They're there for a reason."

"And what's that?" she asked. "To control the masses? To avoid anarchy? Listen, I believe in rules, but up to a point. The trouble is, right now as a separated woman, those rules seem pretty one-sided. I want to be happy again, and if that means doing things that someone else might not, even if it's climbing Bowman's Hill in the dead of winter, then so be it. I really don't care any more what any one else thinks."

"You don't?"

She shook her head. "I've spent my life caring about others' opinions. Was I a good enough wife? A devoted mother? I made sure we showed up in church every Sunday, even if I didn't want to be there. I worked my rear end off in the PTA, because I thought that's what I was supposed to do. I was a good neighbor, but was it because I really wanted to be? Or was I afraid what they would think of me if I wasn't?"

They approached the tower and Maureen stopped to look at Bobby. "I've done a lot of thinking about this. Do we do what we really want, or what we're told? And who's happier in the end?"

"I don't know, Maureen," Bobby said slowly. "Only you can answer that. Were you happy when you were doing all those things?"

"I thought I was. I guess I was doing what I was supposed to be doing at that time. I don't regret any of it because I can look back and know I was a good wife and mother and neighbor. But it just doesn't work anymore. Now I feel . . . I don't know, I guess I feel free to be the person I really am."

He gazed into her eyes. "And who are you, Maureen?"

She smiled. "I don't know yet. But I'm going to try and find out." Turning her head, she looked up at the tower. The huge stone structure had been used as a watchtower for Washington's ragged army and two hundred years later, teenagers prided themselves on climbing the five hundred steps to get to the top.

"Are you ready?" she asked Bobby while reaching for the door.

"I still say this is crazy." He waited as she pulled on the massive brass handle.

"It's locked!" Maureen exclaimed in disbelief.

"What did you expect? Everything's closed."

She was filled with disappointment. "But I wanted—" Suddenly, she turned to him. "You can do it."

"Do what?"

"Open it."

His jaw dropped in surprise. "You want me to open this door?"

She nodded. "Look, if you can turn on my radio, make lights flicker and all that other stuff, then this should be simple. C'mon, Bobby, I want to go in."

He looked around them to the surrounding woods. "You realize this would be breaking the law? What if somebody caught us?"

"Well, they wouldn't catch you; they can't see you. I'm the one taking the risk, and it's worth it. Now, do your magic bit and we can go in."

He hesitated.

"Please."

She watched as he stared at the door, concentrating. He closed his eyes and stood before her as if in a trance. Finally he opened his eyes, sighed deeply, and whispered, "Try it."

Her breath was caught in her throat as her hand reached for the handle. Very slowly, she pressed her thumb down on the latch and smiled when she heard a distinctive click. "You did it!"

she pronounced, her voice filling with awe as the door creaked open. "Tell me how."

"Forget it," he answered, almost pushing her inside.

She grabbed his sleeve. "No, really. Can you tell me how you did it?"

"I thought about it," he said impatiently. "I tried to visualize the tumbler and align—oh, forget it. Will you please get in before we're caught?"

Walking into the cold interior, she marveled at his abilities. "That is so neat. Just think if we could do that with our minds. Think of all the places we could get into—" She stopped and stared at the strange doors ahead of her. "I don't believe it! They put in an elevator. God! Everything is changed! How could they ruin it like this?"

Bobby stood with his arms crossed over his chest. His head was thrown back as he looked up the long circular stone steps. "I think it's a good idea."

"Well, I don't," she countered in a stubborn voice. "I'm going to climb the stairs. Just like we always did." She walked over and proceeded up, holding onto the cold stone walls since there wasn't any railing. She had climbed no more than fifty steps when her calf muscles felt like they were going into spasms. Glancing back down to Bobby, who still stood at the bottom, she grabbed hold of a large stone to keep her balance as a wave of dizziness swept over her.

"Aren't you coming?" she called down, trying to ignore the weakness in her knees.

"If you're determined to do this, I'll meet you at the top." His grin held more than a hint of smugness. "There's only about four hundred and fifty to go."

She turned back and looked upward through the spiral of never-ending steps. Why was it so difficult now? She wasn't *that* out of shape, and she never remembered being dizzy when she was young. Almost dragging her feet, she forced herself to continue. Three steps later, she knew she was beaten.

"I can't," she muttered, hating to admit defeat.

"Maureen?"

Suddenly he was at her side, holding her shoulders for support.

"Why can't I do this?" she demanded, fighting back tears. "I used to race up these steps."

"Because you're a different person now. You're not a teenager. You're an adult and your mind has stored life experiences that tell you this is dangerous. C'mon, let's go back down."

He kept his arm around her shoulders as he turned and led her down the stairs. When they reached the bottom, she felt depressed and more than a little silly for insisting on this adventure. "I guess you can't go back," she muttered.

Grinning, Bobby reached out and pressed the button on the elevator. As the doors magically opened, he said, "Maybe we can't go back, but we can go up. Your transportation, madam?" He waved his arm to the inside of the tiny elevator.

Her eyes sparkled with happiness. Getting inside, she gazed at him as he pressed the only button on the panel. "Sometimes, Bobby O'Connor, you're a real pleasure to have around."

Their eyes met as the elevator began its ascent. "Why, thank you, Maureen. It isn't every woman I would break the law for."

"We're not going to get caught."

"I wasn't just talking about the laws of man," Bobby said. "You're not the only one who has to answer for what you've done."

"Oh . . ." She thought about his statement, and everything he had done for her. "Are you going to get into trouble over this?"

He shrugged his shoulders. "Let's just say some of what I've been doing lately is highly unorthodox."

The elevator abruptly stopped and when the doors opened they were presented with a spectacular view of rural Bucks County. "Look at this," Maureen murmured, as she walked out to the battlement. Even in winter it was a sight that stirred the soul. She could picture the farms below her as they had looked in summer—a patchwork quilt of green that spread out as far as the eye could see. The wind lifted her hair from her shoulders as she viewed the Delaware River and parts of New Jersey that lay beyond.

Closing her eyes, she deeply inhaled and felt a strange peace enter her body. "Thank you," she whispered, yet she wasn't sure who she was thanking. Was it Bobby for getting her up here, or God for this wonderful view of nature? And if it were God, she quickly added a small prayer that Bobby wouldn't get into any trouble because of her.

He stood near, looking over the tops of the trees to the surrounding countryside. "Are you happy?"

She smiled. "Yes. Right now I am."

"Good. Then it was worth it."

She turned her head to look at him and felt a wave of love so strong that she had to fight the urge to wrap herself in his arms.

"Bobby?"

"Hmm?"

"The other night? Was that you, or a dream?" She had to know.

"What do you think?" he answered in a low voice.

"I thought it was a dream, but now you look older—just like then. Did you hold me? Did you lie in bed with me and hold me until I fell asleep? Are you real? I mean, is any of this really happening, or is it all in my mind?"

"I've told you, I'm real for you."

"But nobody can see you, except me. How do I know what's actually happening? Like when I dreamed of us dancing at Boulevard Ballroom.

The night I got caught by my father? We only danced. We never kissed. And yet I dreamed that we did. And the next time I saw you, you knew about that kiss. And all these dreams I've been having. Going back and being with the old crowd. What about that teddy bear? How could you give it to me in a dream, and when I wake up it's on my bed?"

He didn't say anything. He kept looking out at the countryside, so she continued. "And Saturday night. I thought I was going to die from the pain, the betrayal, and there you were. Holding me. Comforting me. Telling me about how I was like a dormant flower. And then you laid down with me, and stayed with me until I fell asleep. Did that really happen, Bobby? Or am I just imagining these things because . . ." She couldn't finish her thought.

"Because why?" he persisted.

She took a deep breath. "Because I wanted them to happen. Because I've loved you since I was nine years old and we never had a chance. I have to know . . ."

He looked down to the stone flooring. "Look, we'd better go back now. It's cold and—"

"Bobby?" She touched his arm and he raised his head to look in her eyes. "Tell me what's real."

"You're real, Maureen. I'm not. I exist for you in your mind because you need me right now. And I love you. God help me, but I do love you. Is that what you want to know?"

"Yes," she whispered, tears filling her eyes.

"And what good does it do you knowing? I can't have you. I can't be with you, give you what you need, what you deserve. And if I let my feelings interfere with my reason for being here, then I might not ever see you again." His expression appeared tortured as he continued, "Don't you understand? I can't bear to see you unhappy, to see your life so screwed up. And yet when you make it through this, and you will, I have no reason for staying. I'll be gone."

She clutched at the material of his jacket. "I don't want you to go! I can't believe I'm saying this, but I want you to stay with me."

"I can't. And you know it. You have to go on with your life. Just like you're going to do tonight."

Their gaze locked and held. "It's just a date," she whispered. "Dinner and a movie."

He didn't say anything for a moment. Then he inhaled deeply and took her hand away from his sleeve. "I can never be anything but a friend to you, Maureen. Go on with your life."

Stung, she spun around and withdrew to the opposite side of the balcony. She grabbed hold of the jutting stones that formed a small barricade and demanded, "What do you expect from me? I can't have Dan. I can't have you. And now you act upset because I've met someone who makes me laugh, someone who shares the same interests. Someone who's *real!* Weren't you the one that said I should go out, do things that make me happy?"

In the silence that followed, she felt the wind whip around her and she pulled her coat closer to her body for warmth. Waiting for his answer, she suddenly realized that none was forthcoming. Very slowly, she turned around.

He was gone.

"Damn you," she yelled out to the sky. Anger filled her as she walked into the elevator and hit the button. "How can you just leave like that? And I know you can hear me or this stupid elevator wouldn't be working!"

Silence.

She reached the bottom and stormed out of the elevator while muttering to herself. "Just leave me alone from now on. Stay away. And this time I mean it. If I make mistakes, then let me make them." She couldn't take any more rejection. Not from her husband, not from a ghost! "Get out of my life, Bobby O'Connor, and stay out!"

Furious, she pushed open the heavy tower door and walked right into the iron-hard chest of a park guard!

Even though she was staring at the man she couldn't believe he was real. His words, however, left no doubt.

"Put your hands in the air and step back. You're under arrest for breaking and entering a Federal monument."

"What?"

"Put your hands in the air and step back," he repeated, bringing out handcuffs. "Now where's your friend? The one you were talking to?"

Just seeing the handcuffs made her raise her hands and back up a step. "I didn't do anything wrong, officer. I swear it. And . . . and I wasn't talking to anybody but myself." She issued a helpless, nervous laugh. "I do that sometimes. Talk to myself." *Dear God, don't let me get arrested,* she fervently prayed.

"Nobody was in there with you?"

She shook her head. "Just me. The door was open and I walked through." No lies yet.

The officer looked at her, trying to judge if she were telling the truth. He glanced to the door and reached out to touch the lock. Looking inside briefly, he shut the door and took out a ring of keys. He bolted the door shut, saying, "If there is anybody in there, they're not going anywhere."

Satisfied that the tower was secure, he pulled on the lock to double check. "Nothing's broke. Looks like somebody got in here with a key. I don't suppose you know anything about this?"

Again she shook her head. Okay. One lie. A small one. "I'm from New Jersey, but I grew up not too far from here and I just wanted to see the tower again." She tried a friendly smile. "I'm sorry if I was trespassing, but—"

"Look, I'm going to have to take you in and report this. Now do you have identification?"

So the friendly smile didn't work either. She

really was going to be arrested. She could just see it. Her children. Her father. Dan. Her publisher. She wrote children's books . . . wait a minute. She had a date tonight! "Officer, please. I didn't do anything wrong. Nothing is damaged. Nobody would even know I was here if—"

"I said, do you have identification?"

She felt like crying as she patted her empty pockets. "I left my purse in the car."

"That's your MG down there?" He indicated the bottom of the hill with a turn of his head.

She nodded. "I just got it today," she muttered under her breath.

"Then let's get an ID. All right?" He pointed to the hill, indicating that she was to proceed him.

All the way down Maureen mentally called Bobby O'Connor every rotten name she had ever heard, and made up a few new ones, too. She would just bet he did this so she'd get arrested and have to call off her date. *Men!* Can't live with 'em, and you can't live without 'em! That's all there was to it. Maybe the nuns were smarter than she'd thought.

When they reached the car, Maureen took out her keys and unlocked the door. She reached in and brought out her purse. Taking out her wallet, she flipped it open to her driver's license and showed the cop.

"Please take it out of the plastic and hand it to me."

Exasperated, she ripped the license free and held it out. "Here."

He studied the document and looked back up to her. "You're Maureen Malone?"

"Yes?" Right now she wished she were anyone else.

"And you said you lived in Bucks County at one time?"

She nodded, waiting for him to arrest her.

"Did you ever attend Bishop McDevlin High school?"

Her eyes narrowed with confusion. "What?"

"Did you used to go to Bishop McDevlin?"

She didn't say anything, just continued to stare at him.

"Graduated in '66? You're Maureen Henessey, aren't you?"

"Who are *you?*"

The man smiled and handed her license back to her. "Dominick Wallinski. You probably don't remember me."

Her jaw dropped open in shock. "Dominick?" she asked in disbelief.

It was his turn to nod with embarrassment.

Her mouth opened into a wide grin. "Dominick! I don't believe it! How are you?"

"I'm doing okay. How are you?"

She was nodding again. "Okay . . . until I decided to go up Bowman's Hill."

He laughed. "Sorry about that. We'll just forget it. Probably some kids jimmied the lock."

She couldn't stop staring at him. "Dominick, you look so . . . so different." He did. The thick glasses were gone. His face had cleared up. Even his curls had disappeared with his closely trimmed hair.

He laughed self-consciously. "Yeah, well, I guess we all grow up, or maybe just grow out of the awkward stages. Contacts and Clearasil helped."

"Are you married?" she asked eagerly. "Do you have children?"

He nodded. "Married with four kids."

"Four?" Maureen was happy for him.

"Yup. How about you?"

"I have twins. A boy and a girl."

"No kidding?"

She laughed. "No kidding. They're teenagers, can you believe it?"

He leaned his elbow on the roof of her car. "My girls read your books. I saw your picture on the back of one and told them we went to school together. They don't believe me, but wait until I get home tonight."

Maureen was so happy to see him again, and happier to hear about his life. "Listen, why don't you give me your address and I'll send them autographed copies."

"You don't have to do that," he said.

"I know. I want to."

He took out a notepad from the breast pocket of his uniform and wrote down his address, adding the names of his daughters. Handing it to her, he said, "It's really nice of you to do this."

She shook her head. "What's nice is running into you again, Dominick. Are you happy?" It was important to her.

He looked about the park and shrugged. "I suppose so. It's quiet here, especially in winter. I got hurt about five years ago. Walked right into a robbery at an old mom and pop grocery. Funny thing is I was off duty and didn't even have my gun with me. Anyway, after I left the force I took this job with the government. It's peaceful, and I bring my books along with me to study."

"Study?"

He looked up to the sky and then back down at her. "I never finished college. I'm going at night, so I'll probably be the first senior citizen to pass the bar exam. But I don't care. It's something I've always wanted to do."

She smiled at him with warmth and affection. "I know. And you'll do it."

She could see he was embarrassed. "It's cold. You should get in the car."

Smiling broadly, she asked, "I'm free to go then?"

"Get in the car, Maureen, and go home."

"Yes, sir, officer. I promise never to tresspass again."

He laughed. "See that you don't. Next time you might not be so lucky." He closed the door and waited until she started her car.

As she shifted into reverse, he knocked on the window and she rolled it down.

"Did you hear about the reunion?"

A reunion? She shook her head. "No. When is it?"

"I think it's being planned for September. Make sure you come."

"I will," she promised. "Good bye, Dominick. It was wonderful seeing you again." And she meant it with all her heart.

"Take care, Maureen. Save a dance for me at the reunion."

Nodding, she pulled out and drove away. She didn't know if Bobby had this whole thing planned, or if it was fate that had brought her and Dominick together. Whatever it was, she was grateful it had happened. But it wasn't until she was out of the park that she recalled Dominick's parting words: *Save a dance for me at the reunion.* Remembering her dream of St. Michael's Fair, a chill ran down her spine.

Nahhhh . . . it never happened.

She would simply put it out of her mind and get back to the business of the day. She would visit her father, make supper for the kids, and then meet Matt Shannon for dinner. And if any ethereal beings showed up again, like Bobby-I'm-leaving-you-to-get-caught-O'Connor, she was calling Ghostbusters.

* * *

"What do you mean, you're separated?"

Her father sat back in his chair at the kitchen table, a look of disbelief changing his expression.

She warmed her fingers on her mug of tea. "Just what I said, Pop, Dan and I have separated."

"Why? What did you do?"

She felt a rush of anger heat her face. "What did *I* do? Why do you assume I did something wrong?"

"Dan's always been a good husband. A good father and provider."

She shook her head. "I don't know why I expected support from you. For your information, I've been a good wife. A good mother. And I make as much money as my husband. I, too, have provided for my family."

Her father pulled on the cuff of his flannel shirt. "Then if it's not you, what did he do?"

She took a deep breath and said it. "He's been having affairs with other women. His behavior was unacceptable and I threw him out."

Martin Henessey was not a man that was comfortable speaking of personal things, especially with his daughter. His world was orderly, from his spotless kitchen to his graying, crew cut hair, and he had little patience for emotions.

"Look, Maureen, you and Dan made a good life for yourselves. You don't break up a marriage, a family, over a little straying."

Her jaw clenched. "What's a little straying,

Pop? A quickie out in the parking lot of some club? Or spending the night with the secretary in some motel? How do we define it?"

Her father scowled at her. "You're being crude."

"I'm being realistic. Where do you draw the line?"

"What about the children? You don't pull your family apart because your feelings are hurt. You'll get over it. You have to get over it, for the sake of the kids."

She almost laughed. "For the kids? Pop, listen to me. I did it as much for the kids as for me. Abbie and Josh suspected even before I faced it. What kind of example would I be giving them if I ignored it? Would Josh grow up thinking that being unfaithful was acceptable? No. He's seen what it does. He knows now that you have to answer for your actions. And what about Abbie? What message would I be sending to my daughter if I allowed Dan to remain in the house? That it was okay to let your husband lie to you and betray you? Believe me, I did the right thing. For my kids, and for me. I can't live a lie, Pop. And that's what you're expecting me to do."

Her father hung his head, as if he were grieving. "I could never talk sense to you. You always had a mind of your own."

She wanted to reach across the table and touch his cheek. He looked so old all of a sudden. "You never tried talking to me. You wanted to control me. I don't blame you for it, Pop. You did the best you could after Mom died. But I'm an adult now, and I'm entitled to a life of happiness." She touched his arm under the heavy flannel and was surprised. He no longer felt like a man of steel. "I do have a mind of my own, and you should be glad that I turned out like that. I know what I'm doing is right."

He didn't respond, just continued to look into his mug of tea, as if somewhere in its dark depths there was an answer he couldn't find.

She knew if she sat at the table any longer she would start crying, and those tears would not only be for the breakup of her marriage but also for her lost childhood, the closeness she never achieved with her father. "Hey, how would you like to see the MG's engine before I leave? I want to cross the bridge before rush hour."

He took a deep breath and slowly pulled himself up from his chair. "That's another thing, Maureen. I simply don't understand you. Why in the world would you buy such a car? A used car, too."

She grinned as she picked up her purse and led him out the front door. "I'll tell you what I'm telling everybody else. Because I wanted it, Pop. It's that simple."

She would never be ready in time. Pulling the chicken out of the oven, she placed the hot pan on the stove and was opening the refrigerator when the phone rang. "Get that, would you Abbie? And then tell Josh to leave the car alone and come in for dinner."

As she squeezed the lemons over the chicken she heard her daughter's short answers and knew it was Dan on the phone. Placing the receiver on the table, Abbie said, "It's Dad. He wants to talk to you. I'll get Josh."

Wiping her hands on a towel, Maureen picked up the phone. "Yes?"

"Hi. How are you?" Dan sounded hesitant, like a child that had been caught and was afraid he wouldn't be forgiven.

"I'm fine," Maureen answered. "How are you?" God, it was so stiff, so formal, almost like talking to a stranger.

"I don't know. I feel just terrible about the weekend. I thought I'd come over tonight and we could talk."

She closed her eyes for a moment, trying to draw strength from some inner source, "I'm sorry. I won't be here. I have plans tonight."

"Plans? You're going out?"

"Yes, Dan. I'm going out."

"I guess I don't have the right to ask where."

"No, you don't. But I'm glad you called. There is something I have to tell you."

"Okay."

She could tell by his voice that Dan thought she was going to bring up his infidelity. But that wasn't what was on her mind. "I withdrew forty thousand dollars today and opened my own bank account."

"You did *what?*"

"I think you heard me. There's ten thousand left in the account and the next time you come over we can sit down and work out some sort of financial agreement."

"How could you do that?" he demanded, anger clear in his voice. "Haven't I always taken care of you? How could you turn on me like this? Damn it. Forty thousand! You're acting like a cold-blooded bitch!"

"I'm going to ignore that, Dan. To answer your question, yes, you took care of me but now I intend to take care of myself, and my children. Listen, I don't have time to discuss this right now. Here's Josh. I'm sure you want to talk to him." She held out the phone to her son while listening to Dan scream out her name.

"Sorry, honey, but Dad's not in a good mood," she whispered to Josh before handing over the phone.

"Hey, Dad. Wait until you see Mom's new car. An MG! And it's red! I'm talking beautiful . . . huh? Yeah, she got a car. I don't know. Wait a minute." Josh held the phone to his chest.

"Mom, he wants to talk to you again."

Maureen sliced the lemon in half. "Tell him to call me tomorrow. I don't have time right now."

Very carefully, she carved his secretary's name

into the lemon's moist center. She held it up for inspection and was filled with a sense of satisfaction. Picking up the other half, she slowly carved out Dan's name, and placed them, side by side, on a plate on the windowsill. She hoped they both were sucked dry.

Quickly, Maureen put the chicken, the salad and the rice on the table. She kissed each of her children on the forehead and said, "Here's dinner, guys. I'm already late."

"Where are you going again?" Abbie asked.

She was racing up the stairs as she called out, "Gina Rosa's for dinner with a friend."

Ten minutes later when she came out of the shower, she turned on the television and dried her hair as she watched her "friend" tell the Delaware Valley about a pulled groin injury one of the Sixers had sustained the night before.

It was the weirdest sensation, watching him on television and knowing she would be sitting across a table from him in an hour. A smile appeared at her lips.

After the day she'd had, she couldn't wait.

Chapter Twelve

"Great car!"

She smiled as she accepted the valet check from the young man. "Thanks. Take good care of it." Pocketing the ticket, Maureen walked up to the entrance of the restaurant and a shot of excitement ran through her as she saw Matt waiting inside.

Holding open the door, he smiled and said, "Hi. That's your car?"

She nodded and smiled back. "Just got it this morning."

He watched the parking lot attendant drive it away. "Congratulations. It's a beauty."

Maureen appreciated the fact that he didn't question her motives like everyone else. "I'm sorry I'm late," she said, observing how nice he looked in his suit. For a split second that sense of unreality came over her. Only an hour ago, she had watched him on television in this same suit and tie, and now he was here with her.

"It's okay," he said, taking her coat from her shoulders. "I don't think our table was ready anyway."

After Matt checked in her coat, he handed her the ticket. "See. I remember," he teased, referring to her speech the night before.

She grinned as she put the stub into her purse. "Thanks."

He smiled back and said, "You look beautiful, Maureen."

She stared at him, completely flustered. She didn't have time to agonize over an outfit and had picked a simple navy blue, wedge-shaped dress with gold earrings. But he had said she looked beautiful—how long had it been since she had felt beautiful?

"Your table is ready, Mr. Shannon."

They both turned to the tuxedoed maitre d'. Matt put his hand on her back and they followed the head waiter to their table. Again, she noted the many stares of recognition as they passed the other diners. When they were seated in a secluded booth in the back, she waited until they were alone and said, "Does that always happen to you? The stares?"

"Not always. Does it bother you?"

She shrugged. "I don't know. It must be tough to give up your privacy."

"There are times, like tonight, that I wish I were an electrician. I don't want you to feel uncomfortable."

255

They ordered Perrier and were looking over the menu when Maureen felt his gaze on her. When she glanced up, she caught him staring.

"All day long I was waiting for a phone call at the station. I thought you were going to cancel out." He looked at her hair, her lips, her eyes. "I'm glad you didn't."

As incredible as it seemed, Matt Shannon acted like he couldn't believe how lucky he was that she was sitting across from him. Flattered, yet embarrassed, Maureen could actually feel a blush creep up her throat to cover her cheeks. "I didn't even think of canceling," she admitted, and was relieved when the waiter came for their order.

It was a wonderful dinner. They talked non-stop. About his job. About hers. He was interested in the children and asked dozens of questions about each one. She could hear the real affection in his voice when he talked about his daughter, relating her latest antics in nursery school. They discussed politics and religion and realized they both leaned more toward liberal views than conservative. They got to know each other away from the pressures of a singles club and liked what they were discovering.

When the booth next to theirs ordered wine, Maureen knew what was coming and waited to see Matt's reaction. The waiter began to sing about the Chianti grapes in a beautiful operatic voice. Surprised with his fork in mid-air, Matt froze and stared at her as the aria began. She could see he was fighting the urge to laugh and she almost giggled as she leaned closer to the table.

"Isn't his voice beautiful?"

"It sure is loud," he muttered under his breath. "My God, that guy's got a set of pipes on him!"

This time she gave into the urge and laughed along with him. And when the short song ended, they joined the others around them by loudly applauding. It was a delightful dinner, right up until the check was presented.

They both reached for it at the same time.

Matt beat her to it. "Now, come on, Maureen. Let me get it."

She was adamant. "No. We agreed."

"But this is so silly."

She took a deep breath and tried to find the right words. "Matt, I don't think you realize how important this is to me. I don't want you to pay for me. I know it's going to sound stubborn, but I have to do this my way. It's all too scary, too frightening—"

"Okay," he interrupted, putting the check between them so they could both see it. "If you insist on this, then let's split it down the middle. Thirty-six dollars each, including tip."

She took out the money and placed it on the silver tray. He did the same. "You're going to do this at the movies, too, aren't you?"

She nodded. "You aren't upset, are you?"

"I'm not upset. This is just the damndest date

I've ever had."

She stood up and grinned back at him. "That's the whole point of it. This isn't a date, Matt."

"Right," he muttered as they turned to leave. "Then this is the damndest non-date date I've ever had."

"Good," she said under her breath while walking through the restaurant. She didn't want to be compared with anyone else. Lately, she had come up short in that department.

He got her coat and was holding it out for her. "Great dinner, Maureen. Thanks for thinking of this place."

"Thanks for sharing it with me. What movie are we going to see?" She slipped her arms into the sleeves of her good black raincoat.

Standing behind her, he held her shoulders as he leaned down and said into her ear. "Cyrano. In French."

His breath tickled her ear and sent a delicious ripple of excitement racing like crazy down her arms to her breasts and below. "But . . . but I don't speak French," she managed to reply, fighting this latest wave of reaction to him.

"Neither do I," he admitted. "I asked our movie critic for a recommendation and Cyrano was it. There are subtitles for those of us who took Spanish or German in high school."

He held the door open for her.

"Gracias," she said with a laugh as she stepped out into the night.

"Ahh, a Spanish student, I take it?"

"And you?"

He grinned. "I speak a little Spanish."

Handing her ticket to the attendant, she said, "No kidding? More than high school sentences?"

He gave the attendant his ticket and turned to her. *"Venga se conmigo, una mujer bella."*

She was impressed. "What did you say?"

He only continued to smile at her.

"C'mon. It sounded great. What was it?" she persisted.

Their cars were brought up to the front of the restaurant. His was a gray Lincoln. He tipped the driver and she did the same for the kid who held open the door of her MG.

"You're not going to tell me?" she asked over the hood of his car.

He looked at her and laughed. "You really want to know?"

"Of course."

He hesitated for just a moment. "I said, Come away with me, beautiful woman."

Completely bewildered, she could only stare at him.

"You asked," he said when her voice seemed lost. "Do you want me to follow you to the movies?"

Nodding, she got in her car and shifted into first. As she left the parking lot, Maureen pressed her fingertips to her burning cheeks. This man thought she was beautiful. Her! Somehow God must have put a veil over Matt's eyes and he saw something the rest of the world ignored. He acted as if he were the one that was privileged to be in her company, as if he couldn't believe she found him attractive. It was as if the world tilted once more, shifting in a new direction, and she'd lost the map along the way. All of it was new to her, and not totally unwelcome.

She was in big trouble here!

The woman sitting next to him was like a wounded animal that shied away from attention or any act of kindness. Matt silently cursed her husband, knowing he had caused this reaction in Maureen. He could tell from their conversations that her self-esteem was almost totally destroyed, and he wondered what kind of human being could do that to another. In the darkness of the movie theater, he thought of his own marriage and remembered the fighting, the sniping away at each other, and knew it was possible, although Claire's image of herself was definitely intact.

He pulled his gaze away from the screen and looked at Maureen out of the corner of his eye. She was sitting stiffly beside him, her legs crossed, her hands clasped tightly together. It didn't take a genius to understand her body language. She was obviously frightened of him. He wanted to reach out and touch her, take her hand and soothe her, but he knew she would fight him.

Matt acknowledged that he'd have to go slowly or she'd run away. And he didn't want her to run away. He wanted to get to know her better. For the first time since his separation, he wanted to spend time with someone for more than sex. Maureen was unlike the other women he had dated. She wasn't obsessed with her body and her appeal to others. When he was with her she looked directly at him, not over his shoulder to make sure everyone else was paying attention. Maureen was soft and warm and pretty. Intelligent and funny. She was real.

At first he had dated women he knew would make Claire jealous, women who looked good on his arm and made him forget his own sense of failure in his marriage. But he tired of that. Quickly. He had found nothing in common with them outside of bed.

Maureen was different. It was scary how alike they were, and he had found himself thinking about her when he should have been concentrating on work. Even when he was playing with Kelly, he wondered if Maureen would like his daughter, if the two of them could ever meet. He wanted to meet her children and see if they had their mother's beautiful smile. He wanted to see Josh play basketball and take away Abbie's anger with her father. He wanted to be a part of Maureen's life. His feelings were totally irrational. It was all happening too quickly and he knew it. He should pull back, give her the time to adjust to being separated, maybe even the chance to reconcile with her husband.

That thought made his stomach muscles tighten with anger. He didn't want her hurt again. He wanted to protect her, to make her laugh, to watch as she regained her confidence in herself.

Everything he was feeling was crazy. He hardly knew her, yet he felt as if he had known her for years. He also knew the symptoms of a man who was falling in love. Love was the last thing either of them needed at the moment, yet the thought of not seeing her was completely unacceptable.

He felt like a teenager, sitting next to her, contemplating whether or not he should take her hand. Christ, how many years had passed since he'd felt this insecure? Just do it, he told himself. She's built a stone fortress around herself and if you want to knock it down you have to begin somewhere.

With the same fear of rejection he had felt at fourteen, Matt slowly reached for her hand.

When she felt his touch, Maureen was startled and pulled her hand back. "No—please. I . . . I don't think . . ."

"Shh. It's okay," he whispered while searching her eyes. "I'm not going to hurt you." He took her hand in his and sat back, looking completely absorbed in the movie.

Maureen turned to the screen, her heart pounding behind her rib cage. She had danced with him, so why was this bothering her? Because it was more intimate than dancing, that's why.

He held her hand in his larger one and softly began tracing each finger, as if to familiarize himself with every line, the length of every nail, each knuckle and bone. Again she was astonished by his touch and how similar it was to her own. It was amazing what could be conveyed by skin touching skin, she thought as she leaned her head back against the seat and enjoyed the attention. Dan never liked to hold hands. He never voluntarily played with her hair or rubbed her back. If she asked him to, it was clear in his touch that he was doing her a favor. But this man, Matt Shannon, liked touching her. She could feel it through his fingers. Watching the big lumbering actor on the screen, she smiled, thinking how alike they were. For a man Matt's size, he had the soul and the gentleness of a romantic.

As if reading her thoughts, he rested his elbows on the sides of the chair and brought her hand up to his chest. Maureen sighed deeply and closed her eyes while listening to the lyrical French language and feeling the strong, sure heartbeat of the man sitting next to her in the dark. It was wonderful and so romantic. And in that moment, she knew if they continued to see each other that it would lead to something more serious. Could she handle it? Could he? God Almighty, she hadn't been with any man except her husband in twenty years. And there had been only one man before Dan, a brief night when she'd lost her virginity. Hell, as far as affairs went, she was practically a virgin all over again. A forty-two year old virgin—it was laughable! Stop it, Maureen, she mentally scolded. Why do you have to dissect every situation? Why can't you just sit back and enjoy it while it lasts?

Opening her eyes she found Matt staring at her, and even in the dark she could see the hunger in his eyes. She was sure it mirrored her own.

"Oh, give me a break!"

Shocked, Maureen pulled her hand away and jolted upright as she stared at the previously empty seat next to her.

Bobby!

"I mean, can you believe this?" He waved to the screen. "Subtitles! I hate subtitles."

"Maureen, are you okay?" Matt whispered.

She tore her gaze away from Bobby to look at Matt.

"Huh?"

"Are you all right?" He appeared confused by her sudden withdrawal.

"Yes, I'm fine," she whispered back and turned to glare at Bobby. Her Guardian Angel was shaking his head at the movie, as if disgusted.

What are you doing? she mentally screamed at him. *I know you can hear me, so answer! How dare you come here—*

"If you'll stop yelling, I'll tell you," he interrupted. He sat back in his seat and crossed his arms over his chest. "I wanted to check out Prince Charming here. Boy, he really knows how to turn it on, doesn't he?"

She was seething. Her brain actually hurt as she silently shrieked at him. *Who gave you the right to interfere in my life? You made yourself perfectly clear this afternoon. You even left me alone, I practically got arrested. Now go away! Get out of here right now, or I swear to God I'll—*

"Don't swear to God, you'll get in trouble, Maureen. I'm just checking the movie out, okay?"

You are not! You're ruining this for me, and you know it. I don't want you in my life anymore. Can't you understand that? You're driving me crazy. Now, leave . . . me . . . alone!"

She stared at the screen, not really seeing the actors. She was furious. Her heart was beating so loud she thought everyone in the theater must surely hear it. She was breathing as if she'd just run a mile. And her head was pounding as though a crew of carpenters were at work inside it. There was also a good possibility that she might throw up.

"What were you looking at? Are you all right? Do you want to leave?"

She turned to Matt and tried to smile. "I wasn't looking at anything," she managed to say between her clenched teeth. "And no. I won't be leaving."

265

Maybe at another time she wouldn't have had the courage, but she really didn't even think about it as she reached out and placed her hand back in his. From the corner of her eye she saw that the seat to her left was now empty.

"Let's enjoy the rest of the movie." Her vision clouded as she viewed the actors on screen and fought the tears forming at her eyes.

Bobby stood in the back of the theater and watched them. Why was he capable of feeling this heartache? She was angry with him and wanted him out of her life. He had done his job, and she was ready to go on now. So why did he torture himself by witnessing her awakening to another man? He told himself that Maureen was starved for affection and the man really cared for her. It was as it should be. Wasn't it? Then why couldn't he leave her alone? Surely whatever awaited him was better than watching her want another man. Yet he needed to stay and make sure she wasn't making a mistake. He would guard her from afar, and he wouldn't interfere anymore. If she wanted this man, then somehow he would accept it and pray for her happiness.

But as he felt the longing taking place between them, a sharp twist of anguish grabbed hold of him and he turned away. Leaving the theater, he wondered what he had ever done in his past to pay like this.

* * *

When the movie was over, Matt continued to hold her hand as he walked her to her car in the darkened parking lot.

"Would you like to go somewhere? Maybe for a cup of coffee?"

She smiled up to him. "I don't think so. It's late. I should be going home."

He nodded, as if understanding. "Can I see you again?"

She didn't even think twice about it. "Sure. I'd like that."

He smiled back, "Good. Does that mean I get your phone number?"

She laughed. "I was pretty protective about that, wasn't I?"

"I don't blame you. You have every right to protect yourself."

Reaching inside her purse, she took out a business card and gave it to him.

He glanced at it and put it in his coat pocket. "I had a wonderful time, Maureen."

"So did I," she said truthfully, while shivering in the night wind.

"You're cold," he said, pulling up her collar to cover her neck. "You should get in the car."

"I know."

He kept his hands at her neck and stared into her eyes. She knew he was going to kiss her and she experienced a moment of panic. What if it was awkward? What if their lips didn't match

267

right? What if he was a bad kisser? What if she was? She'd only kissed one man in the last two decades!

There was no more time to think as he lowered his mouth to hers.

Their noses bumped and they both laughed nervously, and tried again. This time it worked. It was more of a caress than a kiss. His lips were warm and soft and gentle as they grazed over hers, and she felt a pleasurable tingling begin on her inner thighs and shoot upward.

When she moaned with desire, Matt pulled away and said in a husky voice, "I think you'd better go home."

She attempted to pull herself together and speak rationally. "Yes. You're right. Thank you for tonight."

Concentrating on unlocking her car, Maureen flushed with embarrassment.

"I'll call you tomorrow. Okay?"

Getting in the car, she nodded as he closed the door and waved good night to her. She started the engine and slammed it into first gear as she returned his wave. The MG took off like a rocket, yet she could still feel him watching as she drove away.

"You *moaned*, Maureen!" she cried out to the night. "How could you? You moaned out loud. He *heard* you! Damn it. He probably thinks you're some sex starved, Cat-on-a-Hot-Tin-Roof woman.

Turning onto the interstate, she touched her lips and recalled his kiss. When the tingling in her legs started again, she blew out her breath in a rush, figuring her earlier description wasn't far off the mark.

She wanted him.

Chapter Thirteen

They were sitting at a table that overlooked the Delaware River.

"This is so unfair," Lisa complained. "I can't get laid and you find Mr. Wonderful first night out on the town!"

Maureen almost spit her drink out onto the snowy white tablecloth. Wiping her mouth, she laughed. "I didn't say he was Mr. Wonderful. He's just a very nice man."

"Oh right. A very nice man who happens to also be a perfect gentleman *and* the sports anchor for the hottest TV station in town." Lisa shook her head. "Not bad, Maureen. Now just tell me how you did it."

"I didn't do anything. Except hit him with my raincoat. Everything just happened after that."

Lisa jammed a bread stick into her mouth and muttered, "I'll have to try that. Sort of a reversal on the caveman tactic. Hit 'em and drag 'em off to your lair."

Maureen couldn't help laughing. "I didn't drag him off. I invited him for coffee. I swear, Lisa, the words just came out of my mouth before I could stop them."

Shaking her head, Lisa picked up her wine. "And I always thought you were this sweet little writer. You give me hope, Malone."

"But what do I do, Lisa?"

"What do you mean? You enjoy it, that's what you do. Honey, you've earned a little happiness."

Their meal was brought and they both waited until the waitress left before resuming their conversation.

"I'm scared," Maureen admitted.

Cutting her fish, Lisa asked, "Of what? A man?"

Maureen nodded. "A man. The possibility of a relationship. I haven't *been* with anyone but Dan for the last twenty years."

"So?" Lisa chewed and waited for an answer.

The spinach salad looked colorful and bright, yet Maureen merely pushed the greens around her plate. "So, it's almost like dancing. Remember when you were married? You know how you were comfortable with your husband? He'd been your partner for years. You knew how he moved, what he liked . . . it's like sex. When you've been married for twenty years, you're used to one partner. You know his moves, what turns him on. You know the signals. I don't know anything anymore. It would be like starting all over again."

Lisa grinned wickedly. "Discovery can be fun."

Scowling, Maureen countered with, "Right now discovery seems like torture. God, I'd be so embarrassed. I can't even imagine myself in bed with another man."

Lisa gave Maureen a look of disbelief. "Try going without it for two years and your imagination turns fertile. Believe me. I know." She sipped her wine and smirked. "I was getting turned on when you were describing him holding your hand and listening to French love sonnets in the movie."

Maureen smiled at the memory. "It was nice. It's crazy, Lisa, but when he touches me . . . it's like he has my touch. We're so alike it's frightening. And it isn't the possibility of sex that gets to me. It's the attention. The interest in my work. The kids. My life. The touching of my hand, my hair, pulling my collar up so I don't get cold." She stopped and slowly shook her head. "God, I sound pathetic."

"You sound like a woman that hasn't had any attention in a long time. But not pathetic." Lisa suddenly chuckled. "*I'm* pathetic! I'm the one that doesn't even have a prospect on the horizon."

Suddenly feeling very selfish, Maureen touched her friend's arm. "I'm sorry. Here I'm going on about this and you're—"

"Don't be sorry," Lisa interrupted. "If it can't be me, I'm happy it's you. Besides, I want all the details as this thing progresses. I intend to live vicariously through you."

They ate in silence, each with their own thoughts, until Maureen whispered, "I did the thing with the lemons."

Lisa looked over to her. "What?"

"That thing, that spell, you told me about. I carved Dan's name in one half and his secretary's in the other."

Lisa threw back her head and howled with laughter. "You didn't!"

Maureen felt foolish, but nodded. "I did. I don't know why—yes, I do. I had just told Dan over the phone about pulling out my money from the joint account and he went nuts. I was angry and preparing dinner and there it was, sitting on the counter. It seemed like the right thing to do at the time. And I have to admit it made me feel better, less powerless."

Still laughing, Lisa reached over and patted her back. "Good for you."

"Yes, but now I feel stupid and childish. I mean, I really don't want anything bad to happen to Dan, or that woman."

"You don't believe in it, so nothing can happen. It was just a story I remembered from college."

"I still think I'm going to take them off the windowsill and throw them away," Maureen said. "I'll feel less vindictive."

Sitting back in her chair, Lisa smiled with affection. "You know something, Maureen? I'm really proud of you."

Maureen was surprised. "Me? Why?"

"Because it would have been easy to go under with this one. Plenty of women have done it. We've both seen it. The husband leaves and the wife goes into deep depression. But you didn't. Sure you've had your bad days. Maybe they aren't completely over, but you didn't let them defeat you. You didn't let him take you down with him. You survived." She pointed out the window to where Maureen's little red MG was parked. "I'll bet he had a fit when he heard you'd bought his dream car."

Maureen nodded. "Poor Josh told him and I could hear Dan yelling across the kitchen. Funny thing is, Lisa, it was always *my* dream car, not Dan's. Yet he was going to buy it. And not so the two of us could enjoy it." Maureen looked out to the car and admitted, "I couldn't stand the thought of him in it. You should have seen him when we took it out for a test drive. It was selfish, but I'm glad I bought it."

"I'm glad for you. You are the one person I know that deserves some happiness."

Maureen thought about it while she continued to eat. "I just don't understand it all."

"What?"

"You know how you hear the horror stories about women and dating? Look at you. You haven't met anyone you want to chance a relationship with, and it was the same with the women in the support group. When Dan left, I expected to be alone for the rest of my life. I had this picture I held in my mind, of the two of us growing old together, of sitting on rocking chairs on a porch, Dan making me laugh and wiping the dribble off each other's chin because we'd grown too

274

feeble . . ." Maureen's eyes filled with tears. "I knew that was how it was going to be after we'd spent our lives together. I mean, I knew it, Lisa. I would be an old woman with Dan Malone at my side. But now I have to alter the image, and it's so damn hard to give it up. Before, it was comforting to know what my future held. Now, it's so scary."

Lisa sighed. "I know."

"I have the children now, but what happens after they leave? What if I get sick? I'm going to be all alone."

"Don't think about it. You're healthy as a horse and you've got a terrific man in your life."

"But why did he come into my life so fast? It scares me."

Thinking about it for a moment, Lisa said, "You want to know why?" She didn't wait for a reply. "Because you're a good person, Maureen, that's why. Maybe this is your payback for all those years of doing the right thing. Don't question it. Enjoy it."

"Nothing may come of it anyway. He could just be a nice man who's going through a tough time in his life and—"

"And wants to be with you," Lisa interrupted. "We're not talking about happily ever after here. This is just two people who have a lot in common and enjoy each other. Take it for what it is. When is he calling you?"

"He said sometime today. God, I have to make sure I answer the phone. I don't know what to do about Abbie and Josh." Maureen pushed the plate away from her. "Josh gave me a hard time about going to the Woodcrest Inn. I can't imagine his reaction if he knew a man was calling for a date." She cringed. "A date! I still can't believe I'm going through all this again."

"Don't worry about the kids. They love you and want to see you happy. If this man can do that, then they'll come around."

Maureen sighed. "Well, I could be worried about nothing. He may not even call."

Wiping her mouth with the crisp linen napkin, Lisa shook her head and laughed. "You are the most insecure person I have ever known."

Maureen silently admitted the truth behind that statement.

She was sitting in front of her computer, struggling to get the scene written correctly. Nothing was coming. She could see it on the mental screen in her brain. She knew what the characters were supposed to be doing. She could hear the dialogue they were supposed to be saying, yet she just couldn't get it from her head to the computer.

After she had returned from lunch, she went right into her office to work. She was behind in her deadline for the mainstream and a manuscript for the *Cotillion* line was waiting to be edited.

Staring at the blank screen, Maureen could feel a panic begin deep in her belly. Two hours had passed and she had four paragraphs, and she wasn't exactly happy with those. What was happening to her? This was the book she was fighting to write, so why couldn't she write it?

Because your brain is filled with junk, she thought to herself. *You're not thinking about plotting and characterization. You're thinking about your failed marriage, your crazy dreams, about Matt Shannon's touch, how his smile completely changes his face, how his lips felt—*

"Maureen?"

She spun around from the computer. "Dan!"

She felt an absurd moment of guilt for Dan catching her thinking about Matt, and she quickly brushed it aside. "What are you doing here?"

"We have to talk. I thought we should do it before the kids came home from school."

He walked into her office and sat on the small sofa across from her desk. Even though he was dressed in an impeccable Italian suit, he looked worn, tired, and she had a ridiculous urge to take care of him. That impulse, too, she dismissed.

"How's the car?" She could read the annoyance in his expression.

"The car is fine," she said calmly.

"Why did you do it, Maureen?"

She was sick of the question. "Because I was the one that always wanted an MG, not you. Because I found it. It was there. I wanted it. And I bought it."

She could see his jaw muscle working as he clenched his teeth. "What about the money?"

"Most of it was mine and I wanted to protect it."

"What are you talking about? Protect it? From what?"

"From you," she said simply. "You're a stranger to me. I have no idea what you're going to do from week to week. You gave someone at work a loan of two thousand dollars, and you never even discussed it with me. You're not yourself, Dan." She took a deep breath and added, "You're drinking too much. I . . . I think you need help."

He continued to stare at her. "What are you saying?"

"I'm saying I think you have a problem. If you don't want to see the counselor that I found, then find one on your own, but do something. Don't do it for me, or even the children. Do it for yourself."

Shaking his head, he laughed. "You're something, you know that? I reject you and you immediately think I need professional help. Why don't you just admit it? You're doing all this—the car, the money, to punish me. And you think I'm a stranger? *You're* the stranger, Maureen. You wouldn't believe how much you've changed in the last month."

"Oh, yes, I would," she said, sitting back in her chair. "I have changed, and I'm glad. I always put you and the children before me, and it wasn't healthy. I had no life, Dan—"

"You had a life," he interrupted.

She nodded. "Sure. I was your wife and the children's mother. The only time I felt like me was when I was writing, or going to conferences, when I was away and had an identity of my own. Don't

278

misunderstand me — I was a good wife and a mother. I know that. And it was my choice. No one made me do it. But somewhere along the way, I lost me."

"Why didn't you ever say this before?"

"I never knew it before. Not until you left and I had to face my life alone." She felt the emotion well up inside her and she forced it back down. "Don't you see, Dan? I don't blame you. Not for that. This marriage didn't fall apart because of one person. Both of us are to blame."

"Why you? What did you do?"

"When you married me, I was your lover. Then the children came. They needed me more and I switched hats from being someone's lover to being a full-time mother. Then I started mothering you. I picked out your suits and ties. Bought your shirts and underwear. Told you when you needed a haircut. Made appointments for you with a doctor when you were sick; the dentist when your teeth needed cleaning."

He shook his head. "That's caring about someone."

"No, it's not," she insisted. "That's mothering, and you had a mother. I was your wife. You were an adult. You should have taken care of those things yourself, and I should have let you. No wonder you didn't feel any passion for me. Somewhere in your subconscious you saw me as your mother, not your lover — "

"This is ridiculous," Dan said, clearly embarrassed.

"No, it isn't," she persisted. "If you had trouble making the switch, well, so did I. I was constantly exchanging hats, and it was becoming more and more difficult." She thought for a moment and then added, "I'll give you an example. Do you remember when Josh had the chicken pox? Abbie had just finished and it was Josh's turn. I was already exhausted, and I knew I wasn't going to be getting much rest for the next week. But you wanted to make love. And I wanted it too, except I was tired. Right in the middle of making love, Josh called out to me and I went to him. When I came back to bed, you immediately wanted to resume where we had left off. I was expected to be a siren, but in my mind I was still a mother. I was worrying about Josh's fever, not how seductive I was to you. I didn't make the transition easily and as the years went by I guess I stopped trying. I felt responsible for my family's emotional and physical well-being. I was a mother . . . to everyone."

He sat, staring at her. "So what does all this mean?"

"It means I can't take care of you anymore, Dan. I have two children, and I have to start taking care of myself."

Neither of them spoke for a few moments, a slice of time that seemed longer by the strained silence.

"I don't know what to say." Dan shifted on the sofa. "You're never going to forgive me, are you?"

She closed her eyes briefly and tried to stop the pain that quickly wrapped around her heart. "I'm sure someday I'll get past the fact that you don't find me attractive any longer. I just don't know how to deal with the deception. It's strange . . . it isn't the actuality of you being intimate with another woman that makes me sick—it's all the lies. It's the betrayal by my best friend."

He looked as miserable as she felt. "So now what?"

She shrugged. "So I guess we work out a financial arrangement—"

"Are you saying you want a divorce?" he interrupted.

Shaking her head, she answered, "I don't know what I want right now, except time to heal."

"And you can't do that with me?" he asked hopefully.

She had a flash of insight, of how their roles had reversed in the last month. Now she didn't know if she wanted him and the life that came with him. "I need to do it alone. Just as you have to. It's time for both of us to grow up."

He didn't say anything, so she continued. "If you pay the mortgage, I'll take care of everything else. You can see the children whenever you want, as long as you call first. I won't be here when you come. You need time with them alone. You have to work out this problem with Abbie and Josh needs his father. It's tough on him living with two women."

Dan nodded. "I'll spend time with him. I don't know what to do about Abbie."

"I can't help you there. She feels angry and betrayed. Funny thing is, she knew about your infidelity before I did. She's very intelligent, and she'll see right through you if you avoid the real issues."

"God, Maureen, you make me sound like a son of a bitch."

She didn't say anything.

"That's what you believe, isn't it?" he asked.

"I'm too angry to answer that."

"Go ahead, say what you're thinking," he challenged.

She could actually feel his defenses rise to the surface, and her own rose swiftly in return. "I think you're going through a mid-life crisis and you risked everything—your family, the people who loved you—for your ego and strangers, some females who made you feel young again. I think you trampled over our marriage vows and took the easy way out, instead of trying to work through it. And I think you made a mockery out of the love I showed you for twenty years."

"Well . . . I guess that about says it all. You don't like me very much, do you?" He stood up and straightened his suit jacket.

Realizing he was leaving, she left her desk and faced him. "Right now I don't like you, but what's worse is I don't respect you." Her throat tightened with unshed tears. But she would not cry in front of him again.

"I'll pay the mortgage," he said, ignoring her last statement.

She followed him out of her office. When they reached the kitchen, he added, "And I'll call the kids tonight. Maybe they'd like to come over into the city on Saturday."

"Dan?" She stood in front of the sink and waited for him to turn around before saying anything more.

He had an expectant look on his face, as if she might have changed her mind.

Holding out her hand with her palm up, she said, "I'd like the key to the house."

He appeared shocked. "What do you mean? This is my house. I'm paying for it."

She forced herself to stay calm and said in a quiet voice, "No, this *was* your house. The first night you got in bed with another woman, you made a choice. And that choice was not your family. This is my house. Mine and the children's. I don't have a key to your apartment, and I don't think you should continue to have a key for this house. You have your privacy and I want mine."

He didn't do anything, except stare at her as if seeing a stranger.

"Unless, of course, you want to give me a key to your apartment."

He dug into the pocket of his trousers and brought out his keys. Fumbling with the ring, he finally managed to pull out the house key. He nearly jammed it into her palm.

She smiled sadly. "I didn't think so." She resisted making a smart remark about why he didn't want her to have access to his living quarters. Privacy. It was such a touchy subject with wandering males.

He turned around and left her in the kitchen. Hearing the front door slam, Maureen felt the tears roll down her cheeks as she reached for the plate on the window sill.

She dumped the lemons down the sink and turned on the garbage disposal. She didn't want Dan, or anyone else, to be harmed. She only wanted some peace.

He had an overpowering urge to walk up to her and wrap her in his arms. He wanted to take away her pain, to make her smile again. He hated to see her cry. It reminded him of another time, twenty-five years ago, when he had caused tears to appear at her eyes, when he had hurt her so much that she had run away from him. But he couldn't do anything. Not now. He had promised to stay out of her life, to let her work out her own problems. So he kept his distance, loving her in silence, and he watched . . .

Chapter Fourteen

"Will you pass me the salad, Mom?"

Maureen handed the wooden bowl to her son and stared down at her plate. How was she supposed to tell them that in two hours she was meeting Matt Shannon and then going to a hockey game? The idea of lying occurred to her, but she didn't want to deceive her children. It was too reminiscent of Dan. She wasn't doing anything wrong. She was separated. She had a right to see anyone she wanted. But how to convince Abbie and Josh of that?

"What are you doing tonight?" she asked Josh.

He swallowed a mouthful of meatloaf and reached for his milk. "I'm going out with the guys. I guess we'll hang out at Kevin's and then maybe go to Mandi Santelli's party later."

"And who's taking and picking you up?"

"Kevin's parents."

"What about you?" she asked Abbie.

Her daughter pushed her long hair behind her shoulders. "Scott and I are going to the mall. That sweater I wanted at The Gap is on sale. Then we're going to the ten o'clock movie."

Everyone had plans, including her. *Okay, you can do this,* she told herself. *Just open your mouth and tell them. They'll understand. You've put it off for three days. Now face this and get it over with; you're an adult. You're only going to a Flyers game, not getting remarried.*

"I'm going out, too," she began with a smile.

"Yeah?" Josh looked up. "Where?"

She swallowed. "The Flyers game."

Abbie and Josh stared at her. "The Flyers game?" they both repeated.

She nodded. "That's right."

"Why are you going to a hockey game?" Josh questioned, his food forgotten.

"Because someone asked me. It's better than sitting home."

Abbie's eyes widened. "Who? Who asked you?"

"Yeah. Who?" Josh demanded.

Her children were looking at her as if she'd just grown horns on her head. "Someone I've met. Someone very nice."

"Mom!"

Abbie looked surprised. Josh was plainly shocked.

"You have a date?" Abbie was obviously amazed.

Maureen felt like giggling and she actually had

286

to bite the inside of her cheek to control the urge. "Well . . . I guess you could call it that."

"Who is it?" Josh again demanded. He was definitely not pleased by the thought of his mother dating.

It didn't really surprise Maureen. She took a deep breath to steady her nerves. "He . . . his name is Matt. And he's very nice."

Abbie was shaking her head in astonishment. "I can't believe my mother is dating. I mean, *I'm* dating . . ."

"I'm not over the hill yet, Abbie," Maureen said in her own defense.

"Matt what?" Josh nearly growled across the table.

Here it comes, she thought as she took another deep breath and said it. "Matt Shannon."

Silence.

She looked at her children who were staring right back at her. "I just wanted the two of you to know where I am tonight."

"Matt *Shannon?*" Josh pushed his plate away from him. "Matt Shannon—on television?"

She nodded.

Abbie and Josh glanced to each other and suddenly burst into laughter. "Oh, yeah. Right, Mom," Josh managed to get out. He was obviously relieved. "This big deal sports announcer is taking you to the Flyers game. That's a good one."

"You had us going there, Mom," Abbie announced, looking at Josh and laughing again.

"I'm serious," she said in a defensive voice. "I am going out with Matt Shannon tonight."

"Right."

"Okay, Mom . . . whatever you say."

They didn't believe her. She didn't know whether to be relieved or insulted. "You don't think he would go out with me?" she asked, deciding she was insulted.

Josh pulled his plate back in front of him. Still chuckling, he said, "Mom, Matt Shannon could get anyone he . . ." Realizing he was making a mistake, her son tried again. "He's—you know, a big deal. He probably dates models or TV people. You're . . . a mom."

It was like her conversation with Dan earlier in the week. No one saw her as anything but a mother, a caretaker. "Let me tell you two something," she said, clearly annoyed. "Besides being your mother I am also a woman. I am not old and decrepit yet. I have wants and needs just like you. I need friendship, laughter, and a little happiness in my life. Some people actually think I'm intelligent, funny, even pretty."

She stood up and placed her napkin on the table. "And I'm going to the Flyers game tonight with one of them. Now if you'll both excuse me, I have to get ready. I don't care whose turn it is to do the dishes tonight, I just want them done before I leave. Any questions?"

Their mouths hung open in shock.

"Are you serious?" Josh whispered.

"Completely."

She walked out of the kitchen to get ready for her date.

Yes, a date. A full fledged, no sneaking-around date.

She sat next to him, not really watching the game. Hockey. It was a sport she had never liked. It was too fast, and she hated the senseless eruptions of violence. But tonight . . . well, tonight she was fascinated. Not by the game. She wasn't even sure of the score. It was the man next to her that consumed her thoughts.

Matt had met her at the garage where she had parked her car. They'd decided that her car was too small for him, and took his to Philadelphia. Once they got to the Spectrum, Matt took her into the press booth and introduced her to his colleagues. He seemed proud of her, telling everyone that she was a bestselling author. When he found out that she had never been to a hockey game, he led her into Ovations and they had Cokes while more people surrounded them, eager for a chance to speak with a sports announcer. Even though he didn't introduce her to his fans he held her hand, including her in the conversation. And now . . . now they sat together, side by side, and it was wonderful. She felt happy. How ironic, she thought, that a month ago she had been miserable. She had thought her life was over. And now here she was, sitting next to a man that was not her husband, a man that seemed just as happy to be with her.

He held her hand and played with the back of her hair when she leaned forward. He kept touching her. It wasn't annoying. It seemed natural, unconscious, as if they had known each other for years. She couldn't focus on the game. She was fighting the hypnotic effect of his touch. If she didn't concentrate on keeping her eyes open, she would lean back, snuggle up against him, and revel in the attention. It really was pathetic, for a part of her realized how deprived she had been. Another part, a part she didn't want to examine, recalled the words of her children. Matt Shannon was a big deal. He could go out with models and celebrities. Why would he want to be with her, an insecure homemaker and writer? Her own children had trouble believing it.

"Are you all right?" he asked, interrupting her thoughts.

Nodding, she turned her head and looked at him. "I'm fine," she answered. He really wasn't all that handsome. Not until he smiled. But there was something about him, something very male and yet tender.

"You're quiet. Are you bored?" He was still smiling.

"I'm okay," she murmured, still looking into his eyes. He had wonderful eyes. She could actually see kindness, a sense of humor and intelligence in them. A warm excitement started in her belly as they connected on a level that left those around them stuck in reality.

He broke the intense gaze and looked out to the ice. "Why don't we leave? The Flyers are ahead by three goals. We might as well beat the traffic."

"Okay. If you want . . ."

He grinned back at her as he picked up her purse and handed it to her. "Let's go," he said in a rough voice.

Twenty minutes later they were driving past Penns Landing when he pulled the car over to the waterfront.

"Is something wrong?" Maureen asked.

He shut the car off. "Do you want to go for a walk? Will you be warm enough?" He looked at her slacks and sweater, her suede jacket.

Maureen, in turn, looked out the window to the tall ships and thought how nice it would be to walk hand and hand with him. "Sure," she agreed and opened the car door.

He came around the car and locked the door. Taking her hand, he led her to the waterfront. "Why don't you ever let me open the door for you? Is it a feminist thing?"

She was surprised. "No. I just . . . just normally open the car door myself." Dan used to hold open the door for her, when they were dating, right after they were married, and when she was pregnant. But he had stopped a long time ago. She had simply forgotten that some men considered it a courtesy.

Exhaling into the cool night air, she watched the condensation of her breath and said, "I'll tell you what. You can open the door for me, but I won't expect it."

"What do you expect, Maureen?" He stopped and held both of her hands, making her face him. "From us?"

Flustered by his question, she could feel herself blush. "I . . . I don't know. Friendship, I guess."

"Just friendship?" He was staring into her eyes, as if looking for something.

She laughed nervously. "I don't know what you want me to say. I guess I'm not handling this well. It's been a long time since I've dated and I—"

"Come here," he interrupted, and gathered her into his arms. His lips came down on hers, cutting off any further conversation. This time they didn't bump noses. There was no awkwardness about it. This time their mouths met and matched perfectly. His lips nudged hers, softly, gently, waiting for a response.

Maureen gladly gave it. She was astonished by the crazy excitement that raced through her body. A tight coil of anticipation was building inside of her, spreading a delicious heat to her limbs, and she shyly wrapped her arms around him, needing to feel him close.

He pulled her into him and whispered, "My God, I've wanted to do that all night. I've been thinking about it since I left you on Monday."

She stared up at him. "I don't know how to handle all this, Matt."

"Why? Do you feel guilty, because of your husband?"

She shook her head. "No. I . . . I'm scared of where all this is leading."

"I think we both know where it's leading. I've never met anyone like you before, Maureen. I know that sounds like a line, but I swear it's true. I feel as if we've known each other for years, like we were separated and now we've found each other again." He looked up to the sky and grinned. "Now that sounded corny."

She smiled. "But I know what you mean. After Dan left, if I thought about dating it made me break out in a cold sweat. I never believed it would be this easy, this natural."

He looked down to her again. "Is it easy?"

"This part of it. Talking. Sharing things."

"Then what are you afraid of?"

She shrugged. "Everything that comes after this, I guess."

He wound his fingers through her hair and turned her face up to him. Lowering his head, he whispered into her mouth, "Don't be afraid, Maureen. I told you we would go slow. You'll let me know when your ready."

His words and his kiss sent a shock through

her system. She wanted to scream at him not to go slow, to take her right here on the waterfront, because she'd never have the nerve if she thought about it. Her body started to shake from a desperate need she hadn't even known existed, a deep, piercing longing for this gentle man. Startled by her reaction, she pulled her mouth away from his and placed her head on his chest.

"C'mon," he said. "You're shivering. Let's go back to the car." He wrapped an arm around her shoulders and led her away from the tall ships.

She let him open the car door for her and while he walked around the front of the car, she reached over and unlocked his side. He got in and gathered her into his arms. "Do you want me to turn on the heater?"

She shook her head. "Not unless you want it."

"You know what I would like?"

She merely looked at him, afraid of what he was going to say, yet secretly wanting him to continue.

"I'd like to meet your children."

"What?" Somehow this conversation had veered way off course.

"I'd like to meet Abbie and Josh. What do you think?"

Shaking her head, she chuckled. "I think they'd be speechless. You see, I told them I was meeting you tonight and they both laughed at me."

"Why?"

"They didn't believe you could possibly be interested in their mother."

"Well, let me talk to them. I'll tell them what they don't see in their mother—that she's young and beautiful, funny and intelligent. And sexy as all hell. Any man would be lucky to spend time with her."

She was surprised. *Sexy? Her?*

"Maureen? How about tomorrow night? We could all go out to dinner."

Blinking a few times, she tried to concentrate on what he was saying. "Ahh . . . tomorrow they're going to spend time with their father."

"Okay. Sunday or Monday then. What about you? Do you want to go out tomorrow?"

"Tomorrow? Sure, I'd like that." It would be her first Saturday night date in twenty years.

"Where do you want to go?"

"I don't care," she answered truthfully. She just wanted to be with him.

He looked out the car window for a few seconds and then said, "You know what I'd like to do?" He didn't wait for her answer. "I want to take you out dancing again."

Dancing. She liked that. "Where?"

He pulled her back into his arms. "Somewhere that plays a lot of slow songs." He kissed her again, and this time he was less controlled. His lips seemed to possess hers and when his tongue entered her mouth, teasing and exploring, she

295

found herself moaning with pleasure and a desire for something more.

He kissed her lips, her cheeks, her eyes. His mouth traced an intricate pattern down the slope of her neck and she gasped as he stopped at the point where her neck and shoulder met. It was an erogenous zone she hadn't even known existed! As his tongue drew small circles, she wound her fingers through his hair and drew him closer. He kissed her skin and then nibbled at the tender flesh. She was almost squirming, wanting more, and more . . .

After a few moments, he lifted his head and looked into her eyes. "I think I'd better get you home," he said in a rough voice: "Any more of this and I'm not going to stop."

"Okay," she answered softly while fighting disappointment. As crazy as it seemed, she didn't want him to stop. And that wasn't like her. She had always been the sensible one, but she didn't feel sensible. Not now. She felt as if every nerve ending in her body was raw, and craved his soothing touch. Sitting up, she smoothed her hair back into place and felt like a teenager that had been making out in the car.

As Matt started the engine, Maureen was quiet and he reached out for her hand. "Can I pick you up at your home tomorrow night?"

She thought about it for a moment. The kids would be in Philly. There really wasn't any reason why he couldn't.

"All right. If you have the time, you can follow me home tonight and that way you won't get lost."

"Okay. What time should I pick you up? Do you want to go to dinner first?"

She was about to suggest that she cook dinner for him, but stopped herself from offering. It was too soon. And she wasn't ready to have another man sit at her kitchen table.

"It's up to you," she said, liking the fact that he still held her hand.

"Then I'll pick you up at seven. We'll have dinner and be dancing by nine-thirty. How does that sound?"

For a woman who had spent the last twenty years catering to everyone else's needs, it sounded wonderful.

And that's exactly what she told him.

The kids were with Dan. The house was spotless — well, at least as spotless as it could be when she was behind in a deadline. She was wearing a brand new green dress and silently admitted she'd bought it because Matt had once said that she looked pretty in green. The grooming fairies had smiled down on her and her hair had dried to perfection. Even her makeup looked flawless. Nervously checking her appearance in the foyer mirror, Maureen moved closer to the glass.

My God, she looked . . . almost radiant!

For just a moment, a split-second in time, she

saw herself at seventeen with that same look of enthusiasm and expectation, waiting for Bobby to pick her up for her fake babysitting job. It was as if time had stood still as she waited for a male to drive up to her house, to whisk her away from unhappiness and provide her with laughter. Here she was again, dating after all these years. She had the creepy feeling that Bobby was looking over her shoulder and she spun around, as if to catch him in the act. But he wasn't there. Relieved, Maureen glanced back to the mirror and saw the excitement in her eyes.

"This is absolutely and positively pathetic, Malone," she told herself as she left the mirror to pace in front of the door. "To think that a man could do this to you. Someone pays you a little attention and you glow! Well, he was paying more than a little attention," she conceded. But still . . . why was it that a woman's self-esteem was so damned dependent on a man's opinion? Every feminist instinct rejected the theory, but she had to admit it was true. It didn't matter that Lisa thought she was a strong, intelligent woman. Hearing compliments from other women just didn't do it. A man, her husband, had stripped away her confidence, and she now knew she needed another male to restore it.

But where was that male? She stopped pacing to glance down at her watch. Six fifty-four. He wasn't late. Not yet. She peered out the door window and searched the dark street. What if her neighbors saw him getting out of the car? Did any of them know she and Dan were separated? Had the children told their friends? She was sure Abbie had told Scott. Josh's buddies had been over to the house and must have noticed Dan's absence. Did all of the parents know? It must be all over town. Avondale was small. Everybody knew everyone's business. Come to think of it, didn't Marcy Daniels look at her strangely in ShopRite this morning? And Carol Sanders had acted as if she didn't even see her in the dog food aisle.

The doorbell rang and she was so startled that she nearly jumped out of her skin as she grabbed the door and flung it open.

"Where have you been?" she demanded of the shocked man who stood on her threshold holding three white roses tied together with a tiny scarlet ribbon.

Trying to recover, he asked, "Am I late?"

He was about to bring up his wrist to check his watch when Maureen had visions of her neighbors pulling aside curtains and making notes for Divorce Court. *Why yes, your Honor, she had men over to her house, a house where her children lived, and she was still legally married. Disgraceful!* She grabbed his arm and thrust him into the foyer. "Get in," she whispered in a frightened voice.

"What's wrong?" Matt demanded, staring at her as though she'd lost her mind.

"Everyone can see you. You can't just stand out on my porch like that!"

"Like what? I rang your doorbell. What was I supposed to do? Beep my horn?"

She thought about it. "Maybe you should the next time."

"I am not going to beep for you like a sixteen-year-old kid," he said in a determined voice. "Are you ashamed of me, or something?"

"Of course not!" She exhaled loudly and tried to compose herself. "Look, this my first real . . . date in twenty years. And just this morning when I was shopping these women were looking at me funny in ShopRite and I have the kids to think about and—"

"And I think you're getting paranoid," he interrupted.

"I'm not," she persisted, wringing her hands together and then moving him away from the glass sidelights by the door. "If they knew I was seeing someone, dating, and if they knew it was *you*—God, this town hasn't had anything this juicy to gossip about since Mary Steward left her kids and ran off with Carpenter Carl, who was eight years her junior. And we all thought she was merely getting extensive remodeling done!"

"Maureen . . . will you calm down? I am not Carpenter Carl and I am not going to ravish you here in your house—though the idea is tempting. Here," he shoved the flowers to her chest. "These are for you."

She held them and took a deep breath. The scent of the roses seemed to soothe her frazzled nerves for a moment. "Thank you. They're beautiful." She brushed past him. "I'll put them in a vase and we can get going."

"This is not our first date," he called after her. "By my count this is the fifth time we've been together. This is just the first time I've been in your house."

Half way up the steps, she stopped and turned back to him, as if seeing him for the first time this evening. "Why are you dressed like that?" she asked, looking at his jeans and shirt and sweater. "I thought you said we were going dancing."

He nodded apologetically. "I know. I'm sorry. I just thought we would be more relaxed if we were casual. And I was afraid to call you. I mean, I didn't know what you'd told the kids about tonight. I didn't know if Dan was here, or, who'd answer the phone. Do you mind? If you do, we could go back to my place and I could change."

That meant she'd have to find something else to wear. She touched her green silk dress.

"You look really pretty. I'm sorry for the confusion and I don't mind changing . . ."

She shook her head. "No, that's all right. I'll change. Here. Sit here in the living room. You can turn on the light. But don't move around or do anything to attract attention, okay?"

He laughed. "Will you stop it? Go and change. And hurry up before Carpenter Carl's reputation becomes a mere blur in Avondale history. *The separated author secretly meets the TV guy who is also separated while no one else is home* . . . Pretty juicy stuff, don't you think? It might make a great lead story on the Sunday Six O'clock. Sundays are always slow; think I ought to call in a news team on this one?"

She couldn't help grinning at him. "Your sarcasm is not lost on me, Mr. Shannon, but I do have two children that I want to protect."

"I promise I won't move. My breathing will remain shallow. If someone looks into your living room, they'll think I'm part of the furniture. Now put some jeans on and we can go." He smiled at her with affection. "Nobody really cares, Maureen. They have their own lives to get through."

She nodded and raced into the bedroom. Maybe he believed that, but fifteen minutes later as she walked up to his car Maureen swore that she saw more than one curtain fall softly back into place.

She figured he brought her to the Sports Bar because he had a secret desire to impress her. The place was enormous, the old Lit Brothers Building in Center City. Mike Schmidt had a restaurant there displaying all his trophies and Maureen promised herself to bring Josh to see it. They were treated as special guests at dinner and afterward walked into the bar. He was immediately surrounded but showed the same polite reserve as

302

he held her hand and pulled her away with him to the basketball cages that lined one wall. They ordered Cokes and he made sixteen straight free throws. Satisfied, he moved onto the pitching machines. Again, he showed his athletic prowess by throwing strikeouts that registered seventy-one miles an hour.

It was a male thing. She was sure of it. On some level he wanted to show her that he was as good as any other man in the place. She laughed to herself. Men really didn't understand women at all. When they moved closer to the pool tables, Maureen grabbed his arm and pulled him in the other direction.

"C'mon, Shannon," she laughed. "Enough of this. You've had your choice. Now it's my turn."

He looked down to her. "I'm sorry. I asked if you wanted to try, but you said—"

"I think I've just found my game," she interrupted and pointed to the center of the building.

A full size boxing ring made up the dance floor.

"I believe you promised me an evening of dancing."

The look he gave her as he led her up to the other dancers made her blood run hot through her veins. And when he gathered her into his arms, she knew this was exactly where she had wanted to be all evening. She was again amazed at how well they fit together. It felt so natural. So right.

The place was packed, and one song led into another. Despite the fact that it was the dead of winter, along with everyone else on the crowded dance floor, they were sweating. And it was the mixture of body heat and moisture, the scents and the textures, the slow, sensuous swaying that made Maureen realize she was going to make love with this man. Sometime in her future, it would happen, or she would regret it for the rest of her life.

She pulled her face back to look at him and could read the same desire etched onto his expression. They stared at each other for endless moments before Matt leaned forward and gently kissed her lips. "I think we're in trouble, Maureen," he whispered into her mouth.

"I think you're right," she breathed back, wanting him so much that it shocked her.

From the corner of his eye, he looked around the crowded dance floor and muttered, "C'mon, let's get out of here and talk."

She gladly followed, and had to just about run to keep up with him. He rushed her into her coat, grabbed her hand, and led her along the street until they reached the garage where they had parked his car. No words were spoken in the tiny elevator that took them up to the third floor. He was holding her hand so tightly, as though afraid she might disappear, that Maureen was totally unprepared when he reached his car and leaned her up against it.

His mouth came down on hers in a kiss that was almost desperate with longing. He held her head between his hands and devoured her mouth, muttering, "My God, I want you so much I can't stand it. I'll keep waiting for you . . ." He kissed her eyes, her cheeks, her ears. "I know you're scared. I won't hurt you. I promise . . ."

She kissed him back, pulling him closer, needing to feel the length of him against her. It wasn't until they heard the elevator doors open that they reluctantly pulled apart. Both of them were breathing heavily and Matt fumbled with his key as he unlocked the door. She got in the car and opened his side, while pressing a shaking palm against her chest to quiet her heart.

When he shut his door, he leaned back and closed his eyes as he drew in a deep breath. "I think we have to talk," he said in a serious voice.

She nodded. "But not here."

He looked at her. "Where? Do you want to come to my apartment?"

"No." She shook her head. "Let's go back to Jersey. Do you know that park outside Moorestown?"

"Yes."

"Let's go there. It'll be quiet." She buckled her seat belt and tried to calm her nerves as Matt pulled out. But she knew, as they made their way down the winding exit ramp, that she was at a crossroads in her life. She would never be the same after this. It was a decision that couldn't be taken back.

But would she have the courage to make it?

"If I do this . . . if *we* do this," she said hesitantly, as she sat with his arms around her and looked out to the barren trees, "then I want to do it right."

"So do I," he agreed. "But what do you mean by *right?*"

"I mean it has to be my way, or I won't have the courage to go through with it."

He brushed the hair back behind her ear and kissed her temple. "You make it sound like it's something terrible. We're talking about making love, Maureen."

She closed her eyes and tried to gather her strength. "I know. But even though I want to, I can't even imagine myself . . . you know, *with* someone else."

"Why?" He sounded concerned, yet slightly amused.

"Because I don't know anything about you, about that . . . I don't know what you like. You don't know what I like. It's all so embarrassing. And I honestly don't know if I want to put myself through it."

He tightened his arms around her. "So you're saying that if we first got all this awkwardness out of the way—all the likes and dislikes, the

306

things that you're comfortable doing, or not doing—then we might be able to take this relationship further?"

Maureen thought about it for a few seconds. "Yes. I guess that's what I'm saying. But I don't know how I could talk about it. I mean, how comfortable are we going to be revealing such personal things about ourselves? I know I'm scared."

He laughed. "Why are you scared? Do you trust me?"

"I don't even know the definition of that word any longer," she answered truthfully. "I don't think I'm capable of trusting anyone, any male— maybe not for a long time."

"Okay, I understand that. But you can't close yourself off to life. You can't punish yourself and me for something your husband did. It wouldn't be fair to either one of us. But it would be especially sad for you, Maureen."

They sat in silence, holding each other. She could almost hear him thinking, wondering what she was going to say next. He was a good man. She knew that. He was gentle and kind. He'd already proven that. What was holding her back? Sheer terror to find herself in this position after twenty years was the only answer. But as she sat and thought about her life, she realized that she had been blessed with fortitude. She'd beaten cancer, a hysterectomy, a lifetime of disillusionment, kids' crises; she'd built a successful career out of taking a chance and she'd survived a husband who'd trampled all over her marriage and her heart. Somewhere inside of her there had to be a spark of courage left, a tiny bit of herself that she could risk with this man.

Deeply inhaling, she then whispered, "So where do we begin?"

He released his own breath with a sense of relief. "Well . . ." he started, "let's begin with what we don't like. Beastiality. That's a definite turnoff for me, along with necrophilia."

She burst out laughing and hit his arm. "Stop it," she demanded. "This is supposed to be serious."

Laughing, he brought her back into the circle of his arm. "I am serious. Sex with animals and dead people leaves me cold—no pun intended."

She giggled and relaxed against him. "Okay, you broke the tension, now what else?"

"It's your turn."

She thought for a moment and said what was uppermost in her mind. "I'm self-conscious about my body. I'm not young any longer and—"

"Why are you self-conscious of your body?" he interrupted.

She shrugged, not wanting to point out her flaws in case he'd been struck blind and hadn't felt them already. "I had a hysterectomy about eight years ago and my body hasn't been the same since."

He lowered his hand to her abdomen and

started to caress it, but she quickly grabbed his fingers and pulled them away. "Please don't," she begged, feeling her throat tighten. She knew Dan found that part of her repulsive and couldn't bear to go through another rejection.

"Listen to me, Maureen," he whispered, "Everyone's got something about them that they wish would just go away, something they would change if they could. I think a lot of it has to do with the business both of us are in. Television, movies, commercials—they all push this perfect image on us of how we're supposed to look and dress and feel. And I know it's even worse for women. But you have to admit even the books you write are like that in a way, furthering that false image of the perfect man and woman. I know it's a business and everybody feeds off everybody else, but it just isn't a true picture of reality."

"I know," she admitted. "Maybe no one wants to face reality, that we're all just human beings with big noses or thin hair or chunky bodies or crooked teeth, that we aren't carbon copies of what *they* declare as perfection. But don't you see, Matt? We all bought into it. Everyone's terrified of growing old and losing their appeal. What happens when the plastic surgery, the gyms, the youthful clothing, the makeup, can't hide it any longer? How are we ever supposed to grow old and be comfortable with the person we are inside when we never got to know that person? When we refuse to allow ourselves to just be, *however* God created us? How did we allow this to happen to us? It makes no sense."

"Maureen?"

"Hmm?"

"I know this is getting away from our philosophical discussion, but I think I have to say something here."

"Yes?" She held her breath.

"I have a lot of chest hair. Some women don't like it."

She almost laughed. "You do?"

She felt him nod above her head.

"Will that bother you?"

She really never cared for an abundance of chest hair and couldn't understand the fascination some women had for it. Dan had almost none. But this wasn't Dan. Tonight she felt closer to Matt than she had ever felt to her husband. And it was time to do something about that.

Turning around, she faced him and started to unbutton his shirt. "Why don't we see?" she gently asked while smiling into his eyes. "I'm sorry I steered you away from our original discussion." She kept talking in a low voice to ease away any uncertainty. "I think we were at likes and dislikes." There was one more button to his shirt. She pushed his sweater up to his chest. "I like it when you play with my hair. When you touch me or hold my hand. You have my touch, Matt Shannon. I know this is going to sound like

310

an *Obsession* commercial, but when you caress me I can feel the emotion behind your touch and it's so like mine that it's almost as if I'm touching me too."

She could feel the steady heartbeat behind his chest. Pulling his shirt apart, Maureen saw the thick, dark hair and reached out to bury her hand in its depth.

He was very still, barely breathing, as he waited for her reaction. She looked up to him and smiled. "It's so soft," she said and her voice was filled with wonder. She ran her fingertips over his skin, liking the way he deeply inhaled as if she had given him the greatest gift imaginable. "I like it," she whispered, as her nail grazed over his nipple. He grabbed her hand and sat up straight.

"Maureen, you can't do that."

"I can't?" She smiled.

He shook his head. "Not here. Not now. Not if you want to continue this discussion."

Her grin widened. "So I can safely assume that playing with your chest hair is definitely on your list of likes?"

He grinned back at her and kissed her quickly. "Definitely. Now what about you? Do you have any chest hair I can play with?"

Laughing, she realized that she really did want to take this relationship as far as it would go. "No. No chest hair."

"But a very nice chest."

"Please. Don't embarrass me," she asked. She

had always been self-conscious about her breasts. They were too big.

"You shouldn't be embarrassed. Didn't we just talk about people accepting themselves the way God created them? I love your breasts. I haven't even touched them, yet I know what they'll feel like."

Now it was her turn to hold her breath as his fingers slowly slid beneath her sweater. Softly, gently, almost reverently, Matt traced the outline of one breast with his fingertip, and then moved to the other. Her nipples immediately hardened in response and when he cupped them in his hands, she and Matt nearly moaned in unison.

"See how they fit perfectly in my hands?" He leaned forward and kissed her, exploring her mouth while his hands explored her body.

She was not prepared for the white-hot rush of pleasure that raced through her system and she broke his kiss and pressed her chest to his. "Not like this," she whispered against his neck, while struggling for air, sanity, control.

"I know," he nearly groaned and held her tightly to him. "Let's get on with this discussion so we can make plans. I'm too old and getting too frustrated with this petting in the car stuff."

"I'm sorry—"

He squeezed her. "Don't be sorry. Let's just get to the next item on the agenda. We covered your body, my chest hair. I guess the next thing is sex. The actual act."

She shook her head and tried to pull away. "I can't do this. It's the most bizarre conversation I've ever had. I simply can't discuss the act of sex with you."

"Did you ever with Dan?"

The question came out of left field and stopped her cold when she realized the answer. "No," she said in a tiny voice. "I tried, but he wasn't comfortable talking about it."

"So how did you tell him what you liked, what you wanted him to do?"

She didn't say anything.

"Maureen?"

She could feel the tears welling up in her eyes. "I . . . I . . . ," shrugging her shoulders, she bit her bottom lip to stop from crying. "I tried to show him, but—"

"But you were too embarrassed to tell him the truth?"

Nodding, Maureen wanted to curl up away from him. This was not working out as she had planned. Instead of letting her move away, he held on to her more tightly.

"Listen to me, Maureen," he softly commanded. "You made a mistake about that. You should have told him what you needed. But I'm not going to let you make that same mistake with me. Now," and he took a deep breath. "How do you feel about oral sex?"

She stiffened in his arms. "My God! You certainly are blunt!"

"I don't care if you're shocked. I'm asking how you feel about a normal, enjoyable, part of intimacy. And you're going to answer, or we'll sit here with the ducks until the sun comes up."

"Is this the pushy reporter coming out in you?"

"Yes. Now, do you like it, or not? We've got others on the list to cover."

"I don't know how to answer that question."

"It requires a yes or no answer."

"Dan seemed to like it."

"And you didn't?"

"I never had a chance to find out."

He stared at her for a few seconds before whispering, "You mean—"

She was getting angry, tired of his relentless questions. "What I mean, Matt," she said in a precise voice, "is that Dan was the first man with whom I had ever been intimate. Since he enjoyed receiving that particular attention, but never reciprocated, I have no basis from which to answer your original question. Are you satisfied now? Do you have all your answers?"

Silence.

He didn't say a word, for words would seem insignificant at the moment and he sensed she needed a little time. Instead, he soothed her by playing with her hair and watched her as she tried to bring her breathing back under control.

Two or three minutes must have passed before he tried talking to her. "Maureen?"

"What?" She sounded like a hurt child.

"This is going to be even better than I had fantasized."

She shot him a disbelieving look. "You've got to be kidding."

"No, listen . . . I think discovery is the most exciting part of sex. It's the closest you can get to another human being. And we're going to discover things about you that no one else knows." He brought her back to his arms and held her tightly. Leaning down he whispered in her ear, "Because I like being intimate with a woman like that. Sometimes I think it's more of a turn on for me than it is for her, watching her reactions and knowing I have the power to make her feel like that. God, I can't wait! Now what's next?"

In spite of everything, she laughed and turned to him. She reached up and touched his cheek, softly running her fingers over his skin as the tears spilled over her eyelids. "How did you ever come into my life, Matt Shannon?"

"You hit me with your raincoat, remember? Now let's finish this damned discussion. Is there anything else?"

She leaned back against him and looked out to the silhouettes of the trees. "I guess we should talk about safety."

"Safety? But you said you had a . . . that you can't get pregnant."

"That isn't what I'm talking about," she answered in a quiet voice. "Should we first get tests, or something?"

"An AIDS test?" He didn't sound happy.

"Well, it would be the right thing to do. Neither one of us should have to be at risk."

"You would feel better about being together if we got tested?"

"I don't think I would be able to go through with it if we didn't. I do care for you, Matt, a great deal more than I should at this point. But I don't intend to get sick or die for you. I have a life and two children I want to protect."

"Enough. We'll get the tests. Do you know how?"

She shook her head. "No, but I'll make a few phone calls and find out."

Forgetting his strength, he hugged her so tightly that for a moment she couldn't breathe. "Do it tomorrow!" he said in a frustrated voice.

Maureen smiled, happy with his answer.

Somehow, from somewhere, she would find the courage to go through with it and maybe, just maybe, she would find a way back to happiness.

He watched her as she fell asleep with a smile on her face. He wanted to reach out and touch her, or hold her in his arms, but he knew he couldn't protect her from her future. She thinks she's getting her life together, but he had a strange feeling about this new turn of events. Matt Shannon. How could he trust this man with Maureen's heart? And yet, what choice did he have?

And what was it that was holding him here, grounding him to this dimension? The answer came quickly.

A scared little girl with a ribbon slipping out of her hair and her knee socks falling down had once looked him straight in the eye and asked for friendship. He hadn't let her down then. And he wouldn't now. Only once had he failed her. That summer of their senior year. He had hurt her deeply by what she had perceived as a rejection. And that single moment had changed their lives, their fates. This time, even though it hurt to see her with another, this time he was staying and seeing it through.

He owed her that.

Chapter Fifteen

She was staring at the phone when it suddenly rang and she nearly flew out of her chair. Grabbing up the receiver, she asked breathlessly, "Hello? Yes?"

"Maureen?"

She held her breath. "Yes?"

"I just called the doctor . . ."

"Yes?" Oh God, she could actually feel a heaviness settle over her heart.

"The nurse said the results were negative. She's going to send a confirmation."

Maureen slowly let out her breath and collapsed back in her chair. She was relieved. Of course she was relieved, but she knew down deep a terrible part of her was hoping something, anything, would come up to stop her from going through with *it*.

"Did you hear me?" Matt asked. "I've got a clean bill of health!"

Closing her eyes, she smiled. "Yes. I heard you.

Congratulations. I called my doctor about a half hour ago. I'm . . . my results were also negative."

"All right! I swear, Maureen, I feel like I've just found out that I have a second lease on life, like I can do it over. And do it right this time."

There was a pause that seemed to be drawn out for endless seconds.

"Why don't you sound as excited as I am?" Matt asked in a more serious voice.

"Because I'm scared," Maureen said truthfully.

"Of what? Of me?"

"Of everything. I don't know—"

"Listen," he said, "do you want to come here to my apartment? We can talk about it. I won't—"

"No," she interrupted. "I don't want to go to your apartment. I told you, we have to do this my way."

"Okay? What's your way?"

She delayed answering. She had thought about it for three days, going over in her mind how she wanted to proceed. Staring at her blank computer screen, Maureen knew it was now or never. She could stop this now and never know what it was like to be with him, to always be frightened, or she could find the courage and answer him.

Taking a deep breath, she decided to go forward with her life, wherever it took her. "I'll meet you in the bar of the Hilton on Route 73 at seven-thirty tomorrow night."

"The Hilton? Maureen, are you sure you want to go to a hotel? You've never even seen my apartment. I could make dinner. We could relax—"

"No, Matt. I want it to be at the Hilton. And I'll get the room."

"Now that's ridiculous. If it has to be the Hilton, I'll get the room. I don't want you going up to the desk and registering."

"You still don't understand, do you?" she asked gently. "This time, this first time, has to be my way. Please, just be patient with me. I'm nervous enough without you making this a contest over who's paying for the room." She took a deep breath and tried to make him understand. "Look, I know this isn't going to make any sense to you, but I feel like I'm losing my virginity all over again. Twenty years ago, I felt like a victim. This time I want it to be right, and to do that, I have to be in control."

For a few seconds he didn't respond. Finally, he said, "You are the strangest woman I have ever known, Maureen Malone."

"You can back out," she answered, realizing that a small part of her was hoping he would do just that.

"Not a chance," he said. "Okay. Tomorrow night. Seven-thirty at the Hilton bar. What are you doing tonight?"

She smiled. "I'm going to spend time with the kids, and I'll probably do a lot of thinking."

"Me, too."

"I'll see you tomorrow."

"I'll be there."

And she knew he would.

"They found Dad's car. The police say it was used in a robbery. Can you believe it?" Her children were laying across her bed, while Maureen sat on the loveseat a few feet away.

"Really?" It was all she could think to say in answer to her son's question.

"And now he'll probably have to go to court and testify that he didn't give them permission to take it. It's all trashed. They must have poured gasoline all over it." Josh was clearly upset.

Abbie leaned back against the pillows. "He said the insurance company isn't going to total it. So now he'll have to get it fixed."

"No new car?" Maureen asked casually.

Josh shook his head. "Nope."

No one said anything. Maureen had asked them to come into her room after their homework was finished so they could talk, but she hadn't planned on talking about their father. "Well, I'm sure everything will work out. Now, look, the reason I wanted to speak with both of you is because I've done some thinking about your birthday. It's in a few weeks and I thought maybe we could have a small party here."

"Family?" Abbie asked with a raised eyebrow, as if to say it would be a very strange party.

"Not necessarily, if you don't want it. Would

you like to ask some friends? I don't want any more than twenty kids here. Which means each of you could ask ten, or five couples—however you'd like to work it out."

Josh looked up at his sister and Abbie shrugged. "I guess so," she said.

Nodding, Josh agreed. "Okay. A party. Will you be here?"

Maureen grinned. "Yes, I'll be here. Upstairs. You can have your privacy as long as both of you are responsible with the house and you make sure no one, and I mean no one, goes near the bar. I'm going to lock it anyway."

"You don't trust us?" Josh looked insulted.

Maureen said, "I trust you, I don't trust anyone else. And if the party's in this house, then I'm responsible for what goes on. And there will not be any drinking, so make that clear when you do the inviting."

"No problem," Abbie said. "Most of my friends have joined SADD anyway."

Maureen nodded. She was very proud that her daughter had been instrumental in forming a division of Students Against Drunk Driving at the high school. "Okay. Now here's my second idea. For your birthday, I'm giving the two of you driving lessons. It'll help with insurance rates since I plan to give you my station wagon. I don't know how you'll both work out the driving time, but I can't afford two cars and this one is paid off. Both of you will get part time jobs in the summer to pay me back for the insurance which, considering your ages, is going to be a hefty sum. What do you think?"

Abbie nodded. "It seems okay to me. I've wanted to get a job in the mall anyway."

Josh looked less happy. "Both of us sharing the same car? What about Dad? Maybe he could buy me a car."

Maureen's jaw tightened. "You will not ask your father for a car, nor will you try to play your parents off against each other because we're separated. I won't allow it, Josh. I'm offering you the use of a car, free and clear. You have to pay the insurance, but I'm willing to foot the bill until the summer. That's the deal. You either take it or leave it. And if you leave it, Abbie will get the car and the insurance will be cut in half because male teenage drivers are the most expensive to insure."

"Geez, Mom, don't get all bent out of shape. I was just thinking out loud. I'll take it."

She looked at her children. She had devoted sixteen years to them; every single day that they had drawn breath they had been the focal point of her life. She knew every child was self-centered, and she didn't expect the twins to shower her with kisses of undying love and gratitude. But still, something about them irritated her.

They expected so much.

"You know something," she said slowly. "Your father and I have worked very hard over the years to make a good life for you two. We gave you a good home, made sure you went to good schools. You always had the best food and clothes, the best sports equipment. We ran you to church and cub scouts, little league and brownies. We cheered you on and wanted you to feel you were special, that you could succeed in anything you tried. We gave you the best, and now I don't know if we did you any favors. Do you realize that neither one of you has even said thank you yet? Not for the party, the car, the insurance. You both expect everything handed to you on a silver platter. You take too much for granted."

"I said I was sorry, Mom," Josh nearly moaned, knowing nothing was going to stop the lecture. "And we are grateful."

"Really, Mom," Abbie joined in. "Thanks for everything."

Maureen shook her head. "In a few years the two of you will be out on your own. I only hope you can provide for yourselves as well as your parents have done. If you've never known any hardship, if you've never had to work for anything, how will you ever appreciate the good times, or know how to survive the tough ones?"

Her eyes filled with tears as she gazed at each of her children. "I think it's about time we all started to grow up in this house. Abbie, you and I are going to learn how to fix that leaky faucet in the powder room. Somewhere there's a repair book in this house with instructions. We're both intelligent women. We can read. We can learn."

Chuckling, Josh cast his sister a sympathetic look.

"And, Josh . . ." Her son stopped laughing and turned to her. "I want you to get up right now and pick up your laundry basket. I'm about to introduce you to the washing machine."

"Aww, mom! Not now!"

She stood her ground and rose to her feet. "Yes. Right now. You know, Josh, all these years you've acted like the elves came into your room during the night and took away your filthy clothes, only to have them cleaned and pressed when you came home from school the next day. Well, guess what? This isn't a fairy tale. This is reality. And the real truth is I'm tired of picking up after someone who's almost grown. You need to know how to take care of yourself, so you'll learn how to do laundry. And you'll also learn to cook. But do you want to know why I'm really doing this?"

Josh's scowl of displeasure was more than apparent and Maureen knew he'd never admit to curiosity, so she merely continued.

"I'm doing this for your wife. Someday you'll marry and I don't want this woman to turn to me after a year of marriage and ask me why I didn't do my real job as a parent and why she's paying for my mistakes. You will learn, my dear, how to take care of yourself. And, if you choose to marry, you'll know how to live within a relationship. It's not too late for you."

"Oh, so now I'm paying 'cause you're pissed at Dad."

There was dead silence as the room crackled with tension. Maureen stared at him, then surprised both her children by smiling. "No, Josh," she said calmly. "This had nothing to do with your dad. This is because I love you. Now let's get started."

Filled with a sense of purpose, of taking back the control in her life, she walked out and left them in her bedroom.

She fell asleep thinking about the next evening. She knew exactly what she was going to do, what she would wear. And how many rum and Cokes she intended to drink before Matt showed up. Everything was planned. And she was going through with it. Even as she drifted into the welcome languor of sleep she couldn't stop the mental shudder as images rose sharply in her mind, swirling around and around until she settled on one.

Sex.

First kiss.

First grope.

First time . . .

She knew it was a mistake to go out with someone Robin had fixed her up with. Tony Fowler just wasn't her type. He lived in Bristol and drove a motorcycle, though tonight he had his dad's car. It wasn't just because Tony was socially different and that through three years of high school they had never hung out with the same crowd. They simply had nothing in common. They couldn't agree on a movie, or where to go after. She wanted to go to Joe's Pizza and hopefully catch up with her friends. He wanted to go parking at Silver Lake. Since he had the car and a one-track mind, they found themselves sitting in the dark with nothing to say to one another. Maureen just wanted to go home, call Robin and tell her never, ever, to think of her when her new boyfriend's buddies were lonely on a Saturday night. God, she would rather stay in and clean out under her bed than go through this again!

"So are you thinking about going to school?" Maureen asked, trying once more for conversation.

"I am going to school," Tony muttered.

She forced herself not to sigh. "I mean after high school. Do you want to go to college?"

"Nah. Goin' to work with my Uncle Johnny in Philly. Gonna get me in the Plumbers Union."

"Really? That's nice." What more could she say?

"Gotta know somebody to get in, ya know?"

"No, I didn't." Struggling for words, she blurted out, "I'm going to college. Maybe I'd like to be a teacher or a—"

"Yeah, great," Tony interrupted and grabbed her.

He pulled her into his arms and ground his mouth against hers. She was so shocked she couldn't react, except to push against his chest. She never could figure out how or when he did it, but after a few seconds Tony reached up and pulled one of her hands down to his lap.

And that was the first time Maureen Henessey found her hand wrapped around a penis. She couldn't move. She could barely breathe.

Tony stopped kissing her and sighed with pleasure. "There now," he said, as if she had stopped struggling because she was finally happy. "C'mon, Maureen," he urged in a husky voice while squeezing his hand over hers. "You know what to do. Hard and fast . . ."

She simply couldn't move. She was paralyzed with fear and revulsion. And no amount of urging or instruction on Tony's part could rouse her from her near-comatose state. She kept blinking and staring out the side window, not daring to look at him, or . . . or anything else.

"What's wrong with you?" Tony demanded, getting quickly frustrated by her lack of response.

All she could think about was how big and wet and ugly it felt. She tried to pull her hand away, but Tony held hers tighter to him.

"Please . . ." she managed to whisper beyond the lump in her throat. "Please don't do this."

"Look, I didn't even want to take you out," he just about snarled at her. "I was doing Robin a favor. Everybody knows your knees are welded together, but I thought—" He released her hand, as if disgusted. "What the hell? I shelled out two bucks for a movie. Might as well try and get my money's worth back."

She quickly moved next to the car window, as far away from him as she could get. "I want to go home," she whispered in a shocked voice.

"With pleasure," he answered and his father's car roared into reverse.

Neither one of them spoke the entire way back to Makefield. Maureen kept her hand out in front of her, as though it had been contaminated. When they reached her street, she used her left hand to dig into her purse.

He stopped at her home and she opened the car door. Throwing her precious babysitting money onto the front seat, Maureen said, "Here's your two dollars." And then walked with as much dignity as possible up to her front door, while keeping her right hand away from her body.

The house was quiet. Her dad was at a Knights of Columbus meeting and her brother was sleeping over Jeff Clark's. Maureen dropped her purse onto the sofa and hurried into the laundry room like a woman possessed. She pulled up the sleeve to her sweater and turned on the hot water. Grabbing a stiff brush she started scrubbing her hand, over and over again, but nothing could take the scent of Tony Fowler away from her fingers. In desperation, she took the huge bottle of Clorox and poured it over her hand, wincing as it stung her raw skin. Surely the bleach would take away every trace.

Instead, for the rest of her life, the distinct odor of Clorox would remind her of sex and Tony Fowler. No wonder she hated doing laundry so much . . .

She sat straight up in bed and stared at her darkened room. What a crazy dream. What in the world would make her relive an incident that happened over twenty-five years ago? Of course, Maureen thought, dropping back to her pillow. Tomorrow you're planning a sexual liaison, your first with a new partner in twenty years. Though Matt wasn't Tony Fowler, thank God.

But what if it was distasteful? What if she froze up, like with Tony? What if it was humiliating and embarrassing? What if she wasn't any *good?*

Something had made her husband turn to strange women.

She clamped her eyes shut and shook her head. No. She refused to think it. This was a second chance, and she was taking it. She *had* to take it. Not for Matt. Not even to prove Dan wrong. She had to do it for herself.

Chapter Sixteen

"I would like a room, please."

Maureen held her gold card out to the woman behind the front desk of the Hilton Hotel. The young woman smiled, yet Maureen was sure the reservation clerk knew exactly what she was up to, even down to what was in her overly large shoulder bag.

"A single or a double?"

Maureen swallowed. "A double."

"We have king size or queen size mattresses—"

"A queen will be fine," Maureen interrupted.

"Would you prefer to be on the east side or the west? The west has a lovely view of the countryside."

"I really don't care."

"Would you like a stocked bar in your room?"

"No, that won't be necessary," Maureen said, while mentally screaming *I plan on getting drunk in the bar. Just give me the room key!*

After a few minutes at the computer terminal, the desk clerk placed a charge receipt on the marble counter. "If you'll just sign here, Ms. Malone."

Ms. Malone signed quickly and scooped up the large key. "Thank you very much," she managed to say and headed for the bar, her head held high, her dignity still intact.

Well, barely.

She was on her fourth rum and Coke and absolutely sure every salesman in the bar knew she was meeting her future lover. Lover! Just thinking the word made her stomach muscles tighten with fear. She felt as if she had a neon brand on her forehead, flashing *About to Commit a Mortal Sin*. But it wasn't. Was it? She was separated. Matt was separated. They had actually talked about it, like mature sensible adults. And they both had a clean bill of health. She had done everything right so far.

And she wanted this, didn't she?

Didn't she?

Staring into her drink, Maureen felt his presence even before he sat down.

"Hi. Are you okay?"

She looked up and smiled. "I'm fine," she murmured, conscious of a tingling in her lips.

He was dressed in a suit and looked as if he had come from a business meeting. Knowing he had just finished the Six O'clock Sports, she simply continued to smile when a waitress came up to their table and asked Matt if he wanted a drink. He looked at Maureen's glass and ordered a beer.

"How many of them have you had?" he asked when the woman left.

"I believe this is my fourth."

"Fourth?" He appeared shocked. "Maureen, you don't drink."

She laughed. "I do tonight. Don't lecture me, Matt. I'm nervous enough."

He reached for her hand and held it. "We don't have to go through with this, you know."

"Oh, but we do. I mean I want to," she corrected. "If I don't, I'll always regret it." Taking a deep breath, she added, "I have enough things to regret in my life. I don't want you to be one of them."

"But if you're this nervous . . ."

"I know what I'm doing, Matt. Okay?"

The waitress brought his beer and Maureen watched him pour it into a tall glass. "Aren't you nervous?" she asked when they were alone.

"I'm not going to answer that," he said.

"You're not?"

Shaking his head, Matt grinned. "One of us ought to be calm and sober." He looked out to the bar. "How long do we have to stay here?"

She gulped the remainder of her rum and Coke and signaled the waitress for another. "Just until I get this drink."

"Maureen, what are you doing?" He was obviously shocked. "You're not used to drinking. You'll get sick. And knowing you, you'll take it as a sign from God that we weren't meant to be together."

Her head felt fuzzy and her lips continued to tingle, as if just kissed. Running her fingernail over her bottom lip, she smiled at Matt and knew she was finally relaxed. "I'm bringing this drink up to the room with me. I may not even touch it."

Matt quickly paid the bar tab and they stood up. Maureen felt a rush of dizziness and held onto the table for a few seconds until her equilibrium settled. Giving Matt a nod, she picked up the glass and said, "I'm ready."

She knew several people were staring at them as they walked out, but she told herself that it was because Matt was a celebrity and not that they were being obvious in their intentions. After four rum and Cokes, she really didn't care what anyone thought. Holding her head high, she walked beside Matt. Past the desk clerk. Past the new arrivals checking in. They stood in front of the elevators and Maureen whispered, "Are you afraid someone will gossip about you being here?"

Matt shook his head. "Most people aren't sure it's me, unless I speak with them. If this elevator would come, we wouldn't have to worry."

The doors opened and they walked inside. "I'm sorry," Maureen said. "You wanted to go to your apartment. I should have listened. It would have been more discreet."

He squeezed her shoulder. "We're here. Let's not think of anyone but us."

Maureen nodded and tried to swallow down the fear that was quickly returning with each floor they passed.

She handed him the key and watched as he opened the door to Room 528, knowing she would never forget the number.

Maureen walked in and flipped on the light. She looked around. It was nice . . . and serviceable. A loveseat was placed in front of the window, with a table and chair next to it. Except for the dresser, the rest of the room seemed filled with the massive bed. Didn't she ask for a queen size? Surely this bed was larger than hers at home. Unsure what to do, she placed her drink on the night table and dropped her purse onto the chair.

Matt was searching through the radio stations for one that played soft romantic music. When he found it, he turned to her and took off his suit jacket. "I'll be right back," he said, and headed for the bathroom.

Maureen knew her eyes had widened with apprehension and she told herself to relax her facial muscles. She swallowed deeply and nodded. "Okay," she said, surprised by the tremor in her voice.

She heard the bathroom fan begin to hum

when he turned on the light and closed the door. Oh God, this is so personal! She didn't want to hear the water running. She didn't want to hear him going to the bathroom. She didn't know him well enough . . .

"But you think you know him well enough to get into bed with him?" she muttered, closing the drapes and sitting on the mattress. Immediately, she jumped up and sat on one of the chairs. How could it be possible to feel like a virgin all over again? How pitiful. A forty-two year old virgin! Poor Matt.

Less than three minutes had passed until he walked back into the bedroom.

"Are you okay?" he asked, seeing her stricken expression.

Maureen nodded and stood up. Taking her purse with her, she passed him and said, "I'll just be a few minutes."

When she was safely behind the bathroom door Maureen leaned against it, clamped her eyes shut and took several deep, steadying breaths. Realizing Matt was waiting for her, she pushed herself forward and placed her huge shoulder bag on the vanity. Inside was everything she could think of to get through this night. Deodorant. Toothpaste. Feminine Hygiene Products. Makeup. Perfume. And an ivory silk teddy and matching kimono.

It was a lot longer than three minutes before she emerged from the bathroom.

A lot longer.

He had turned down the bed and was sitting in his baby blue boxer shorts when she walked back into the bedroom. Immediately, Matt stood up and came over to her. Maureen marveled at the ability of men to bare their bodies so easily, without any self-consciousness, while her own legs were shaking. She wanted to look sexy, but was afraid she looked like a female Sumo wrestler masquerading as Madame Butterfly.

"You look beautiful," he whispered, gathering her into his arms.

They kissed long and tenderly. It wasn't until Matt slid his finger under the material at her neck and tried to push the kimono down her shoulder that Maureen jerked back.

"No," she said, pulling the robe closer around her. "I want to leave it on."

He looked puzzled. "Leave it on?"

She nodded.

"But . . . but how? I mean, you have underwear on underneath it."

"The robe opens. See?" She draped it by her sides. "And this isn't underwear. It's called a teddy."

"But, Maureen . . . do you intend to make love with clothes on?"

She felt like crying. Instead, she bit the inside of her lip to cause her enough pain so that she wouldn't allow tears. "Please, Matt. Please let me do this my way. The teddy opens. It has snaps. Can we turn off the light?"

His brow furrowed. "What are you so afraid of? You're beautiful."

"Please, Matt. Just this once."

He shook his head and walked over to the window. "I'll turn off the light, but I'm opening the drapes. I want to see you. I've waited too long for this moment to have it in total darkness."

When he opened the drapes, Maureen went to the night table and picked up her drink. Taking a long, deep gulp, she sat on the edge of the mattress. She could see him in the moonlight as he walked up to her. He stood before her, caressing her hair, her face . . .

And then he did the most incredible thing. He knelt down in front of her. He was so tall that, even kneeling, his head was above hers.

Lifting her chin, she stared into his eyes as he whispered, "Don't be afraid."

She fought the tears that were building inside of her. "I'm sorry, Matt. I know I'm making this difficult—"

He kissed her lips to silence her. "Shh. Relax. Just let it happen. You're a beautiful, sensual woman and I want to make love to you." He kissed her temple. "Now spread your legs."

She stiffened. "What?"

He chuckled. "Wrong phrase. I just want to move closer to you. Your knees are digging into my stomach."

"Oh." Relaxing, Maureen slowly made room for him and both of them sighed with pleasure as the heat of his chest touched hers.

She wrapped her arms around him and caressed his back while his lips roamed over hers, softly, gently, slowly becoming more demanding. Their tongues met and tasted, feeling, licking, rolling and entwining. Maureen felt breathless when Matt pulled his mouth away from hers and traced a course down her jaw and her neck to the cleft between her breasts.

She ran her fingers through his hair as he untied the tiny satin ribbon of her teddy and kissed her breasts. Reveling in the intimacy, she closed her eyes and sighed deeply and happily.

"Lie back, Maureen," he whispered.

She opened her eyes. "What?"

"Just relax. Lie back on the bed."

Trusting him, she sank onto the crisp white sheet. He caressed her thighs, her knees, her calves. Every nerve ending on her skin came alive at his touch. It was slow and sensual, as if he wanted to familiarize himself with every inch of her. Lifting her leg, he turned his head and ran his tongue over her heel and ankle, making his way back up her leg. Maureen pulled herself up on her elbows and reached for his head to stop him.

"Matt, please. Don't . . ." she pleaded, knowing full well his intentions.

He lifted his head and, reaching for her hand, he kissed her palm. "Will you trust me?"

She wanted to. God knows she wanted to trust

him. But this . . . this was something her husband hadn't wanted to do and had avoided for twenty years. How could another man, a man she had only known for a few weeks, really want to?

"I just don't know," she murmured, tracing his lips with her fingers.

He captured them between his teeth and sucked her fingers deep into his mouth. The act was so erotic that Maureen could only stare at his face, as a wild yearning started deep within her.

"I'm going to make love to you, to all of you. I won't hurt you. If you want me to stop, I will. But we are going to try. Now lie back, or sit up and watch. Do whatever you want, Maureen. Just enjoy yourself. Enjoy your body, and me."

He held her leg up to his mouth and ran the tip of his tongue over the inside of her thigh. Almost squirming with desire, Maureen sighed deeply and collapsed back onto the bed.

One leg. Then the other. Always avoiding where they were joined together. He was driving her crazy and he knew it. She kept hoping, wanting, dreading, needing, him to make contact, yet it was only his hot breath that touched her as he passed over to explore her legs.

She was moaning aloud and she didn't even care. Her arms were above her head and she wrapped her fingers through her hair and held on, as if it might be the only thing keeping her anchored. It wasn't until she felt him unfasten the snaps of her teddy that she held her breath in an irrational mixture of fear and anticipation.

It was soft and wet and warm, and it was better than any fantasy she had ever had. "Oh my God," she groaned, as his mouth adored her. His tongue explored, tasting, feeling, flicking, until it settled in the place where she wanted him.

And then it started to happen, building slowly as he continued . . . over and over . . . faster and constant . . . until her body was off the bed, offering herself to him, begging him not to stop. She felt as if she were fighting to get out of her body, losing all self-control, as she ascended higher and higher, until she was suddenly exploding into a burst of exquisite, intense pleasure that went on and on, and on . . .

Slowly she came back to reality as tremors continued to pass through her. Never in her life had she experienced such pleasure, such intimacy, with another human being. Grateful to him, Maureen pulled him up to her and kissed him with an urgency that frightened her. She could taste herself on his lips, the scent of her mixing with her perfume, and it was so sexual that she whispered into his mouth, "I want you, Matt. I want you inside of me now."

She became the aggressor, pulling off his shorts, impatient for him to lie down on the bed. Before he could touch her or kiss her again, she straddled him and held her breath as he slid easily into her. He moaned with pleasure and suddenly Maureen became a different woman. She was

341

confident, self-assured, and knew she was desirous.

"My God, Maureen," Matt whispered. "I've never seen anybody react like that."

"And now it's your turn," she answered, running her fingernails over his chest and through the soft silky hair that covered it.

The robe slid off one shoulder and her breast was exposed, but she didn't mind. She stared at the man before her and knew that he cared for her . . . just the way she was. She didn't have to be younger, or thinner, or prettier. She just had to be herself.

And for the first time in her life that's who she was. Maureen Henessey. Not daughter. Not wife. Not mother, or author. Just a woman, discovering her true self. This was starting over, without any preconceptions.

This was freedom.

It was a sacred dance of lovemaking and they participated as one, moving together naturally, spontaneously, until she led him with her over the edge. Maureen's only regret was that she couldn't read the expression on Matt's face as he called out her name.

She collapsed next to him and he gathered her into his arms. He sighed gently. "I knew it was going to be good between us, Maureen. I just never imagined how good." He brushed the tendrils of damp hair off her forehead and tenderly kissed her temple. "There's so much I want to say to you, but I know it's too soon."

She took several deep breaths and ran her hand over the smooth skin of his back. "Don't say anything. Don't promise me anything. And don't even think about the "L" word. It isn't a part of my vocabulary anymore."

He closed his eyes and shook his head, as if saddened by her statement. Holding her closer, he whispered above her head. "He hurt you that much?"

She felt tears come into her eyes and nodded. "He took away all my beliefs—about myself and about my life. But maybe it wasn't such a terrible thing. If I didn't go through all that pain, I wouldn't be here with you. And I would have missed so much, Matt." She kissed his chest. "Thank you for tonight, for giving me back myself."

His lips were warm and tender on her forehead. "You made the decision. I know you were scared, but you did it anyway. And considering the last hour, I should be thanking you."

She was pleased with his answer and couldn't stop the giggle. "It *was* pretty good."

"Are you kidding? It was phenomenal." He laughed and hugged her with affection. "You know, I was a little worried myself."

"You? Why?"

He shrugged. "I hate to admit this, but you are the shortest woman I've ever been with. And well,

343

I thought we wouldn't fit together right, or something."

Maureen smiled. "I'm glad I wasn't the only insecure person in this bed. I do think, however, that we put your fear to rest."

"We certainly did. Now what about your worries? When are you going to take off this robe? Don't you think it's pretty silly, considering what we've just experienced?"

She shook her head. "I can't. Not yet."

"Why? What did he do to you?"

He sat up against the pillows and she put her head on his chest. As if it were the most natural thing in the world, Matt started to caress her hair as she began to tell him . . .

"Eight years ago I went to my doctor for a routine office visit. I thought everything was fine until I got a call a few days later. My Pap smear showed the possibility of cervical cancer. To make a long story short, some of the doctors thought I had it and others told me it was a precancerous condition. I was so scared. I thought my life was over. I had even picked out my best dress to be buried in." She cringed, remembering the painful time in her life.

"I kept thinking about the twins and who would take care of them. I guess I was a basket case. I couldn't eat or sleep. I just kept thinking that my life was over and there was so much I would miss. Graduations and weddings and grandchildren . . . Anyway, my doctor said I could have a hysterectomy and the cancer would be gone. I thought how grateful I was to have two healthy children and that I really didn't want any more so I told him to schedule it. But while I was on the phone it occurred to me that I was feeling queasy all the time. I thought it was stress, but my doctor said I should have a blood test before I came to the hospital."

She felt the lump in her throat cut off her next words, and she forced herself to get past it. "I found out that day that I was pregnant. I had cancer and I was pregnant. It was a nightmare that wouldn't end."

"God, Maureen, what did you do?"

She shook her head. "I didn't do anything. I couldn't. I remember getting the phone call from the lab and sinking to the kitchen floor. I must have stared at the refrigerator for half an hour. That's where Dan found me when he came home. He said the decision was mine, but he thought I should terminate the pregnancy."

Wiping the tears from her eyes, Maureen sniffled and Matt kissed the top of her head. "Maybe it's easier for a man," she finally said. "But for a woman it's so physical and emotional. I couldn't say take this mixture of cells out of my body because I don't want it. I would wake up in the middle of the night and look at the twins while they slept and sob for that poor creature I carried, the child I knew I couldn't give life to. But I simply couldn't make the decision. It had nothing to do with being Catholic. It had everything to do with being a woman, and knowing I'd never be able to have another child."

"What happened?"

"After four days of constant grief, Dan came home from work. I was standing at the kitchen sink and he walked up behind me and put his arms around me. He said enough was enough and he was making the decision. He got on the phone and called the doctor and made all the arrangements. All I had to do was show up." She was crying freely as the memories flooded back at her. "No matter what he's done, or how much he's destroyed, I will always be grateful to him for that, for taking that terrible decision away from me."

"It's all right," Matt soothed. "You're allowed to love him. He was your husband for almost twenty years. There have to be good memories mixed with the bad."

"But he couldn't handle what happened to me later. He was turned off by the scar and that my body was different. I was never thin, but my metabolism changed after the operation. He made me feel, I don't know, deformed. That there was something wrong with me. Our sex life took a definite turn for the worse. Then he got busy with his job. I sold a few books and my career took off. And neither one of us took the time to face what was happening. I guess it all just fell apart . . ."

"It happens," Matt murmured, and Maureen knew he was thinking about his own marriage. His wife and his daughter.

Silence filled the small room.

"God, Maureen, what a nightmare you've been through, but I'm glad you told me," Matt said gently, and hugged her to his chest. "It explains a lot."

She sniffled and wiped at her eyes. "It does?"

"Sure. Now I know why you insisted on keeping clothing on during lovemaking. I just thought you were kinky, or something."

In spite of everything, she laughed. "You do make me laugh, Matt Shannon. And I need laughter. I've missed it."

"Anything to accommodate."

Raising her head, she kissed his cheek. "I'll be right back. I want to use the bathroom."

She hurried down the short hallway and closed the bathroom door. Turning on the cold water to muffle any sounds, she rushed to the toilet. Glad she had left her shoulder bag in the small room, Maureen brought out several items to freshen up. Minutes later, as she was brushing her hair, she looked at her reflection in the mirror.

"I can't believe I actually did it," she whispered to herself.

"I can't believe it either. What's wrong with you, Maureen? How long have you known this guy, and you jump into the sack with him?"

Her eyes widened with shock. Her hand froze

347

in mid air, as she spun around to face him.

"Bobby! What the hell are you *doing* here?"

He shook his head, as if disappointed with her. "That's my question exactly."

Chapter Seventeen

"This is unforgivable! How *dare* you?"

Bobby crossed his arms over his chest and stared at her. "Maureen, what the hell are you doing here? Do you have any idea what you're getting into?"

"What business is it of yours?" she demanded, wrapping her robe tightly around her. Mortified that he should witness this night, Maureen tried to control the trembling of her chin. "Get *out* of here! How could you intrude like this?" Her voice was a hoarse whisper of outrage. "This is *my* night. Do you understand? And you're not going to screw it up for me!"

"Somebody's got to talk to you. He isn't the answer—"

"I never thought he was," she interrupted.

"It has to come from inside of you."

"Oh, go away, Bobby. I'm tired of listening to your sixties version of wisdom. I've got a life here and I'm trying to get through it. God, this is so embarrassing! Why do you keep popping up in bathrooms? Especially *this* bathroom. Tonight—"

"Maureen? Are you okay?"

She and Bobby both turned to the door. It was Matt.

Maureen glared at Bobby and cleared her throat. "Yes, I'm fine," she said in a voice that hopefully sounded normal. "I—ah—I sometimes talk to myself. I'll be right out."

Bobby rolled his eyes, as if making fun of Matt. "Oh, brother . . ."

She was so angry that she punched Bobby's arm. "Will you get the hell out of my life?" she demanded through clenched teeth. "I know what I'm doing."

He was rubbing the spot where she'd hit him. "No you don't, Maureen. You only think you do."

Making a childish face, she turned back to the mirror to see if she appeared normal. What must Matt be thinking, hearing her muttering all by herself in the bathroom? "I'm telling you one last time, leave me alone and get out of—" When she looked over her shoulder Bobby was gone.

"Good," she whispered, and took several deep breaths before opening the bathroom door. Imagine the nerve of the guy! Popping up *here*! On this night! Shaking off all thoughts of Bobby O'Connor, Maureen walked back into the bedroom.

She made sure, however, to keep the bathroom light on for the rest of the evening.

Ten of two. My God, she had never come home this late. Driving down her street, she wondered if the children would wake up. And what she would tell them. As she neared her driveway, she applied the brakes and stared at the rental car in front of her house.

It was Dan's.

Closing her eyes, she took a deep breath and tried to stay calm. Just what she needed. Another confrontation.

She pulled into the driveway, locked her car, and walked up to the front door.

There was silence.

Turning off the light in the living room, she proceeded into the kitchen. It was when she placed her shoulder bag on the table that she heard him.

"Where have you been? Do you know what time it is?"

Dan was sitting in the family room and she turned around to face him. "I'm not one of the children with a curfew. A more important question is why are you here?"

He looked tired and rumpled, as if he had fallen asleep while waiting for her. "I came to see the kids."

She glanced toward the stairway. "I imagine

they've been in bed for hours. So I'll repeat my question. Why are you still here?"

"I wanted to talk to you. Where were you?"

"Out."

"I know you were out, Maureen."

She refused to allow him to ruin this night. "What is it you wanted to say?"

He was staring at her and Maureen felt he could surely see where she had been and what she'd been doing. The glow of sexual fulfillment had to be written all over her face.

"I wanted to talk to you about the kids' birthday. They said you were giving them a party."

"That's right. And driving lessons." He didn't know! It didn't even cross his mind that his wife, his separated wife, had just been to bed with another man. That stung her even more than a confrontation. As far as Dan was concerned, her sexuality wasn't even an issue. Only his counted.

"Look," she said, trying to control her voice. "It's late. We can discuss this another time. I want to go to bed—go to sleep," she corrected. "I have to work tomorrow, and so do you."

Coming into the kitchen, he stood in front of her and examined her face. He was staring at her lips when he said, "You never told me where you were tonight."

Now she knew what thoughts were starting to churn around in his brain and she wondered if her slip of the tongue was really an accident. Did she want him to know?

"It's none of your business where I was tonight. It stopped being your business when you left this home . . . and this marriage." She picked up her bag and added, "Why don't you call me tomorrow about the birthday party and we can discuss it? It's late and I think you should leave."

They stared at each other for the longest time, neither saying a word, until Dan nodded and picked up his jacket. She followed him to the front door and locked it behind him. She didn't even wait until he reached his car before shutting off the porch light.

Snuggled beneath the warm comforter, Maureen smiled as she recalled the evening with Matt. It had turned out even better than her fantasies. And she now knew a secret, one that made her grin even wider. Dan Malone wasn't the great lover that he thought he was. In fact, he had a lot to learn about pleasing a woman.

How ironic that had he left her to find passion and happiness, and she was the one to find it.

Maybe there was justice in this world after all. Closing her eyes, she immediately fell into a deep and dreamless sleep.

Maureen stood in the hallway and listened to her children.

"But I don't want to meet him. I don't care who he is. I'm going to be rude and embarrass her so much that we'll have to leave."

"Oh, Josh, knock it off. We owe it to her to meet him. I don't know about you, but I want to check him out. She's been dating him for over a month now. Don't you think it's time?"

"But what about Dad?"

"What about him?" Abbie asked. "Do you honestly think he's staying in his apartment every night? Why do you think he left to begin with?"

"What do you mean? They were fighting all the time—"

"Get real," his sister demanded. "All those nights he came home late. He was cheating on Mom before he ever left."

"He was not!" Josh defended his father. "Mom said he left because he was unhappy and he needed to . . . to find himself."

"Oh, c'mon. What was she supposed to say to us? Sorry, kids, your dad is screwing around and I can't live like that? She was protecting him, and us. Use your brain, Josh. It all adds up."

Walking to the front of the hall, Maureen called out, "Are you two ready? We're going to be late." She couldn't believe her children were discussing her like that. She was nearly overwhelmed with apprehension. Josh was going to go out of his way to be rude! She thought about talking to him, but then decided to play it by ear. They were her children, and probably as nervous as she was.

Maureen watched as they came out of Abbie's room and forced a smile. "Hey," she said cheerfully. "It's only dinner." Abbie smiled back at her but Josh was dragging his feet as if he were being led to an execution.

"I can't stay all night. I have to study for a geometry test," he mumbled.

Maureen patted his shoulder as he passed in front of her. "Okay. We have dinner and we leave. I appreciate you both coming with me tonight."

The kids nodded and Maureen sighed deeply as they all walked out of the house. This was going to be a long night. For all of them.

Even though it was still early spring, the weather felt like winter. Dressed in a heavy overcoat, Matt was waiting for them outside the restaurant.

"Why didn't he go inside?" Josh asked as they found a parking space. "Pretty stupid to wait in the cold."

"I think it's nice," Abbie answered. "It shows he's a gentleman."

Josh made a face at his sister as they got out of the car. "It shows he's got no brains."

Maureen locked the car and looked at her children. "Please, let's all try and get along. Okay? Do this for me. It's only a couple of hours."

Abbie nodded and gave her brother a meaningful glance.

In return, Josh shot his sister a disgusted look before saying, "Yeah. Sure. Why not?"

If it were possible, Maureen was more nervous about this evening than meeting Matt at the Hilton that first time. In the last six weeks they had been together almost every night. They went to the movies and the theater. He took her to the Art Museum, where they had stood in awe of the great masters and then giggled over the modern art. They joined the crowds on South Street in Philly and browsed through the strange little shops, devouring Italian water ice along with everyone else. They took in sporting events and concerts, but Maureen's favorite times were the quiet evenings when Matt would cook dinner for her and they would watch television and then make love in his king size bed.

She held a deep fear that she was becoming a sex addict, for during the week he had been at spring training, her limbs had actually ached for him. She had found herself aroused just speaking to him on the phone when he called her every night from Florida.

But now he was home. And the first thing he had asked to do was meet her children.

He smiled as they walked up to him.

"Matt, I'd like you to meet my daughter, Abbie, and my son, Josh." She watched as Matt shook hands with her children.

"Abbie, I've heard so much about you. Here . . ." With his left hand he brought out a pink rose with baby's breath and handed it to her.

"Thank you," Abbie breathed, clearly pleased.

Matt turned to her son. He grinned as he reached into the pocket of his overcoat. "Your mom told me how you've been following Ricky

Jordan's career since the minor leagues." He placed a new baseball in Josh's palm. "I picked this up at spring training."

Josh held the ball up to the light outside the restaurant. "Oh my God, Mom . . . look at this!"

She read the autograph. *For Josh, my biggest fan. Regards, Ricky Jordan.* Handing the baseball back to her son, she glanced at Matt and her eyes almost filled with tears.

"That's great, Josh," she said. He wasn't buying her kid's affections. He just knew what would break the ice and was doing what came naturally to him . . . being nice.

"Hey," Matt said. "I've already checked. Our table is ready. Let's go in where it's warm."

Everyone agreed, and somehow she found herself walking with Abbie in front of Josh and Matt, while her son talked a mile a minute to the man he never intended to like.

"How'd he do in spring training?"

"Not bad," Matt answered as they waited to be seated. "But he's going to have to work for his position at first base. This is going to be a tough year rebuilding the Phillies . . ."

Sniffing her rose, Abbie leaned closer to Maureen and whispered, "He's nice, Mom. And Josh—I don't think you have anything to worry about."

Maureen put her arm around her daughter's shoulders and kissed her temple. "Thanks, honey. I know you helped me out on this one."

357

Abbie looked up at her mother and grinned. "Hey, you're happy. I'd have to be blind not to see that."

It was a strange moment. Her son and her lover were deep in conversation about baseball and she and her daughter had just conversed like two women.

Times were certainly changing.

And then she looked at Matt, grinning at her son's rapid questions. He had wanted this meeting, even pushed for it, and now she knew the reason. He missed his family. If he couldn't have his own back, perhaps being with hers would take away some of the pain and longing.

The phone rang, waking her up, and she squinted toward the alarm clock. Twelve twenty-three. Who in the world . . . ?

Picking up the receiver, she hoped her father was all right. "Hello?"

"Maureen, were you asleep?"

She laid back against the pillow and let out her breath. "Yes, Dan, I was. Is something wrong?"

"Can I come over and talk to you?"

"Now?"

"I know it's late, but I need to talk to you."

"Where are you?" she asked, hearing the slur of his speech. He'd been drinking.

"I'm up at the 7-Eleven. I can be there in three minutes. Please. We have to talk."

She could hear the desperation in his voice and reluctantly said, "All right. I'll unlock the front door."

She hung up the phone, got up and put on her robe. She brushed her hair and then walked through her silent house, flipping on the kitchen light and the one on the porch.

She was boiling water for tea when he came in the front door. He walked into the kitchen and she turned around to face him. "What's going on, Dan?"

He looked tired and rumpled, his suit jacket hanging open. Sitting down at the table, he tried grinning at her. "I need to talk to you."

The grin didn't work. Maureen poured out the tea and placed the mug before him. Sitting down, she crossed her arms on the table and said, "Okay, let's talk. What's wrong?"

He played with the tea bag, staring into the mug as if mesmerized. Finally, he raised his head. "I can't believe you're dating someone."

Her face remained expressionless. She'd been waiting for this discussion. "And why is that? You find it hard to believe that someone else is interested in me?"

"No, that's not it. But this, this television person—"

"His name is Matt," she interrupted.

"Matt. Matt Shannon. Christ, it's probably not even his real name."

"I believe it is," she said calmly. "What is it you

want to discuss?"

He looked like he was going to cry. "How can you have this affair with him? You're still my wife."

She could only blink for a few seconds before her voice kicked in. "Excuse me? I'm still your *wife?* Are you saying that I should respect our marriage vows even though we've been separated almost six months, when you never respected them while you were living here with me?"

He shook his head. "I never had an affair. I only had one night stands—"

"Oh, so in your mind it's all right if you're just out there looking for sex," she interjected. "But because I'm involved in a relationship, you find it unacceptable. Do you realize how sick that sounds? You'd rather I pick up a string of men in singles bars then be happy, secure and safe with one?"

His jaw clenched and she knew he didn't like her response. "I'm just saying that you're still legally my wife. And I don't like the fact that this man is coming into my home, eating food I pay for and taking my son out to the goddamned batting cages. They're *my* kids, not his. And you're still my wife."

"First of all, you pay the mortgage and the gas and electric. That's it. I pay for the food and everything else to run this home. And you're not here. That was your choice, remember? Tryouts for baseball are next week and Josh asked him to go to the batting cages." Staring at him, it suddenly came to her. "You're not angry with me for being involved with another man. That isn't it, is it? You're jealous of him, because he's more successful than you. Because your kids get along with him. And because Abbie probably told you that he makes me happy. I know the kids have talked to you. How else would you know about the batting cages?"

He was looking at her with an expression of near hatred. "I just want that man to stay away from my kids. Christ, Maureen, you want to sleep with the guy, do it. Just know he's only in it for the sex. I thought you'd have more respect for yourself than that."

"It won't work, Dan," she said with a steady voice. "You can't manipulate me any more. You see, you judge everyone else by your own motives. *You* may be only looking for sex, to make yourself feel young again, but there really are men out there who want more." She stood, and picked up his untouched mug of tea. "Now I think you'd better go."

As she watched him leave she knew she didn't want to spend the rest of her life with this man. It was so strange. Six months ago she had been devastated when he'd walked out of her life. Now, when she looked at him, she felt only sadness. It was as if he were her brother, someone she had lived with for a long time.

When did it happen? When did she fall out of

love with him?

"Do you love him?"

Sighing, Maureen looked at the late spring peonies that bloomed with a brilliant profusion outside her kitchen window. In a few weeks, when summer began, they would disappear. "I don't know," she whispered, trying to remember what Bobby had once said to her about blooming like a flower. Wasn't it something about turning her face up to the sun? Bobby. She hadn't seen him since that first night at the Hilton. Maybe he was gone for good. Would that make her happy? She honestly didn't know.

"You are not paying attention, and that was a very important question." Lisa picked up her coffee and sat back in her chair. "Well, you look like you're in love, and you certainly act like it. My vote is you are."

Turning to face her friend, Maureen shook her head. "But I don't want to be in love. I don't want the inevitable heartache that comes with it."

"Hey, that's life. Would you rather have not known Matt?"

"Never." Her answer was immediate. "He makes me happy." She actually giggled. "He makes me happy and crazy. We laugh all the time. We go out and he makes me feel special and pretty. He even reads my work. Dan never read anything I had written."

"How do the kids feel about him?"

Maureen smiled. "I can't believe it. Abbie likes him. The two of them cook dinner together at least once a week. And Josh—well, Josh has found a soul mate. They're constantly talking sports or telling jokes, or out playing basketball. He even goes to some of Josh's high school baseball games. He sits out in the outfield so no one will recognize him. Sometimes I'm actually jealous of the time he spends with my son. That's sick, isn't it?"

Lisa laughed. "No. I'm telling you, you're in love."

Maureen covered her face with her hands and shook her head. "I can't be. It isn't possible. I'm forty-three years old and I feel like a teenager."

"It's love."

She looked at her dearest friend. "Will you please stop saying that?"

"Okay." Lisa sipped her coffee and grinned at Maureen. "Then tell me about the sex. Is it good? It has to be if you're in love." She covered her mouth with her fingers. "Oops. Sorry. Slip of the tongue. To hell with love, what's the sex like?"

"None of your business!" Maureen answered, clearly embarrassed.

"Hey, we had a pact. Remember? I support you in whatever you do and in return I get to live vicariously. Give me a break, Maureen, it's been two and a half years. Do you know that I ride by one of those tacky little adult bookstores every day to work? Lately, I've actually been considering going in and seeing if they have a vibrator. I'm getting desperate," she said to her laughing friend. "So save me the humiliation of doing business with those people and spill your guts about this media guy. Every man fantasizes about going to bed with Madonna or Elle McPherson, and women dream of Mel Gibson or Tom Selleck. Or is it just us thirty and fortysomething babes who still go for Selleck?"

Still chuckling, Maureen wiped at her eyes. "I wonder what all those corporate execs would think if they ever heard you talk like this."

Lisa laughed. "They wouldn't believe it from the Iron Skirt, as they lovingly call me. Heck, you're the only one I let my hair down with, so don't disappoint me." She held her spoon in her hand like a microphone. "What is Mr. Matt Shannon, Channel Seven Sports, like in the sack?"

Giving up, Maureen sighed. "He's not Tom Selleck, but he is wonderful."

Lisa held the spoon to Maureen's chin, as if interviewing her. "Oh, golly gee whiz. He's wonderful. How boring. I want details, girl."

Maureen pushed the spoon away. "I don't know. He's gentle and romantic and exciting. He's discovered erogenous zones on my body that I didn't even know existed."

"Yeah? Like where? This is more like it."

Maureen grinned at her friend. "Like the small of my back. When he runs his tongue across the small of—"

"Oh God, his tongue . . ." Lisa groaned.

Waving her hand through the air, Maureen said, "I'm not telling you any more."

"Oh, please. Please." Lisa looked truly penitent. "I promise I won't interrupt anymore. Remember you'll be saving your best friend from the degradation found inside one of those tawdry shops. Besides, I've always suspected that the soles of everybody's shoes must stick to the floor from certain bodily emissions. And you know I always wear really good shoes to work."

Maureen burst into laughter. "Will you stop it? We both know you would never go into one of those places, but the picture of you in sun glasses and a bad wig and trying to purchase a vibrator will stay with me for months."

Laughing along with Maureen, Lisa somehow managed to get out, "I'm desperate! Try being celibate for almost three years. No wonder monks always have their hands buried in their robes. This is not a natural state!"

"Okay, I'll tell you about an argument we had last week."

"What? I don't want to hear about a fight."

Maureen smiled. "I don't think you'll be disappointed."

Picking up her cold coffee, Lisa definitely looked disappointed.

"We were at his apartment," Maureen began. "Everything was great. Or I thought it was great, but then he stopped . . . Well, I guess I should tell you that I've never been nude with him."

"What?" Lisa's jaw hung open. "How long have you been dating this guy?"

Maureen nodded. "A long time. I know, but I have this thing, this hang up. I always wear a silk blouse and keep it open. God, I must have bought a dozen new blouses since I've met him. Well, anyway, Matt stopped right in the middle of making love and insisted that I take off my blouse."

"About time," Lisa announced and then shook her head, as if apologizing for interrupting again.

Maureen ignored her. "I tried to make a joke out of it, but he refused to be put off. He kept after me, telling me it wasn't funny anymore, that it was weird, and I jumped out of bed and started to find my clothes. I was crying, telling him I couldn't take any more adventures. I mean, the things he's taught me . . . I'm not just talking about positions. I'm talking about discovering my body and his . . . I can't believe how naive I was."

"Yeah? So?" Lisa was now clearly interested. "What happened?"

"He got out of bed and grabbed the panties out of my hand. He said he'd come to hate my blouses. That he felt there were three people in bed every time we made love. Him. Me. And Dan. That it was Dan who made me feel self-conscious about my body, and he, Matt, was paying the price. Every time he touched one of my blouses, he thought of Dan and how he had put this barrier between us. He told me I was beautiful, that he couldn't believe how lucky he was to be with me, and that I was special, all of me, even those things Dan thought of as imperfections. And then . . ." Maureen's throat almost closed as she pictured the scene in her mind. "And then he knelt down in front of me and . . . and kissed my . . . my scar. He kissed it and I could feel the tenderness in his lips. I swear, Lisa, I couldn't believe it. I started sobbing like a baby and he just held me and I held him."

Lisa swiped at the tears rolling down her cheeks. "Oh God, what did you do then?"

Smiling, Maureen blinked away her own tears. "I took off my blouse."

After clearing her throat, Lisa muttered, "Damn, Maureen, if you don't love him, I think I will."

Maureen could only stare at her friend as the truth rushed in on her, slamming into her brain with the force of a Mack Truck. She couldn't deny it any longer. "What am I going to do?" she whispered, her chin quivering with the realization.

No explanations were needed as Lisa reached across the table and squeezed her hand. "You're going to love him and be happy. For as long as it lasts. You deserve it."

"But there are so many complications. His

daughter. My kids. His wife. Dan. I know we're both separated, but . . . Did I tell you Dan came over here in the middle of the night to lecture me? He said I was still his wife. That Matt shouldn't come here, be in his house, or with his children—"

"Hey, did I ever explain my theory that men are like dogs?"

Lisa always had the ability to make a confusing situation even more confusing. "Dogs?" Maureen asked, not seeing the connection.

"Sure. They're like male dogs that lift their leg to mark their territory."

"Oh, Lisa, really."

"Wait. Then they feel free to walk away, secure that no other male would dare to trespass. And when one does, they can't believe it. I think it threatens their position in the pack, or something."

Maureen wasn't sure whether the moisture at her eyes was from laughter or fear.

She was in love. Again. For the first time in twenty years.

It was most definitely fear.

Chapter Eighteen

Matt was sitting at the kitchen table playing poker with Josh and Mike when she walked into the room. He glanced up at her and winked. "Loser has to make a crank phone call."

"And he's losing," Mike announced before throwing out a couple of cards. "I'll take two," he said to Josh.

Her son dealt out the cards. "How about you, Matt?"

"I'll take three," Matt said, and Josh and Mike started laughing.

"This is it," Mike pronounced. "The moment of truth. Matt's broke. If he doesn't win this one, he's got to make the call."

Maureen again thought how desperately Matt wanted to be part of a family and how much he must miss his own. He talked constantly about Kelly and seemed wistful about his lost family and dreams. She always listened in silence, unsure how to help him.

Maureen pushed it out of her mind. She grinned and walked closer to the table as everyone showed their hand. Matt Shannon may be a lot of things, she thought. But he certainly wasn't lucky at cards.

"Okay," Josh said gleefully as he stood up and handed Matt the phone. "You gotta crank somebody."

Maureen stepped in. "All right. Enough. No one is making a crank call from this house."

Matt pushed his chair back and stood beside her. Taking the phone from Josh, he said, "Hey. A deal's a deal."

"You are not going to do this," Maureen insisted, using her mother voice. Josh and Mike were still laughing.

Matt shrugged and punched in random numbers. "I can't back out now, Maureen. I won't be obscene, or anything. Wait! Quiet!" He held his hand up for silence and the boys watched him with naughty expectation.

"Hello? Is this the lady of the house? Yes?"

Maureen shook her head and walked back to the sink, leaving the three males to the phone.

"This is John . . . Wooley. I'm calling to introduce a new lawn service that fertilizes and cuts your grass at the same time. No. I'm serious. It's ecologically safe and has been around for centuries, and it's just now being rediscovered by smart home owners like yourself."

There was a pause as the woman actually answered Matt and Maureen shook her head, although she had to bite the inside of her lip not to laugh with the kids.

"No, Ma'am. It doesn't cost much at all. Are you interested? You are? The name of our company?"

He paused for effect.

"We call ourselves *Sheep Are Us!*"

The boys nearly fell over each other laughing while Matt kept repeating into the phone, "Hello? Hello?"

Hanging up the receiver, he accepted the pats on the back from Josh and Mike and looked to Maureen, as if apologizing. "I had to do it."

She couldn't help it. She laughed. It was so stupid, it was funny. He was always making her laugh, and she felt young and happy . . . and in love.

"Hey," Matt said, "let's all go to Baltimore."

Maureen stopped laughing. "Baltimore?" she asked in disbelief. She looked to the clock on the wall. "It's almost four o'clock."

"I know, but if we leave now we can be at Memorial Stadium before they throw out the first ball."

Josh and Mike agreed. "All right! Let's go," Josh announced.

Mike picked up the phone. "I'll call my mom."

"Wait a minute!" Maureen interrupted. "You want to drive three hours just to see a ball game?"

Matt gave her one of those little boys looks, and she knew why he got along so well with her son. Neither one of them had grown up yet. "Oh, c'mon, Maureen. What else did you have planned for tonight?"

She thought about it. "Well, nothing, but—"

"Then let's do it."

She knew when she was defeated. Shrugging, she watched as Mike grabbed the phone and got permission.

Three and a half hours later, she and Matt left the boys in their seats behind third base to get hot dogs and Cokes. She was at the refreshment stand preparing seven hot dogs while Matt was trying to find a way to carry four large Cokes.

"What did Mike want on his?" she asked. "Mustard and ketchup?" She shuddered as she squirted the runny yellow stuff down one side of the hot dog. "How can anyone eat this?"

"He's young. He can eat anything."

She tried to remember everyone's order. Josh's was mustard, relish and onions. Matt only wanted mustard, with just a tiny bit of relish on one side. There was more liquid than substance in the mustard container and Maureen shook it up while spooning on the relish.

"Oh, no!" She looked down to her pale blue tee shirt. Several lines of yellow streaked the front.

Matt took one look at her and started laughing.

She glared at him as she reached for the napkins. "It's not funny."

"Yes, it is," he said. "You are the clumsiest woman I have ever known."

"I am not!"

"Yes, you are. That's one of the reasons why I love you."

She stopped mopping up the mustard and stared at him. "What did you say?"

He was smiling at her. "I know. I said the terrible "L" word. And I don't care. You have to know how I feel about you. Why can't I say it? I want to get on the PA system and announce it to all of Baltimore."

"You love me?" she asked stupidly.

Still grinning, he nodded. "I think I must have fallen in love with you when you hit me with your raincoat. I love you, Maureen Malone. And I don't give a damn who knows it."

"Well, congratulations," a man wearing an Orioles tee shirt said. "Now could I have the mustard?"

Maureen shoved the container into the man's hand and rushed into Matt's arms. "I love you, too," she whispered, fighting back tears. "And I'm still so damn scared."

Squeezing her tightly, Matt kissed the top of her head. "What's there to be scared about? We're only saying out loud what we've both known for months. Don't be afraid of love, Maureen. Let's be happy."

Happy? Could she allow herself that freedom, knowing what must surely follow? For love doesn't last. Life had taught her that. And she was opening herself up to heartache. But hadn't she already done that when she'd allowed him into her life and into her heart? Lifting her face, she gazed into his eyes.

"I do love you, Matt Shannon," she said while strangers milled past them.

The look in his eyes spoke volumes. "Too bad we have such lousy timing. We couldn't be back at my apartment when we finally put the rest of the letters behind the *L?*" Shrugging his shoulders, he shook his head. "No, I do it in the middle of Memorial Stadium. Well, I'm at least going to kiss you."

He leaned down and his mouth captured hers.

Breaking apart, they heard the beginning of the National Anthem and the two of them started laughing as they looked at Matt's shirt.

It was smeared in mustard.

"Look what I've done," Maureen said.

"I know what you've done," Matt answered. "And I wouldn't take back a minute of it."

Grinning like two teenagers with a secret, they finished fixing the hot dogs and returned to the boys.

The ride home was interminable. Maureen kept looking into the back seat, hoping that Mike and Josh would fall asleep. But they didn't. Frustration was sharp as a razor, slicing through her and making her silent. She wanted to snuggle against Matt as he drove. He held her hand, running his fingers over hers, yet she had an almost desperate need to touch him, to be close to him, . . . to make love to him. And listening to two teenaged boys in the back seat playing baseball trivia was not her idea of foreplay.

It was well past one o'clock before they arrived home. Mike was sleeping over and he and Josh thanked Matt before going upstairs. They were both dragging their feet and Maureen knew it would be only minutes before they fell asleep. She checked on Abbie and when she returned to the foyer, Matt was standing at the steps.

She almost slid into his arms. "I have waited all night for this," she murmured against his neck.

His hands moved up and down her back, only to settle on her hips. Pulling her into him, he muttered, "It's late. Too late for you to come to my apartment."

His lips found hers and he kissed her deeply.

"But I want you, Matt," she said.

"And I want you," he answered. "What can we do?"

She thought of her children sleeping upstairs and made a decision. "We can make love here."

"Here? Are you sure?"

"We've been going to your apartment for months now. This is my house. And the kids never wake up. I've waited through a baseball game and a three hour ride home. I don't want to wait any longer." *Yes, yes, you are definitely a sex addict,* she thought, for nothing save her children's appearance was going to stop her.

He stared at her for a few seconds before saying, "Take off your jeans and sit down."

"Sit down?"

"On the top step."

She pulled off her jeans and underpants and threw them on the rug. Sitting down, she waited for him.

"Now lie back," he ordered in a rough voice.

With only her bra and tee shirt on, she did as he requested. She knew what he wanted, what he was going to do. And, God help her, she wanted it, too. Even if it was on her foyer steps.

As he made love to the most intimate part of her, Maureen listened to the crickets while remembering how Matt told her that he loved her. He loved her. Matt Shannon loved her. As incredible as it seemed, it was true. Rising up on her elbows she watched him and knew this night would be branded into her memory. It was more than special.

It was a keeper.

In the weeks that followed Maureen was never happier. Being in love changed her in ways that she never thought possible. She was carefree and it showed. Even the kids remarked on it and she hid a secret smile. She and Matt did everything together. Every spare minute was spent in each other's company. Movies. Ball games. Late night walks on the banks of the Delaware River. He spent more and more time at her house, leaving after David Letterman was over. They were settling in, becoming a couple. Life couldn't have been better. Even her writing flowed and she was ready to send out the proposal for the mainstream. When Matt talked about moving in with her and the children, she actually considered it. How wonderful it would be to wake up to him every morning. Ah, yes, love. Who was it that said love is an exploding cigar we willingly smoke? She couldn't remember. And even if she did, she wouldn't have listened.

"Abbie. Josh. This is Kelly, Matt's daughter."

Maureen made the introductions and watched as her children said hello. Kelly, tiny, blond, with wide blue eyes just like her father's, stared back. The five-year-old held Matt's hand in a tight grip and turned her face into his leg.

"She's shy," Matt said, as if explaining why she had done the same thing at the front door when she'd met Maureen.

"That's okay," Maureen said gently, wanting to make the child as comfortable as possible. "It's not easy meeting three people all at once. Why don't we just go to the restaurant? I bet Kelly's as hungry as the rest of us."

Everyone got up and followed Matt and Kelly out the front door. "You know," Maureen added, "I've heard this place has great desserts, especially the ice cream. Almost as many flavors as Baskin Robbins. Do you like ice cream, Kelly?"

The child didn't answer.

Dinner was strained as everyone tried to include Kelly in the conversation. But Kelly was silent. The only time she spoke was to whisper to her father what she wanted to eat. She struggled with her spaghetti and Maureen found that she was clasping her hands together to stop herself from helping the child. Instinct told her that Kelly would not have appreciated the offer. Finally, Matt pulled his daughter's chair close to his and cut up the spaghetti into small pieces for her. When dessert came, Kelly climbed up onto her daddy's lap to eat it. She had mint chocolate chip ice cream over her face and down the front of her dress.

Maureen was sure Kelly's mother would somehow blame her for not keeping the child clean. She desperately wanted Matt's daughter to like her, but that didn't seem to be happening. All day long she had been nervous about the meeting. It had been her idea. She had heard so much about the child from Matt that she couldn't wait any longer. Besides, this was the daughter of the man she loved. She would be patient, understanding—

"Is she your girlfriend?"

Everyone stopped what they were doing when Kelly finally spoke.

Matt seemed embarrassed. "Maureen is my friend, my good friend" he explained. "Just like Abbie and Josh are."

"Are you going to marry her?"

Abbie and Josh laughed. Matt was speechless. It was Maureen who answered. "Honey, your daddy and I are friends. That's all." Okay, a lie. But this child didn't need to hear the truth yet. "I'd like to be your friend, too."

Kelly turned to her father. "I don't want you to have a girlfriend."

Matt looked crushed and he quickly brought the napkin up to wipe away the chocolate ice cream. "Don't be rude, Kelly. We can talk about this later."

Maureen stared at father and daughter and saw the writing on the wall. This poor kid wanted her daddy back home.

In the weeks following the dinner it became obvious that Maureen's analysis of the situation was on the mark. Every time she saw Matt, he would tell her of his conversations with Claire— how Kelly was acting up in kindergarten, interrupting the teacher, hitting other children. And now this:

"Claire says she's starting to bite the other kids. God! Biting? What's wrong with Kelly? Claire wants me to come with her to the school tomorrow. We have an appointment with a Dr. Walker, the school district's psychiatrist. Can you believe it? A psychiatrist! For my baby . . ."

They were in his apartment and Maureen was sitting next to him with her head on his shoulder. "Maybe it's just a phase—"

"A phase? Biting other children?"

"She wants attention." Maureen experienced a heaviness in her heart. Something was going to happen. She could feel it.

The next night she cooked dinner for him. Last month he had given her the key to his apartment and she was becoming familiar with his kitchen, even to the point of bringing fresh flowers to brighten the table. Since he had to do the sports at six and six-thirty, she had told Matt that she'd have dinner ready for him when he came home. While she cooked his favorite meal she'd watched him on TV. He wasn't at his best; he'd seemed distracted, as if he were just reading lines. Shaking off a sense of foreboding, she set the table and waited.

"Hi," she said sympathetically when he walked in the front door. "Tough day?"

He dropped his suit jacket onto the back of the sofa. "That's an understatement."

She poured him a Coke. "What happened? You met with the school doctor?"

Matt looked tired, almost drained. He accepted the Coke. "Thanks. Something smells good."

Even though he was avoiding her questions, she smiled and went into the small kitchen. "Beef stew. Good. Hearty. Builds blood. Of course, that was in the days before cholesterol."

He walked up behind her as she ladled out the stew into a bowl. "Thanks honey. It smells great."

She put a bright smile on her face. "As long as you appreciate it, Mr. Shannon. Not every woman would cook stew in the middle of August."

"We could have gone out to eat."

"Stop it. I'm kidding," she said as she put the salad on the table. "C'mon, sit down. You really have had a bad day, haven't you?"

He sat down and sighed. "I don't want to talk about it. Not yet."

Oh God, this isn't going to be good, Maureen thought as she handed him the stew. "Guess what?" she asked, wanting to take his mind off his troubles. "My agent called. She's received an offer for my mainstream. A very good offer . . ."

She talked for most of the meal. Matt tried to be enthusiastic, but she knew he was forcing it. Finally, when she saw that he wasn't going to eat anymore, she sat back in her chair and said, "Okay, tell me. What happened?"

He ran his hand over his eyes. "Dr. Walker says Kelly is acting out her anger with me by taking it out on the kids in her class. He says it isn't all that abnormal for kids whose parents have separated."

She knew it. "What did he say you should do?"

"Spend more time with her."

Maureen nodded. "That's a good idea." But there was something else. She could tell by the expression on his face. And she could feel it in the pit of her stomach. "What is it, Matt? What's really bothering you?"

He looked at her and she held her breath. If she didn't know better, she would swear he was about to cry.

"Claire . . ." He stopped talking and cleared his throat. "We talked for about three hours after we left the school. And . . ."

"And?" Maureen prompted, even though she knew she really didn't want to hear what was coming.

"And we talked about me moving back temporarily."

Maureen was stunned. "Moving back?"

He took her hand and held it tightly. "Not getting back together. I love you, Maureen. Claire knows that. It's just that Kelly needs me right now. I'd still see you after Kelly went to bed. Claire and I—we'd have an open marriage. We would still be technically separated and be free to see other people."

Maureen couldn't think. Her whole body was rigid with shock.

"Say something," Matt whispered.

"I don't know what to say," Maureen muttered, staring down at her plate. The gravy surrounding an uneaten carrot was starting to congeal. Maybe she'd used too much flour . . .

"Maureen? Please, this doesn't have to make a difference with us."

She looked up at him. "Of course it does. You're moving back home."

"But we'd still be separated."

She shook her head. "There is no such thing as legal separation in New Jersey. I've looked into that. You and Claire would be living as husband and wife and . . . and I couldn't do to her what was done to me. I couldn't be with you and know your wife was home waiting for you. I couldn't, Matt."

She pushed the chair back and stood up to gather the dishes. Matt grabbed her hand. "Please try and understand the position I'm in. My family—"

Pulling her hand away, she said, "I do. Kelly has to come first. I understand. My children's welfare will always be a priority for me." She walked to the sink and placed the dishes down. It had been too good to last, she should have known that, yet she felt like her heart was breaking. The right thing would be to send him back to Claire and his daughter, tell him to try again, but she didn't want to give him up. She didn't want to be noble. She wanted to be loved.

He came up behind her and pulled her back against him. "I don't want to lose you."

She fought the tears that were building up inside of her. "Please, Matt. Don't." Leaving the sink, she picked up her purse. "I have to leave—"

"No, don't," he interrupted, coming toward her.

She held up her hand to stop him. "I'm sorry about the dishes, but I have to go. I need some time to think and so do you. I don't blame you, Matt. Really, I don't. There are just too many complications right now."

"Please, Maureen. Don't do this. You're too important to me." He looked stricken.

"Your family is what's important right now. Concentrate on them. Don't call me. Promise me you won't call. Give me some time."

Before she walked out, she left his key on the small table by the door.

Nobility hurt like hell.

She stared at the blank computer screen and wiped her eyes. God, she was sick of crying! Why couldn't she write? Why was every scene, every bit of dialogue, stuck in the recesses of her brain? *Because you're miserable,* she told herself. *Because your skin actually aches for his touch. You haven't laughed in two weeks and you're scared to leave the house in case he calls.*

But he hadn't called.

He was giving her time, just as she had asked. The writer in her visualized vivid scenes of Matt and his wife. She could see them together, cozy and happy with their daughter. Of course, she wanted him happy. She just couldn't stand feeling so miserable herself. In the last two weeks her hand had reached for the phone over fifty times. But she didn't do it. Instead, she moped around the house. She'd tried to lose herself in work, but her brain was blocked and so she'd thrown herself into housecleaning. Her home was spotless, yet every time she vacuumed the foyer steps she broke down and cried. She missed him so damned much that it hurt like a fresh, raw wound.

Staring at the phone she told herself that all she wanted to do was hear his voice and she would be okay . . .

Picking up the receiver, she dialed his line at the television station. Maybe he wasn't there. He could be out on an assignment, she thought, as her heart pounded behind her rib cage.

"Hello? Sports."

She didn't say anything for a few seconds. Then she whispered, "Matt?"

She could hear him let out his breath. "Maureen." He said her name softly, gently. "Thank God you called. How are you?"

"I'm miserable," she said truthfully, starting to cry.

"So am I. Are the kids okay?"

"Yes. How's Kelly?"

"She's doing better. No more biting."

"That's good."

There was a prolonged silence.

Finally, Matt said, "I have to see you. Please. Can I come over tonight?"

Maureen's heart lifted. She forgot all about her

reservations. She didn't care anymore. She needed him. It was all that mattered.

"What time?"

"As soon as I'm finished here. About seven-thirty?"

"Okay." She was going to see him!

"Why don't you come to the apartment? I never gave it up."

"I'll be there," Maureen said, already impatient for the time to pass.

"I'll see you then. I love you, Maureen."

She smiled. "I love you, too."

It was going to work out. Somehow they'd make it all work out.

Chapter Nineteen

Everything was perfect. She had to go to New York for a meeting with her agent and publisher, and Matt was covering the Mets game against the Phillies. They were finally going to spend the night together. She had fantasized about it for months. To make love and fall asleep and then wake up in each others arms . . . the old adage was true. Good things come to those who wait.

Gazing about the beautiful hotel room that overlooked Central Park, Maureen asked, "What time do you have to be at the ball park?"

"Around four-thirty. What time's your meeting again?"

"Three."

"And what time is it now?"

She looked at her watch. "Twelve twenty-two."

They grinned at each other. Words weren't necessary. Quickly shedding their clothes, they came together on the bed and made exquisite love. They were like two kids let loose in a candy store, eager to sample everything and determined to make good use of the freedom. They even bathed together.

"I'm going to have to take a shower after this," Matt said and chuckled as he brought a handful of bubbles up to his nose. "It smells like my grandmother's garden."

Maureen laughed and relaxed against him in the huge jacuzzi. "This is heaven," she breathed, relishing the feel of Matt behind her and the water caressing her skin. "I don't ever want to leave this bathroom."

"What about food?" he asked, kissing the back of her neck.

Maureen shrugged. "We'll use room service."

"How about your career?"

"You brought your lap top computer. I can use that."

"And what about me? How will I do the sports from inside a jacuzzi? Invite the camera crew into the bathroom like Howard Stern? The news is a family show, remember? Besides, I don't want anyone to see you like this." He cupped her breasts in his hands and sighed.

"And then there are the children," Maureen added, being drawn back to reality. Even though they were together again, she could sense Matt was torn between two homes, two women, two families. It was an uneasy situation, but right now she was too full of love to think about Matt's marital problems. This was their one night together and she wasn't going to spoil it.

"The children . . ." Matt repeated in a low voice. There wasn't any easy way around that issue. It was the main complication in their relationship. The one that was destined to keep them apart. "Listen," he said, pulling her back against his chest. "I hate to be the one to burst this fantasy bubble, but we both have to start getting ready. Especially you. You're going to be late unless you get moving."

She knew he was right, but she didn't want to leave him yet. And not like this when they were both thinking about the real world and all its problems that awaited them in New Jersey. "Then let's take a shower to rinse the bubbles off." She looked over her shoulder to see him.

He was grinning. "C'mon."

She left her publisher's office and went to Bloomingdale's to buy an outrageously expensive nightgown and robe. It was a celebration, for she had just been offered two hundred thousand dollars for the mainstream. And hardcover. She was going to be published in hardcover! She could hardly believe it. All those hours, all those years, in front of the computer had paid off. If someone asked her in fifty years what was the best day of her life, this one would certainly be at the top.

She was walking around the streets of New York on air, especially since she had traded in her black heels for a newly bought pair of Keds. Not wanting to fight the five o'clock traffic, and knowing it would be nearly impossible to hail a cab, Maureen carried her purchases as she made her way back to Central Park. She smiled at the grumpy New Yorkers who rushed past her, bought a bunch of yellow roses from a street vendor and felt that for one day, just one, she was a part of the city. She came, she saw, and she had conquered. Two hundred thousand dollars . . . and hardcover. She couldn't wait to tell Matt.

After ordering room service, Maureen watched the game on television. In the ninth inning, with the Mets winning, she shut off the TV and took a shower. She felt almost like a bride as she slipped the nightgown over her head. Fine white cotton with tiny tucks and silk embroidery felt wonderfully luxurious next to her skin. She put on the matching robe and looked into the mirror. There was no doubt about it. She looked like a woman in love. Her hair hung down her back in a thick wave. Her makeup was light, almost nonexistent, yet her face glowed with happiness. Splashing French perfume in all the right places, Maureen smiled as she walked over to the ice bucket to check on the champagne. He should be back to the hotel in an hour or so. And that was more than enough time to get everything ready.

Tonight they would celebrate.

* * *

"Maureen? Wake up."

She blinked several times and stared at the man who stood over her. "Matt? What time is it?"

"Quarter to two," he said, throwing his brief-case onto the chair. "Did you see the fight?"

"Fight?" she asked, sitting up and trying to sound alert. "What fight?"

"The Phillies and the Mets. Didn't you watch the game?" He looked sweaty and tired.

"I turned it off at the end of the eighth inning. What happened?"

"The Mets had just put in a reliever and—listen, I'll tell you about it later. Right now I have to do a story for tomorrow's paper. Thank God I didn't forget the laptop." He brought the computer over to the desk and plugged a modem into the hotel phone. "Do we have any Coke?" he asked over his shoulder. He sounded excited, eager to send the story to Philadelphia.

Maureen slipped off the bed. "Sure, but how about some champagne?"

"Huh?" He was already getting organized at the desk. "Champagne? No, the Coke's fine."

She took some ice from the champagne cooler and poured the soda into a glass. Bringing it to him, she said, "Guess what? They want to buy the mainstream."

Distracted, Matt looked at her and answered, "Hey, that's great." He gulped the Coke and went right back to work.

"They want to publish it in hardcover. And they

offered me two hundred thousand dollars."

He stopped fooling with the computer and stared at her. "Are you kidding?"

She smiled. "I'm serious."

Matt pulled her down and kissed her cheek. "Congratulations. We'll celebrate tomorrow, okay? I'm sorry about this, but, you know, duty calls . . ." He started typing out his lead sentence, and Maureen knew she was dismissed.

She watched him for a few seconds and turned back to the bed. Her feelings were hurt. All her plans for tonight were for nothing . . . She tried to be understanding. She knew his work had to come first. But why was it that she always wound up taking the back seat to every important man in her life? Her father. Her husband. And now her lover. Disappointment was sharp and bitter as she took off her beautiful robe and pulled the covers up to her chin. He didn't even notice how she was dressed.

"Is this typing going to bother you?" Matt asked without looking at her.

"Not at all," she mumbled and closed her eyes.

Sometime during the early hours of the morning, Matt came to bed. He cuddled her up against him and fell fast asleep. Maureen was still awake. She had done a lot of thinking in the last few hours. About herself and Matt. About Dan and the children. Even about Bobby. She missed Bobby, but knew he had to go. Even the crazy dreams had stopped. She had to get on with her life and make her own decisions, without any ghostly help. But that was just it. She simply couldn't make any decisions.

She'd been separated from her husband for over eight months and still didn't know if she wanted a divorce. It wasn't easy to flush twenty years down the drain. And Matt . . . what about Matt? He was back with his wife. Oh, he didn't sleep in the same bedroom, or so he said. But how would she really know if he did? She didn't see Matt as often as before because of Kelly. She understood that, it's just that she was starting to feel like the other woman, the one a man tries to fit in after his family. And it wasn't a good feeling.

Matt started to snore in her ear. The noise was loud and annoying, and she moved away to the far end of the mattress. It suddenly occurred to her that she wanted to go home. She wanted to be in her own house, in her own bed.

Alone.

"You just take off like that? Leave your kids and go to New York?"

Maureen pulled the weeds away from her tomato plants. Without looking up at him, she said, "I didn't just leave the kids, Dan. I had a meeting with my publisher. Abbie and Josh knew the number of the hotel, and you're twenty minutes away. They're sixteen years old, not babies.

393

Everything was fine. Nothing happened."

"Yeah. This time."

She dug her fingers into the dark earth to suppress her anger. "Look, if it makes you feel better I'll call the next time I have to go out of town."

"I suppose it was only an accident that your *boyfriend* was also in New York City covering a game at the same time."

"That's none of your business." She threw some weeds onto the grass. They landed inches from Dan's feet.

"Oh, that's where you're wrong, Maureen. I lost my house and my kids because I was seeing another woman. Let me ask you this . . . how much better are you for seeing a married man?"

She pulled her gloves off and stood up. "He is not married. He's separated."

Dan looked at her with contempt. "I've done some checking up on him. He is not separated. I've even driven by his house and he was mowing the lawn. His daughter was there and so was his wife, and they looked pretty chummy to me. He's living there, Maureen, and seeing you on the side."

She felt a sickening pull of her stomach muscles. "How could you do that? You can't possibly understand the situation. It's complicated. His daughter—he's—"

"He's doing the exact same thing I did when you threw me out," Dan interrupted. "How do you justify that in your mind?"

Squinting in the strong sun, she shaded her eyes. "I'm not going to discuss this with you. I don't know who you're seeing, or what you're doing with them. That's your business. Give me the same courtesy." She wiped the sweat off her forehead. "You seem to forget that you were the one that started this. You were the one that tore the marriage apart. I'm just trying to get through it the best way I can. Now if you came to see the kids, they're in the house." She continued to stare at him, not daring to show him how shaken she was by his words.

He held her gaze, looking at her as if seeing a stranger. "I know you don't think much of me, but how much better are you for seeing a married man? What's happened to you?"

He didn't wait for her to answer. Turning, he walked toward the house.

Maureen watched him until he opened the back door. Sinking to her knees, she picked up her gloves and stared at the dirt embedded from years of gardening. My God, could it be true? Was Matt really back with his wife? Dan's words had brought all her fears to the surface. All the nagging doubts that had been lurking at the back of her mind since New York City came rushing up at her. They didn't see each other as often. He was busier than usual. When they were together it was hurried, as if he had to answer to someone for his time. And that could only be one person. His wife.

* * *

"How come Matt doesn't come over as much anymore?"

Maureen stirred the spaghetti sauce and glanced at her son. "He's busy now that the season is winding down." She looked back at the sauce. Maybe it wasn't such a good idea that Matt and Josh had become so close. Now that Matt spent less time with them, Josh was feeling the loss almost as much as she did.

"Well, the Phillies aren't going to make the playoffs, that's for sure." Josh slid the plates onto the table. Four of them. Matt was coming to dinner.

"There's always next year," Maureen said, wondering why Matt was late. He was always late and preoccupied. Something was going on. When she tried to talk to him about it, he would assure her it was only because he was so busy. He kept telling her that he loved her, yet wouldn't call her for days at a time. Instinct told her that she didn't have to accept that kind of behavior, but she did. She wanted to be understanding. She told herself that she was the one who had called him and started everything up again after he went back home for Kelly. That all of this is part of the bargain when you're involved with someone who isn't totally free of commitments. But it still hurt to cling so desperately, stubbornly, to the idea that all their problems would somehow work out.

She felt attached to the telephone, afraid to leave the house in case he called. But the worst part was looking in the mirror, for it was then that Dan's words haunted her. She was beginning to feel like she really was the other woman.

Angry that he was late, again, Maureen slammed the lid on the pot and picked up the phone. There were three other people waiting for him. And they were hungry.

"Hello, sports."

"Matt?"

"Hi, what's up?"

She hated it when he said that, for it forced her to state her reason for calling. She felt as if she were bothering him. "Are you held up at the station? It's almost eight-thirty and the kids are hungry."

"Hungry? Oh God, I—"

"You forgot," she supplied, closing her eyes and trying to control her anger. "Well I guess we'll just eat without you."

"Did I say I was coming?" He sounded slightly defensive.

"I invited you for dinner and you said you'd call if there was a problem. I didn't hear from you so I assumed you'd be here. But then again, you've forgotten to call quite a bit lately, so I really shouldn't be so surprised." Damn, she sounded just like a nagging wife.

"Look, I'll come as soon as I'm finished here."

"Well, we'll save you something. I'm going to

feed the children."

"Don't save anything for me. I had an early dinner with . . . with Kelly."

Maureen didn't miss the hesitation. He'd already had dinner with his family. His wife and daughter. It kept repeating itself in her brain. His wife and daughter. His wife. His wife. That was it. The man had a wife. This was becoming impossible, and she couldn't stand much more. What was really eating away at her was the feeling of losing her self-respect.

"Don't bother to come," she said quietly. "I won't be here."

"Look, Maureen, I'm sorry I forgot. This is so confusing. I'm trying to keep everyone happy and—"

"And it's not working," she interrupted. She had to get off the phone before she broke down. "I'll talk to you later, Matt. Okay?"

"I'll call you tomorrow. I'm really sorry, Maureen. I do love you."

She clenched her back teeth to keep from saying that she loved him too. "Bye."

She hung up the phone to find her son staring at her. Taking a deep breath, she managed to say, "It looks like it's just going to be the three of us tonight. Do you want to call Abbie?"

"What's going on, Mom? Are you and Matt breaking up?"

Please God, not this. Not now, Maureen silently prayed. She swallowed down the lump in her throat and said, "I don't know, Josh. He's having trouble with Kelly and he's moved back with her. It just doesn't seem to be working out."

"So you're not going to see him anymore?" Josh looked crushed, and Maureen felt terrible for involving her son in this relationship.

"I don't know," she repeated. "It's all so complicated. But this doesn't have anything to do with your relationship with Matt. You can still—"

"Oh, yeah! Right!" Josh interrupted in an angry voice. "First Dad. Now Matt." He shook his head and walked out of the kitchen mumbling, "What the hell is going on here?"

Her chin started quivering and she pressed her fingers to her mouth to stop the tears. "I don't know anymore," she answered to the empty room. "I just don't know."

It was a habit she was trying to break. It didn't matter where she went. As soon as she came in the house she would go into her office and check the answering machine for his call. Nine times out of ten, there was no message. Days went by and she was miserable, knowing full well that his silence was all the message she should need.

When the phone rang, she almost jumped onto her desk as she reached for the receiver. It had to be him. He would tell her he was sorry, that he missed her and—

"Hello?" She waited breathlessly for his deep,

warm voice.

"Is this Maureen? Maureen Malone?"

It was a woman. Disappointment was sharp as she absently answered, "Yes."

There was a slight hesitation before the woman said, "This is Claire Shannon. Matt's wife."

Chapter Twenty

Maureen's mouth hung open and her eyes widened in shock. Matt's wife! "Yes . . . hello," she said in a anxious voice. *Why was the woman calling her?*

It was as if she had said the words aloud. "This is awkward, but I'm calling because . . . because Matt's been in an accident and I know . . ." Claire sounded like she was crying. "And I know that Matt cared for . . . for you . . . and . . ."

"An accident?" Maureen tried to keep the hysteria under control. "Where? What happened? Is he all right?" Dear God, an accident!

"He's in Jefferson Hospital. I don't know if he's going to make it. I . . . I mean the doctors aren't saying anything right now and . . ."

Maureen felt like she was going to throw up and she covered her mouth as she listened.

"He was in Reading doing a story on someone from the minor leagues when the van he was in was hit on the Schuykill Expressway. I . . . I think he would want you to know," she managed to get out before she started crying.

"Claire? Claire, can I come there? Would it be all right?" Maureen couldn't believe she was having this conversation. It had to be a bad nightmare.

"He's on the fifth floor."

"Thank you," Maureen whispered and hung up the phone.

Clairessa Shannon was everything Maureen wasn't. Tall. Thin. Beautiful, even in her grief. It's funny how women notice those things, even in times of trouble. Like how perfectly Claire's summer skirt floated about her ankles while Maureen was dressed in jeans and a tee shirt. The differences between them were striking.

Maureen left the elevator on the fifth floor and saw Claire down the hallway. She was sitting in the small lobby by the nurse's station and Maureen recognized her immediately from Matt's description. Unsure whether she should first talk to Claire, or see Matt, she hesitated in front of the elevator.

She watched as Claire spoke to a man on her left and soon the man started walking in Maureen's direction.

"I'm Jack Stoner," the older man whispered. "Matt and I worked together. Claire said to tell you he's in Room 528. They're waiting for a specialist before they take him to surgery."

Maureen only nodded and turned down the hall. She stood before the door and stared at the number. 528. It was the same number of the room at the Hilton that first time. What was all this? Was it some punishment for loving each other? Did they do something wrong? What kind of cruel God would play these tricks?

Her hand was shaking as she pushed open the door.

He looked smaller. He was such a big man that to see him in the hospital bed somehow diminished him. There were tubes going in and out of him. Monitors. Machines. Noises of suction and heartbeats. None of it seemed real.

She came closer to the bed.

"Matt?" Her voice was barely audible. There were bruises all over him and the left side of his face was bandaged. She knew he couldn't hear her, yet she had the need to speak to him, to tell him.

"Hey, big guy," she whispered, letting the tears come. "This is a hell of a way to get out of doing the Six O'Clock News." Reaching out, she touched his hand that lay stilled on top of the white sheet. She remembered his touch, light and caressing, how his fingers would automatically connect with hers whether they were walking or watching a movie or eating dinner together. The idea that he might never do any of those things again broke her heart.

Clutching his hand, she tried to give him her

strength, her love. "You saved my life, Matt Shannon. You gave me back myself, and the funny thing is I didn't even know what I was missing until I met you. You came into my life when I was drowning and you loved me for me. I didn't have to be a good wife, or mother, or daughter, or writer. You didn't care. All I had to do was breathe for you, and you accepted me. Nobody, not in my entire life, loved me like that. And maybe never will again."

The tears ran off her face and fell onto the bed. "I love you. I always will. And you made me laugh again. God, how I missed the laughter and you gave it back to me. When I'm an old lady sitting in my rocker on the porch, I'll be thinking about you. And all my grandchildren will wonder why I have such a smile on my face. Thank you, Matt. Thank you for the memories and for giving me the best time in my life."

She squeezed his hand and reached down to kiss his forehead. It was cold and clammy, and frightened her far more than the machines. "Now you listen to me. You're going to fight this. Do you hear me?" She sniffled and wiped her nose on the back of her hand. "Think of everybody who needs you. Think of your family, of Kelly. You love her and . . . and Claire. You still love her. I guess you were trying to tell me these last weeks, and I wasn't listening. It doesn't matter anymore. Just find the strength somewhere and come back to your family. They need you."

"I'm sorry, you'll have to leave. We're taking him down to surgery now."

Maureen wiped her eyes and nodded to the nurse who was directing two male attendants. Kissing him one last time, she ran from the room.

The chapel was quiet and nondenominational. Compared to the churches of her youth, it was austere. There were no statues, or candles. Not even an altar. Sinking into the last pew, Maureen stared at the arrangement of summer flowers in front of a huge stained-glass window.

Please, God, she prayed, *don't let him die. If we were doing something wrong, we didn't know it. Don't punish him like this. Don't take him now. I . . . I'll give him up. He can go back to his family and I'll never see him again. I won't even talk to him. I promise. Just don't let him die. Please . . .*

The tears were streaming down her cheeks and she didn't bother to wipe them away. She felt ten years old again, making a deal with God. Wrapping her arms around herself, she watched the sun sparkle through a brilliant ruby shard of glass and remembered running all the way to church when her dog was sick. She had knelt for over an hour, begging, pleading, dealing. She would take better care of Sooty. She would walk him every day. His fur would never be matted again. She would even give him part of her dinner every night, if only God would let him live. But the big brown mutt had been over twelve years old and had died later that night.

Maureen covered her face in her hands and sobbed. Even at ten years old she should have known you can't strike a deal with God. *Okay, then,* she mentally screamed. *You've got him. He's in your hands. Just remember he's a good man, and he deserves to live a full life. Please be merciful. And . . . and Bobby? If you can hear me, I'm sorry. I'm sorry for the way I treated you. Please do what you can for Matt. Please . . . ?"*

"Maureen?"

She dropped her hands and stared at the person sitting next to her.

"Claire. How is he?" *Oh God, don't let there be a scene or a confrontation,* she silently pleaded. *Not now.*

Matt's wife shook her head. "I don't know," she whispered, trying to control her voice. "He's still in surgery. I . . . I thought I would come in here and wait. Did I disturb you?"

Maureen's chin quivered and her eyes filled again with tears. "No. Not at all. Thank you for calling me." How strange to be sitting here talking with Matt's wife. She was even prettier close up. Her black hair was pulled back off her face and tied in a small knot at her neck, in the style that only someone completely confident about her looks could wear. Her features were finely chiseled and Maureen knew that when she walked into a room, both men and women would find her striking.

Claire nodded and studied the multicolored window. "I called because I knew he would want you here. You . . . you're important to him."

Maureen could see how hard it was for this lovely woman to admit that. Swallowing down the lump in her throat, she said, "Claire? He loves his family. You and Kelly are more important to him than anything else. I know that now. We . . . we were two lonely, hurt people that connected and tried to find some happiness. To take away the pain. I felt like I was drowning and I reached out for his hand because I knew he would pull me out and save me. But it's over now, and we both knew it. I . . . I just have a tougher time letting go, I guess."

Claire wiped at her eyes and sighed deeply. "I've hurt him so much, and now I might never have the chance to tell him how sorry I am. I don't blame you, Maureen. I drove him out because he didn't fulfill my dreams. And now . . . now that . . . I might lose him, all I can think of is how selfish I was. And how foolish. I love him and . . . and . . ." She couldn't finish as sobs overwhelmed her.

"I know," Maureen whispered soothingly. "We have to believe that he will pull through this. He's big and strong and stubborn as hell sometimes. He won't let this defeat him."

Despite her grief, Claire smiled and nodded.

"He is a big overgrown kid."

"With a good heart," Maureen added. "And he loves life. He wouldn't give it up easily."

"You're right," Claire whispered and clutched at the tissue in her hand.

"And when he does get better, because I know he will, maybe you could tell him that I was here? And that I said goodbye."

Claire turned her head and looked at Maureen. "I will," she promised. "I can see why he cared for you. You're just like him." Tears ran down her cheeks. "Thank you for taking care of him when . . . when we were apart."

Maureen nodded and reached for her hand. They sat in silence and looked back to the front of the chapel, for there was nothing more that needed to be said.

Two women—one beautiful, one average— clutched each other's hand and prayed for the man they both loved.

Snuggling against the smooth cotton pillowcase, Maureen listened to the rain as it hit the roof top. Ever since she was a child, she had loved the sound. It made her feel warm and secure. The house was dark and quiet. The bed was soft and cozy. The only thing missing was someone to share the moment.

But there wasn't anyone.

Claire had called that morning to tell her Matt

was leaving the hospital. After three weeks all the internal injuries had healed and he was acting like a caged bear, anxious to get home.

Maureen smiled, thinking of Matt. It still hurt sometimes, not seeing him or sharing something important with him, but she had wonderful memories and she didn't regret a moment that she had spent with him. How strange to end a love affair by becoming friends with the man's wife. But it was a friendship that ended today with Claire's phone call. They both knew it would be their final conversation. And that was the way it should be . . . everyone had to go on with their lives.

Pulling the comforter up to her chin, she closed her eyes and sighed deeply. Why was it so painful to grow up and go on with her life? School started earlier in the month and the kids were now seniors. Seniors. And driving. It was hard to believe. One more year before she had to let them go. It seemed like she was forever letting people go. First Dan, then Matt, and soon it would be her children.

In the end, who was left? Just herself. But she had friends, her work, and the kids would come back from college to visit. And next month she would be attending her twenty-fifth high school reunion. Twenty five years had brought so many changes to her life. What about her friends? What would they be like now? What would they think of her? She was excited, envisioning the reunion, but a part of her was dreading facing the changes that were inevitable. For such an occasion was a vivid reminder that time was quickly passing.

Just one day at a time, that's all she had to deal with now. Tonight. Just get through the rest of the night. Listen to the rain and sleep . . .

She sat in front of the mirror and grinned. It was her twentieth birthday and she was waiting for Dan to pick her up. He was taking her to a fancy restaurant in Philadelphia to celebrate. Dan Malone. God, he was gorgeous. And sexy. Ah, yes . . . Just looking at him made her knees go weak. He had taken her virginity and made love to her in one wonderful night. Okay, so maybe the beginning wasn't that great, but he had made up for it. Her cheeks flushed when she remembered him bringing hot towels to her afterward. Maybe it was that gesture that made her fall in love. Who knew?

Picking up a pen, she tore off a piece of flowered stationery and started doodling. Dan Malone. Maureen Malone. Mrs. Daniel Malone . . . Something told her this was it. This was the man with whom she would spend the rest of her life.

"Maureen! You have company."

Bolting up, Maureen yelled downstairs, "I'm coming!" She ran a brush through her hair, flipping the ends up, and smoothed down her miniskirt. Her eyeliner was dark and drawn to perfection and her lipstick was pale blushing pink, almost white. Going against the current fashion style, Maureen pinched her cheeks to bring color to them.

"I'll be right there, Dad," she shouted, grabbing her purse as she left her bedroom. Why did her father always announce that she had *company?* Why couldn't he use Dan's name? She hurried to the stairs, yet controlled her impatience as she slowly walked down. No need to be obvious, she told herself, while composing her expression to one of welcome.

The smile froze on her face when she saw who waited for her by the front door. "Bobby?"

Bobby O'Connor grinned as she stood before him. He looked nervous, though not as nervous as Maureen felt. Dan was coming at any moment.

"Hi," Bobby said, holding a thin box in his hand that was wrapped in silver foil.

"Hi," she answered, confused by his visit. The last time she had seen him was at Muzzy's party a month ago, before she had met Dan. "How come you're here? I thought you'd be on your way to Florida. Doesn't school start this week?"

Nodding, Bobby said, "I'm leaving tonight." He looked down to the present in his hand. "This is for you. Your birthday's next month. I don't know, I just thought I would give it to you before I left."

She didn't know what to do. "Bobby . . . I . . . Gee, thanks, but I'm waiting for my date and if he saw you he might get the wrong idea and . . . and we never gave each other birthday presents before—"

"Hey, no problem," Bobby said, clearly embarrassed. "It was a stupid thing to do I guess. I don't know. I just saw it and thought of you. Here, take it." He shoved the box into her hands.

"I can't take this," Maureen protested. "I never gave you anything for your birthday. Not ever. It wouldn't be right."

He looked up to the ceiling and shook his head. "Just take it, all right? Look, I got to go." He yelled into the kitchen, "Goodbye, Mr. Henessey."

"Take care, Bobby. Good luck to you at school this year."

"Thank you, sir."

Bobby raked his fingers through his hair, that same gesture she had seen him do since fourth grade. He did it everytime he was nervous. Looking at Maureen, he shrugged. "See you around, kid."

She watched him walk down her sidewalk and get into his baby blue Chevy Impala, feeling terribly sad for not having the time to spend with him. "Thanks for the present," she shouted from the door, still not sure why he had given it to her. They never gave each other presents.

He started his engine and waved, as if dismissing the entire episode.

It was the last time she had seen him alive.

Sipping her morning coffee, Maureen thought back to her dream of the night before. Suddenly, she had the overwhelming urge to connect with the past. She left her coffee on the counter and walked into the hallway. Pulling down the attic stairs, she knew somewhere in the recesses of her home was a big box with dried corsages, old notes that had been passed during religion class, love letters from old boyfriends, her high school yearbook and Bobby's present.

A silver heart pendant outlined in purple glass. She would wear it for the reunion.

She'd wear it for Bobby, who couldn't be there.

Chapter Twenty-one

"*Maureen Henessey! You look wonderful, damn you!*"

She had just pinned on her name tag when she heard Robin's distinctive throaty voice. Turning, Maureen found herself enveloped in her old friend's ample arms.

"So do you," Maureen said with a laugh. "It's great to see you again." They parted and looked at each other with fondness.

"Don't tell me I look wonderful. It took me six stores before I could find a dress that fit. Five kids," Robin's voice filled with sarcasm. "Brats. Every single one of them. And they've destroyed my body." She grinned. "But I wouldn't trade in any of them." She paused for effect. "Except Jason. He keeps lizards in his bedroom and feeds them mealy worms that have to be refrigerated." Grimacing, Robin added, "He takes after his father."

"Is Timmy here?" Maureen asked. It was wonderful seeing her again. How strange that Robin looked exactly like her mother did twenty-five years ago. Had they all turned into their parents?

"Of course he's here. Timmy wouldn't miss this for anything. He's at the table." She linked arms with Maureen and led her into the ballroom. "We've saved a place for you. Everybody's here. Colleen. Margie. Jake. Mike. Ted. Everybody. Wait until you see Colleen. She was a budding feminist twenty-five years ago, and now she's some hot shot politician with the county. Wouldn't you know it?"

"No kidding?" Maureen smiled as she looked out to the crowd of middle-aged couples moving to a Martha and the Vandellas song. The room was decorated in blue and gray, their school colors, and a big silver ball spun multicolored lights over the dancers in an effort to recreate a sixties atmosphere.

"God, Robin," she muttered, "Twenty-five years . . . I can't believe it."

"I know what you mean. It feels like yesterday we were grinding in McDevlin's gym, and Father Canaise would crack that paddle over the boys back to straighten them up."

Maureen laughed, remembering the scene. "Nobody grinds anymore. The last time I saw it was in *Dirty Dancing*."

"Ahh, those were the days," Robin sighed. "Look, would you believe that's Joey Harrington?"

Maureen followed Robin's gaze and saw a tall, balding man that resembled Jackie Gleason. "No! You're kidding? That can't be him." Joey Harrington used to be the star football player for McDevlin. He had also been gorgeous, conceited, and Maureen had dated him briefly.

"And there—there! That's Barry Pillary talking to him. Remember how crazy we were for all that black hair? Where is it?"

Maureen shook her head, feeling like she had walked into a "Twilight Zone" episode. "He looks so old . . ."

"I'm telling you, Maureen, it's the weirdest thing. All the cute guys in high school? The boys we drooled over? Now they're balding, fat or obnoxious. And the geeks, the ones we used to laugh at? *They're* handsome, successful and downright charming. I can't figure it out. What happened?"

"Just late bloomers, I guess."

"Yeah, well, makes me wish I was a geek in high school just so I could show up at this reunion looking fantastic. Take a peek at Cara Soledaz." Robin pointed to a table by the dance floor.

A tall attractive woman was surrounded by four men, all laughing and flirting with her. "That's Cara?" Maureen asked in disbelief. In her mind's eye she pictured Cara twenty-five years ago—shy, studious, with thick glasses that had made her seem perpetually astonished. "Talk about blossoming," Maureen whispered as she saw Cara's

416

tight, red-sequined dress. "Good for her!"

"Easy for you to be charitable. You look like a million bucks. I wish I could fit into something like that." Robin looked with envy to Maureen's outfit.

"You're just saying that to make me feel better. I'm probably the only one here without a spouse or a date." She had debated long and hard over what to wear, and had finally gone to I. Magnin's and charged a long, black silk jacket, scattered with tiny pearls and silver bugle beads. Under the jacket, she wore a black georgette camisole and tapered pants. Her only jewelry was Bobby's pendant that she wore on a thirty-inch silver chain.

"My guess is there's plenty of people here tonight that are divorced," Robin said. "That seems to be the curse of our generation. You know Margie's on her second marriage, don't you?"

"Really? I didn't know."

Nodding, Robin led her to a table by the DJ. "Hey, everybody," she announced in a loud voice. "Look who I found!"

"Maureen Malone!"

"God, you look great!"

"You've hardly changed at all."

"Good to see you, Irish. Still as pretty as ever . . ."

"Oh, Maureen, it's been too long. My kids all read your books . . ."

She felt breathless by the time she worked her way around the table to Colleen and Margie. She

417

stood, looking at the women who were once her best friends. She felt a moment of awkwardness and smiled shyly. "Margie, Colleen—it's so good to see you two again. I'm sorry I haven't kept in touch."

Colleen, red hair falling down her back in a sensuous wave, pulled Maureen down to give her a kiss. "Everybody feels the same way. I'm just glad you came."

Margie was still pretty, yet there were lines deeply etched around her eyes and mouth. Lines that spoke of worry and disappointment and sorrow. Emotions they had all experienced in the last two decades. But when Margie smiled, they seemed to disappear. "Just like always, Henessey, I'm saving you a seat." She pulled back the chair next to her and said, "It's about time you got here."

Maureen bent down and kissed her on the cheek. "I didn't know until right now how much I missed you. I should have kept in touch." Seated, she looked out to her old friends and smiled. "I can't believe it's been twenty-five years."

"I know!" came the resounding chorus.

She met the husbands and wives and dates. She heard about the children, the jobs, the businesses. They talked about teachers and gossiped about everyone they recognized, recalling incidents from the past. Almost every other sentence started with, "Do you remember . . . ?"

The music of their youth blared around them

418

while they drank a lot and laughed even more. Dinner was served and seemed especially long because no one could stop talking long enough to eat.

She was the only one at the table without a partner and Ted, Mike and Jimmy took it upon themselves to keep her dancing. When she saw that their wives didn't exactly appreciate being left by themselves, she pleaded a combination of exhaustion and age, and sat alone at the table while everyone else danced. Sipping her drink, she looked out to the couples and tried to identify them. There was something so wonderful about seeing all her high school friends again, and yet it was also depressing. Not because they were getting older; that was as it should be. They were no longer the younger generation. The torch had been passed on, and it was their children's turn to make a difference in the world. What depressed her was that something was missing.

She touched the silver pendant at her chest and knew it wasn't something. It was someone. Bobby. He should have been here.

"Would you like to dance?"

Startled, she turned around. "Dominick! Where have you been hiding yourself all evening?"

Dominick Wallinski smiled. "Catching up with old friends, like everybody else." He nodded to the dance floor. "How about it?"

She stood up. "I'd love to."

They joined the others and Maureen said,

"Thanks for not arresting me up at Bowman's Hill."

Dominick laughed. "You looked pretty upset. I didn't think taking you in was going to help."

Nodding, Maureen said, "I had just gotten separated and . . . I don't know, I guess I was just trying to recapture a time when I was happy."

"You better now?"

She smiled. "Much better. Thanks." Embarrassed, Maureen changed the subject as Dominick easily led her around the floor. "Hey, you turned out to be some dancer. I'm impressed."

It was his turn to be embarrassed. Shrugging, he said, "My wife loves to dance, so I took lessons."

Maureen looked at him and grinned. "She's a lucky woman, Dominick."

He stared at her and she could tell he wanted to say something more. "What is it?" she asked. "What's wrong?"

"Maureen, we *did* dance, didn't we?"

A chill ran down her back. "What do you mean?"

He shook his head. "It's kind of crazy, but I have this vague memory of you asking me to dance at St. Michael's Fair. It's so dumb. Sometimes I'm not sure if it even happened. I mean, a quarter of a century ago, this pretty, popular girl asked me to dance in front of all her friends and we talked about me becoming a lawyer." He shook his head. "I still don't know whether it happened. But it changed my life."

She could only stare at him. That was her dream, not his!

"I'm sorry. I embarrassed you," he apologized. "It's just that it was important to me and I wanted to know I didn't imagine the whole thing."

Maureen felt close to tears. "Dominick? What I remember is wiping a smudge of chocolate ice cream off your cheek before we danced. That was when you told me about wanting to become a lawyer."

"You remember?" he asked with relief.

She smiled. "I remember."

"I'd like you to meet my wife, okay? That's one of the reasons she wanted to come tonight. Thanks for sending the books to my kids. They took them into school and showed their friends . . ."

He kept up a steady stream of conversation, but Maureen was barely listening. Dominick remembered her dream. How could that be? Unless it really did happen? But that was impossible, wasn't it?

Toward the end of the evening, the class president of 1966 took the microphone and did his best to entertain them with anecdotes from the past. He introduced the Prom King and Queen and it was funny to watch them being crowned again. Then he asked for a moment of silence as an overhead projector came on and pictures of classmates who couldn't be with them were shown, friends who had died in the war or on a trip up north from college . . .

She pressed her fingers to her lips to stop the tears as Kevin Reed's graduation picture lit up the darkened room. Everyone at their table was silent. Muzzy was one of theirs, and his death was such a waste. And then it happened. She knew it was coming, but nothing could have prepared her for it.

He looked so handsome, so young, so full of promise.

Dressed in his graduation gown, Bobby looked out at her from the screen with eyes that hinted at mischief. His smile was wonderful, even the dimples were there. She half expected him to jump off the screen and walk over to their table to make a joke.

But he wasn't here. He was gone from her life. She listened to Ted and Mike talk about him and she wanted to tell them that she'd seen him, that he had come to her and saved her life. That he had driven her crazy with his interference and they had fought. She had told him to stay away, but now she missed him. God, how she missed him . . . and loved him. She had loved him almost all of her life, since fourth grade, but they never had a chance.

Looking at her friends, she knew she couldn't say a word. No one would believe her. Before she broke down in front of them, she excused herself and quickly headed for the ladies room.

She didn't see Robin, Colleen and Margie follow her.

When she came out of the stall they were standing in front of the mirror fixing their hair and makeup.

Margie turned around and wrapped her arm over Maureen's shoulders. "I think you were the only one that didn't know you loved him," she said, looking toward the others.

Colleen dropped her lipstick into her purse and nodded. "Everybody saw it. The looks you two used to give each other all through high school—"

"Even after that," Robin interrupted. "I remember one party the summer before he was . . . before he went back to college. You came with Jake, but spent all night talking to Bobby. Do you remember that?" she asked them. "We stood off to the side and made bets that you would end up marrying him. The way you were looking at each other . . . it was like a smoldering flame waiting to explode." Robin sniffled and swiped at her nose. "That was pretty good. Maybe I should be the writer."

Maureen brushed the tears away from her face and smiled. "A flame doesn't explode. It ignites."

"Who gives a damn?" Robin asked with a laugh. "The point I was trying to make is that you and Bobby had something, for as long as I can remember, and you never did anything about it. Now it's too late and you're feeling lousy. But that's normal. Hell, I was looking at George Barker tonight and telling myself I was a jerk to have turned him down in junior year. Have you *seen* him? He's gorgeous!"

They all laughed. Margie squeezed Maureen and let her go. "And you don't think the men are all out there thinking the same thing about passing over Cara Soladaz? It's natural to have pangs of regret on a night like this. It forces you to look back and examine your life. And that's not easy for a lot of us. Yours is just sad because Bobby's not here, and there's nothing you can do about it."

"You're right," Maureen said, bringing out a stick of concealer to repair her eye makeup. "There isn't anything that I can do."

Colleen snapped her purse shut. "Hey, will you look at us? The Terrible Four are together again and we're standing here weeping. We've got a reputation to uphold. I say we make a date to meet for dinner and talk about husbands and lovers and sex. All the stuff we *really* want to hear about the last twenty-five years."

They looked at each other and smiled.

"Sounds great."

"Count me in."

"Me, too," Maureen said, grinning at the others. "It'll be fun."

Robin held open the door and announced, "Now let's get back out there. I'll kill Timmy if he's drooling over Cara Soladaz like all those other middle-aged men."

As they were walking back to their table, Colleen said, "Do any of you remember that conversation we had at Joe's Pizza? The one where Maureen told us all about sex?"

Margie howled with laughter. "Remember? How could I ever forget? I shocked the hell out of my first husband by introducing him to my erogenous zones—one in particular."

Robin agreed. "I think we all have to thank you, Henessey, for our great sex lives. How did you know that stuff way back then?"

Maureen only shook her head and shrugged. How could she explain it to them? How could she tell them that it was only a shared memory of a dream?

By the time she walked out to the parking lot, Maureen felt strong, confident, successful—even pretty. It had been a wonderful night and she was glad she'd come, but it was time to leave. Everyone was pairing up. Husbands and wives. Friends and their dates. The slow songs were winding down the night and she didn't want to be around to hear them. Not tonight. Not when she was all alone. She could still hear the loud music coming through the opened front door as she inserted her key into the lock of her MG.

"Can I have this dance?"

Shaken by his voice, she jumped and spun around to face him.

"*Bobby . . .*"

He was grinning at her. "Hey, you didn't think I was going to miss this, did you?"

She flung herself into his arms and hugged him to her. "I thought I'd never see you again! Oh, Bobby, I'm so sorry I yelled at you. I've missed you . . ."

He kissed the top of her head. "I've missed you, too, kid. Now, c'mon, the song's almost over."

She didn't care who saw her, or what they might think. Holding him close, she let him lead her around in a small circle in front of her car.

"You should have seen everybody. Colleen's in politics and Ted had his own accounting business. Dominick Wallinski. Remember him? He was in the police force, but he got hurt a couple of years ago and now he's studying to be a lawyer."

"I wanted to be an architect."

"You did?"

"That's what I was studying. Shh . . . listen to the song." He started singing the words in her ear, very softly, and a shiver of longing and hunger ran through her body. Wrapping her arm tighter around his shoulder, she listened as he sang the old Dion and the Belmonts song "Where or When." It was perfect. He was telling her that they had stood and talked just like this before, that they had danced before and loved before. And right then she wanted so much more than that. She wanted what was taken away from them, and she didn't care about anything else at the moment. It was Bobby that she had been longing for all this time. She wanted him. Whether he was real, or not. If she was losing her mind, she would gladly lose it to him, for she couldn't fight it any longer.

"Come home with me, Bobby," she whispered.

He pulled back and stared down at her. "Maureen, I—"

"Please. Just come with me," she interrupted in an urgent voice. "We messed up twenty years ago. This may be our only chance."

He seemed to be weighing her words, fighting something that was taking place within him. He held her face between his hands and stared into her eyes, looking at her with such love that Maureen felt her throat tighten with emotion. She forced the word past her lips. "Please . . ."

Finally, he said in a rough voice, "Let's go."

She broke every speed limit, knowing Bobby would take care of her. She didn't care whose laws she was breaking. It would be worth it to spend one night with him. One night that had been stolen from them—that was all she asked.

The kids were in Philadelphia and Maureen held Bobby's hand as she led him through her darkened house. When they were in her bedroom, she dropped her purse onto the loveseat and turned to him.

"I love you, Bobby O'Connor," she whispered, fighting down the emotion that threatened to overwhelm her. "I've waited almost my entire lifetime to say that."

He took her jacket off and ran his fingers down her bare arms, not believing she was standing before him, wanting her, loving her. He clasped the silver pendant in his fist and gazed into her eyes. "Maureen, I love you. I love you. I was coming home to tell you when I . . ."

"Oh my God, no. Oh, please no . . ." Maureen pulled him to her and cried against his chest. "You were coming home to *me?*"

"I was going to tell you how I felt, that we had played around the edges of it for too long, and it was time to be honest."

She stood back and stared at him in the moonlight. Bobby knew he would never forget how her eyes sparkled with tears and love.

"Then let's be honest now," she begged. "All we might ever have is this moment."

His mouth came down on hers in a fierce, possessive kiss—a kiss that shocked both of them with its intensity. He wanted to touch her, taste her, brand her skin with his love so that after he was gone she would remember. He didn't care if it was wrong, or if he was breaking all the rules. It couldn't be wrong. Not this, not this sweet passion so long denied him.

Maureen ripped off her top and fumbled with his buttons. When his shirt was opened, she pressed herself to him and said, "I have to feel your skin against mine." They both gasped at the searing naked contact.

He closed his eyes and held her tightly, never wanting to let go. "Oh God, Maureen, I've waited so long for you . . ." He captured her mouth again and ran his hands down the slope of her back, pulling her into him, wanting to make her a part of him forever.

And that's when it happened. He had no control over it. The familiar buzzing started in his ears and quickly spread down his body, making him weak and compliant, forcing him into obedience.

She felt it, too, and suddenly lifted her head to stare at him. "Don't do it," she pleaded in a frightened voice. "Don't leave me now. Please—stay with me!"

His eyes filled with tears. "I can't! I've gone too far. I've broken too many rules . . ."

His hands dropped away from her body and she reached for him, desperate to keep him with her, but her fingers passed through him, leaving her with a slight electrical shock.

"I love you," he cried, trying to touch her again but unable. "I love you, Maureen . . . I'm so sorry . . . I'm sorry . . ."

It was as if a wind had entered her bedroom and stirred up a luminous fairy dust that swirled for mere seconds before abruptly disappearing, taking the man she loved along with it.

Wrapping her arms around her waist, she stood in the center of the room and screamed out his name. *"Bobby!"*

There was no answer.

Only a silence that seemed more loud, more cruel, than anything she had ever heard in her life.

Sinking to the rug, she cried out, "Come back. Please, please . . . come back." She clutched the woolen fibers, digging her fingernails into the rug, and sobbed with grief. "Why is every man I have ever loved taken away from me? *Why?* Why couldn't we have one night? We deserved one night . . ."

Chapter Twenty-two

"Mom, you sure you want to be alone tonight?"

Maureen threw the skirt onto the loveseat and looked up at her children. Smiling, she said, "Cleaning out my closets is the perfect way for me to spend New Year's Eve. Out with the old, right?"

"I don't know," Josh said, coming further into the room. "Can't you call somebody? How about Lisa?"

Maureen's eyes widened with news. "Didn't I tell you? Lisa is dating."

"Dating?" Abbie, ever anxious for gossip, grinned.

Nodding, Maureen looked back into her closet and pulled out the red silk blouse. She slipped it off the hanger and tossed it onto the pile she intended to give away. "Yup. He's an artist. Can you believe it? Super Yuppie falls for shy, sensitive painter. They've gone to New York for the holiday. Some party in the Village, I think."

Josh looked at Abbie and then back at his mother. "Well, what about one of those women? Robin or Margie? Every time they come over all of you laugh and have a good time. Can't you call one of them?"

Maureen gazed with love at her two children. They'd grown up so much in the last year. Everyone had. "I don't want to call them up. I want to be alone."

"Oh, Mom, you'll just feel bad. You know . . . too many memories of last year and everything." Abbie picked up the red blouse and held it against her chest for size. Throwing it back down to the pile, she added, "You should get out and do something."

"I am doing something. I'm cleaning my closet." Maureen walked up to her son and gently pushed his hair back from his forehead. "You look handsome. Big date?"

"Can't be a big date as long as Abbie's got the car. You sure I can't borrow yours?"

She laughed. "No way. That was part of the deal you made with your sister. You got it during Christmas and she has it tonight." Picking a piece of lint from his sweater, she asked, "Did you both call your dad and wish him Happy New Year?"

Josh nodded. "Yeah. We called. He said he'd try and come over tomorrow, if that's okay with you."

"That's fine."

"He's taking Melanie to a big party at some hotel in Center City," Abbie said with more than a trace of sarcasm.

"I hope they have a good time," Maureen answered, and realized she actually meant it. Things really have changed, she thought with a smile. That was how she knew it was time to file for a divorce. When Abbie had first told her about Dan's new young girlfriend last month, she hadn't run to the bathroom to throw up. She'd merely shrugged, as if it were inevitable. Dan's new love didn't bother her in the least. It was time to move on. The trouble was, she didn't know what she was moving toward.

"Go on, you two. Enjoy yourselves, but be careful. There are lots of crazy drivers out there tonight." She looked at Abbie. "You're staying in Avondale, right?"

"Right. Billy Appleton's party. You know his parents."

Nodding, Maureen slid her arms through her children's as she walked them from her bedroom. "Okay," she said as they stood at the front door. "Have a good time, and don't worry about me. I need to be alone tonight. I promise. I'm fine."

Josh bent down and kissed her cheek. "Happy New Years, Mom. I love you."

She hugged him and whispered, "I love you, too. Have fun."

Embarrassed, Josh took the keys from his sister

and muttered something about warming up the car.

Maureen looked at her daughter. "You look beautiful, Abbie. You're almost a grown woman. I can't believe you and Josh will be off to college in less than a year." Maureen searched her child's face. "Where did my little girl go?"

"I grew up—thanks to you. You know, I wasn't going to tell you this," she said, buttoning her coat so she wouldn't have to meet her mother's gaze. "But we had to fill in some information for our yearbook. The bio and everything. They asked a lot of stupid questions like your favorite class. Your favorite song and movie. Then they wanted to know my heroes, the people I look up to." Lifting her head, Abbie said, "I wrote down Margaret Thatcher. And you."

Trying not to cry, Maureen forced a smile. "Boy, pretty heady company to be in." She wrapped her arms around her daughter and closed her eyes as the tears came. "Thanks, Abbie. I can't tell you how proud that makes me." All those years of trying to balance mothering and friendship came down to this moment.

"I'd better go, Mom. Happy New Year."

She kissed her child. "Happy New Year, Abbie."

Watching as they drove away, Maureen couldn't remember a better one.

* * *

Why do we save so much? she thought as she folded another sweater and started a new pile. It was so hard for her to let go of anything. Clothes that no longer fit. Purses that were worn and frayed. Mother's Day cards the kids sent ten years ago. Report cards from grade school. And people. Especially people.

Something caught her eye in the bottom of the closet. She reached in and pulled out the blouse she had worn the first night she'd made love to Matt. Smiling, she ran her fingers over the silk material. He was back on the news, but she didn't watch him. It was a bittersweet reminder that was better off in her past. They had been two lonely people that had come together out of a mutual need. He had done so much for her, giving her back her femininity and her self-esteem. Wrinkling the shirt in her hand, she remembered a time when she'd been too ashamed to undress for the man she loved. But it was never meant to be. She could see that now. He was back where he belonged. Happy with his family, but she would always be grateful for what he had given her at the time.

Turning back to her task, she reached up for another sweater and was surprised when a bundle of yellow fur dropped into her hands.

A teddy bear.

Bobby's teddy bear.

She held it before her, running her fingers over the fake fur. *Bobby* . . . How she missed him.

But he was gone. Just like Dan. Just like Matt.

She was alone. Really alone, for the first time in her life. What surprised her was that it was okay. She didn't need a man to feel good. All she ever really needed was herself. Bobby taught her that.

An overwhelming sense of sadness came over her as she held his gift close to her heart. If she could see him, just one more time. Talk to him. Say goodbye . . .

But she knew he wouldn't come to her. Not anymore. They had crossed some invisible line, and he was gone.

Could she go to him? Where? Her mind raced with possibilities. Not Bowman's Hill. Not even the parking lot where they had danced. Where was the first place he had kissed her? It was down at the shore. Wildwood. He had kissed her and then insulted her, or something, and she had run away. What would have happened if she had stayed? If they had talked? Been honest with each other? Dear God, their lives would have been so different.

Suddenly she knew where she was going on New Year's Eve. The one place he might show up.

Wildwood By The Sea . . .

Okay, so it was crazy. Who else would be sitting on the beach, in the dead of winter, waiting

436

for a ghost to appear? Shivering, she realized what a dumb idea it was but she wanted to see him again. There was something that wasn't completed between them. It haunted her, and she couldn't release him until it was finished.

She wrapped her arms around her legs and exhaled, watching the cloud of her breath as it faded into the starry night. Was it only one year ago that he had come into her life and turned it upside down? What a New Year's Eve that had been! And now here she was, almost divorced, and—

"Maureen . . . you shouldn't be here."

She sensed him even before he spoke. Startled, she turned to her side. He was sitting next to her on the sand. "Bobby! You came!"

"For the last time," he said, smiling at her. "What brings you here, to the beach, on New Year's Eve?"

"You do. I had to see you. Talk to you . . ."

He shook his head. "Maureen, we made a mistake that night of the reunion. I went too far. I should never have allowed it."

"Don't say that," she whispered, wanting to hold him, yet afraid he would disappear if she touched him. "It wasn't a mistake. When two people that love each other—"

"Don't you understand?" he interrupted. "I had my chance. Right here. Twenty-five years ago. And I blew it."

"What are you talking about?" Maureen shivered as she looked at him in the moonlight.

He smiled back at her with tenderness and she was immediately filled with a comforting warmth. The cold wind seemed like a soft, summer breeze. Knowing he had done it, her eyes filled with tears. "What chance? I don't understand."

"When we were here, that summer after graduation," Bobby said, looking out to the dark ocean. "I spent four years of high school watching you date others because I didn't have the nerve to tell you I wanted to be more than your friend. And after school was out and we were down here . . . I'm sorry I hurt you that night of the party. I guess that's what I wanted to tell you all along. And somehow make up for it."

Seeing the regret and anguish in his expression, she shook her head slowly. "Bobby, I don't even remember what you said."

He looked at her. "Of course you do. The pain that was in your eyes has stayed with me, haunting me. You ran away from me. You have to remember."

"I don't," she whispered. "We were just kids. Whatever it was, I forgave you a long time ago."

Closing his eyes, he raked his fingers through his hair. "All this time . . . When I . . . it happened so quickly that I never felt any pain. There was a blinding white light, and all I could see was your face, the way you looked the night you ran away from me, and the pain I had caused you. And now you're saying you don't even remember?" He turned to stare at her.

Again, she shook her head. "I'm sorry. It was so long ago."

Looking up, he studied the clear sky and sighed deeply. "I guess I'm the one that had to be taught a lesson. Maybe this whole thing, coming back to you, wasn't just because your life was falling apart and I was supposed to help you. Maybe it was for me, too."

"For you?" Dear God, she wanted to hold him, feel him next to her, for she knew time was running out and she would soon lose him.

He picked up a handful of sand and let it sift through his fingers. "When we hurt someone, it's so easy to say we're sorry and believe that takes care of it. No one ever thinks about making restitution anymore. I'm not talking about getting even. I'm saying that we have to try and change the wrong we've done. I guess that's what I was trying to do for you, Maureen. But it was really for me, too." He held her gaze. "Now I can let you go."

"I don't want you to," she whispered. "I know I argued with you and told you to get out of my life—"

"You said I was driving you crazy."

In spite of everything, she laughed. "You were! How many people meet up with old boyfriends in as many bathrooms as I did?"

"You'd be surprised."

Her eyes widened. "I'm not the only one?"

"With a guardian? There's a lot of people in trouble out there."

"This is happening all over? Ghosts—I'm sorry, I know you don't like that word, angels are—"

"I'm not an angel," he interrupted. "And if I was on my way to being one, I think I've slipped down the ladder a few rungs after our last meeting."

She shook her head and smiled with sadness. "Boy, talk about premature evaporation . . ."

He smiled at her. "I had a mission to accomplish," he said, ignoring her attempt at a joke. "And I've done it. You're okay now. You're better than okay. Most people never get to examine their lives like you did. They just go through it, making the same mistakes over and over, because they don't know how to change. Change was forced on you, but you're one of the lucky ones."

He looked at her eyes, her nose, her mouth, as if memorizing each feature, and she was filled with love.

"You're going to be happy, Maureen. You've finally grown up. And you know real happiness doesn't depend on a husband, or even your children. It all has to do with you, and whether you like the person you've become."

"It was a hard lesson," she murmured, thinking back on the last year.

"But you learned," he answered, and suddenly

grinned. "I may not have handled everything right, but my first assignment was a success. Thanks, kid."

"You mean you're going to do this again?"

He shrugged. "If they trust me with someone else. They'll just have to make sure it isn't someone I love."

"I'm never going to see you again, am I?" she asked as tears ran down her cheeks. "I love you, Bobby O'Connor. I always have. I always will."

He reached out, lightly touching her face, and a warm, peaceful feeling spread throughout her body. "Sometimes I don't wonder why we die, I wonder why we're born." Smiling sadly, he said, "Listen to me, Maureen. When it's your turn? When you leave this world? The first thing you'll see will be my hand reaching out for you."

Turning, she kissed his palm. "You promise?" she demanded through her tears.

"I promise. Now, don't cry. A part of me will always be with you."

Wiping her eyes, she looked up at him. "It will?" Her voice sounded like a little child's, begging for reassurance. She didn't want him to leave her, yet knew it was coming.

He nodded. "You're going to recognize it soon."

"How? I want to know. I have to—"

"Don't worry. You'll know. Look," he said, pointing to the sky. "A falling star."

When she turned back, he was gone.

Was it only her imagination, or did she really hear the words, *I love you* whispered into the night?

She sat for a few more minutes on the deserted beach, listening to the sounds of the wind and the ocean, thinking how blessed she was to have known him, until a chill forced her to get up and leave. Stamping her feet on the boardwalk to remove the sand from her sneakers, she suddenly felt stronger and more at peace than she had ever been at any other time in her life.

It should have been sad, saying goodbye to Bobby, but it wasn't. He had given her so much in the last year, taught her so many lessons, and the most important one was to value herself. She had spent her entire life trying to please others and it hadn't worked. Now she knew her happiness, her sense of wholeness, was merely a reflection of how she felt inside. Loving herself . . . it was a totally new idea to her.

Looking out to the darkened stores that lined the boardwalk, Maureen thought how different life seemed now. It was as if she knew a secret the rest of the world hadn't yet learned. Smiling, she walked off the boardwalk, confident, happy, secure.

And then she saw the man standing by her car.

She had parked the MG in front of a small convenience store because it was well lit. Now, as she came closer, she could see the man was writing something and placing it on her windshield.

"I'm not getting a ticket, am I?" she asked, wondering if he could be a plainclothes policeman. She could not be getting a parking ticket on New Years Eve!

He turned to her and Maureen stopped walking as she stared back at him. He looked upset, distressed over something.

"Is this your car?" he asked.

Maureen walked closer. "Yes? Is something wrong?"

The wind whipped his thick black hair across his forehead, and he raked it back with his fingers. "Hey, I'm really sorry."

"Sorry about what?" She jammed her fists into the pockets of her jacket. She really didn't feel like standing out in the cold windy night playing guessing games.

"I was picking up some cigarettes and I just backed up. I guess I didn't—"

"You hit my car?" she practically yelled, rushing up to examine the MG. There was a dent on the right front fender and the headlight was smashed. *"You hit my car!"* she repeated, running her hand over the damage. "Oh, no . . ."

"I'm sorry," he said again, and sounded sincere.

"I love this car," she murmured, more to herself than him. "You don't know what it means to me." Purchasing it was her first real act of independence.

"I can't tell you how bad I feel. I was leaving

my name and number when you—"

She spun around to him. "Why weren't you careful? What could you have been thinking, hitting someone's car, in the middle of the night? What were you doing? Drinking?"

And then she looked at him. Directly, for the first time.

He was good looking. He appeared to be in his late forties. Weathered handsome. That's how she would describe him.

"I wasn't drinking," he said in a defensive voice, while jerking up the collar of his suede jacket to keep out the wind. "I haven't even been to any parties tonight. I must have been preoccupied." He pulled his fingers through his hair again and looked down at her. "I'm sorry. I wish it didn't happen. But it did. Do you want me to call the police?"

She couldn't answer. She could only stare back up at him. He did it just like Bobby, that frustrated habit of pushing back his hair. And his eyes . . . his eyes were blue, a deep blue, as blue as the ocean would be in summer. She knew those eyes; she'd been looking into them since she was a kid.

She felt mesmerized, seeing something in them beyond color and expression. It was that same incomplete longing that she and Bobby had shared for so long. The revelation was sudden and startling.

A part of me will always be with you . . .

You're going to recognize it soon.

She heard the words in her brain and desperately tried to find meaning in them. Could it be? Was this man . . . *Bobby?* It was crazy. She thought of wish fulfillment, repressed needs, delusional behavior. She was looking for a sign and this poor man had stepped into her path on the wrong night.

"Are you okay?" His voice was concerned.

She blinked several times, trying to come back to reality, and finally nodded. "What's your name?" she whispered, still trying to reason out the sudden connection.

"Jim. Jim Brennan." He smiled and held out his hand.

Placing hers inside his, she said, "I'm Maureen Malone," and waited to see his reaction.

"Well, Maureen, do you want me to call the police?" He looked at his watch. "I'm sure they're going to love it at five minutes before midnight on New Years Eve."

She glanced at his Volvo station wagon and noticed the fine lettering on the door. *Brennan Associates.* "What do you do?" she asked.

"Are you wondering if I'm insured?" He grinned. "I'm an architect. I have an office in Philadelphia."

When he smiled, dimples appeared and his whole face lit up with friendliness. Maureen could only stare at him as she felt the beginnings of something that scared her. An architect . . .

"Do you live down here?" She needed to know.

He shook his head. "I have a house here for the summer." Gazing out to the ocean, he added, "I didn't feel like being alone in the city tonight, so I came down. I thought it was going to be a quiet, uneventful night." Looking back down to her, he grinned sheepishly, "Little did I guess I would bump into you."

"You bumped into my car."

He held her gaze. "Right."

After a moment, Maureen looked away shyly.

"If you don't want to call the police, shouldn't we exchange cards?"

"Cards?" Maureen asked, shaken by the encounter. "Business cards?"

He laughed. It was deep and warm . . . and very nice. "Insurance cards. That way I get to find out where you live without being obvious."

"I live in Avondale," she said, digging into her purse.

"That's a long way from Wildwood."

She held the insurance information in her hand. "I was . . . was saying goodbye to an old friend."

He recognized the sadness in her expression and smiled with understanding. Holding out his hand, he said, "Maybe you could say hello to a new one?"

Just as she shook his hand, horns started beeping, people came out and banged cooking pots. A fire siren even went off.

Suddenly happy, she giggled. "Happy New Year, Jim Brennan."

He pumped her hand and laughed. "Happy New Year, Maureen Malone."

She wasn't going to cry. Not this time.

It was a new year . . . and a new beginning.

Afterword

She must not swing her arms as though they
*   were dangling ropes,*
She must not switch herself this way and
*   that;*
She must not shout and she must not,
*   while wearing her bridal veil,*
smoke a cigarette.

Emily Post (1873–1960)
American hostess and writer

One is not born a woman, one becomes one.
*   Thank God.*

Simone De Beauvoir (1908–1986)
French writer and philosopher